“I have given you my soul.

“Will you not give me anything in return?” Desmond murmured.

“I will play you a game of cards for it,” Marianne replied. “If you win, you may have me. I will come to your bed, willingly, wearing nothing but a smile of invitation. There will be no damnable tears.”

“And if you win?” he asked.

“I get Kingsbrook.”

There was a stunned silence. One could almost see the workings in Desmond’s head as he tried to collect his faculties.

“You would get Kingsbrook?” he finally asked, very slowly and carefully.

“Or you would get me,” Marianne said.

Desmond narrowed his eyelids and appeared to be considering very seriously. “You value yourself very highly, Miss Trenton, to put your worth equivalent to this grand estate.”

“Rather, Mr. Desmond,” the girl said coolly, “it is a question of how highly *you* value *me*…!”

Dear Reader,

This month, author Sally Cheney returns with her fifth historical for Harlequin, *The Wager*. Known for her ability to capture the flavor of 19th-century England, the author's new title tells the story of a young woman who sets out to destroy the man who won her in a card game, only to fall in love with him in the process. We hope you enjoy it.

Beloved Outcast by Pat Tracy is a dramatic Western about an Eastern spinster who is hired by a man with a notorious reputation to tutor his adopted daughter. *Affaire de Coeur* recently labeled Pat as "one author definitely worth watching," and we hope you agree. This talented author just keeps getting better and better.

Whether writing atmospheric Medievals or sexy Regencies, Deborah Simmons continues to delight readers. In this month's *Maiden Bride*, the sequel to *The Devil's Lady,* Nicholas de Laci transfers his blood lust to his enemy's niece, Gillian, his future wife by royal decree. And fans of *Romantic Times* Career Achievement Award winner Veronica Sattler will be thrilled to see this month's reissue of her Worldwide Library release, *Jesse's Lady.* We hope you'll enjoy this exciting story of a young heiress and her handsome guardian.

We hope you'll keep a lookout for all four titles wherever Harlequin Historicals are sold.

Sincerely,

Tracy Farrell
Senior Editor

Harlequin Books

TORONTO • NEW YORK • LONDON
AMSTERDAM • PARIS • SYDNEY • HAMBURG
STOCKHOLM • ATHENS • TOKYO • MILAN
MADRID • WARSAW • BUDAPEST • AUCKLAND

ISBN 0-373-28934-0

THE WAGER

This edition published by arrangement with Harlequin Books S.A.

Printed in U.S.A.

Books by Sally Cheney

Harlequin Historicals

Game of Hearts #36
Thief in the Night #112
Tender Journey #148
Tapestry #192
The Wager #334

SALLY CHENEY

was a bookstore owner before coming to her first love—writing. She has traveled extensively in the United States, but is happiest with the peaceful rural life in her home state of Idaho. When she is not writing, she is active in community affairs and enjoys cooking and gardening.

To Ursula, in appreciation for her invaluable input

Prologue

London, 1855

"One card."

"Two."

"I'll play these."

The cards were dealt around the table as requested. Finally the dealer snapped a number of cards off the deck for himself.

"Dealer takes three," he announced.

The four men sat studying the little rectangles of pasteboard they held with expressions of varying degrees of grimness. The least forbidding of them seemed to be that of the dealer himself, his insouciance owing, no doubt, to the impressive pile of coins and banknotes on the table before him.

"Mr. Phillips, I believe the bid is to you," he softly reminded the man at his side.

Mr. Phillips's scowl deepened. "One pound," he growled at last, adding a heavy coin to the kitty, challenging the player to his left with a scowl.

Mr. Abbot would have faced down his fellow gamester, despite his stern expression, if the gentleman dealing had given him one more face card, but with this hand...

Abbot sighed heavily and pushed his cards together. "Discretion dictates my retreat from the field of battle, I fear," he said, laying the cards facedown in front of him.

"Mr. Carstairs?" the dealer prompted.

"I'm in," the third man said sourly, removing several coins from the short stack left before him.

"The dealer meets the bet." A banknote was added to the collection.

The four men—Phillips, Abbot, Carstairs and the dealer, Mr. Peter Desmond—were not close intimates. *Friends* was too strong a word. Even *acquaintances* was. It was not at all certain that if two of them met on the street in daylight they would recognize each other, or, if recognizing the other, would exchange greetings. They met several times a year to play cards. One or more of them always went away a loser, which did nothing to endear them to one another.

"Mr. Phillips? Do you wish to raise or call?" the dealer prompted now.

"I *wish* to do many things," Phillips said. "But one's wishes are not always granted, are they? I fold."

"Well, Mr. Carstairs, once again it appears only you and I will play out the hand," the man dealing said. His voice was low, his manner suave and perfectly charming.

Mr. Carstairs pictured his nose smashed and bleeding and wondered how suave and charming he would be then. Although the winners and losers varied with each game the four men played, Mr. Desmond usually left the table with money in his pocket, and Mr. Carstairs usually left with none in his.

"You have most of the money I brought with me, and I would like very much to recoup some of those losses. Let us waste no time. It is all or nothing, Desmond."

Carstairs pushed the rest of his funds into the center of the table.

Desmond picked up the cigar smoldering in the ashtray at his elbow and put it to his lips as he carefully studied the cards he held and, even more carefully, the man sitting next to him. He squinted against the aromatic cloud of smoke he exhaled, but neither the smoke nor the squint could disguise the fact that he was a vividly handsome man, with dark brown hair, dark gray eyes and a set to his jaw suggesting an iron will.

He tapped the ash from the end of his cigar, then returned it to his mouth, holding it between his teeth. "Unfortunately, Mr. Carstairs, you are in no position to dictate terms," he said, a silken smile on his lips. "I need only to increase your bet and you lose."

He began to gather enough coins and bills to do exactly that, but Carstairs, almost frantically, stopped him. "Wait!" he cried. "I said all or nothing."

"You did," Desmond agreed. "And you have wagered all and have nothing left."

"No, no. I have..."

"What, Mr. Carstairs?"

"I have... here, give me a piece of paper."

"Now, Mr. Carstairs, you know our policy. We have agreed to play only for the monies we brought to the table." The gentleman sounded genuinely grieved by the fact.

"Not money," Carstairs murmured, finding a paper and pen on his own person and scribbling something as he spoke. "Better than money." He reached inside his coat again, found a little pocketbook and, after rummaging through its contents for a moment, extracted a bent and tattered daguerreotype. He passed it and the paper across the table.

"Better than money? I doubt it," Desmond said, picking up the items Mr. Carstairs had passed to him and studying them both. He raised one eyebrow and then looked up at his fellow gambler for confirmation. "Indeed?" he asked.

"I guarantee it," Carstairs said firmly.

Desmond took the cigar from between his teeth and laid it carefully in the ashtray again. "I will admit you pique my curiosity."

"You accept the wager, then?" Carstairs urged.

Desmond hesitated for another moment, but finally nodded. "Very well," he said. "It might prove something of a . . . lark. My winnings against this." He held up the paper and the daguerreotype. "What have you got, Mr. Carstairs?"

Carstairs smiled gloatingly and turned his cards over for the others to see.

"Full house!" he announced triumphantly, splaying the cards on the table before him.

Mr. Phillips and Mr. Abbot murmured in appropriate tones of awe.

Mr. Desmond studied the three knaves and the pair of twos and shook his head slightly.

"Well," he said, "that beats three of a kind." Carefully he laid down three threes.

Carstairs chuckled and reached across the table to claim the money.

"However," the younger gentleman continued, "a full house does not beat four of a kind," and he coolly laid down a fourth three.

Carstairs fell back in his chair as if he had been dealt a physical blow.

"Buck up, old man," Desmond said, pulling the winnings across the table, including the scrap of paper and the sepia-toned photograph. "Here's a little something to get you home." He selected the heavy coin that had been Mr. Phillips's last bet and tossed it across the table to the other man. "I would not want to discourage you from letting me win more money from you the next time. Ah, but this—" he picked up the picture and studied it gloatingly "—on this I will expect full payment."

"Of course," Carstairs said. "We are at your convenience."

"What is that?" Mr. Phillips asked curiously, nodding toward Desmond and the picture he held.

"I thought we determined not to play for notes of debenture," Abbot said reproachfully.

"Indeed we did. But Mr. Carstairs did not offer me a promissory note. It seems he has given me title to his *ward,* a Miss Marianne Trenton."

The other two gentlemen laughed as Desmond took up his cigar again with a broad wink.

Chapter One

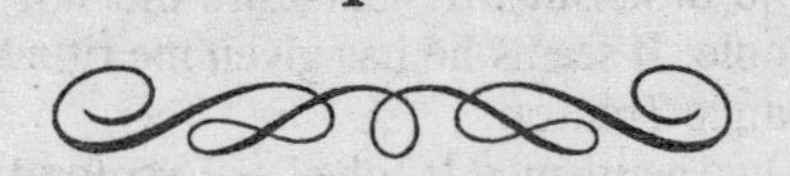

The night was warm for so early in the summer. The windows were open, inviting every passing breath of fresh air to enter, but they were few and far between and often merely flirted with the window shade.

A young girl sat on the end of the bed, fully dressed.

The ensemble she wore was too warm for the season and too complete for the hour, so it was not surprising if little droplets of sweat had gathered on her brow. But, in fact, the perspiration was there, and running down her back in hot, lazy rivulets, for another reason.

Marianne was waiting for her uncle Horace. His temper was usually vile, but he became violent if he lost at cards. And unfortunately, more often than not, when Horace Carstairs gambled he lost.

The man was not actually her uncle. After the death of her parents the previous year, her father to a hunting accident and her mother three months later to an influenza that found her in a weakened condition owing to her grief, the girl had been assigned by the court to Mr. Carstairs, whose misfortune it had been to be bequeathed some monies in her father's will to clear an outstanding debt.

"I cannot take the girl," Carstairs had objected. "I am unmarried. Surely you would not burden an old bachelor like myself with such a responsibility?"

But the court reminded Mr. Carstairs that with the girl a ward of the state, it could, in fact, dispose of her and her modest legacy as it saw fit. Carstairs might have objected further, but the judge agreed to pay him, as guardian, an annual stipend out of the girl's inheritance.

Mr. Carstairs pursued various ventures in order to make money—some, but not all of them, legal—and being no more an astute businessman than he was a clever card player, he often found himself in need of extra cash. The payment the judge named appeared very attractive to him just then.

Thus it was that Marianne Trenton, so recently part of a loving home and family, had her grief compounded by suddenly becoming the ward of a man she did not know and soon found detestable.

Her schooling had been haphazard, and at the death of her parents, her formal education ended abruptly. But Marianne, alone and largely unnoticed in Mr. Carstairs's house, became an avaricious reader—almost exclusively of the penny dreadfuls she was able to purchase with the small allowance her "uncle" afforded her.

Tonight, though, as she waited for her guardian, she was too distracted and tense to concentrate on her latest novel, *Leonore, Jeune Fille*. And when she finally heard Uncle Horace's key grating in the lock, she jumped in alarm.

Fearfully she listened to her uncle's progress through the house. She could hear him hanging his overcoat on the tree by the front door. He paused by the table in the foyer to look through the mail. She thought he might turn into the sitting room to read the paper, but after a pause, during which she could imagine him scanning the headlines, his footsteps continued to the stairs.

The heavy clump of shod feet on the risers sounded as if they were produced by a large man. Though relatively tall, Mr. Carstairs was not heavyset, but lean and lanky. His shoulders were narrow, his face, with its pursed lips, pinched nose and close-set eyes, long and thin. Yet his slow, heavy steps up the stairwell seemed almost to shake the house with their weight.

Marianne stiffened, the book in her hands entirely forgotten. If all had gone well tonight Uncle Horace would continue down the hall to his room, and she could finally undress and go to bed. But if he had lost, he would kick the door open and would be upon her before she could assume a position of defense. The amount of abuse she would suffer—the shouts of rage, the blows to her face and body—would depend on the size of his losses.

His steps neared her door and slowed. Her green eyes opened wide; her breathing grew shallow and almost stopped. "Go on, go on," she whispered, as he stopped and turned to her door. She sucked in her breath and held it, waiting for his boot to hit the thin panel that separated them.

Instead, there was a soft tap at her door.

Surprised, she released the breath she had been holding. "Come in," she said.

The door opened slowly. Uncle Horace peeked carefully around the corner, for all the world as if he were making sure she was decent. Such a concern had never suggested itself to him before.

"You are still up," he said.

"I am," she replied.

"You were unable to sleep?"

"No, I was waiting..." Her voice trailed away to silence.

"Waiting? For me? I am touched, Marianne."

She did not reply.

"I have been reviewing our situation here," he continued when the brief pause indicated the girl was not going to speak. "You know that I am ill suited to raise a young woman, and I suspect you have not been happy here, alone so often, with no young people for companions, no chance to socialize. You are of an age when you *should* be socializing."

The girl shifted her feet uncomfortably, one toe nudging the book she had dropped when Carstairs knocked. She had pictured herself of late in situations similar to the ones Leonore, the young heroine, encountered.

"I suppose—" she began.

But the man cut her off. "Perhaps it is time we looked into a new position for you. Something with broader perspectives." He had half turned, his voice casual, as if he were speaking the thoughts as they occurred to him, but now he peered at her from the side, studying her face.

"Another position? You sound as if I should be seeking employment. *Am* I seeking employment, Uncle Horace?" she asked.

"No, no. I misspoke. You misunderstood. But another house, a broader acquaintance, that is what I am suggesting."

"I am to visit someone? An old friend of mine, perhaps?" she said.

"Not exactly," Carstairs said, hedging.

"Then what, exactly?"

"Not an old friend of yours. A gentleman of my acquaintance. You will be leaving at the end of the week."

"Leaving?" If Marianne sounded more surprised than saddened by Carstairs's announcement, it was due to the fact that leaving this house had been her fondest wish since the day she had entered.

"A coach will be by to collect you on Friday morning. You must be prepared to leave by then."

"A coach? Where am I to go?" Marianne asked, making every effort to understand the frightening man who was her guardian.

"The gentleman has a private estate outside of Reading. I believe he intends for you to stay there."

"I am to leave London?"

"It is not far," Carstairs told her. "And you will doubtless be returning in a few weeks."

Horace Carstairs was embarrassed to admit that until tonight he had never seen the possibilities Marianne presented. She was a fresh young girl, as far as he knew, a virgin. When Desmond was finished with her, Carstairs could sell her services again.

Surprisingly, especially if one knew Carstairs and the depths to which he was willing to descend in the name of business, that had not been his intention when he offered Marianne to the gentleman. He had honestly expected to win when he wrote his little IOU. He'd had three jacks and two twos. A full house would have won any of the other hands all night long. But it did not win that hand, and consequently Carstairs had finally realized the practical value Marianne represented.

"You need not worry about me," Marianne said, in response to his promise she would soon be returning to him. "I will stay away as long as you like."

"We shall see how things turn out," Carstairs said.

"And who is this person I am to visit?" Marianne asked, at last coming to the question of most pressing interest.

But her guardian shook his head and shrugged his shoulders. "You do not know him," he said.

"A philanthropic gentleman." It was not a question. To Marianne it was an obvious statement of fact that any man who would take her away from Uncle Horace was a philanthropist.

But the next morning, when Marianne arose, she learned that Mr. Carstairs had left very early for Barnet, to collect on a loan.

She was confused and alarmed. Uncle Horace had left without telling her anything about her new placement or the situation facing her. When Bette first informed her of Mr. Carstairs's unannounced business trip, the girl was not at all certain she had not dreamed the episode of the night before. It had gotten late, and perhaps she had fallen asleep. In her uncomfortable position at the foot of her bed she must have had a particularly vivid dream.

A letter arrived with the four o'clock post, though, which confirmed her flickering memory.

Miss Trenton,
Your guardian has by now, I am sure, informed you of your approaching relocation. I am looking forward to meeting you. My man will be there at seven o'clock Friday morning. The drive to Kingsbrook will take the better part of the day, so you will have to make an early start. Until then, *je suis le tiens, ma biche.*

P. Desmond.

Marianne, having quit her schooling after only a few French lessons, did not know Mr. Desmond had called her "his fawn," nor did she realize how indecently familiar the gentleman had been in his concluding sentence.

She rose with the sun on Friday morning and was dressed to greet Mr. Desmond's coachman when he rang the bell, a little before seven o'clock.

As Mr. Desmond had said in his letter, the trip to his home and lands outside of Reading took all of that morning and most of the afternoon. The day was unseasonably hot for so early in the summer. By eight o'clock Marianne regretted that she had chosen her three-piece ensemble, which required the jacket to look complete.

They stopped at a little roadside tavern for lunch. As always, Marianne's finances were meager, and she was not sure she could afford to buy even the plainest meal on the menu. She was relieved, touched even, when the coachman produced two pound notes and told her Mr. Desmond had sent them, for any expenses she might incur along the way.

She therefore enjoyed her meal immensely, even drinking a glass of wine, and as a result was able to sleep very comfortably in the jogging, sweltering coach for the remainder of the journey.

She woke with a jerk when the coachman, who had identified himself as Rickers, opened the carriage door.

"Just 'Rickers'?" Marianne had asked him doubtfully.

"Rickers usually suffices, miss, unless the missus gets impatient with me, as she does every now and again, and then it's *'Eus-tice!'*"

"We're there, miss," he said now.

"There?" Marianne felt as if her wits had been scrambled by an eggbeater, which was a fair description of the coach ride and its effects.

"Kingsbrook." With a flourish Rickers opened both doors of the coach, and Marianne caught her breath.

They had just crossed a wooden bridge over the brook after which the estate was no doubt called. Its banks were covered with moss and pretty pink centaury blossoms. The untamed beauty of the landscape continued into the park itself, which Marianne knew must be planted and cared for to some degree because of the buddleia and poppies, the dahlias and azaleas growing in such colorful beds among the shrubs and trees.

To complete the picture, a delicate doe tiptoed down to the brook, mindful but not fearful of their presence.

And then Marianne raised her eyes to the house and drew in her breath again. Kingsbrook Manor, rising from the ferns and meadows surrounding it, looked like a fairy-tale castle to the young girl. Then her breathing evened out, her wine-induced sleepiness lifted completely from her brain, leaving behind the dull throb of a headache, and she saw that of course the structure was not quite as awe-inspiring as she had first thought.

There were three stories, with tall windows all along the bottom floor, to the right and left of the big double doors set squarely in the middle. The upstairs windows were smaller, and the panes under the gables mere pigeonholes.

Rickers helped her down from the carriage, and as he accompanied her to the house, she realized some of the impression of overwhelming magnitude was due to the structure rising starkly from its wild setting. If it had been surrounded by a paved courtyard, with a wide, winding drive in front of it, it would not have startled the senses so, nor seemed so colossal.

Still, it was the largest private dwelling she had ever stayed in, and she had to force herself to keep her mouth from dropping open as she looked up at it.

At first Rickers seemed to be leading her aimlessly through the tall grass, but in a moment she realized there were flat, even stones under her feet. The path, like the beds of multicolored poppies, had been carefully and meticulously planned to convey the impression of artless natural beauty.

When they had nearly reached the doors, the path finally widened and the grass was cut back. Mr. Desmond had evidently made a minor concession to visitors and guests who might prefer civilization. There was a paved walkway around the house, and the flowers blooming near the windows were confined in planter boxes. But one had to be very near the structure before the illusion of a fairy castle in an enchanted glen was disturbed.

Rickers stopped before the large double doors.

"Mrs. River will get you situated," the man said.

"Mrs. River?"

"Housekeeper here at Kingsbrook."

"And where is Mr. Desmond?" Marianne asked. She was anxious to meet the gentleman, to thank him for his generosity.

"Oh, 'e's 'ere about someplace, I would wager. Let Mrs. River show you around a bit and you'll 'ear about it when 'imself gets in." Rickers put her belongings down and touched his cap.

"Miss Trenton?" Startled, Marianne turned to face the speaker, a tall, angular woman, who had opened the door. With her hair turning gray at the temples and pulled back into a knot, she was not beautiful, but her face was interesting. Her eyes saw a great deal, Marianne suspected. Her ears heard more than what was said and her mouth spoke the truth. The girl instinctively liked Mrs. River the moment she saw her.

"Miss Trenton, I believe. We have been awaiting your arrival. Will you come in?" Judging from her icy tone, the housekeeper did not reciprocate with her own favorable impression.

"Yes. Thank you," Marianne mumbled, reaching down for one of her bags.

"Leave them. James will take them up for you."

Mrs. River turned sideways to allow Marianne to pass, and the girl stepped across the threshold into the dark receiving hall. "Mr. Desmond is . . . ?"

"Mr. Desmond was attending to business this morning. He left instructions to serve tea when you arrived, and said that he would try to be back in time to join you. Tea is ready, Miss Trenton, but perhaps you would like a chance to freshen up first?"

Mrs. River had modified her unfriendly tones so that her voice was now perfectly expressionless. But if her eyes saw a great deal, they revealed certain things, too. Marianne felt a sinking sensation in her stomach at the housekeeper's unmistakable disapproval of her.

She smiled sweetly, though, at the woman's offer to freshen herself, and hoped it would mean a cool, damp washcloth—her head still ached a bit from her luncheon wine—and a brush. "I would like very much to wash my face and hands, if I could."

"Certainly, Miss Trenton. Alice, show Miss Trenton to her rooms and then bring her down to the front sitting room when she is ready," Mrs. River said, and Marianne was startled to see a maid in a dark skirt with a white cap and white apron suddenly materialize at her elbow.

"Yes, Mrs. River. Will you follow me, miss?" the maid inquired.

Alice led her through the receiving hall, up the stairs and along the balcony. "This is Mr. Desmond's suite," she said, clearing her throat. "And these—" she indicated the next door along, facing, like Mr. Desmond's rooms, the front doors on the ground floor "—are your rooms."

Rooms?

Indeed, the apartment Alice showed her was almost as large as the little cottage where she had grown up, in which she and her parents had lived comfortably.

"Is this all to be mine?" she gasped. "Am I to be in here—alone, I mean?"

"Well, yes, miss. That is, unless you bring...I mean, until such time as you should care to invite—anyone else in. I did not mean to suggest..." The little maid, barely older than Marianne, stammered uncomfortably, colored brilliantly and finally stopped talking altogether.

Marianne was too overcome by the proportions of her chambers to pay much attention the girl's confusion. "I was not expecting anything so...grand," she said softly, looking around her and finally turning wonder-filled eyes on the maid again.

Alice bobbed a curtsy and left her alone, unable to keep from shaking her head slightly as she closed the door. This young woman was not the sort of person she had been expecting, judging from the low-toned conversations between Mrs. River and Mrs. Rawlins she had overheard downstairs in the kitchen.

In her grand apartment, Marianne washed her face in a porcelain bowl, dried her hands on one of the fluffy towels set out in the private washroom, then rearranged her hair with the tortoiseshell brush, part of an elegant set placed in front of the large looking glass. She smiled into the mirror, then drew her face into more serious lines, trying to assume the proper expression of a deserving waif. Before she had the chance to practice her presentation any further, there was a nervous tapping at her door.

"Come in," she called.

Alice slipped into the room. "He's come, miss. Mrs. River sent me straight up to bring you. Mr. Desmond doesn't like to be kept waiting, and in any case, Mrs. River said you would want to see him."

"Mr. Desmond? By all means," Marianne said, putting the brush down, smoothing her dress, checking her reflection one last time. At last she was going to meet the kindly old gentleman and have the chance to offer her heartfelt appreciation for his selfless benevolence.

Chapter Two

He was standing in front of one of the tall windows, looking out at the beautiful wild grounds, holding a teacup and saucer in his hand. The juxtaposition of savagery and civilization was curiously duplicated by the gentleman himself.

Mr. Peter Desmond was dressed in an elegant suit of clothing, of meticulous fit and the finest materials. The pants and jacket were so dark a blue as to be almost black, and the crisp white cravat and shirt were as representative of polite society as the delicate bone-china teacup he held.

But when he turned and looked at Marianne, his face and expression were as untamed and breathtaking as the scene outside the window.

He studied her for a moment without speaking. She was standing in a wash of variegated light, where the sun shone through a loosely woven lace curtain. Her traveling suit was of a light tan shade, to camouflage any dust clinging to the skirt or jacket, and with her dark golden hair and wide green eyes, she reminded him of a jungle cat. A young lioness, carefully stepping from the underbrush to suspiciously survey the landscape before her. The scene through the window behind her completed the image, with its suggestion of a tropical forest.

Her bosom rose and fell quickly and she watched him closely, a nervous creature ready to either attack or flee, depending on his next actions. The idea made him smile ever so slightly.

Marianne did not need the position of light and shadow to enhance the impression she got from the man, of a wild beast about to pounce. This was *not* the kindly older gentleman she had pictured to herself, with snowy white hair and palsied hand waiting to greet her. He was tanned and dark, as muscularly broad as Uncle Horace was narrow. His dark hair was too long, and his eyes, roving deliberately over her person, were a great deal too bold. His nose was straight and would have been prominent on his face if his brows had not been so black or his jawline not so pronounced.

When he turned to her, his black brows were drawn together in a thoughtful frown, almost a glower. In a moment, his fierce expression relaxed ever so slightly, but she did not feel any easier. She felt defenseless and somehow exposed as she stood before him, and the word that came to mind to best describe him was *predator.*

"Miss Trenton, how good of you to join me." His voice was soft and low.

"Mr. D-Desmond," she stammered. After a slight pause she remembered to execute an awkward little curtsy.

His smile deepened. The girl was perfect, just as Carstairs had described her. It was not Desmond's habit, certainly, to gamble for young women, but doubtless among his varied business ventures Carstairs occasionally made certain "arrangements" between gentlemen visiting in the city and women of...free spirit. Desmond was amused that Carstairs had referred to her as his "ward."

The proposition had intrigued him.

He had kept himself aloof from his neighbors since taking possession of Kingsbrook and so did not have any friends among the families living near him. When he was here on his estate he found himself virtually isolated from the surrounding community.

He did not regret the fact. He valued his privacy and saw enough of society in London and abroad to sate him. But the house did, on occasion, seem awfully silent, and it had occurred to him that having a woman in his home, in his bed, now and then, would compensate for any lack of ties to the local gentry.

Of course, bringing a mistress to stay with him in Kingsbrook would effectively bar him from any future ties with the local gentry, so just in case he ever wanted to court local favor, he could, as Mr. Carstairs had, present her as his ward. And she looked the part. From the outfit she wore, the style of her hair, even the youthful timbre of her voice, she almost seemed to be a schoolgirl.

"Come in, Miss Trenton. Sit down. Jenny has prepared an excellent tea for us. Let us not allow it to grow cold." He motioned toward the short divan, and Marianne quickly sat, thankful for the offer to relieve the weight from the uncertain support of her knees.

Unexpectedly, Mr. Desmond joined her, in effect sitting down by her side.

"Tea?"

She nodded.

"Sugar? Milk? I do not see any lemon here. Shall I ring for Mrs. River?"

"Oh, no," Marianne gasped. "Sugar and milk are fine. I like sugar and milk. I never put lemon in my tea. Well, sometimes I do, but I do not like it as well as sugar. And milk."

"Sugar and milk it is then," Desmond said, taking up a lump of sugar with silver tongs and pouring a measure of milk into the cup before passing it to her.

The cup rattled treacherously and Marianne set it down.

"And tell me, Miss Trenton...won't you have a sandwich? Cress, I believe...how do you like Kingsbrook? Somewhat different from Londontown, is it not?"

Marianne, having taken one of the proffered sandwiches and bitten into it, could only nod.

"But then, that has been my goal. To make this place as unlike any town as possible."

He smiled at her over his cup, and Marianne swallowed the bite of sandwich, which then became a heavy, solid lump in her throat. She swallowed again. "It appears you have succeeded," she offered breathlessly at last.

"I hope you will not miss the bustle and noise of London," Mr. Desmond said, his tone of perfect politeness not calming her nerves at all. "I find Kingsbrook very peaceful, though I suppose some could find the quiet oppressive."

"Oh, not me, sir. I love the quiet, but then, Mr. Carstairs's house was not frequented so often that it 'bustled,' anyway."

Marianne gave a wavery smile, but Desmond had looked away. He did not want to hear about Carstairs nor the business that went on in his "house."

"I see," he said, choosing one of the little cakes from the tray Mrs. River had provided. He held the tray out to Marianne, but she shook her head. The idea of the colored icing mixing with the chewed watercress in her throat nearly made her gag.

"I hope by that you mean you will not find your change of abode too jarring," Desmond continued, putting the tray down again.

"Not at all," Marianne said, then, taking a breath, added, "in fact, I have been waiting the opportunity to thank you, Mr. Desmond, for your kindness in bringing me here. Kingsbrook is a lovely place and I shall endeavor to meet your expectations."

"I am sure you will," the gentleman said, smiling into her eyes and then allowing his gaze to slip down even farther.

"And you must tell me if there is anything I can do for you," she offered.

"Oh, you may rely upon that," he said, with a smile that did not brighten his dark eyes.

Another moment of silence ensued, during which he studied her and she studied her teacup.

"It was a long ride," she mumbled at last, the only thing she could think of to say. "And warm. Very warm. Rickers warned me it would be warm today when he came this morning. And it was. And still is. Very warm. One does not notice it as much in the shade outside there, and, of course, inside here it is perfectly cool. But the ride itself was warm. And long."

The dampness at her hairline would have seemed to refute her claim that the house was cool, but it, like her babbling, was a sign of her nervousness.

"Yes, I suppose the ride was exhausting," the gentleman murmured, directly into her ear, so that his breath tickled the fine hairs at the base of her hairline. "You would probably like to rest and unpack before we get any better acquainted."

"Yes. I...that would be lovely," Marianne whispered. But she could still feel his breath on her neck and was not completely clear on what it was that would be lovely.

The gentleman smiled slowly. "Very well," he said. He stood and offered his hand to assist her to her feet, a gesture that was not entirely superfluous, given her nervous state. "Rest yourself, Miss Trenton, and I will meet you at the supper table tonight."

He reached behind her, and for one giddy moment Marianne thought he was going to embrace her. Instead, he pulled a cord hanging against the wall, hidden behind the draperies.

Mrs. River answered the summons promptly. "Mr. Desmond? You wished something?" she asked. She had stopped short the moment she entered the room and discovered the gentleman and the young woman in such close proximity, and her voice was decidedly chill.

"Miss Trenton is feeling exhausted after her trip from London. Take her upstairs and have Tilly or Alice draw a bath."

"Certainly, sir. This way, Miss Trenton."

Marianne left with Mrs. River, not sure if she would rather be in the company of the unfriendly housekeeper or stay with the unnerving Mr. Desmond. Either way, she suspected that by leaving Uncle Horace's she had jumped from the frying pan directly into a roaring bonfire.

Following Mrs. River's brisk orders, Tilly drew a bath, while Alice helped Miss Trenton unpack.

Tilly, the older maid, was a taciturn woman with lined face and dumpy figure. She did not even acknowledge Marianne's presence. Alice offered her a shy smile when Mrs. River summoned her, but after a look at the housekeeper and her dour expression, the little maid withheld any other friendly overtures. With eyes downcast, she silently took the articles Marianne extracted from her bags.

Marianne regretted the coolness she sensed from the staff. But her rooms were very grand and the bath positively decadent in its luxuriance, and she tried to let her troubled thoughts float away with the fragrant steam. She followed the bath with a much-needed nap.

When Alice knocked on her door to announce dinner at half past eight, Marianne was already carefully dressed and prepared, if she ever would be, to dine with the master of the house.

Alice went ahead of her into the dining room, but passed through the door beyond, which led to the kitchen. Marianne found herself alone.

The long table was covered with white linen and set for two with china, crystal and silver, all shined so flawlessly that she could see the reflected image of her forest green gown as she paced, waiting for the disconcerting gentleman. The dining room was at the back of the house, and lined with long windows just as in the front. Darkness had fallen, and she could also glimpse her reflection in gaps between the imperfectly drawn drapes.

She was wearing one of the few dresses that she had brought from her home when she came to stay with Uncle Horace. As she touched the folds of the skirt, she remembered her mother saying it was too old for her, but that she would grow into it someday. And probably she would, though she had not yet. The sleeves were off her shoulders, the bodice was tight and the neckline dipped provocatively. It was a gown made for a mature figure, though with the aid of pins and tucks, and in the dim light, Marianne's scant form appeared to fill it adequately.

Finally, after desperate thoughts began to present themselves about being left in here alone all night, or worse, being required to eat by herself at the forbidding table, the double doors to the dining room were thrown open and there stood Mr. Desmond.

"I thought you had forgotten me," she exclaimed nervously. She had not meant to voice her thoughts, but somehow the words escaped her.

"Miss Trenton. Not at all. The afternoon got away from me, though. I did not even take time to dress for dinner." He stopped to consider the picture the girl presented in her dark dress in the midst of the room filled with light and sparkle. The green gown called to mind his initial impression of the cat and the jungle. "I see now I should have."

"Oh, no. You look wonderful." A dull flush mounted the girl's cheeks.

"Well, let us continue our admiration of each other over a bowl of soup. I assume you are hungry? I am starved, and I had more to eat at tea than half a cress sandwich." Mr. Desmond stepped to the table and rang the little silver bell near one of the plates. Evidently his plate.

Mrs. River answered the summons. Marianne had the distinct impression Mr. Desmond's house and life flowed along so elegantly and effortlessly because of the housekeeper's careful attention.

"We are hungry, Mrs. River. Convey my apologies to Mrs. Rawlins for being late and see that supper is served immediately, if you will."

Mrs. River murmured her acknowledgment and left.

Desmond held out a chair, and Marianne sat. A bowl of clear broth with a hint of onions appeared in front of her. She supposed she ate it, because after a while the dish was cleared away, replaced by a plate holding a lean slice of beef and a selection of hot vegetables. She saw Mr. Desmond eating, and she made a conscious effort to choose the same fork he picked up for whatever course was in front of them. But she honestly did not remember eating.

She did not recall anything about that meal except Mr. Desmond's deepset eyes, which one discovered were dark gray if one was fortunate enough to be very close to him, and his soft, low voice, which was mesmerizing. He spoke of exotic parts of the world, places of which she had never even heard. He recited passages of literature, words full of fire and passion that brought the blood to her face.

The clock struck ten.

He told her she looked bewitching in her gown, with her hair arranged so.

The clock struck eleven.

Five minutes later it struck twelve.

"Listen to the quiet," Desmond murmured, tilting his head as if he were hearing faint strains of stillness wafting to them on the night air. "The house is so solid it does not even creak in the night. And all the servants have gone to bed. Even Mrs. River. There have been times when I thought Mrs. River did not go to bed at all." Desmond smiled and rose. "Let us follow their example," he said, pulling Marianne gently to her feet.

He did not release her hand, but led her through the dim halls and up the darkened staircase. They turned on the landing and started along the balcony overlooking the front hall. Desmond stopped at one of the doors and opened it, drawing her inside. In the darkness, Marianne, being unfamiliar with the house, believed it was her room and stepped across the threshold.

Mr. Desmond followed with the candle, and by the time her senses registered the fact that it was the wrong room, he had closed the door behind them.

"This is not my room," she told him, still believing he, like she, had made an understandable mistake.

"No, it is my room."

At last, at long last, far past the time when such a reaction would have been understandable and advisable, Marianne felt the cold stab of panic in her heart.

"I think it will be better this way, do you not agree?" Desmond said, turning to engage the lock on the door. "By this arrangement, you may keep your rooms to yourself, where you can be alone and enjoy your privacy."

Coolly he began to loosen the buttons of his pants. Horrified, Marianne watched him pull his trousers off completely, exposing long, dark, exceptionally hairy legs.

"Then when we are together," he continued, speaking as casually as if they were exchanging opinions on the weather in a public salon, "we will be in here. Our rooms are even close enough that you may retire to your bed afterward, if you wish. Though I certainly hope you would choose to spend some nights with me."

Marianne's eyes were very large, though in the uncertain light of the single candle, Desmond may not have recognized the fear that filled them. Or perhaps he simply chose to ignore it, or to interpret it as something else. Desire, perhaps.

But it was fear in her eyes, in her mind, in her heart. She took a step away from him, but the distance she put between them was negligible, and without moving, he reached out and grasped her arm, encircling the slender limb with his long fingers. He pulled her against him and was excited to feel her heart pounding in her chest as rapidly as a sparrow's.

"What—what are you doing?" she gasped, pulling her head back, but unable to free her arms.

He wrapped his own arms around her, holding her head with one hand as he bent toward her.

"I am taking you to paradise, my little fawn," he murmured as he nuzzled the creamy indentation of her neck and kissed the pink lobe of her ear. "And I absolutely guarantee you will enjoy it more than anything old Carstairs has given you before."

Suddenly his lips were on hers. For a moment, for a split second, Marianne was lost in the sensual pleasure of their warmth, their moistness, electrified by the feel of his tongue against her lips. His hand at her back, caressing the exposed skin of her shoulder blades, pressed her to him. She was aware of the tense strength of his thigh muscles as he worked his knee between her legs.

But as her legs were forced apart, as he drew his other hand up to the bodice of her dress, her head cleared with the realization of what he was doing, what he was going to do to her. She pulled away, trying to get her arms between them, turning her face away from his kisses.

"No, no!" she gasped.

He stopped his efforts for a moment and looked into her eyes with a puzzled expression.

"Your resistance is not very flattering, my dear. I would not have imagined this was the best way to get ahead in your profession."

"I—I don't know what you mean," she whispered, unable to catch a full breath of air because of his tight embrace.

"I mean, you owe me this. I intend to collect on Carstairs's wager."

"Mr. Carstairs's wager? What wager?"

"The wager he lost and I won. You, Miss Trenton."

"Me? But I am Mr. Carstairs's ward," she gasped.

He smiled. Of course. Rather than being unskilled in her field, the girl was, quite to the contrary, very good. She was acting out her role of "ward." Delightful.

With no further ado, Desmond picked her up in his arms and carried her to the big, dark, four-poster bed in the middle of the room.

"No...no, you mustn't!" she cried. "Oh, please, no."

But Desmond, believing it was all part of her "ward-and-guardian" game, ignored her pleas as he pinned her arms with his left hand and with his right loosened the bodice of her dress. The buttons were frustratingly small and he was tempted to rip the material, but he focused his concentration on the little bits of obsidian and at last unhooked them all, without pulling any of them loose.

The dress fell open and he quickly pushed her confining undergarments out of the way.

As he freed her firm, young breasts, he released her arms, meaning to cup the tender morsels to his mouth. But the girl beneath him swung her freed hand, delivering a resounding slap to the side of his face.

Intoxicated by passion, Desmond only flinched in surprise and then chuckled. It was a dark sound, a sound without mercy, and Marianne's heart clenched tightly.

"You are a little spitfire, are you not?" he said with a laugh.

He captured her hands again and started to pull at the material of her skirts and petticoats. He had expected cooperation, but the girl was *very* good, determined to make it exciting for him.

Her gown was like a maze. He would work his hand under one length of material only to find another blocking his path. But at last his fingers touched the smooth skin of her thigh, warm and yielding. He rubbed the inside of her leg delicately, trailing his palm over the silky skin, pushing aside confining undergarments here, as well. He nuzzled her exposed bosom, taking the tender mounds into his mouth.

By now he had raised all her skirts and petticoats out of the way. He was excited to feel the smooth, cool length of her bare legs against his own. He pushed his thigh between hers and began to rock gently.

At any moment she would begin to relax and respond. She would move beneath him, shifting to accommodate him. They would push against each other, the heat building between them, until they melted into one another.

With his lips against her ivory skin, he moaned softly, lost in the smell and feel of her. He expected to hear a soft murmur from her in response.

But she did not give voice to her passion. The form beneath him did not relax, did not move to accommodate him. She remained cold and stiff. She might have been petrified. And then he noticed a hitch in the rise and fall of her chest against his mouth.

He freed his hand from the intricacies of her undergarments and raised himself to look into her face.

Tears were streaming from under her clenched eyelids, wetting the hair at her temples and the pillow under her head. Her lips moved, and in the sudden stillness in the room he heard her murmur, "Please, no. Oh, dear Lord, please do not let him do this to me. Please, no."

He released her hands and rolled off of her, sitting up on the edge of the bed. He glanced behind him and pushed his fingers through the wild tangle of his hair.

What did she mean by this? What was happening? This was not what Carstairs had promised him.

Desmond took a breath and told himself to think. His breathing became deeper and slower, as the fire in his loins cooled. What exactly *had* Carstairs promised him? The man had offered him his "ward." His ward? Was it possible...?

"Marianne?" he said at last, very softly.

The girl did not open her eyes, but her lips stopped moving.

"How old are you, Marianne?" he asked.

There was a long pause, during which the girl hiccupped and Desmond gently smoothed away the tears on one of her cheeks with his thumb.

"Sixteen," she whispered.

Sixteen? Was she as young as that? He studied her unlined face.

There was no question. He had been a blind fool.

"And you...you have never done this before, have you?"

She shook her head.

Desmond withdrew his hand from her face, almost expecting to see her cheek stained by his touch. He was suddenly filled with a great revulsion. A revulsion for Carstairs, who had delivered the young woman to him, fully aware of her probable fate. The wager had been offered and accepted with a mutual understanding as to what they were playing for.

But he also felt revulsion for himself. Carstairs was a pig, but what was he?

It was very silent for two or three minutes. The girl's tears had ceased, though her sobs occasionally shook the mattress.

Desmond appeared to be completely lost in thought, totally unaware of the girl, but in fact he was consumed by thoughts of her, considering what her life must have been like, wondering what had brought her to this place tonight and where the path on which Carstairs had planted her would eventually lead her. If this was her first time, Carstairs must not have tried this ploy before. But since his wager had been accepted once, it would be again. Probably often. Until she was no longer worth the bet. Even though Desmond would not touch the girl again, if he sent her back he would be delivering her straight into a life of prostitution, into the the jaws of hell. He would be no better than Carstairs.

He grimaced. He was no better than Carstairs now, for he had brought her here expecting to collect his "winnings."

"Mr. Desmond?" the girl whispered.

Desmond started in surprise and turned to look at her.

Her eyes were open, red rimmed and swollen, focused on him with an expression Desmond would have thought only executioners saw in the eyes of the condemned.

"Are you finished?" she asked.

"What?"

"Is it over? Can I go back to my room?"

"Yes. Go. Go," he said hoarsely, turning his face so he would not have to watch her struggle from the bed.

She rolled to her side and swung her legs toward the edge. She had to work her way across the wide mattress before she could reach the floor, but at last she stood. Aware of the man on the bed behind her but not daring to look in his direction, she pushed her skirts down self-consciously and fumbled to refasten the bodice of her dress.

With slumped shoulders and heavy tread, she walked to the door and struggled to release the lock. He could not help raising his eyes to watch her when a relieved sigh signaled that she had finally succeeded. He saw her pull open the door of his room. Before stepping out into the hallway, she pushed the hair back from her face, squared her shoulders and raised her chin.

He was touched by her bravery and determination. But before his door shut her completely from view, he saw the line of her shoulders slump again as if with a terrible weight.

Desmond felt crushed with remorse. There was no question about the physical damage he had almost done to her, but what spiritual blow had he actually delivered?

He could not keep her here at Kingsbrook, subjecting himself to the accusations of her presence. But neither could he send her back to her former home.

He had played for a ward and he had won a ward, but now that he had her, what was he to do with her?

Chapter Three

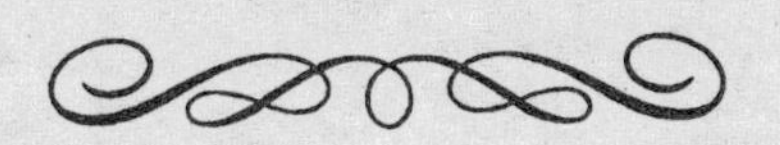

To Marianne, her short lifetime seemed to be a succession of frightful nights. Endless nights spent waiting for Uncle Horace to return to the town house, fearfully wondering what abuse and indignity she would be required to endure this time. That ghastly night she had spent at her mother's bedside, watching her become weaker and weaker, unable to do anything to overturn the awful verdict, to bar entrance to the merciless reaper.

But not even the memory of that night seemed as horrible as this night in Kingsbrook.

Marianne undressed slowly, careful to keep her eyes turned from the mirror, fearful of the physical evidence she would see of what had happened.

She pulled the green gown off her shoulders and dropped it to the floor at her feet. It lay in a crumpled heap, and automatically she picked it up and hung it in her closet, though she knew she could never bear to wear it again.

She removed her underthings, then poured some of the lukewarm water from her pitcher into the basin. She washed slowly, carefully, but not with any obsessive effort to cleanse herself. A tear rolled down her cheek as she told herself that was impossible now.

Her muscles were sore, owing to her struggle with the larger, stronger man. Her head ached and her breasts were tender. She did not feel a deeper, more intimate pain, but she was too distracted and too ignorant to wonder at that. Besides, more painful to her than any physical injury was her burning shame.

She pulled a long flannel nightgown from the drawer where Alice had put it earlier that afternoon. She slipped it over her head and then crawled between the sheets of her bed. She pulled the blankets up around her neck as if chilled by the cold of winter, though it was so far an unseasonably warm summer. The cold she felt was deeper and darker than any she had known before.

Marianne did not want to think about what had happened, but self-accusations swirled around in her head like feathers caught in a hurricane. What had she done to provoke such an assault? Nothing consciously or intentionally, that she could recall, but she had been so fascinated by him. She had been flattered by his attention, eager for his approval. Her admiring gaze had no doubt seemed provocative. She had probably leaned too far toward him as he spoke to her, or perhaps her eyes or the movement of her lips or hands could have been interpreted as an invitation.

She moaned softly and turned onto her side.

Her anguish was compounded because she was so lonely. There was no one here, no one in her life to whom she could turn for help and comfort. No one to advise her or give her any explanations. Marianne had to reach her own conclusions about everything, and she was a very young girl with a very limited field of reference.

All night long she tossed and turned, her brief snatches of sleep filled with dreams of strange longings, from which she awoke drenched in sweat and even further shamed.

But at long last the sun rose and began to climb higher in the sky. Wide-awake and uncomfortably warm, Marianne still lay abed, the blankets clutched to her chin.

When she had crawled into this bed last night, she had wished with all the strength of her being that she could die.

But she had not died, and as she turned fretfully, restlessly, she realized she did not really want to spend the rest of her life in this bed.

True, when she rose she would have to leave this room again. She would have to walk down the stairs, speak to Alice and Mrs. River. *He* would be there.

The thought made her stomach churn, and she tried to imagine what she would say or do the next time she saw him.

She could not escape him, though, lying in this bed. If he was there, he was there. In fact, if he so desired, he could force open her door and drag her out, just as her uncle Horace had. She could do nothing to prevent that, as she had been unable to fight Desmond off last night. Somehow she would have to deal with the terrible uncertainties in her life and get on with it.

Her lips firmed as they had last night just before she left his room. She pushed the blankets back and swung her legs from the bed.

"Mrs. River!"

"Miss Trenton?"

They had surprised each other in the dining room. Marianne was relieved to find the room deserted when she arrived there and was doing her best not to alert anyone in the house as to her presence. She was gratified to find a few breakfast things still on the sideboard. The congealed eggs and cold oatmeal did not tempt her, but she found a few fresh strawberries and two muffins, which she was hungrily munching when Mrs. River entered the room through the kitchen door.

The housekeeper took a moment to collect herself. She was very confused by the situation here at Kingsbrook. She had known the young master and his family too long for her to be taken in by Mr. Desmond's very thin story of bringing his "ward" to stay at Kingsbrook for a while. In the rooms directly adjacent to his own.

In fact, she had known Mr. Desmond since he was "Mister Peter" and came to visit his grandfather occasionally. He had been a pleasant enough child, but it was her understanding that he had acquired certain unfortunate habits while away at school. It was known in the servants' quarters—and what was known in the servants' quarters was invariably true, though no one could say precisely from whence the knowledge had come—that the boy was a great disappointment to his parents and had been virtually abandoned by them as a hopeless cause.

But Mrs. River knew her place, and Mr. Desmond was welcome to indulge himself and his base appetites without asking leave of his housekeeper or even hearing her opinion on the subject. Mrs. River firmly believed that she could distance herself enough from the gentleman's private life that his crotchets need not come to her attention at all, as long as he kept such goings-on in London or across the Channel. But to bring a loose woman into this fine old house, to bed and board her behind these walls, deeply offended the Kingsbrook housekeeper.

Then Alice had reported this morning, in breathless undertones, that Mr. Desmond had slept *alone* in his bed, as had Miss Trenton in hers. Alice had added that Miss Trenton really did seem a perfect lady, whatever her profession might be, if Mrs. Rawlins and Tilly caught her meaning.

Mrs. River was disapproving of such tittle-tattle, naturally, and dismissed Alice's opinion as the silly romanticism of a child. Now, though, as she stood facing the young woman in question, she could not help but admit that the adventuress of last night and this sweet young thing with crumbs on her fingers and a tiny smear of strawberry on her chin might not have been the same person.

This morning Miss Trenton was dressed in a light smock with a homey pinafore over it. Her hair was mussed and her eyes looked tired and red. Mrs. River felt her moral outrage being replaced by motherly compassion. Had she been wrong?

It was a new idea for Mrs. River.

She had been the unquestioned authority on every subject here in Kingsbrook for so long that she had almost forgotten the concept of "being wrong."

"Excuse me. I found these things still out. I know it is terribly late and I certainly was not expecting breakfast, but I thought, since they were here... Oh, I—I hope they were not being reserved for someone!" Marianne stammered, as guiltily as if Mrs. River had surprised her stashing the house silverware in her undergarments.

"It is quite all right, Miss Trenton. You are welcome to anything on the sideboard, or Jenny will prepare something fresh for you if you would like."

"Oh, no," Marianne gasped, apparently appalled by the suggestion that something be prepared especially for her. "This is fine. The strawberries are very good, and if I can just take this second muffin up to my room, I will get out of your way."

The girl fumbled with the muffin, attempting to wrap it in a napkin, reducing it to little more than a mass of crumbs.

"Here now," Mrs. River said. Marianne looked up in astonishment, for the woman's voice sounded kind and helpful.

Tears sprang to the girl's eyes. She understood the housekeeper's coolness of yesterday, knowing now the reason Mr. Desmond had brought her here. They all thought she was a tart. And perhaps she was, she thought miserably.

She had been unhappy staying with Uncle Horace, always lonely, sometimes even mistreated, but she had never been as frightened and confused as she was here now. Never since her mother's death had she needed a comforting arm more.

"Oh, my dear," Mrs. River cooed, the last barrier of disapproval melted by the tears in the girl's eyes. The housekeeper stepped forward and put her arm around Marianne's shoulders, and the young woman collapsed against her bosom.

Dismissing Marianne's mature gown of last night, the impression she had given of flirting with Mr. Desmond, Mrs. River concluded she had made a deplorable mistake, that the young woman *was* here as the ward of her master, doubtless suffering from the recent loss of one or both of her parents. The tears were easily explained, and Mrs. River had only to gently pat the girl's back as she wept. "Hush, now," she said softly after several minutes.

Marianne, who had imagined her grief to be depthless, was surprised to find herself running out of tears. She sniffled, and Mrs. River withdrew her handkerchief from her waist and offered it to her. Like a dutiful child, Marianne blew into it heartily and felt herself even further recovered.

"Better?" Mrs. River asked.

Marianne nodded, hiccupping pitifully. "A little," she said. "I am sorry. . . ."

"Tut tut, child. I understand completely."

Marianne looked into the woman's face and was relieved to see she did not understand at all. Whatever trouble Mrs. River was imagining, it was not Marianne's seduction and fall from innocence.

"Now you go on up to your room and wash your face and brush your hair. It is almost noon, and by the time you come down again Jenny will have a nice bowl of soup ready for you."

The soup was delicious. Eaten in the privacy of a little nook in the kitchen, it was the most delicious meal Marianne could remember having in this place. Mrs. River was in and out of the kitchen several times, seeing to household affairs, entering again just in time to see Marianne mop up the last drop with her slice of bread.

"There now," the housekeeper said, wiping her hands on her apron as if she had finished some taxing chore. "Mr. Desmond—"

Marianne jerked her head up, wiping her mouth with the back of her hand as she looked around wildly. "Where? Where is Mr. Desmond?" she cried.

"Not here. Not here," Mrs. River said soothingly. Goodness, the girl was as skittish as a thoroughbred colt. "I was only going to say Mr. Desmond left early this morning. He said he would be away for a few days and that you are to enjoy free access to the house and the park while he is away, so I merely wondered what you would like to do now?" The housekeeper smiled, and Marianne smiled back, though hers was a little weak and trembling.

"I do not know," she said, genuinely at a loss.

"Well, you cannot stay tucked away in your room until the master returns," Mrs. River chided.

But Mrs. River's suggestion sounded very attractive to Marianne. She hurried back to her room and spent most of the day there, and the first half of the next. But by then she was growing bored and restless, indeed, and had quite caught up on her sleep.

"So you have come down at last?" Mrs. River said in greeting the next afternoon.

Marianne flushed slightly. "What are you going to do today, Mrs. River?" she inquired timidly.

"Why, I am going to shell peas for Mrs. Rawlins and set Alice to polishing the glassware," the housekeeper replied.

"May I help?" Marianne offered.

So Mrs. River and she shelled peas, and then Marianne and Alice polished crystal under the housekeeper's watchful gaze. Marianne took supper that night in the servants' quarters and for the first time felt quite comfortable, almost jolly here at Kingsbrook.

By the next day she was ready to explore the estate. "Might I go about on the grounds?" she asked Mrs. River.

The woman smiled. "Indeed you may, child. A breath of fresh air will do you a world of good."

Mrs. River pulled a loosely woven shawl from a hook and gently pushed Marianne toward the open doorway. She pointed out the walkway and suggested a route that would take her past the most charming sights of the Kingsbrook estate.

Marianne carefully put her foot outside the door, as if she was testing the frigid waters of some mountain spring before plunging in. She took another step. As soon as she was across the threshold, Mrs. River, with a soft chuckle, shut the door behind her.

At first Marianne wandered at random. After an excursion or two across meadows and flower beds left her with a muddied hem and a torn seam, she found that following the flagstone walkway was definitely the path of least resistance. And Mrs. River had been correct: whoever had plotted the route had done so with an eye to displaying all of the charms of the lovely estate.

The dense woods appeared to be clogged with a riot of ferns, mosses and ivy. The meadows were bejeweled with dahlias and delphiniums, and wild orchids and red campion were placed to achieve exactly the right balance and effect.

The pathway took Marianne across an arched wooden bridge over the bubbling brook. She saw another deer and wondered if the animals were treated as pets on Mr. Desmond's lands. She did not have a lump of sugar with her, but was quite certain the delicate doe would have taken it from her hand if she had.

She was watching her footing carefully because the trailblazer, in what must have been a moment of irrepressible mischief, had laid the path stones perilously close to the bank of the stream, when she looked up and found herself standing in front of a squat stone enclosure. Walking around to inspect it, she discovered it to be open to the air, with pillars of stacked stones supporting a sloping slate roof. It was evidently a gazebo, with the same primitive quality as the landscape and as painstakingly created.

From the bright, sunlit meadow, the place appeared dark and forbidding to Marianne. She peered around anxiously, feeling unaccountably threatened by the heavy pile of stones. Taking a breath to bolster her courage, she mounted the steps. Walking between two of the pillars into the shady interior was like entering a cave. But once inside, she found it a very pleasant retreat, with a smooth stone bench to rest upon. The curious acoustics seemed to deaden the sounds of the woodland as effectively as the closing of a door.

Marianne sat down.

She looked out onto the meadow, straining to hear the rustle of the breeze stirring the grasses. Gazing between the dark stone pillars at the sun-dappled scene was like looking at another world—a brighter, more innocent world. Marianne's eyes stung and tears began to flow down her cheeks. It was a world she could not be a part of now.

Not just because of what had happened, but because of the dark, more secret thoughts that pushed into her head: the image of him standing before her, half-clad, his bare legs pressed against her skirts; the remembered sensation of his heavy hand and strong fingers on her breasts, against the sensitive skin of her upper thigh. She wondered, though she did not like to and pushed the guilty thought away as quickly as she could, what it would have been like had Mr. Desmond gone slower, if she had been a willing partner. A great deal of whispering and sniggering went on about the subject, and Marianne wondered what on earth all the interest was about. She had experienced no great pleasure in the act. In fact, she could not remember "the act" at all. She wondered if, under the right circumstances, it could be as pleasant as people said. She tried to imagine what the right circumstances would be, and as a number of indecent scenes appeared before her mind's eye, she attempted to push those thoughts away as well.

Without a doubt, she was irredeemably vile and sinful.

She buried her face in her hands, trying to block out the images, trying to return to the girl she had been a week ago, knowing in her heart that girl was now part of her irretrievable past.

If Peter Desmond felt guilty about nothing else, he should feel guilty for that.

She was not alerted to another presence in the peaceful little glade until she heard the scuff of a shoe on the stone steps leading into the gazebo. She jerked her head up to meet the very eyes she was trying to forget, though their depth and intensity seemed almost to have burned their impression into her living flesh.

She gasped.

Desmond winced as if she had spat in his face.

She looked like a rosebud as she drew away from him, folding tightly within herself, pink and tender, young and immature, but with great promise in her delicate petals. Desmond realized he had bruised the bud, and his cheeks grew warm with an unfamiliar shame.

It had been many years since Peter Desmond had felt shame. He would have thought his conscience had atrophied completely by now. He remembered vaguely feeling ashamed when young Ronny Withers had gotten him drunk that first time, there at Ketterling, and he had missed classes the next day and been called into the dean's office.

"What have you to say for yourself, Master Desmond?" Dean Stampos had inquired darkly. Dean Stampos had been a big man, with heavy black brows and the voice of doom.

"I—I believe I was intoxicated, sir," young Desmond had gulped.

"Believe?" Dean Stampos thundered.

"I was intoxicated, sir."

"Six lashes, boy, and do not let me hear of such a thing again."

If Dean Oliver Stampos had ended his direful sentence merely with "Six lashes," Desmond really believed he would not have fallen from grace—at least not so quickly—nor plummeted to such depths. But the awesome symbol of authority in his young life had added those next eleven words, *and do not let me hear of such a thing again,* and the exceptionally bright boy had at last felt challenged by his schooling.

It became a contest of wit and ingenuity to find out how much he could get away with, how many rules he could break, in what misconduct he could indulge without Dean Stampos hearing of it. Desmond found he could quaff any strong drink his money could buy and his schoolboy stomach could hold. He found he could gamble away every cent of money his father sent him, his mother sent him, his grandfather advanced or he could beg, borrow or steal from the other boys. He believed it was Ronny Withers who also introduced him to the ladies who introduced him to pleasures of the flesh, though he was drunk at the time and did not really remember the painted jade who led him into one of the little cubicles, or what had happened there in the dark, let alone the schoolmate who had accompanied him to the den the night they sneaked away from Ketterling.

Yet in the end, Desmond was not as clever as he supposed, and when one day his father arrived at the school and Peter was called to a meeting in the dean's office, Stampos was able to produce a file of proof of the boy's misbehavior. Desmond was summarily dismissed.

He returned to the family home in Birmingham. His mother thought it was to her watchful care, but it was to a city that offered vice with as much increase over that available at the Ketterling school as a stream realizes when it enters a lake. Desmond eventually became a skilled gambler, but that education cost him the legacy an uncle had left him, all of the money his grandfather had meant for him to have after his death, when the boy took over Kingsbrook, and his father's good graces.

And though in the beginning, there at Ketterling, and even when he returned home, he felt a twinge of conscience now and then, the nudges became fainter, the remorse negligible. He was not aware of feeling particularly ashamed even when, at last, his father summoned him to his office in town and told him that after the escapade of the weekend before—Desmond did not remember what had happened; he only knew his gold watch and chain were gone again and one of the carriages was wrecked beyond repair—Mr. Desmond could not allow his son to stay in the family home any longer.

Mr. Desmond did not like to suggest that the boy go to live with his wife's father at the estate the old man was determined to leave him, and felt guilty at the relief he felt when Georgia tearfully suggested it herself. Sir Arthur Chadburn was a straitlaced old gentleman who would not countenance his grandson's debauchery, and Peter, Mr. Desmond knew from experience, was bound and determined to be debauched. Mr. Desmond did not like to imagine the result of the stress Peter would cause the elderly gentleman.

As it turned out, though, even as father and son were having their grim confrontation, a letter was being delivered to Mrs. Desmond announcing the death of her father. So Peter assumed ownership of the Kingsbrook manor and estate outside of Reading, and his father, with a stony face but a clear conscience, sent the boy away, vowing he would never see him again.

It was unbeknownst to his father, young Desmond was sure, that his mother sent him a semiannual stipend that more or less kept him afloat. It was meant to supplement the estate upkeep, but more often than not it supplemented Desmond's gambling expenses. Fortunately, his gaming had improved to the point where he could pay the few Kingsbrook servants with fair regularity and travel to all the great gambling Meccas here in England and on the Continent to make additional monies for himself and the estate.

It was a difficult, strenuous life he had chosen for himself. Despite his dismissal from boarding school, he was accepted into the Reading University on his scholastic merit. Though the lessons came easily, he would not focus on his education and left the university after four years with no better idea of what to do. By then he had been disowned by his family; he had lost the generous remembrances of his uncle and grandfather. His father had roared and his mother had wept, and through it all Desmond kept his jaw stubbornly squared and refused to admit to any shame.

Now, though, as he stood between the pillars of the little stone gazebo, facing the girl he had claimed as prize in his latest game of cards, his cheeks grew warm and he was forced to acknowledge his own ignominy.

He would have given anything to have relegated this meeting to someone else, but to have taken that happy option would have required a fuller disclosure than Desmond intended to ever give anyone about what had happened that night.

He cleared his throat. "Good day, Miss Trenton," he said.

She did not answer, only continued to watch him warily.

He took another step into the gazebo, and she hitched herself farther away from him on the bench, as far as she could without falling to the stone flooring.

He sighed.

"Miss Trenton, I wish I could convince you that you do not have to fear me, but I do not suppose that is possible now. Here, I will stand with my back against this pillar. I will not take another step toward you the entire time I am here. And you, if you could, may relax your hold on the edge of the bench there so your knuckles are not quite so white."

He nodded toward where she gripped the stone seat, apparently clinging for dear life. She released her hold and then looked up at the man standing on the other side of the little enclosure, his back dutifully flat against the supporting pillar. She folded her hands in her lap, but dismay and terror still filled her eyes with dark shadows.

Peter Desmond, though an admitted roué, having advanced from dark dens to glittering palaces of prostitution, had never taken a woman against her will or even below her top price. It was his habit, though hardly a regular one, to meet with such ladies and leave them satisfied, as well as pleased, as it were. Despite his decidedly wicked ways, he had never expected to see in a young lady's eyes the expression he saw in Marianne's.

He cleared his throat gruffly. "I will come directly to the point," he said. "I have spent a number of sleepless nights contemplating your immediate future, as I am sure you have."

The girl nodded slightly.

"If I understood you correctly that night . . ." the young woman's pale cheeks suddenly blazed at the mere mention of the episode, and Desmond uncomfortably cleared his throat again ". . . you are not a regular girl of Mr. Carstairs's then?"

Marianne looked at him blankly, furrowing her brow slightly in her attempt to understand his meaning.

"You do not . . . *work* for Carstairs?"

"I am the ward of Uncle Horace," Marianne whispered.

They were the same words Carstairs had said to him, the same words he had laughed over and repeated to Abbot and Phillips, almost the exact words Mrs. River had employed to announce Miss Trenton's arrival. Why, then, did they mean something so very different when the girl whispered them?

"Yes, of course," Desmond murmured. "Nevertheless, I do not believe you should return to Mr. Carstairs's establishment."

He watched her carefully, trying to gauge her reaction to his decision. Would she quarrel with him and be difficult? Did she *want* to return to that pit?

She shook her head, but did not venture any comment.

Desmond nodded briskly. "Right. I should tell you then, I have been into London to consult with legal counsel, reviewing the situation in which we find ourselves."

Marianne's expressive face registered surprise. After what Mr. Desmond had done, how could he go to a representative of the law?

"I do not know if you are fully aware of the circumstances that brought you here, Miss Trenton, but Mr. Carstairs wagered his guardianship of you and lost. I won." He could not keep the ironic tone from his voice. "My lawyer informs me that, though unusual, such a transfer of responsibility can be legal. There are papers and signatures involved, but Mr. Bradley assures me that dating from my meeting with Carstairs and the others at the Grand Hotel, you may be considered in my legal custody."

"Oh."

It was a very small sound, but Desmond hoped there was more surprise in it than fright. But there was some fright in her eyes, which cut him to the quick. Seeing her here, clothed in dress and pinafore that made her look like a child fresh from the nursery, Mr. Desmond was, as his housekeeper had been, struck by how young she appeared. If she had arrived at Kingsbrook dressed this way, or had come to supper that night in this outfit instead of that indecently provocative green gown that seemed to set her hair ablaze, Desmond would never have attempted what he had.

Now the gentleman hitched his back in discomfort against the hard rocks, but kept his shoulders squarely against the pillar. "It is my intention to enroll you in a respectable boarding school."

He had arrived at that happy solution in the long waking hours of that night before he left for London, though he was not prepared for the amount of money such a solution would cost. Mr. Bradley, his solicitor, had informed him a "good" school would cost every bit of the money his mother sent him each year. It was lucky for Desmond that he had done the girl no physical harm, or this damned conscience of his, which had chosen a most inconvenient time to reintroduce itself, would have had him selling Kingsbrook to recompense her.

As it was, he would be required to tighten his belt and pass up his forays to Paris and Monte Carlo for the next few years. As he discussed the proposition with Bradley and contemplated the sacrifices that would be required of him, his resolve had faltered a bit. He might have been willing to seek another solution, but as the lovely young girl sat quivering on the cold stone bench before him, his chin firmed and he determined to limit his gambling trips to London and Liverpool as long as she was enrolled, if need be.

By gad, it felt good to be noble!

"I have made no inquiries yet, so if you have a preference for the part of the country in which you wish to be located, or for a school you may have heard about, I will certainly give your choice consideration."

"I—I attended Miss Willmington's classroom on Miller Street for a while," she whispered.

"You have had some schooling?" Desmond asked, surprised. He had assumed the girl, though not a professional yet, was merely some street urchin Carstairs had picked up, preparing her for market.

The girl nodded.

"You can read and write, then?"

She nodded again.

"And work figures?"

Her lips turned up unconsciously, and Desmond drew in his breath at the delightfully whimsical effect the slight change in her expression produced.

"Some," she said softly. Marianne's introduction to, and practice with, numbers had been grueling, the difficulty compounded by any help her father tried to give.

At the thought of her father, the glimmer of a smile left her lips, and Desmond exhaled in disappointment. "Well, that will make a difference, of course," he said. "Do you wish to return to Miss Willmington's school?"

"I finished there," she said softly. "It was for children."

"I see." He swallowed heavily. The girl before him was still barely more than a child. "Very well. We must find another place then, but now I see I do not have to look for a classroom that offers the most elementary instruction, but can place you with girls your own age."

Marianne continued to stare at him wordlessly, with large, disconcerting eyes.

"I shall set the works in motion then," he said. "It may take a week or two, but I will take rooms in Reading until I find a place for you. You may make yourself at home here in Kingsbrook, and Mrs. River will help you with anything you need. Do you have any questions about your schooling?"

He paused to give the girl a chance to speak, but she shook her head.

"If you think of something, you may ask Mrs. River. I will leave complete instructions with her. If I do not see you again before you leave, Miss Trenton, once more allow me to express my regrets over our little misunderstanding."

He took a deep breath of relief. There. It was over. He had done all he could in redemption for bringing the girl here and behaving like an animal, and now, if he was lucky, he would never have to see her again and could put this episode behind him. In the future, he would be happy for the solitude of Kingsbrook, thankful for the privacy of his bed.

He was even tempted to give up gambling, though he did not go so far as to make the personal pledge. His losses he could cover; it was his winnings that were so appalling.

He pushed himself away from the pillar.

Marianne had dropped her eyes, seeming to be fascinated by the fingers twisting in her lap. "Mr. Desmond, what if..." she began softly, timidly, unable to let him go without asking her most fearful question.

"Yes?" he said, encouraging her as gently as he could when it appeared she would not finish her sentence.

"What if I am pregnant?" she whispered.

Desmond's shoulders fell back heavily against the pillar. In fact, it was fortunate the solid pile of stones was there to catch him.

"You are not pregnant, Marianne," he said. There was a gruffness in his voice that suggested how touched he was by the child and her anguished question.

"But after that night..."

"Nothing happened that night."

"Nothing?" She looked up at him, her beautiful eyes opened wide in doubtful wonder. "But you—you..."

"I behaved like a brute, but I assure you the act was not consummated that night. You are as pure and inviolate now as you were when you left Mr. Carstairs's home in London. And you are safer here than you ever were there."

The girl's eyes filled with tears of relief. "Really?" she asked uncertainly, hopefully.

He wanted more than he had ever wanted anything in his life—more than he had wanted Galston's Way to win the Derby that year when he might still have repaid his grandfather; more than he had wanted that ace of clubs that would have finished his straight flush and sent him home victorious at least once before his father threw him out of the house; more even than he wished, sometimes late at night as he lay in some narrow cot in a strange city, that good old Ronny Withers had sunk to the bottom of the

English Channel before he ever came to Ketterling—to gather this trembling girl in his arms and smooth away the fear and distrust he had taught her. But he had promised he would stay where he was, and the finger of God could not have moved him from this place.

"Really," he replied earnestly.

She gave a shuddering sigh and dropped her eyes again.

She was not going to have a baby.

Marianne had been terrified by the events of that night and totally confused. Her perception of the sexual act was based solely on the cheap novels she read. In them the man kissed the woman—very much as Mr. Desmond had kissed her—clothes were discarded and body parts exposed, and in the next chapter the woman was with child.

Her fear had been practically paralyzing, and now her relief made her bones feel gelatinous. But she believed Mr. Desmond. Not only because he knew more than she did about what had happened that night and how much more was actually required to produce a baby, but because of the look on his face and the timbre of his voice when he spoke.

"Good," she whispered, but he did not answer, and when she looked up she was alone in the gazebo again.

As she stared across the empty space, out into the deep green of the bower beyond the columns of stone, her mind was cleared of the dark pall of fear that had held her in its grip. But in its place, she heard Mr. Desmond's words again and was free to contemplate their meaning.

"I assure you the act was not consummated *that evening,*" he had said. Mr. Desmond, she knew, was very rich. And very wicked. He was sending her to a fine boarding school, but was he taking such action only to save her for himself another day?

It was not the first time Marianne misunderstood the gentleman's motives, nor would it be the last.

Chapter Four

It was not a week later that Mrs. River received news and instructions from Mr. Desmond informing her, and his ward, of an upstanding women's institute of education that he had located near Farnham. A place had already been secured for Miss Trenton.

During the interim, as he had promised, Mr. Desmond left Kingsbrook to allow Marianne privacy. Feeling curiously at home in the big house now, she spent the days flitting from room to room, most often coming to rest in the library, with its tall shelves packed with books, collected over decades.

That the library was not the compilation of one person was evidenced by the varying topics of interest represented: birds, history, tropical plants, political essays, even a few slim volumes of poetry produced by obscure poets whose names Marianne had never heard before. There were books about rocks and books about etiquette, and a rather large selection about horses and horsemanship, horse equipage and shoeing, feeding, bedding and medicine. That last, the book on horse medicine, was a very old volume that included a chapter on demonic possession and another on the use of equine leeches.

On a low shelf along the north wall of the room, easily within reach and just a little above the girl's eye level, were books with some rather intriguing titles: *Medea, Antigone,* the *Iliad,* the *Aeneid.* One whose cover was nearly torn off, and which fell open easily and lay flat, suggesting it was often taken from the shelf and read, was entitled the *Odyssey.*

But Marianne was disappointed when she opened them to find them all, and many more besides, written in a foreign language, some even in a foreign alphabet that looked like bird scratchings and mystic symbols.

In all the immense inventory of the room, there was not one book of the sort Marianne was used to reading. No *Berkshire Maiden,* no *Eleanor Simple,* no *The Life of Roman Charles and the Ladies He Encountered,* subtitled *A Misspent Youth.* Nevertheless, she was enthralled by the new ideas suddenly available to her.

She was in the library reading, in fact, several days later, when Mrs. River brought her a letter that had just arrived in the post.

"It is from Mr. Desmond," the housekeeper said, holding the letter and empty envelope before her. "He says he has found a school for you. He says...well here, let me read it to you. 'The Farnham Academy is outside of the town proper. I believe Miss Trenton will enjoy the quiet, and Mrs. Avery, headmistress of the school, assures me they provide the finest education befitting a young woman of our advanced day.' There now, does that not sound grand? He says you are to leave Kingsbrook a week from the day he wrote the letter, which would make it...let me see. Day after tomorrow."

Marianne felt her stomach tighten, but she was not sure whether it was from anticipation or dread.

"Though he adds if that is too soon, you are to be allowed all the time you need. But I do not think that is the case. Alice can have you packed in one afternoon. Do you not agree?"

Marianne had little choice but to nod in response to Mrs. River's brisk question.

Without any further discussion, Marianne Trenton found herself two days later once again behind Rickers, in an open coach on her way to the Farnham Academy for the Edification of Young Ladies of Quality.

She had been at Kingsbrook for just twenty-one days, but they had been the most tumultuous days of her young life. She was surprised to feel an ache of homesickness in her throat as a turn in the road concealed the manor house and parkland surrounding it. Her days at Kingsbrook had perhaps not been happy, but they had become an important part of her.

The academy was housed in an unremarkable gray stone building of three floors, with two smaller adjoining buildings. One of the outbuildings served as the kitchen, from which food never arrived hot at the long table in the dining room, though the room was on the ground floor, with a door that opened directly onto the walk leading from the cookhouse.

The other outbuilding was for physical exertion and exercise, "as necessary to the well-being of the body as nourishment." Mrs. Avery, a spiky woman of rail-like thinness, was a great advocate of the benefits of physical exertion and exercise.

The main portion of the school, where the girls spent most of their time, was inside the big center building.

Mr. Desmond's careful inquiries had indeed located a very creditable institute of learning for "young women of quality of that advanced day." Occasionally, though, as Marianne attended Miss Gransby's elocution classes, Mrs. Lynk's deportment classes or Mr. Brannon's ancient history classes, her attention strayed, and she wondered if a school slightly less tailored to young women of quality might not have been more interesting.

Mrs. Avery taught the Latin classes. "Not all schools for young ladies include the study of Latin," she often reminded them. "Young women are taught to speak softly and work their needlepoint, while all the most sublime thoughts of mankind are locked away in the classic languages. Young men are taught Latin. Boys of eight years old are taught Latin. You young women are extremely fortunate to receive that same mystic key."

Rickers delivered Marianne to the gaunt stone edifice on the afternoon of this fine day in the latter part of June.

"Miss Trenton." It was Mrs. Avery herself who greeted the new student. "Welcome to the Farnham Academy. I hope you will be happy here."

Marianne hoped she would, too, and murmured vague words of agreement. She was shown to her room, or rather, to the dormitory where half the girls in the school slept. The other half, the younger girls, ages eight to twelve, slept below stairs in much more cramped quarters.

Next to her bed was a stand with two drawers for her smallclothes and other personal possessions. Marianne, like everyone else, was issued a lightweight, brown woolen skirt and two muslin blouses to be worn to classes. The skirts, blouses and any dresses the girls might have brought with them from home hung in a long common closet at the end of the room.

Owing to Mrs. Avery's emphasis on exercise, and the laundry being done only once a week, the odor that issued forth from the closet when she folded back the screen was heady, and Marianne was not at all sure she wanted to hang her things in there. But she had little choice, so she changed dutifully from the frock she had worn from Kingsbrook into the school uniform. Rejoining Mrs. Avery in the receiving hall, she was shown to her classes.

"'There is a place within the depths of Hell/ Call'd Malebolge...'" A thin, pale girl, who looked younger than Marianne was reading aloud from a worn book she and her deskmate were sharing. The little woman at the head of the class clapped her hands sharply and the reader stopped, looking up, like the rest of the girls, to curiously study the new student disturbing their lessons.

"Girls, this is Miss Marianne Trenton. Miss Trenton, you may sit there, in the last desk. Judith, see that Miss Trenton has a copy of Mr. Aligheiri's *Divina Commedia.* Nedra, you may continue. We are in Hell, Miss Trenton...."

The girls were pleasant enough, but Marianne was slow to make friends in the school. It was a week before she said a complete sentence to anyone, two before she divulged any personal information about herself, and that was only to reveal her age and birthday to Nedra, the pale reader in that first class.

Marianne and Nedra Stevens were drawn together the same way two falling leaves are thrown together atop a swirling stream.

More or less isolated for the past two, pivotal years of her life, Marianne did not know how girls her age were supposed to behave. So she withdrew into a shell that, even a month later, had been only slightly eroded by Nedra's gentle personality.

A year younger than Marianne, she presented no threat, and so colorless both in body and spirit as to be practically transparent, she did not intimidate Marianne, nor overshadow her. When Marianne could be dragged from her books, the two girls spent quiet afternoons together.

Nedra told her she lived in a house overlooking the ocean. Marianne described the mysterious wonders of Kingsbrook. Nedra told Marianne of her two brothers, both older than she was; of her mother, who suffered from poor health; of her father and his business of selling water-resistant clothing to the local seamen; and of her cousin, with whom she had been hopelessly in love since she was seven.

For her part, Marianne supposed she may have mentioned her guardian and his physical attributes a time or two.

In fact, Marianne was somewhat distressed to find Mr. Desmond so often in her thoughts. For one thing, there was that envelope she received from Mr. Bradley, Esq., every week. "Mr. Desmond has arranged for you to receive a small allowance to provide for the miscellaneous necessaries of a young woman," Mr. Bradley explained in a letter accompanying the first banknote. Her clothes were provided, her food was provided, her living quarters and books were provided, and there were very few additional "miscellaneous necessaries" on which to spend the money. She took the bill from the envelope every week and put it in the first very stiff, very white, very solemn-looking envelope she had received from the solicitor's office. At the end of two months that envelope was becoming quite thick and could not help but remind Marianne of the man and the favors for which perhaps he thought he was paying in advance.

The other reason it was so difficult to dismiss thoughts of Mr. Desmond was, having had Uncle Horace and now Mr. Brannon, the history teacher, as points of comparison, she was beginning to realize how unusually good-looking her guardian was.

"Now, young ladies, I trust you will conduct yourselves as such today. Miss Gransby, Mrs. Grey and myself are here to direct you, but not to tend you as if you were infants. Reading, as you have been told, offers a very fine art gallery where, it is hoped, some of you will be inspired to improve your own artistic efforts. In the Reading museum we will find a number of ancient relics, some dating from the time of Henry I. You remember the remains of the Benedictine abbey we saw. That was founded by Henry I, converted by Henry VIII into a palace. . . ."

Mrs. Avery lectured dryly over her shoulder at the brood of young girls trailing at her heels, all of them agog at the sights and sounds to behold in the town, at the thrill of being on an outing of such magnitude.

Calling it a "marvelous learning opportunity," Mrs. Avery had already lectured them for hours on the wonders they were to behold at the Reading museum and art gallery, "not to mention—" though she did, often, at great length "—the free lending library, and, of course, the university."

Whenever Mrs. Avery spoke of the university, she raised her eyebrows and looked over the top of her reading spectacles at the girls. She had warned them that Reading was a university town, but that they were to take no notice of young college men they might see on the streets of the city.

Such warnings were useless. How could the girls, all of them in their teen years, not notice the handsome young men who thronged the streets of Reading, looking terribly serious as they hurried along?

Mrs. Avery had also advised her charges to keep their heads down, their voices low, and to stay in step with the girl in front of them at all times. Instead they clustered together in excited little groups, pointing and giggling shrilly and tending to wander away from the main body, where Mrs. Avery, Miss Gransby and Mrs. Grey could control them.

The schoolgirls' presence in the art gallery disturbed air that had floated silent and still for decades. Art patrons certainly frequented the gallery, but came singly or in pairs, some of them as old as the paintings themselves. In contrast, these twenty-eight teenage girls moved through the rooms like a fresh breeze.

The paintings were named and described in undertones by Miss Gransby, owing to her passing acquaintance with art and her possession of the guidebook. The task diverted Miss Gransby's attention from her charges, leaving gentle Mrs. Grey to keep track of all the young women, most of them taller than herself, all of them spryer than she was. When they left the art gallery on their way to the museum, Mrs. Avery stood at the door and counted the girls as they came out. Twenty-eight had gone in; twenty-four came out.

"One or two of the older girls said they were getting a trifle light-headed in the close confines of the gallery and asked if they might step out for a bit of refreshment," Mrs. Grey offered.

"If they miss the museum or delay the coaches, they will be walking back to the academy," Mrs. Avery said grimly.

But the girls could not contain themselves. When Mrs. Avery discovered who was missing, she naturally assumed the desertion was of Judith's, or even Sylvia's, instigation. She would have been surprised to learn it was Marianne who had first prodded Nedra in the ribs and motioned toward the open side door of the gallery the group was passing.

"Let us go outside," she whispered.

"*Outside?*" Nedra gasped. "We mustn't. They will discover we are gone."

"Then I shall ask permission," Marianne said coolly, turning toward Mrs. Grey and claiming that the room was too close.

The two girls slipped out, closely followed by Judith and her friend, who recognized a golden opportunity when they saw one.

"What are we going to do?" Nedra asked fretfully, looking longingly over her shoulder at the dark walls of the gallery.

"We are going to explore a little of Reading. I can see all the dank, dimly lit rooms I want to back at the academy," Marianne replied.

"What if we are left behind?" the other girl asked.

Marianne, who did not consider the possibility as dire a one as did her friend, patted Nedra's arm reassuringly. "You must not worry," she said, though she offered no reason why not.

Reading was a town accustomed to serving travelers and students, the sort of people looking for inexpensive amusement and food, not necessarily in that order. The walkways teemed with cafés and little shops, selling everything from apples to zebra pelts, though those last, upon closer inspection, resembled nothing more exotic than painted cowhides. Marianne was fascinated by it all, and poor little Nedra trailed miserably behind her, sure that the next store proprietor they passed was going to point an accusatory finger at them and demand to know why they were separated from their group.

In fact, it was Nedra, with her nervous paranoia, who noticed the two men huddled over one of the tables placed on the sidewalk to tempt passersby in the warm summer weather. She drew closer to Marianne, who followed her friend's suspicious gaze with an indulgent smile on her lips. The smile froze. Marianne stopped suddenly in her tracks and then pulled Nedra to one side, first around two or three other pedestrians and then into the open doorway of a bookstore.

"What is it?" Nedra cried in alarm.

Marianne hushed her and motioned toward the two men at the table. "It is my guardian," she whispered. "It is *both* my guardians."

And indeed it was Mr. Desmond, in consultation with her uncle Horace.

With wide eyes the girls watched the two men at the table. They were in earnest discussion, but owing to the distance, Marianne was unable to determine their mood. Both seemed serious, but if either was expressing more volatile emotions, she could not tell.

In a few moments, Mr. Desmond reached into his coat and withdrew a pocketbook. He opened the purse and extricated a sizeable stack of banknotes. Without counting them, he passed the notes across the table to Carstairs, who snatched them up and immediately began to lay them out on the table, doubtlessly in piles of different denominations.

"What are they talking about?" Nedra asked. "Why is he giving him money? What did he pay him for?"

Marianne shook her head silently, watching the two men with wide-eyed fascination. She was very troubled by what she was seeing. She had allowed herself to assume when she left the dark rooms where Uncle Horace lived that that was the last she would see of him, that their relationship was severed. She knew, of course, that he and Mr. Desmond were acquaintances, but she had not thought they had commerce with one another. She believed *she* was the only business they had transacted.

Now Mr. Desmond held up two fingers and nodded to one of the waiters just inside the door of the coffeehouse. In a few moments drinks were served to the men. Desmond picked up his glass, said something to Carstairs and emptied it in one gulp. Carstairs smiled thinly and sipped at his drink. He nodded and gathered up the money, placing it in the purse attached to a chain he kept in his pocket. Evidently he was satisfied with the amount Desmond had given him and allowed himself another sip of his drink.

Desmond pushed away from the table, but Carstairs did not offer to join him. The younger man turned from the table and walked away, headed toward the bookshop where the two girls huddled just inside the doorway.

With a gasp, Marianne hurriedly stepped back from the door, pulling Nedra to one side, looking behind her to find someplace they could hide if Mr. Desmond came into this shop.

But he did not even glance in their direction as he passed. Marianne kept Nedra hushed and still in the little store for several minutes, long enough so that the clerk approached and loudly asked if he might help them, in a tone of voice suggesting that if he could not, they should leave.

The girls quickly went to the door, but Marianne peeked out and carefully inspected the street and walkways before she ventured out. Mr. Desmond was nowhere in sight. Uncle Horace had also disappeared.

Now it was Nedra who hurried them back along the street toward the museum their schoolmates were visiting, located near the art gallery they had been in earlier. She kept murmuring, "Oh, please, let them still be there," and "I promise never to do this again, Mrs. Avery." She had not enjoyed their little adventure.

Marianne did not say anything, but she had not enjoyed herself, either. Half-formed suspicions were like cod-liver oil, easy to swallow but leaving an abominable aftertaste.

In the same city, but in the opposite direction, Mr. Peter Desmond was walking along briskly toward the stable where he had left his horse. His steps were easy; his shoulders seemed lighter. He had made his final payment to Mr. Horace Carstairs. Desmond had never realized before how much he truly detested the man. In recent years he had been required to court Carstairs's favor owing to his occasional—frequent, really—cash shortfalls.

He had cleared such loans with Carstairs before, but he had never before been aware of this sensation, like the lifting of a pall. Usually when he paid off a loan he was aware in the back of his mind that he would be getting more money from Carstairs in the future. Today was different. Desmond had not actually formed his decision into a decree or sacred pledge, he simply knew he would not again go to Carstairs for money. Not only because he did not like the man, but because he was not going to allow his bills and gambling debts to accumulate to the point where such a loan would be required. Already his finances were in better order as he gave up the trip to the Continent he always took at this time of the year.

But his determination not to deal with Carstairs again had even deeper roots. It had to do with Marianne and her former association with the man, and with Desmond's desire to shield her completely from his influence. But now both of them were free of the moneylender's tentacles, and Peter began to whistle a jaunty tune as he strode along.

Desmond was not a man of great introspection. He only knew it would be a cold day in hell when he crossed paths with Carstairs again.

There were reprimands when Marianne and Nedra caught up with their fellow students in the Reading museum. Judith and Sylvia had returned in good time, having dared only a brief walk up the street. Mrs. Avery had glared at them reproachfully, but the longer they were returned and Marianne and Nedra were away, the less reprehensible Judith's and Sylvia's actions seemed.

As soon as Marianne and Nedra arrived, the outing was summarily ended, the girls herded in the coaches and taken back to Farnham, without the promised stop for refreshments. The reprobates were confined exclusively to their rooms and their classes for a month, which actually was not as severe a punishment as Mrs. Avery meant it to be. It took the full month for the other girls at Farnham to forgive them for marring the expedition.

Marianne was deeply sorry she had insisted on the fateful adventure, not only because of the loss of her teachers' and her schoolmates' favor. She was frightened by the obviously close connection between Mr. Desmond and her uncle Horace.

Curiously, however, she found she actually missed Kingsbrook. She knew how beautiful the house and park were in the spring, and she imagined the glories of the fields during the summer months. And summer, it seemed, would never end. First there were the academy classes, then the trip to Reading, then banishment to her room, and still the summer sky unfurled its glorious blue overhead.

One day in September, it abruptly came to an end. The sky clouded over, the temperature dropped and the rain began to fall.

It did not stop raining until all the leaves had been beaten off the trees, all the birds driven from the sky, all the flowers left sagging and bent. The weather did not change until November, when the drizzling rain was replaced by flurries of snow. It was only then that the misadventures of summer were at last forgiven.

Mrs. River wrote to Marianne regularly. In almost every letter she urged her to come down to Kingsbrook for a day, a weekend, a fortnight. Marianne always replied to the letters, but refused the invitations, offering as an excuse her studies, which could not possibly be interrupted.

But time was inexorable. The days marched steadily onward. And in December, it seemed that every girl, and almost every instructor as well, was leaving the academy to spend the Christmas holiday with family and friends.

Mrs. River's note of December third did not brook any excuse.

> Rickers will be down to pick you up next weekend. Kingsbrook is lovely this time of year and we have all missed you. I even have a promise from Mr. Desmond himself that he will not be completely engaged in Reading or Londontown for the entire month, so if you are lucky you may get to see him.
>
> We are anxious to have you here.
>
> Fondly yours,
> Mrs. River.

"If you are lucky." Marianne's hands started to shake when she read the line, but there was no way to avoid returning to Desmond's home.

Chapter Five

Kingsbrook *was* beautiful.

There was a light dusting of snow across the grounds, but owing to the brook and the protection of the trees, even in the middle of winter the white flakes lay on green undergrowth.

Rickers stopped the carriage at the side entrance this time, where the drive drew closer to the house. Mrs. River, who had been waiting for their arrival, threw open the long French windows of the south sitting room, and even before Marianne entered she could hear the crackles of the fire and feel a soft brush of warmth against her cheek.

"Come in, come in! Well, let me have a look at you. Farnham seems to be agreeing with you, though perhaps not the academy food so much. Let me take your cloak and bonnet. Alice! Al—oh, there you are. Take Miss Trenton's things. And ask Jenny if she has any of that broth still hot from lunch. Take those bags up the back stairs, Mr. Rickers. Come in. Come in."

Marianne felt like the prodigal child returning as the housekeeper ushered her in and clucked over her, imperiously directing the disposal of her effects.

"Now let me get a good look at you," the woman continued, turning Marianne toward the windows in order to catch the full light of the declining day. She shook her head reprovingly. "You only turned seventeen in November and suddenly you are a beautiful young woman. No, no, do not sit down there. Mr. Desmond said you were to wait for him in the library when you got here."

Marianne was obviously wearied by the ride from Farnham, so Mrs. River did not think it unusual for her to be pale. Heedlessly, the housekeeper put her hand at the girl's back and propelled her toward the sitting-room door.

"I trust you remember where the library is. Heaven knows you spent a good deal of time in there when you were here in the spring."

Evidently Mrs. River was not intending to go to the library with her. This was to be a *private* interview.

"Is... is Mr. Desmond waiting to see me?" Marianne asked nervously.

"Not at the moment. He rode across the way to talk to Sir Grissam about the woods they share, but he promised he would not be long, and he did want to see you. I thought surely you could find something in the library with which to occupy yourself," Mrs. River explained.

"Yes, of course," Marianne murmured.

The door was heavy, but never before had that fact seemed so ominous to the girl. She laid her white hand against the dark wood, reminding herself that Mr. Desmond was not in here yet, might not return for some time. She pushed, the catch gave and the door swung inward with a breathy susurration.

The room was deserted, just as Mrs. River had promised. The books were familiar; the long windows admitted a dim light, choked off by the heavy drapes. The first thing Marianne did was push the curtains back to admit as much of the cold glow of winter as possible. Then she turned around and inspected the shelves, desk, chairs, fireplace; the stepladder to reach the higher shelves; the familiar titles on the lower shelves.

The books that had so intrigued her last time she was here, the tempting volumes she could easily reach but not read, she now knew were written in Latin and Greek, though six months of elementary Latin were not sufficient to allow her to decipher any yet.

She dropped into one of the deep leather chairs set in front of the hearth. A moment later there was a gentle tap on the door. Marianne clutched the arms of the chair as she peered around. "Come—" she cleared her throat "—come in."

But the head that appeared was covered with a white lace cap, and the slender form was Alice's. "Mrs. Rawlins sent you in some soup, miss. Welcome home."

"It is very nice to be home," Marianne replied automatically, not stopping to consider that it was true.

The little maid set the tray down on the table next to Marianne. "It's chicken and noodles, Miss Marianne. Mrs. Rawlins does a real fine chicken-and-noodle soup."

"I am sure she does. I am hungry, thank you."

Alice bobbed her head and left the young lady alone again.

Mrs. Rawlins's soup was as good as Alice had promised, and in only moments the bowl was emptied, the spoon laid aside.

Marianne's feet were warm, her hunger quelled. Her nervousness could occupy only a portion of her interest now, she found. There was a volume on the table next to the tray, which she took up and absently began to read. The book was on trees, the various types, their growth and development. It was not riveting reading, though more than one passage was underlined faintly, suggesting someone was perusing the book with interest.

In a few minutes Marianne put the book aside and stood impatiently. She did not remember making a conscious decision to go to Mr. Desmond's desk. Once there, though, she began idly eyeing the papers and personal knickknacks on top of it.

Among other things there was a large foreign coin set in a circlet of glass, which Mr. Desmond used as a paperweight. Marianne had no way of knowing the coin was from the first international card game Desmond had participated in when a mere lad, still in his father's good graces, ostensibly in Paris to study the artwork of some of the old masters. The coin was hardly a symbol of victory; Desmond had lost miserably in that game and was forced to cut his "art expedition" short. But the seasoned player who had taken most of his money was the one who had taught him never to leave his opponents penniless. Monsieur Deveraux had presented him with the coin and invited him back another time. Desmond had had a glassblower set it for him as a remembrance. In recent years when he returned to the games in Paris he was the player who doled out souvenirs to unlucky novices.

On the desk there was a letter opener that resembled a small dagger. In fact, it was a dagger—one with which a disgruntled player in Cologne had threatened him.

"Du Schwindler!" the man had screamed, jumping to his feet, knocking his chair over, brandishing the blade before him. *"Ich bringe dich um!"*

"Oh, do not be ridiculous, old man. I did not cheat you and you certainly are not going to kill me. Give me that little hat pin and go get yourself some good strong coffee," Desmond had replied, taking the knife from the drunken German as easily as if he *had* been an old man wielding a hat pin. "Gentleman, I believe it is Bloomingard's deal."

Through his years of straight-faced card playing he had learned to hide his emotions and appear perfectly calm, but he had been shaken and kept the dagger as a letter opener to remind himself never to play with a man who paid exact change for his drinks and whose eyes gleamed red when he lost.

There was a worn deck of cards on the desk, an ivory thimble, a small velvet pouch holding an unset gem, each with a story behind it. Most of the objects were connected with some gambling escapade or other, though the thimble was a memento of a more romantic adventure. Marianne, unaware of the personal history each represented, fingered them with mild interest, replacing them thoughtlessly before going on to the next item.

Among the various keepsakes were a number of other things, and a smile nudged at her lips as she looked down at the disorder. Pens were scattered about; an inkstand, stained blotter, writing implements and papers mingled together haphazardly. On one corner of the desk was a pile of letters, some delivered long ago, most of them unanswered, she suspected. She picked up the first envelope and, turning it over, discovered it had not even been opened. In amusement she began to look through them, to find out how many had not been read, let alone answered.

Marianne was halfway through the stack when her conscience began to nag her; what she was doing might be interpreted as snooping. She determined to stop, but contrarily picked up one last envelope. This one had been opened. But her eyes fell on the name of the sender in the top lefthand corner, and every good intention she had of leaving Mr. Desmond's papers alone vanished.

The letter was from Mr. Horace Carstairs, East Coventry Lane, Number 16, London. Without the slightest compunction Marianne lifted the flap of the envelope and extracted the sheet of paper within. It was dated two months earlier, a little after the field trip Mrs. Avery had conducted to the Reading museum and art gallery.

Desmond my good fellow,
I have been contemplating our mutually satisfactory business transactions over the years. One in particular I assume you are still enjoying, owing to the fact you

have made no attempt to return the girl to me, nor complained that she has escaped. And as I considered the matter, a rather ingenious idea occurred to me.

Because of your avocation you are acquainted with a number of monied gentlemen who visit London occasionally on business, or merely to participate in a friendly evening of cards. These men, strangers to the city, usually traveling alone, are doubtless in need of companionship, though being gentlemen of quality they would hardly wish to draw from the unwashed pool of street slatterns. And perhaps they hold certain prominent positions that would prevent them from frequenting a more exclusive establishment.

It is therefore my proposition to procure young women for these gentlemen, as fresh and unsullied as was sweet Marianne when you claimed her, acquired in much the same way, at the card table, only with the stakes and the outcome of the game being determined beforehand.

We would, of course, divide the profit, you providing the customers and myself the girls. Granted, I do not have an endless supply of wards to distribute, but I am quite certain I can fulfill my half of the bargain.

I feel I can approach you with this proposal owing to the similar arrangement you are enjoying. Your continued use of the girl is, of course, according to our agreement, and as a gentleman I would never refuse it. But our arrangement, despite your solicitor's very clever document, was very casual and I am not convinced binding.

I eagerly wait to hear from you on my proposal.

Your most humble and obedient servant,
H. Carstairs

Marianne stared at the paper in her hands, aghast. It was too horrible! Uncle Horace was proposing that Mr. Desmond join him in plunging other young women into the same dire circumstances in which she found herself.

Ironically, she glanced around at the luxurious appointments of the Kingsbrook library and admitted these circumstances did not *appear* so very dire, but Mr. Desmond obviously still considered her part of his "winnings."

She would...she would kill herself before she allowed the fiend to have his way with her. But she could not run away, either, or even become an annoyance to Desmond for fear that rather than toy with her longer, he would simply send her back to Carstairs.

For the first time Marianne realized she was teetering on a very fine wire.

There was a noise at the front door, and Marianne started violently. With shaking hands she returned the letter to its envelope and the envelope to the middle of the stack of letters. The commotion drew nearer, the sounds more distinct.

"Has Miss Trenton arrived?" she heard a masculine voice ask, the tones deep and the pronunciation precise. Mr. Desmond, unmistakably.

"She has been waiting in the library for you since she arrived, sir," Mrs. River said.

"Very good," Desmond said. The library door, which Marianne had left ajar, now burst completely open, almost, it seemed, by the force of his personality.

He was wearing a heavy black suit coat, with a high collar over which his dark brown hair fell. His locks had grown even longer since she had seen him last, so he looked like a shaggy hunting dog with its winter coat.

She caught her lower lip between her teeth but could not control the shaking of her hands and legs. This was the villain, with his despicable designs on her and his hellish intentions to join with Uncle Horace in his "business." He was ruthless, a monster and, she was distressed to see, as forbiddingly handsome as she remembered.

His first sentence held none of the threat he represented to her. "Mrs. River says you have been waiting here for me. I hope it has not been long," he said.

"Not long at all," she whispered.

"Long enough, I see," he said.

Marianne blanched and gulped guiltily, afraid she had left a telltale corner of Carstairs's damning letter protruding from the stack. But Desmond's eyes were directed to the tray with the empty bowl on the reading table.

"Oh, yes. Mrs. Rawlins sent in a bowl of soup. I hope that was all right. But no, one should not eat in your library, of course. I will take these things back out to the kitchen," Marianne said, jumbling her words together so quickly that she had picked up the tray before Mr. Desmond sorted out everything she had said.

"No, no, that is quite all right, Miss Trenton. Leave the tray here. Mrs. River will take care of it."

He was all the way in the room now, his presence filling any empty space, but he did not close the door behind him. The fire was reduced to coals and the big room was growing cool, but Marianne did not remind him about the possibility of drafts. She was, in fact, tremendously relieved they would not be shut up together in here.

Desmond went to stand by one of the chairs in front of the fire, the very one she had been sitting in, and motioned to the other. "Sit down," he invited.

To her it sounded like a command, and in dumb obedience she stepped to the indicated chair, perching on the edge of it, the very picture of a nervous bird poised for instant flight. Desmond sat in his chair, rattling the tray when he put his elbow on the armrests.

"You have come for Christmas, then," he said.

His tone was conversational, his comment harmless, even banal. But of their own will, her eyes wandered to the pile of letters atop his desk. How *could* he sound like that, planning what he was planning, engaging in his fiendish plots?

Marianne took a deep breath and dragged her eyes away from the desk. "Mrs. River sent the coach," she offered in her defense, wanting to make it very clear it had not been her idea to come back.

"Of course. You will find Kingsbrook a pleasant place in the winter."

There was a pause. Marianne, in her determination not to look at the letters again, was staring at the floor in front of her. Mr. Desmond shifted in his chair and cleared his throat.

"Do you like your school?" he asked.

"It is very... adequate," she said, pausing to search for the appropriate adjective.

"Adequate," he repeated thoughtfully. "That will have to do, I suppose."

The chairs in which they sat had wide wings and were turned to face the fire, so he could not see her clearly. She was not sorry for that fact and told herself she did not want to see him, either. But her gaze rose from the floor to the sharp creases of his trousers, the polish of his shoes. She pictured in her mind again his tousled hair and wondered absently why a man so careful of his wardrobe would be so careless of his person.

Not that his person was totally abandoned to ruin, she said to herself, and then frowned over her shameful thoughts.

"Mrs. River says you have not returned to Kingsbrook since you were enrolled in the academy," Desmond continued.

"No, sir," Marianne replied faintly. At mention of the housekeeper, she realized suddenly why his wardrobe, at least, was so well cared for.

They sat in silence again for a few moments more. Desmond hitched himself in his chair again and Marianne gulped noisily.

"Really, Miss Trenton, you must not feel exiled to the Farnham Academy," Desmond said at last.

"I am perfectly comfortable there," she quickly averred.

"I hope you are," the gentleman said. "But it is merely an institution. It cannot be pleasant for you to stay shut up there for months at a time. Mrs. River says she has invited you back to Kingsbrook on a number of occasions, but you have always put her off, saying that your studies are too pressing to allow you to leave. Believe me, Miss Trenton, I know something of the dedication of young scholars, and I cannot think you have been completely immersed in your books for a full six months now."

"Usually... though not always," she admitted softly.

"I asked for this semiprivate conference—" he glanced pointedly at the open door, and Marianne was forced to acknowledge that the door had not been forgotten, but purposely left open to put her at ease "—because I was fearful we would have to broach a subject painful for us both." He leaned forward in his chair so he could see her clearly, putting his deep, dark eyes on a level with hers, where he could look unflinchingly into her wide green ones.

"Miss Trenton—Marianne—I know you have stayed away from Kingsbrook to avoid me."

Marianne drew in her breath and made a tiny motion with her head she meant to be a denial. Desmond held up his hand to stop her weak attempt.

"What happened that night was unfortunate," he said. "And it has left painful wounds for both of us. But please, you do not need to entomb yourself at the academy."

"The Farnham Academy is very pleasant—" Marianne began, but the gentleman cut her off.

"You forget, I have seen the Farnham Academy, a few gray buildings on a half acre of ground. How can you stay away from Kingsbrook so long?" he asked, with a quality of genuine wonder in his voice that made him sound like a small boy.

"I did not want—I did not think..." Marianne stammered.

Desmond cleared his throat uncomfortably. "Of course," he said.

They sat in thoughtful silence for a few minutes.

"I have a proposition for you, Miss Trenton," he said at last. Marianne held her breath as she waited for him to finish his thought, mindful of the letter in the middle of the stack on Desmond's desk, suspicious of the man and his proposals.

"I can make arrangements to be away from Kingsbrook when you are here. Though it would be difficult now." He murmured that last to himself.

"I—I could not turn you out of your own home," Marianne protested.

"Only for a few days. It will be no real hardship, I assure you. You could have Kingsbrook to yourself. What do you say?"

He stopped and waited for her answer.

What was this all about? What sort of man was Mr. Desmond? Marianne was young and knew little of the world, and perhaps wickedness was not always easy to detect, but she had known Uncle Horace and she knew he was a bad man. If Mr. Desmond and Uncle Horace were partners in the degrading business her former guardian had proposed in his letter, then surely Mr. Desmond was a bad man, too. Even though every characteristic of Mr. Desmond's seemed opposite to every one of Uncle Horace's... Marianne was confused and befuddled. And weary of trying to detect all the evil in the world around her.

"Kingsbrook *is* lovely," she admitted softly.

"So you will visit," he said, deciding the matter. "Splendid. How often, then? Every week?"

"I do not think once a week would be necessary, or even wise, Mr. Desmond. I really do have studies. Perhaps every three months, though. Then I could see Kingsbrook like a series of still-life paintings in every season of the year." She could not bring herself to smile, but her expression softened to match the tone of her voice as she pictured the estate in spring and summer.

"Every change seems better than the one before it," Desmond said in agreement, trying to coax the gentleness in her tone to stay, sadly aware it would disappear at his next words. "A week every three months, then. Now lastly..." He cleared his throat again. "Holidays can be frightfully dreary at a school, so I would not have you stay in Farnham during Christmas or Easter or All Saints' Day, or even Saint Swithin's Day. But some of those times, like this Christmas, would be awkward for me to be away from Kingsbrook. Can we, do you think, call a truce when necessity demands we be here together?"

"Of course," Marianne said. But her consent was not given wholeheartedly. She feared their every meeting would be marred by a dark undercurrent. Like this one was, she thought, as the image of his tanned, hairy, bared legs suddenly infiltrated her mind.

"In fact," he continued, interrupting her disturbing thoughts, "I am afraid it must be something more than a silent tolerance between us. You must remember you are my ward now. Mrs. River already thinks it odd, I am sure, that you never visit and we never make any attempt to meet, though I trust she assumes you write to me while you are away at school. But in front of the servants we must be civil, and any guests I were to invite to Kingsbrook would expect to meet my ward and to hear us exchange pleasantries and news of the day. What do you think? Are you up to it?"

Marianne gulped noisily. This would be much harder. She could stammer out a greeting when they met, she supposed, or even carry on a conversation of a sort when they were alone together. But she had no control over the blood that retreated and then suddenly rushed back into her cheeks when she caught his eye, over the tremor in her voice or the slight shaking of her hands and knees when he spoke to her. If Mrs. River and Mr. Desmond's guests thought it odd when guardian and ward did not address each other, how would it appear to them when they did?

"Miss Trenton?" he asked. Then, leaning forward so he could see her face again, he said, softening his voice, "Marianne? Can you do it? I do not ask you to forget what happened, I only ask you not stay away on account of one dismal night in your life."

She winced ever so slightly when he mentioned the episode, and as uncomfortable as the memory was to him, he could see it was much worse for her. Still, like that night in his bedchamber when she had squared her shoulders and opened the door, he saw the light of determination enter her eyes. Firming her chin, she nodded her head.

"Yes. Certainly. I see for appearances' sake, for both our sakes, we must try to act as naturally as possible."

"It will not be so very terrible. You will love Kingsbrook, and I most solemnly vow never to be anything but the most perfect gentleman with you. And the vow of a Desmond is absolutely irrevocable," he ended grimly, remembering his father's vow those long years ago, when Desmond had last seen him.

Marianne did not know what else to say, and evidently neither did Mr. Desmond. The crackling of the fire was insufficient to fill the empty air, and after thirty uncomfortable seconds, he then pushed himself up out of his chair. Marianne stood, too.

"Would you care to shake on our agreement, Miss Trenton?" he asked, offering his arm stiffly.

Marianne put her hand in his, and to Desmond it felt like the wing of a dove, as soft and as white and as fragile. He could crush it without effort, though he was dismayed to realize that what he wanted most to do was raise it to his lips and cover it, and her wrist, her arms, her shoulders, in hungry kisses. With never a crack in his expression he solemnly pumped it once and released her.

Despite the nagging recollection of Uncle Horace's letter and Marianne's justifiable distrust of her "guardian," staying at Kingsbrook was not as horrible as it could have been, she supposed. Mr. Desmond insisted that Mrs. River set the big table for them every night, and they sat at opposite ends, with salt cellars, pepper grinders, candlesticks, several drinking goblets, china, a glittering array of silverware and a broad expanse of white damask between them.

He would ask her how she was. She would say she was fine. He would ask her how her chop was. She would say it was delicious. He would ask her what she had been doing that day, and she would answer in as few words as was humanly possible.

Those three questions more or less exhausted their topics of discussion, unless Desmond commented on the weather, which he sometimes did, or Marianne sent a timid compliment on the soup or entree to Jenny via Mrs. River, which she sometimes did.

That first night Alice's bustling to and from the kitchen and Mrs. River's ferrying dishes from one end of the table to the other camouflaged any uneasy silences between Mr. Desmond and his ward. The evening after they reached their agreement, Desmond was joined by two gentlemen from London, and Marianne was allowed to eat with Mrs. River.

"I apologize for your relegation to the kitchen, like some naughty child. But I assure you, rather than being deprived of any pleasure, you have been saved an evening of utter boredom," the housekeeper said. "Mr. Desmond and his guests will not say two words during dinner, and directly thereafter they will excuse themselves to the card table."

"Oh, please, Mrs. River. You do not need to apologize. I think it is perfectly jolly to join you and Alice for supper," Marianne explained with a winning smile. It was a smile Mr.

Desmond had seen once or twice during dinner the night months ago when the girl had first arrived, but had not seen since and did not really have any hope of ever seeing again.

"Well then, have Jenny give you a bowl of good beef stew there and come join us."

The next night Alice had come down with a dripping cold, and Jenny Rawlins barred her from the kitchen and dining room. Mrs. River had been seeing to household accounts all day—Mr. Desmond had given her a fat roll of banknotes that morning and told her Mr. Frederick and Mr. Bartholomew would be paying the bills this month—and was suffering from a headache herself. She instructed Jenny to put the poached fish and creamed potatoes on the sideboard and allow Mr. Desmond and Miss Trenton to serve themselves.

Both guardian and ward felt a sinking in their stomachs when they were informed of the arrangement. That would mean twenty minutes alone in the same room together. Desmond nearly excused himself, until he saw the girl's upper lip actually stiffen.

"Very well, Mrs. River," she said, even managing a small smile.

He really had no choice but to fall in with the plan and assure Mrs. River it would be no inconvenience at all.

Silently they filled their plates, neither one having much of an appetite. But the charade had to be acted out nevertheless.

"Good fish," Desmond mumbled after several minutes of silence, accented by the sounds of chewing and swallowing.

"Excellent. Very good fish," Marianne agreed softly.

While Desmond seemed merely taciturn, her head was treacherously filled with memories of the last time they had shared a private meal—the *first* time they had done so. The conversation then had been lively, Desmond and his stories positively fascinating. He had made her laugh. He had been charming, if treacherous.

Marianne glanced up at the man sitting at the other end of the table. His head was lowered. He was addressing himself to the food on his plate with what appeared to be rare single-mindedness. He did not seem treacherous now. As she watched him, she realized he was not merely being taciturn, but was as uncomfortable at the familiar intimacy of this meal as she was. The faintest glimmer of a smile fluttered across her lips. It would have surprised—*appalled* her—if she had been aware of it.

"Did you enjoy supper with your friends from town last night?" she asked.

Desmond looked up sharply. The question was not particularly amazing, but that Marianne was asking it of him in a perfectly civil tone of voice was. "Yes," he said, a slight, puzzled furrow in his brow.

"It must be very pleasant for you when friends come down to see you here at Kingsbrook."

"It can be," Desmond said. Then he smiled slightly. "Last night it was, definitely."

"Then there are your neighbors here at Kingsbrook. I imagine you are surrounded by friends wherever you go," she said.

"Well, actually, I do not know my neighbors," Desmond confessed. The girl had caught him off guard, and his confession suggested more regret than he had meant to show.

"Not at all?" she asked in surprise.

"I have not been at Kingsbrook for any length of time . . . before," he explained.

"But you are always here," she cried.

"Well, yes, *now*. But I was not previously. Anyway, I have not had the opportunity to become acquainted."

Marianne eyed him seriously. "You must create the opportunity, Mr. Desmond," she told him. "Your neighbors cannot come to you. As the wealthiest landowner in the community, *you* must make the first overture. Surely you are the host of some sort of Christmas party for your neighbors?"

"I really cannot remember ever being at Kingsbrook for Christmas before," he admitted. He was usually on the Continent, where certain people he knew gathered in certain places to play for some very high stakes at this season of the year. The extremely wealthy Count Anistopholes had for two or three years now played the role of Father Christmas by losing enough to keep Kingsbrook running until spring.

"Well, you are here this year," Marianne said, stating the incontrovertible fact.

"Yes," Desmond acknowledged with a sigh, "I am here this year."

"Then you must invite your neighbors in," she said decisively, taking up her fork and absently spearing one of the cubes of potato. "Mrs. River and I can make the arrangements for a Christmas gathering—small, informal, easy and friendly, the perfect theater in which to become acquainted. But you must personally invite your neighbors. I must return to Farnham the first week in January, so, heavens! Mrs. River and I must start making preparations immediately."

"A Christmas gathering?" Desmond asked doubtfully. "Here?"

"Certainly here," Marianne stated emphatically, with the confidence typical of a seventeen-year-old. Not being a parent, Desmond was not sure how or even if he could defend himself against the girl's determination.

"If you think so..." he began uncertainly.

Marianne was looking around the room, making plans as she spoke, but when he gave his reluctant consent, she turned back to him and smiled.

She could not imagine what had possessed her, but at that moment the dreadful man at the other end of the table seemed almost... dear.

Chapter Six

In his family home, when he was a boy, there had been a large Christmas party hosted by the Desmonds every year. Since being exiled from those portals, though, Peter Desmond had always been away at this time of year.

Desmond barely knew his neighbors' names and was hardly on a friendly footing with any of them. But having given his coerced consent for the gathering, which sent Marianne and Mrs. River off in a flurry of planning, he found there was nothing for it but to deliver the invitations.

Mrs. Jacobs, frankly stunned, sat in the parlor of her house as Mr. Desmond offered his hospitality. The young Mr. Desmond had lived in Kingsbrook Manor almost ten years now—he could not even accurately be referred to as the *young* Mr. Desmond anymore—and in all that time he had made no friendly overtures to his neighbors, even when residing in the manor and not off leading his life of dissipation in foreign capitals. And as libertine as his young adult life had been, it did not approach the levels of depravity Mrs. Jacobs and some of the other ladies in the neighborhood imagined.

Now here he was, being positively charming and inviting Mr. and Mrs. Jacobs and their two daughters to Kingsbrook on Christmas Day.

"It will be a small gathering. Of neighbors. I have no doubt you will all know each other."

"No doubt," Mrs. Jacobs agreed.

"Yes, well," Desmond said, with just the slightest touch of boyish timidity in his voice. "I thought it was time I got to know you, too."

"That would be...delightful," Mrs. Jacobs agreed again. Then at last she smiled, committing herself and her husband to both the party and the acquaintanceship. "We would be very pleased to join you at Kingsbrook Christmas evening and are flattered you would remember us."

"Not at all, not at all," Desmond said.

Mrs. Jacobs saw him to the door and stood smiling out at him as he mounted his horse. She waved as he turned the animal, and only then went back inside.

Desmond breathed a sigh of relief. One invitation delivered and accepted, only a few to go. The area around Kingsbrook was, thank a mindful Providence, sparsely populated. In fact, it had not been as difficult as he had feared, and Mrs. Jacobs had appeared to be a perfectly pleasant woman. Not the sort with whom he generally socialized, certainly, but his youth was not so far behind him that he had forgotten how pleasant perfectly respectable women could be.

He also stopped at the Romer home, the Martin home, and rode through the woods to speak to Sir Grissam. All seemed surprised to see him, even old Grissam, with whom he had spoken in the past ten years, twice within the last month about the overgrown forest land between them and an idea for its improvement, the cost of which the two estates might share.

After their initial surprise, though, Desmond found they were all very cordial, and all agreed to attend him on Christmas Day.

That is not to say words were not exchanged about the master of Kingsbrook after he rode away.

"Well, Mrs. Romer, I believe we could call that a bolt out of the blue, what say you?"

"Straight out of the blue, Mr. Romer," his wife agreed.

"For five, ten years the fellow lives like a hermit over there—"

"When he lives over there, though I have heard—"

"Yes, yes, I have heard all the stories, too. Still, seemed a nice enough chap, and with the Chadburn blood in him, we know his lines are good."

"Do you think we ought to take the boys?" Mrs. Romer asked doubtfully. Perhaps her husband had not heard *all* the stories she and some of the other ladies had exchanged over tea.

"Desmond invited them, did he not? Damned cordial he was, in fact. Do you suppose that ward of his has something to do with this? Maybe he wants to introduce her to some of the lads around Kingsbrook. Now there is a tidy little catch," Mr. Romer mused.

Mrs. Romer, usually not one to ignore such tempting bait, did not reply with the enthusiasm he expected. But then, she had heard some stories about Desmond's "ward," too.

Nor were the Romers the only ones to discuss Mr. Desmond's invitation and unexpectedly charming demeanor. But that did not keep any of the neighbors away on Christmas Day.

The house had been in a whirl since Marianne first proposed the party, with Mrs. River and Mrs. Rawlins preparing for guests for the first time since the baron had "gone to his reward."

At eight o'clock on Christmas evening the guests arrived. Marianne, thrilled to see her idea come to such glorious fruition, stood with Mr. Desmond at the door to the dining hall, greeting their neighbors.

"This is Mrs. Jacobs. Mrs. Jacobs, my ward, Miss Marianne Trenton. Miss Trenton had told me how anxious she has been to meet you," Desmond would say, passing the guest along, being surprisingly solicitous to put both guest and ward at ease.

For dinner, Mrs. Rawlins had roasted a goose, three ducks and a cured ham, and filled a pan big enough to bathe a baby in with potatoes, beets, carrots and onions.

After the meal the guests retired to the formal sitting room, Mr. Romer and Mr. Jacobs in some discomfort, having made a concerted effort to empty Mrs. Rawlins's roasting pans.

Mr. Desmond instructed James to bring up a bottle of wine from the cellar.

James brought two.

Sir Grissam told an outrageous story about the very proper Lady Steepleton and Will Pellan, the London tailor who had tried to get from her the measurements for a new suit for Lord Steepleton. Mr. Pellan asked Lady Steepleton about her husband's waist size. She informed him that she and her husband had nearly the same girth, so Pellan was obliged to measure the lady's waist. It turned out that Lord and Lady Steepleton were of very nearly the same build in every part of their anatomies, and Mr. Pellan was required to take all his measurements from Lady Steepleton.

The story, which in the years since, Lady Steepleton and Mr. Pellan tried desperately to suppress, had been shared generously by Lord Steepleton himself, and at Kingsbrook it caused a great deal of laughter, besides summoning some blushes as red as poor Lady Steepleton's and Mr. Pellan's must have been that day. The further into the story Sir Grissam got, the more times James had come around the table with the carafe, so the funnier the telling of it became.

Eventually Mrs. River sent Tilly in with coffee and Alice in with a little plate of petit fours. Mr. Martin put his head down and began to snore softly. The two oldest Romer boys, Teddy and Ross, poked each other in the ribs and snorted with laughter. Mr. Romer scowled at them, and finally Mrs. Romer's airy little voice announced it was time to go home.

Everyone acknowledged that the hour was late, but company so congenial it was difficult to leave.

Mr. Desmond and his ward once again positioned themselves at the door to bid their guests farewell.

"It has been so pleasant to meet you, Miss Trenton," Mrs. Romer cooed over Marianne's captured fingers. "I wonder you do not spend more time here at Kingsbrook. As I have said to Mr. Romer, though, the grounds seems rather wild, and it is perhaps not a place I myself would care to come to alone." What Mrs. Romer had actually said to her husband was that the place was like a jungle and she would not venture onto the grounds for all the tea in China, for fear of being eaten alive by some wild beast. "I cannot help but notice the improvement in the estate *and* Mr. Desmond since your arrival. You have brought a bit of civilization to both Kingsbrook and its owner."

After the guests left there was another flurry of activity as Alice and Tilly collected their things and Rickers got Mr. Desmond's coach rigged one more time to take them all into Reading. Alice was being allowed a week off to stay with her family, and for the first time since she had arrived in this house, more than six months before, Marianne realized Mr. Rickers and Tilly were married. They, too, would be spending a few days in Reading, at Mr. Desmond's expense.

Then, suddenly, Kingsbrook was as still as an empty church. Mrs. River, who moments before had been standing at the open door, waving goodbye and calling motherly advice to Alice, excused herself and disappeared up the stairs before Desmond got the door securely shut and bolted.

When he turned, he saw that he and Marianne were alone in the echoing receiving hall, a fact of which his ward was already acutely aware.

"I believe the evening could be termed an unqualified success, Miss Trenton," he said.

"I hope so," Marianne replied.

"I regret now I have taken so long to meet my neighbors." He turned to snuff out the candles lighting the hall.

"They all seemed very nice," Marianne said, nervously watching the light dim, fearful of being alone here with Mr. Desmond, but not at all sure of how to get away.

"And it was not so very bad, was it? Our show of camaraderie?" the man asked.

"Not so very," Marianne replied. She had not even been aware that it was only a show, though she did not confess that to the gentleman now speaking to her out of the shadows of the receiving hall.

"I have enjoyed the last week—spending it here at Kingsbrook, getting out and about, the busy work and the party. I hope you have enjoyed it as well."

"I have, sir," Marianne said.

Desmond could not see her clearly, but her voice was as soft as the night breeze, as a whispered murmur on the pillow next to his.

"I am pleased. Well, good night then, Miss Trenton," he said quickly, turning as he spoke to hurry away from her and her damnable allure.

"Good night, Mr. Desmond," she replied, aware that she spoke with a sigh in her voice. It was a sigh of relief. She thought.

"The declension of *nauta,* sailor. Miss Prince, begin."

Sylvia Prince was a tall girl with a bony frame and rectangular cheeks and jaw. She and Judith Eastman were best friends, quite inseparable, and their friendship puzzled Marianne when she took the time to consider it as they were two girls who were very different from one another. Miss Eastman was a bright young woman, with strong opinions and a cutting wit. She was quite pretty and presented herself with such self-assurance people always assumed she was prettier than she was. Miss Prince, on the other hand, was dogged rather than bright, imitative rather than opinionated and quite the most humorless person Marianne had ever met.

The Farnham Academy instructors were fond of Miss Prince, though, because Miss Prince always took her lessons seriously. Miss Prince took *everything* seriously.

Now she stood next to her desk and began the declension. "*Nauta, nautae, nautae, nautam, nauta.*"

"Very good, Miss Prince. Miss Baxter, *silva,* forest. Begin."

One by one the girls stood and recited the Latin declension of the nouns Mrs. Avery gave them. It was not a difficult exercise, dating from their very first lesson, yet Marianne was having difficulty concentrating.

It was March. Though the weather was not warm yet, the winter chill had definitely left, and Marianne was unable to focus her attention on her slate and books. And certainly not on Mrs. Avery.

"Miss Trenton, *terra,* land."

Guiltily, Marianne started and stood.

"*Terra,*" she repeated. "*Terrarum, terris—*"

"Not in the plural, Miss Trenton. In the singular. Try again. *Terra.*"

Her studies were actually going very well in Farnham. Dear Mrs. Grey had finally allowed them to expand their study of literature to include a few of *Plutarch's Lives*. The girls at the academy had read about Pericles and Coriolanus. When they had "done away" with Julius Caesar, Mrs. Grey hinted, they might delve into *The Confessions of Saint Augustine.* Some of the girls had hopes that Augustine had led a life of riot and abandon and had committed grievous, colorful sins of which he felt the need to confess himself, but knowing Mrs. Grey, Marianne had no such expectations.

Wistfully, her eyes wandered again to the window. In their free time she and Nedra wandered the country lanes surrounding the Farnham Academy. The grass was just beginning to green, though the few flowers valiant enough to blossom in March were still tight buds, except for daffodils and crocuses, which had unfurled their colors the first time the sun showed its face.

Each new leaf, each chirping insect reminded Marianne of Kingsbrook. She imagined her fingertips brushing the tall grasses of the meadow, dried from last year, only now being replaced by new green growth.

The songbirds would be different at this early season, too. Last June they had seemed cheerful and complacent, but in March they would be loud and raucous, trying to outdo each other with their courting ballads.

And she pictured the gazebo, imagining herself in the cool shadows, one of the books from the Kingsbrook library in her hand. She would find it even more difficult to concentrate on the printed page there than she did in Mrs. Avery's Latin class. Any sudden noise would have her looking up with a start, expecting . . . what?

That same presence that had surprised her the first time she was there? Looking grave, forbidding, with his heavy brows and undisciplined hair? And would she be disappointed when, every time, she saw nothing more than a startled hare or a nervous bird?

But at the Farnham Academy the scene was not quite so idyllic in the cool month of March, and after a week of wandering about in the damp outdoors, poor Nedra came down with fever and chills. Her bed was moved to the infirmary, and she was firmly tucked between its sheets.

"Are you getting any better?" Marianne asked hopefully from the doorway the following day.

"I have forgotten what 'better' feels like," Nedra said, turning on her side with a moan.

Marianne tiptoed away from the sickroom, admitting that it was beastly of her to go out and enjoy the weather while poor Nedra was so ill. But the sun was going to shine and the soft breeze to blow whether she went outside or not, so she wrapped a shawl around her shoulders and quickly left the academy behind her.

There was a wooded hill behind the school, with pathways that led to graded lanes, which eventually put one on the roadway to Portsmouth. The climb could be strenuous, and most of the girls preferred the easier walkways around the school. Marianne, feeling lonely without her friend, turned her steps toward the rise of ground.

The woods began at the very base of the hill, and intrepidly Marianne plunged into the deep shade, to pick her way carefully over the twigs, branches and deep piles of leaves fallen from the deciduous trees. While she and Nedra had occasionally walked out this far, they always drew up short at the dark line of trees, Nedra demurring to venture beneath the low-hanging branches and high-climbing vines.

Nedra was not with her today, though, and Marianne unflinchingly entered the "untamed" depths. Much to her surprise, even before the trees closed completely around her, she found Nedra had been correct to be so reluctant. The air was heavy, the ground damp with leaves and dead undergrowth decaying in a pungent compost beneath her feet. To keep her skirts clean and to enable her to step over or around large branches, boulders and bushes, she had to hike her skirts up well past her knees, to midthigh.

A low-hanging branch pulled at the loosely woven material of the shawl, and it seemed she could not walk past a tree without a stick or twig tangling in her hair, pulling strands free to fall across her eyes or float down her back.

She was paying no attention to the direction she was going, choosing her path solely with an eye to avoiding what difficulties she could now that she was here. Marianne had her eye fixed on the next step directly in front of her, when her attention was suddenly claimed by a rustle beyond the trees ahead. She stopped for a moment to try and assign the noises she heard to a known source.

It was nothing, she told herself firmly after a few nervous moments, and grasping her skirt to take a wide, ungainly step over a fallen tree trunk, exposing ruffles, slips, pantaloons and an indecent expanse of white thigh, she pushed through the branches before her to confront her fear, ready to laugh at herself when she found it was only a curious ground squirrel.

But it was not a timid forest animal twitching its nose on the other side of the tree, and her fearful start was wholly justified. "Uncle Horace!" Marianne cried.

Because of the shock of seeing Carstairs, appearing in the woods like some evil apparition, Marianne was not aware until it was too late that her last step had brought her to the edge of a steep embankment that gave onto a lane.

The man below her looked up before she could drop her skirts. "Why, Marianne," he responded, with some surprise himself.

"What are you—"

Her question was cut short when her heel slipped on the uncertain footing, and with a bounce and a jog she was suddenly at the base of the embankment with her knees up to her chin.

Carstairs watched the spectacle, his thin lips twitching in amusement. "Marianne, Marianne, my poor child. Still as clumsy as a cow, I see," he chided, looking down at her and shaking his head. "Well, up on your feet now, and try to keep them."

"Uncle...Uncle Horace. What are you doing here?" she asked, her eyes wide with disbelief.

"I found myself in this part of the country, collecting on a business transaction, and I said to myself, why not check into this school where Desmond says he has my Marianne? I had to make sure you are comfortable and well cared for, did I not?" he asked, with a display of goodwill that was totally unconvincing.

"I am very well, but you really needn't have bothered," she said, in a tone she could not keep from sounding defensive.

"But of course I did, my pet. You will always be my little Marianne." Carstairs smiled his thin, humorless smile, and Marianne cringed.

She brushed at her skirts to straighten them again. "But I understood I am solely Mr. Desmond's ward now," she said softly, keeping her head down so she would not have to see the hateful man before her.

"Did you? Oh, I know old Desmond has tried to make it all very legal and binding, but a dozen papers cannot break the tie that binds us, can it? But never mind about that now. Come walk with your dear old uncle awhile." Without her leave he took her hand and drew it through the crook of his elbow. When he started to walk, he dragged her behind him, stronger than his emaciated frame would suggest, certainly too strong for her in her subdued condition to resist.

Carstairs looked around approvingly at the dark trees surrounding them. "A very pleasant place, this wood. Do you know there is a boulder up ahead that looks out over your school? A person can see right down onto the lawns from up there, down on you and all your pretty little friends."

A shiver of revulsion shook her frame at the thought of Uncle Horace spying on her, gazing down upon Farnham like a noxious bird of prey. But before she could gather her wits and courage enough to lodge a vocal protest, they came around a bend in the lane and saw the school below them. Carstairs pulled her quickly back under the shade of the trees.

"Look at that," he said. The academy buildings and grounds were spread out before them. Marianne had never stopped to consider how impressive the place really appeared. "All this and Kingsbrook Hall as well. Peter is indulging you shamelessly." Carstairs clicked his tongue disapprovingly. "Who would have imagined that one hand of cards would give you so much? I had a full house. He had four threes. Now you have this." He put an arm around her shoulders and gestured broadly with the other.

Marianne quailed at his embrace, but her uncle held her shoulders tightly and would not allow her to move away.

Suddenly Carstairs released his hold. Mrs. Avery had appeared at the doorway of the main building and began to ring the bell.

"It is time you returned to your classwork. Tell Desmond I send my best regards, will you?" He gave Marianne a push, and she stumbled out of the woods onto the academy grounds. She glanced behind her, but the man had melted into the shadows.

Marianne was pale and withdrawn for many days after, though she did not tell anyone of her meeting with Carstairs or his suggestion that he might be watching the place.

Chapter Seven

Though he acknowledged his responsibility and had assumed the duty with a dedication that would have surprised his father, Desmond, having provided for the girl, honestly endeavored to put her out of his mind.

Why then did images and memories of her constantly plague his thoughts?

Often the way some young woman moved her head or lifted her chin made him turn sharply, the beat of his heart increasing when he thought, for just a moment, that it was Marianne.

As he went about Kingsbrook, various things reminded him of his ward. In the library certain books which had been taken down and returned to different slots, or perhaps replaced at a slightly different angle. He found a hair ribbon that he was quite certain was not Mrs. River's. In some rooms Desmond could even detect the delicate scent of the bath soap she used.

At Christmastime they were together only for the sake of the staff and the neighbors. By mutual consent they had tried not to be alone together, yet at one of those odd moments Marianne had presented him with a gift.

She explained, with some embarrassment, that Mrs. Lynk had insisted that her students practice their handwork, hinting that due to the season of the year their projects might be used as Christmas gifts. Marianne felt required to work up one of the sets of handkerchiefs Mrs. Lynk provided, and once finished, she had a dozen with the initials *P.D.* on them, and what else was she to do with them?

Granted, it was not the most gracious of presentations, but Desmond was touched by the gift. The thought occurred to him that he was putting a part of the girl in his front pocket whenever he took one of the handkerchiefs from his linen drawer. Now it did not even take the back of a girl's head or some distant song to remind him of her; he thought of Marianne Trenton every time he wiped his nose.

As the weeks passed, he admitted to himself that he had an unhealthy fascination for the girl. He was appalled by his interest in her, called himself a cur, a cad and a blackguard. He would not acknowledge the fact that she really did have bewitching green eyes and soft dark golden hair that sparkled with fiery red highlights when the sun shone on it. Or the fact that she was no longer a child, but a young woman not yet eighteen.

The picture of her he called to mind, with which he castigated himself, was of her lying on his bed, eyelids clenched shut, her tears seeping under the lids, down her cheeks onto the pillow. He would always feel that pressure in his chest when he recalled her quavering answer to his question. "Sixteen," she had whispered, and would always whisper in his mind.

Days passed. Weeks slipped away. Winter melted into spring, spring drizzled into summer and summer beat down upon them.

Mr. Desmond, in his sincere effort to forget the girl, did not speak to Mrs. River about her, and naturally assumed he would not meet with her on the Kingsbrook estate. Nor would he have in past years. Since taking possession of Kingsbrook he had often stayed away from the estate for six months at a time, simply sending money to the housekeeper to meet the necessary obligations and not even enclosing a note inquiring after the house or grounds.

Now, though, he was required to spend more time on his property, having assumed a more responsible role at Kingsbrook. He was attempting to earn the upkeep money from the estate itself, rather than from the gaming table, and to his surprise, Desmond was finding it a rather pleasant change. And with Marianne safely entrenched at the Farnham Academy, he felt fairly easy in coming and going from the estate unannounced.

So it happened that he cut short his trip to London in June, deciding not to cross the Channel at all that summer, and returned to the estate to take a more active interest in the planting of his leased lands.

"Mrs. River! Ho, there, Mrs. River! I am returned. Like Odysseus home from the wars at last." Desmond threw open the front doors and dropped his traveling bag on the floor of the receiving hall, calling for the housekeeper so loudly that his voice echoed off the tall ceiling. Then he crossed to the library and pushed open that door, taking the female figure silhouetted against the window to be Mrs. River.

"'Ye dogs, ye said in your hearts that I should never more come home from the land of the Trojans,'" he quoted with a smile. Then his eyes accustomed themselves to the lighting, and his smile froze. "Miss Trenton. I was not expecting you to be here."

"Did you not receive Mrs. River's note? She said she had written to you telling you I would be here for the month."

"For the month? Of June?"

Marianne nodded, and Desmond felt an uncomfortable sinking in the pit of his stomach.

He *had* received a letter from Mrs. River, true enough, and had certainly intended to read it. But being casual about his correspondence, first he had misplaced it, and when he found it again he was busy packing to come to Kingsbrook anyway and had put it aside, assuming he would discover its import when he arrived.

As, in fact, he just had.

"Mrs. Avery dismissed the academy for the summer," Marianne was explaining. "There were repairs to be made in the dormitory before winter, and she was going up to Birmingham to visit an ailing cousin."

"Damned inconvenient, if you ask me," Desmond blurted, without taking time to soften his reaction.

"Well, yes, and I apologize, but I had nowhere else to go," Marianne said with a slight quiver in her voice.

"Of course not," he assured her quickly, guiltily. "I did not mean *you* were not welcome here. As I have said, you must consider Kingsbrook your home."

"Well, here I am until the end of the month," she finished helplessly.

They stood gazing at each other in silence for a few moments, both acutely aware of the tense situation in which this would put them. Marianne would not have looked on it as quite so catastrophic if her meeting with Uncle Horace at Farnham and his insinuations about her guardian did not form such a persistent, unpleasant memory. And Desmond himself could have looked on the development with something closer to equanimity if Marianne had not been clothed in a pale, moss green dress just then, with loose strands of golden red hair trailing across her cheeks and down her neck. She looked as young as the first night she'd come here, and twice as tempting. He couldn't help shamefully noticing the rise and fall of her bosom and the moist fullness of her lips.

"I see. That does pose a problem then. I am committed to my tenants and must be here at Kingsbrook until the first of August." He looked around at the pleasant appointments of the library and then out the window across the waving grass. "It appears I, like you, have nowhere else to go."

"Can you not—" Marianne began, but before she could finish her hopeful suggestion, Mrs. River swept into the room.

"Mr. Desmond. What a delight. And to think you and Miss Marianne will have the whole month together. Has our girl not grown there in Farnham? Getting to be quite the lady." The housekeeper stood beaming at them both.

Marianne blushed furiously and ducked her head. "Mrs. River, please," she protested softly.

"And smart? She is becoming quite the scholar, too. Go ahead, miss, tell Mr. Desmond what you were telling me about Corio... Corialon... Corilus—"

"Coriolanus. And I do not think Mr. Desmond would be interested in *Plutarch's Lives,*" Marianne said.

"On the contrary, Miss Trenton, I am very interested in Coriolanus, Pericles, Demosthenes, Caesar. I have myself been edified by their noble thoughts and deeds and am pleased to learn you are becoming acquainted with them as well," Desmond said.

"Enough of this now," Mrs. River said. The housekeeper was not as imperceptive as they both assumed. She had sensed the unease in the room when she entered and now deemed it time to separate the two of them in order to relax tensions. She had grown very fond of Miss Marianne and had always had a soft place in her heart for Mr. Desmond, despite what seemed to be his hopeless incorrigibility.

"James is taking your things upstairs, Mr. Desmond. Perhaps you would like to join him to oversee the unpacking?" she suggested.

"Yes, of course," Desmond said.

"Dinner will be at seven," she added, following him to the door and almost giving the impression of herding him out of the room. "I am afraid I was not certain when you would arrive, so I left instructions for Mrs. Rawlins to prepare something light. I will go now and tell her she will have both of you for supper. She will want to put on something more, I am sure. A few more potatoes and another chop, perhaps."

The housekeeper ushered the master from the room, but Marianne remained standing before the bookshelves in something of a daze.

A month. An entire, ghastly month. And they were trapped there, the two of them, like two of the trussed rabbits she had seen Rickers bring to Mrs. Rawlins just the other day.

Suddenly fearful that Desmond would burst in on her again, she gathered up the books and papers she had brought with her from the academy and hurried from the room. She spent the remainder of the day barricaded behind her door, feeling very much under siege. Yet the only bombardment she experienced was Alice's gentle tap as afternoon was dimming to evening.

"Miss Marianne? Mrs. River sent me to remind you dinner will be early this evening."

"What time is it now?" Marianne called through the door, without opening it or even rising from the chair in front of her little writing desk.

"A quarter past six. Dinner is to be at seven o'clock."

"All right," Marianne replied. "Thank you, Alice."

"Very good, miss." There was a pause as the serving girl turned uncertainly from the closed door and then back again. "Miss Marianne? Can I do anything to help?" she asked.

The door finally opened partway and Marianne smiled out at her. "No, thank you, Alice. You may tell Mrs. River I am changing now and will be right down."

"Very good."

Marianne's smile seemed to reassure the serving girl, and without further inquiry she crossed the hall and started down the stairs. Mrs. River had said not to make too much of a to-do over Miss Marianne being here at the same time Mr. Desmond was, but she gave the instructions in a tone of voice that suggested some sort of "to-do" *could* be made over the situation.

When Marianne descended from her room, Alice's vague suspicions seemed to be warranted. The young lady's cheeks were flushed, putting two scarlet carnations in her otherwise pale face. Her hair was theoretically confined in a twist at the back of her head, but locks and curls had slipped during her hasty toilette and now fell against her damp neck. And her eyes were dark and sparkling, enlarged with nervous dread until they seemed to fill her face.

"Is Mr. Desmond down yet?" she asked.

"I do not believe so," Mrs. River told her.

Marianne nodded and passed by the housekeeper distractedly. "I shall wait in the dining room," she murmured.

Five minutes later Desmond came down the same staircase. "I shall wait for Miss Trenton in the dining room," he said.

"Miss Marianne is waiting there now, sir," Alice said.

Desmond drew up short. He glanced over his shoulder as if contemplating returning to his room, but almost reluctantly turned toward the dining-room doors again. "In that case you may serve dinner as soon as it is ready," he said.

When he opened the door, Marianne was seated in her place, her hands folded on her lap. She was watching the entrance with bright, feverish eyes.

"'To me, fair friend, you never can be old,/ For as you were when first your eye I eyed/ Such seems your beauty still,'" he quoted spontaneously when he saw her. The words were so appropriate, the sentiment so personal that he was not sure for a moment if he had not composed them himself in that instant. Or if he even spoke aloud, until Marianne responded.

"Shakespeare," she said. "From one of his plays?" she asked.

"A sonnet, I believe," he said.

"Of course."

With something of an effort he went to his place at the head of the table. "I have given instructions that dinner is to be served immediately," he announced, sitting in the chair, while at the same time shaking out his napkin and laying it across his lap. "You must be hungry."

"I believe the early dinner hour and the menu planned are for your benefit," she said.

"Ah. Yes."

Desmond's words were both in agreement with the girl's statement and in approval of Alice and the bowl of boiled beet and noodles the serving girl brought in at that moment. The food was served to them both, and then the platter left near Desmond's plate.

The presentation of the food had been a diverting piece of business, but when Alice left, she took all the animation in the room with her.

Silence, like a dammed wall of water, waited for the tiniest break in the conversation, at which point it would wash over them in suffocating waves. Desmond was determined not to allow that to occur.

"Your studies are going well?" he asked.

"Very well."

The girl was not helping him a great deal in maintaining the dike.

"And they are?" he prompted.

"Not difficult," she returned, unsure what exactly he was asking.

"Figures?"

"Figures? Oh, yes, figures. There are some. Mrs. Avery instructs us in addition and subtraction. And our times tables, certainly." Marianne allowed herself a bite of beet, assuming her conversational duty had been fulfilled.

"I do not suppose anything so demanding as geometry is required of Farnham's young ladies, is it?" he asked ironically, taking a bite himself.

"Not as a formal class, no," she replied when she had swallowed. "But I found a copy of Euclid's *Elements* in the library and have read a bit on the subject."

"Have you? I commend your initiative," Desmond said with genuine admiration. "And your Latin?" he inquired.

"Linguam Latinam doctus sum," Marianne replied solemnly.

"Yes, I see you 'have been taught Latin,'" Desmond said, nodding his approval. *"Pure et Latine loqui."*

"Perhaps not 'elegant Latin,' but the books in your library are not quite so enigmatic anymore," Marianne said.

Desmond raised an eyebrow and nodded slightly. "Very good," he murmured, more to himself than to her. "And what of your other classes?" he continued.

So Marianne told him of Miss Gransby's elocution class, and Mr. Brannon's history. "And deportment from Mrs. Lynk," she said.

Desmond could not restrain his smile. "Deportment?" he asked, barely able to keep the chuckle out of his voice.

Marianne looked at him in surprise. "Certainly," she told him. "Indeed, Mrs. Lynk believes her subject to be the most valuable taught in the academy."

Desmond's grim widened, and at last a tiny crack appeared in Marianne's porcelain expression.

"And what does Mrs. Lynk teach you?" he asked.

"Why, deportment," Marianne said.

"You no doubt stand and walk a good bit."

"And sit down again. It seems sometimes, though I do not suppose it is possible, we sit down more often than we stand up," she said, with a pretty lilt to her voice and what Desmond interpreted as a twinkle in her eye.

"And are you very good at deporting yourself?" he asked.

"Except for my sitting and the way I turn my head."

"The way you turn your head?"

"Well, yes. I turn it too abruptly at times. Mrs. Lynk has warned me on a number of occasions that no gentleman of quality would develop any romantic interest at all in someone who turns her head so quickly. I must admit I have wondered to what fatal flaw in my character the unfortunate mannerism must attest, and have worried over the sort of lowbred fiend I am sure to attract as a result. But other than that, I believe Mrs. Lynk—indeed, all of my instructors—are satisfied with my progress at the academy," Marianne concluded.

The merest hint of a smile curved her lips, and Desmond chuckled softly. "I have no doubt you are a very apt pupil, Miss Trenton," he said. "And allow me to allay any fears you have about your head turning. I knew some perfectly respectable, admirable ladies in my youth who jerked their heads about with the agitation of winter thrushes. One is married to a very wealthy banker now, I believe, and another to a baronet. I think Mrs. Lynk is not so well informed as she believes she is on the subject of what attracts and repels a gentleman's attentions."

"I suspected as much," Marianne said, the curve of her lips deepening.

Desmond had taken a second, even a third helping of chicken and noodles, and offered the bowl to Marianne, who also did Mrs. Rawlins the honor of having more. Alice cleared away the dishes and brought in little tarts the cook had baked as a special treat. The gentleman and the young lady emptied that serving tray as well—to Alice's and James's disgruntlement—as they tarried over the dinner table.

When the meal was over, as evidenced by the consumption of all the food Jenny had provided, both of the diners, having come to the table with grave misgivings, were surprised by how pleasant the meal, and the enforced company, had been.

Marianne was not put entirely at ease, but she was intrigued by the gentleman's obvious education, which she had been too ignorant herself to notice before. And by a certain air of confidence he displayed, which Marianne suspected was something he'd been born with rather than something he had been able to purchase—or win at the card table.

"How peaceful Kingsbrook is. It seems a bit odd that a man like Mr. Desmond should make this his home."

It was the afternoon of the next day. Marianne and Mr. Desmond had parted company after dinner. He had been off making his appointed calls by the time she came downstairs this morning, which was another departure for Desmond, who had accustomed himself to the nightlife in the gaming capitals of the world. But here in the country, folks rose with the sun, and Mr. Desmond had promised to meet the farmers in their fields.

So Marianne had a quiet morning to herself and now sat with Mrs. River in the parlor, solitude being a tonic most easily swallowed in small doses.

Marianne was gazing out the window while Mrs. River did a bit of mending. The housekeeper pulled her thread taut and studied the bit of cloth in her hand for a moment. "The estate was left to Master Peter by his grandfather, Sir Arthur Chadburn," she explained.

Marianne exhaled a breath of laughter and the woman glanced up. "What is it?" she asked.

"It seems so... irreverent to call him 'Master Peter,'" Marianne answered.

Mrs. River returned her smile. "I knew the gentleman as Master Peter long before he took possession of the manor. Sometimes I forget he reached his majority two years ago. I suppose that is because..." But she stopped suddenly when Mr. Desmond himself entered the room.

"You suppose what, Mrs. River?" he asked with a smile, when it became evident she would not continue. Marianne turned to look out the window again, embarrassed to be caught discussing the man.

"I was just telling Miss Marianne about your grandfather Chadburn," Mrs. River said.

"Pulling the old skeletons out of the closet, were you?" he asked playfully, sitting on the arm of the sofa.

"Not at all, sir. You know how admired your grandfather was," Mrs. River assured him.

"Oh, yes, certainly, my grandfather was a saint. The same cannot be said of all the Chadburns, though, can it?" He winked at Mrs. River, who shook her head in mild disapproval. "Has she told you of poor old Cousin Jerome, who beat his wife and drank himself to death? Or Great-Uncle Iverson and his *unfortunate* habit?" he asked Marianne, who was listening with eyes wide, appropriately scandalized.

"Do not pay attention to a word he says, my dear," Mrs. River scolded. "The house of Chadburn is a fine, respectable old family, with laurels crowning its members for generations. Why, it was King Charles II himself who granted Kingsbrook to Wallace, the *first* Baron Chadburn, back in 1662, in appreciation for his services in restoring the king to his throne."

"Indeed?" Marianne said, looking around her at the dark wood and elegant furnishings of the manor. "I would say Kingsbrook constituted a great deal of appreciation."

"What Mrs. River has neglected to tell you is that two hundred years ago the house was not much more than a cottage by a stream," Mr. Desmond added. "So old Wally Chadburn's service and King Charles's gratitude may not have been as profound as you think."

"Of course Kingsbrook was not then as it is now. But over the years improvements were made on the house and grounds—"

"Dependent upon some very colorful Chadburns and their uncertain fortunes," Desmond interjected. "Was it not the third Baron Chadburn who was rather fancied by Mary, or was it William? Whichever way the wind blew, he managed to parlay their favor into a healthy grant from their majesties, monies that were used to make a respectable dwelling out of the country cottage. Then, of course, the sixth Baron Chadburn married very well, and several times, if I am not mistaken, owing to a number of unfortunate accidents suffered by his wives. With their fortunes he was able to add the east wing *and* the third story."

"Mr. Desmond, I will not have you filling Miss Marianne's head with such wicked tales," Mrs. River protested.

"You are quite right, Mrs. River. It has taken years to whitewash certain aspects of Chadburn history, and I will not be the one to rob them of the veneration they so justly deserve. In all seriousness, I will admit the Chadburn name has become very well respected in the kingdom. The current baron and his sons own at least two other estates, if not three. Kingsbrook, it would seem, is considered a very minor property, the sort of unproductive estate generally left to younger sons or—" Desmond put the palm of his hand modestly against his chest "—family blackguards.

"My grandfather's father, the ninth or tenth Baron Chadburn, had two sons, Miss Marianne," Desmond explained patiently. "The eldest, naturally, inherited the other houses, most of the family fortune and his father's title. Baron Chadburn was not completely without feeling for his younger son, though, and left my grandfather Kingsbrook. And strictly between ourselves and these fine old stones, I think my grandfather came away with by far the finest property in all of the corpulent Chadburn holdings."

Mrs. River, who had refrained from saying anything far longer than she liked, pushed apart the securing hoops holding her needlework taut. "And to answer your other question, Miss Marianne, the current master of Kingsbrook could do with a more respectful attitude, but he is not wholly without his estimable qualities."

"Why, la, Mrs. River, you make me blush with such accolades," Desmond said.

A merry little laugh from the windowseat surprised both Mr. Desmond and his housekeeper. It surprised Marianne, as well. This was not what she had expected when she learned Mr. Desmond would be here. But then, nothing about Mr. Desmond had ever been what she expected.

Chapter Eight

The days flew by.

True, at the first of the month Peter Desmond and Marianne tiptoed so carefully around each other it was like the elaborate steps of a complicated quadrille.

"Good morning, Mr. Desmond."

"Ah, Miss Trenton. Down early, I see. I thought I might be finished with breakfast before you came."

"Oh, I am sorry. Go right ahead. I can eat later," she protested hurriedly the morning after the Desmond-family history lesson, even taking a backward step out of the dining room.

But Desmond held up his hand to stop her. "Never mind. Now that you are here, do sit down. Join me. Mrs. River!"

The next morning it was easier.

"Come in, come in," Desmond called from the breakfast table.

"Thank you," Marianne said, with only a little uncertainty in her voice. "It appears it will be a fine day."

"Yes it does."

Marianne sat at the other end of the table. "Something smells good," she said, sniffing the spicy air.

"Mrs. Rawlins has prepared a treat for us this morning. Cinnamon rolls."

By the end of the first week it had become something of

a habit for the two of them to greet each other first thing in the morning and exchange small talk and inconsequential opinions as they shared their breakfast hour.

However, even after the first week was past they could not part without feeling a twinge of guilt at their enjoyment of the time they spent together.

During that first week Marianne spent more hours in her room than she really wanted to. She sewed, read and stared out of her window a good deal.

For his part, though Desmond had always enjoyed his books, he got to feeling rather claustrophobic in the library. And there was just so much overseeing he could do on lands where the farmers had been farming since before he was born. Still, he did not leave for London or even go into Reading. He told himself he could not afford it, and it was true he did not want to be away from Kingsbrook right then, but the expense was not the reason.

So began the second week of June.

Breakfast had included fresh apple sauce and thick cream, and Mr. Desmond, with his characteristic unkempt good looks, had spent most of the meal with a mustache of cream on his lip from tilting his apple sauce bowl to his mouth to empty it. It was Mrs. River, coming to take away the dishes, who cleared her throat and glanced pointedly at Desmond's napkin, finally alerting him to his faux pas.

Like a schoolboy caught with melted chocolate around his mouth, Desmond ducked his head into his napkin and scrubbed at his lip.

Marianne smiled. It was the delight of Desmond's life that Marianne did smile sometimes, here in his house, with him. He looked up and caught her expression, and smiled back, chagrined.

She glanced out the window and cleared her throat. "It looks to me very pleasant out of doors today." She spoke quickly, before he had a chance to put his napkin through its ring and stand up. Once on foot, he was away, and she thought she would not like that to happen quite so soon today.

He turned to look out the window himself. "It does indeed," he agreed.

"I thought I might go for a walk."

Desmond nodded approvingly. "Be sure to take a parasol," he warned. "The cool breeze is undoubtedly camouflaging a blistering sun."

"Do you think?"

"Undoubtedly," he affirmed.

"Perhaps, then, I ought not to venture out?" she asked uncertainly.

"Oh, by all means, venture out. I am sure a walk in the fresh air will do you a world of good."

"Mrs. Avery often says there is nothing so good for the health of the body as a little exercise," Marianne reminded them both. The point was not in question, she only needed to give herself another excuse.

"Very true."

There was a brief moment of uncomfortable silence as Marianne steeled herself to be foolishly impulsive. "In that case, I thought... that is, I wondered if you would care to join me?" she said.

"On your walk?" Desmond asked, surprised both by the invitation and the glow of pleasure it gave him. "This morning? Why, I think I would like that very much."

"Just let me get my shawl," Marianne said hurriedly, before either of them had a chance to reconsider the proposal. She stood and turned from the table, but glanced back at him before she left. "And my parasol."

They left together by the front doors and followed the pathway across the front lawn and through the gardens. For a moment they walked in silence, which Desmond feared would last the entire short length of their walk.

"What are those flowers?" Marianne asked, even while he was cudgeling his brain for some topic of discussion.

Desmond glanced in the direction she was indicating. "Chamomile and wild orchid," he told her.

"Do they grow wild here?"

"As wildly as they are allowed. Mr. Rickers keeps a close watch on them," he said. He had stopped when she asked about the flowers and now studied the flower beds with a careful eye.

"Rickers is your gardener, too?" she asked.

"Rickers and James do some of the gardening for me. I do not have what you would call a 'gardener,'" Desmond said.

"Then who planted this park? Who maintains it?" she demanded.

"The Kingsbrook park and gardens were laid out and planted by generations of Chadburns past. When the estate was demoted to a minor status, though, the grounds were allowed to deteriorate. My grandfather reclaimed the gardens and lawns as far as he was able. In recent months, having had the opportunity to spend more time here, I must confess Kingsbrook park has become something of a personal hobby of my own. I liked very much what the original landscape gardener did with the grounds and have attempted to follow his lead," he explained modestly.

"I see," Marianne said, taking an even more admiring look at the grounds herself as they continued their stroll.

She asked other questions. She wanted to know what kind of tree this was, what animal made that sound or those tracks. She asked about the growing season in this part of the country. She told him she liked sweet william very much and asked why he did not have any of those plants in his park.

"They are too common," Desmond said.

"They are beautiful flowers with a delicious fragrance. How can they be common?" she asked him.

He did not have an answer for her.

The sun grew warm and the bugs annoying, yet neither one of them suggested they terminate their walk and go inside to their separate, solitary confinements. It was not until Mrs. River hailed them for luncheon from the French windows in the sitting room that they returned to the manor house.

After lunch they did not see each other again for the remainder of the day. That evening Marianne learned that Mr. Desmond had been invited out to supper by some friends down from London.

She did not see him the next morning, either. There had been drinking and card playing, and a considerable sum of money lost the night before, and Mr. Desmond did not come down to breakfast or say more than two surly words at lunch.

But nevertheless, a crack had appeared in the sheet of ice between them. They began to go from the breakfast table out into the park regularly. They ate lunch together. Sometimes they would find themselves in the same room after lunch and continue their discussions.

Desmond told Marianne of his childhood home, and was so at ease with the girl as to allow a note of regret and loneliness to creep into his voice. He mentioned that he loved sweet cherries, though he preferred them sweeter than could be found in this part of the world. From his casual reference she was able to gather that he had tasted cherries in a great many places and had arrived at his considered opinion after much comparison.

She told him about the academy, about Judith and Sylvia and a new girl named Myrtle Thane. She told him about her friend Nedra Stevens and confessed, with scarlet cheeks, that she and Nedra sneaked passionate poetry from Mrs. Avery's private library, poring over it as they sat together among the lilac bushes.

By the end of the month Desmond had discovered the young woman had an inquiring mind behind her emerald green eyes. She played the piano passably well and could beat him at chess if he did not pay attention to the game, which was difficult when she was gazing at him across the chess board with those same green eyes.

"I prefer Alexander Pope to Samuel Johnson, Pope being the sharper wit," Mr. Desmond told her.

"Do you think?" Marianne asked. "I have read some of each, though not enough to make an informed judgment, I am afraid."

Desmond smiled to himself. The occasions when Marianne refused to make a decision because of a lack of information were few and far between. "I do not imagine they are very well represented in the Farnham Academy library, either one of them," he offered.

"They are not in the academy library at all. What I have read of them I read here."

Desmond shook his head ruefully. "I see. Well, here on my shelves poor old Johnson and Pope tend to get pushed aside by Mr. Shakespeare, who is, I admit, often displaced himself by Homer and Virgil."

Today they were in the sitting room. Mrs. River was mending a tablecloth, sitting quietly to one side, enjoying the spirited conversation.

"Homer and Virgil. Now there are curious favorites for a man of the modern day. Does it not seem more sensible to read of modern ideas in modern languages?" Marianne demanded.

"I do not believe there are any modern ideas, Miss Marianne. Only ancient ideas rephrased very clumsily for our day. Greed, honor, hate, love, war, peace—these will always exist, and our only hope of understanding and mastering them lies in our learning from the past."

"So the reason you read your classics is to be edified concerning problems facing our society today?" Marianne asked seriously.

Desmond grinned. "That, and because Homer describes decapitations so colorfully in the *Iliad.*"

"I delight in Johann Sebastian Bach," Desmond told her on another occasion. "His works are sublime studies in form and discipline."

"By that same definition, do they not become cold, mechanical exercises?" Marianne asked. "Mr. Bach has always seemed too emotionless to me, though I have played his inventions dutifully to improve my fingering technique."

"Oh, do not make of Bach's works nothing more than exercises in manual dexterity!" Desmond exclaimed, with genuine passion in his voice.

They had come to the little stone gazebo behind the manor. Their steps often led them through the meadows of Kingsbrook, usually to this field and this little gray structure. They had always walked around it. The memory of the day Desmond had come here to tell her she would be his ward was burned too painfully into both their minds.

But today Desmond, lost in his heated remonstrances, climbed the few steps to the cool interior. Marianne followed him. He turned to face her, resting his back against one of the pillars.

"Bach's music, like that of all great composers, is a window to his soul. His joy, his faith, his adulation of spirit is in his work. And if played with that same ebullient emotion, it becomes grand and thrilling, touching our own souls," he said. He took her hand in his. "Allow your soul to be touched, Marianne!"

He spoke earnestly, almost urgently, looking directly into her eyes. His final sentence was a plea, but Marianne was not sure for what he was pleading. For a split second, as a gust of wind outside the gazebo ruffled his tousled hair, the girl forgot what it was they were discussing.

They were three weeks into June by then and had come to feel perfectly comfortable with each other. They could exchange greetings naturally in the mornings. Marianne casually interrupted Peter in his library, and he would often ask her to stay, to read a passage or hand him a book. More remarkable than their easy conversation, however, were the silences between them, which were no longer strained. If he happened across her in a sitting room, or even one of the numerous little private window nooks tucked here and there about Kingsbrook, he might not simply pass by, but claim one of the chairs or an end of the windowseat. If he stayed, he might ask what she was doing or what were her plans for the day, or if she had read the selection he had pointed out to her the night before. Or they might not talk at all. Sometimes he merely put his head back and closed his eyes, or gazed out at the park.

But this moment in the gazebo, as he held her hand and looked at her so intently, and she stood so still and unmoving, was different from their easy companionship. Yet it lasted no longer than other silences between them and seemed no more important than their casual conversations.

It was Desmond who finally disturbed the moment. He did not move, but shifted his eyes to look out at the meadow. An instant later Marianne extracted her hand from his, and by the time they left the gazebo together, discussing the various charms and shortfalls of side dishes that went with roast beef, the moment had passed. Though it was not forgotten. By either of them.

"My father was a merchant," Marianne told him. She spoke suddenly, with no introduction, and Mr. Desmond looked up with interest from the financial records of the estate he was studying.

"He sold dry goods in a little shop outside of London. He was never able to afford the expensive wares of the more exclusive shops uptown, but he always told his customers they were 'every bit as good as.' That was the very phrase he used. 'This lampshade is every bit as good as anything you could buy in Stillworthy and Grey's, Mrs. Markham,' he would say. Dear Papa would never have dreamed of misleading his customers, and I know he believed it when he said it. And his patrons believed in him. So they smiled, bought the wares and forgave him when they were cheap and flimsy." Marianne turned from the library window and smiled at Mr. Desmond, who sat behind his desk across the room.

The month was nearly over. It was June 29. Mr. Desmond had mentioned that he had to go into London tomorrow, and the next day Marianne would be away from Kingsbrook, on her way back to the academy, probably before Desmond returned. Neither one of them spoke of the approaching separation. The idea preyed on their minds, but neither of them acknowledged it.

As the days slipped away from them, especially in this last week, they had come to spend almost every waking hour together, jealous of the interruptions that parted them and robbed them of these last few moments.

The room they usually chose to meet in, by silent, mutual agreement, was Mr. Desmond's library. Not only did they both love the room, but Mrs. River preferred her sitting room and left them alone in here.

Though overcast when they woke, the day had brightened, and they could have been out walking, but neither suggested the open air and wide blue sky today. Mr. Desmond stayed behind his desk, looking over his papers, and Marianne read for a while and then wandered about the room, looking into random volumes she took from the shelves, making comments occasionally, feeling not the least compunction about disturbing the man at his work. She had come to a standstill in front of the long window of the library, lost in reminiscences, and now, in surrender, Mr. Desmond closed the folio cover on his papers and leaned back in his chair.

He felt a calm sense of appreciation, watching the girl in front of the window. The sunlight filtered through her dress and silhouetted the curve of her breasts, the indentation at her waist, the swell of her hips. He could even see the shape of her thighs and the calves of her legs as they tapered away to the fine bones of her delicate ankles. Still, with resolution, Desmond refused to let himself find the picture provocative. She was like a delicate ivory carving, perfect in form yet unattainable in fact. When she turned and smiled at him, he was able to return her innocent smile with a clear conscience.

"And did you help in the shop? Did you wait on customers, telling them the wares were 'every bit at good as'?" he asked her.

Marianne shook her head. "No. That is, I helped in the shop now and then, when time and my mother would allow it, but I did not have my father's conviction concerning our wares. And I fear Papa did not always appreciate the help I did give, for very often I would discourage a purchase and tell a buyer where she could find a better or less expensive item."

"The candor of children. It has often been the bane of our adult world," Desmond said reproachfully.

"You make yourself sound like a hoary Ancient of days," Marianne said with a scornful smile.

Desmond squinted at her and spoke in a palsied voice. "Oh, my child, if you could but know what these eyes have seen."

"Oh, tosh. You have traveled a bit and read a great deal. That does not make you old, it has only made you stuffy."

"You amuse me, Miss Trenton," Desmond said, with just the right note of condescension, he was certain, to infuriate the girl. "Twenty years from today, *ten* years from today, when you recall this conversation, you will blush at the brashness of your youth. Or at least, we can only hope by then that the years will have brought you some degree of maturity."

"The same maturity you enjoy?" she asked mockingly.

He bowed his head gravely.

"If you are so very old and experienced, thou wise and aged one, how have you reached such a doddering maturity without being married?"

Desmond smiled faintly and glanced down at his desk again. The candor of children did indeed catch one unawares at times. "The opportunity never presented itself," he said lightly.

"In all your lengthy existence? I find that difficult to believe," Marianne exclaimed, goading him.

"Perhaps it would be more exact to say, then, that when the opportunity was there, the girl was not."

Mr. Desmond was doing his best to keep his tone light, but the subject, even after ten years, was painful still, and he could not disguise that fact entirely.

"Have you been in love then?" Marianne asked, serious herself at last.

"Once," Desmond admitted softly. He did not look up, but continued to speak in a faraway voice. The spirit of reminiscence had suddenly claimed him, as well. "In Coventry, where I grew up. She came to live with her older sister, who was an absolute tyrant. An omnipresent tyrant. As fond as I was of the young lady, I do not believe I was ever alone with her in our entire acquaintance. Perhaps that is why she is not here today in Kingsbrook as its mistress."

"I am glad," Marianne whispered.

Desmond glanced up curiously at the girl. "Glad I was never alone with her or glad we did not marry?" he asked.

Marianne blushed. "I am glad her sister was a tyrant. I hope she made your life miserable."

"That she did," Desmond admitted, with a shake of his head.

"What was her name?" Marianne asked.

When she had started on this course of questions, her tone had been light and playful. She had not expected to hear Mr. Desmond admit he had been in love before. She had not wanted to hear that and now was not sure she wanted to hear about the girl who had taken his heart and returned it, bruised and broken. . . . Despite Marianne's exposure to the classic works of literature, such phrases from *Leonore, Jeune Fille* and its ilk still colored her thoughts.

"The sister? I do not remember the sister's name. Now is that not curious?" Desmond asked.

But Marianne scowled, suspecting correctly that he was having fun at her expense.

"What was your young lady's name?" she pressed.

"Yes, of course, my young lady. Well, her name *was* Miss Deborah Woodley. Shortly after our break she changed it from Woodley to Chancery."

"She left you for another?" Marianne asked, a breath of disbelief in her voice.

"Your incredulity flatters me," Desmond said, smiling at her, leaving the past for the present at last. "Yes. She preferred a close friend of mine, and I, in our world of flawless manners and good breeding, had no choice but to step aside, to relinquish her hand and heart to another. Unfortunately, ours is not a species that generally fights to the death in order to claim our mates."

"Do you regret it still?" Marianne asked. "Do you think about her often?"

"Yes and no," Desmond answered. "Yes, I regret losing her. One always regrets losing a love, at any time in one's life, regardless of what happiness follows. Pain is never a pleasant memory, and her speech of farewell was very painful, for us both, I believe. At least, I *like* to believe she suffered in some degree as well. Rather base of me, I know. But one cannot always keep from feeling vengeful.

"As to your other question," he continued, "no, I do not think of her often. I do not suppose I have thought of her in months, and only your questions brought her to mind now. I might not have given her a thought for another several months."

"Then I am sorry," Marianne said.

"You need not be. Thoughts of Miss Woodley—that is, Mrs. Chancery—are not all painful. She was a lovely girl, just as I am sure she is a lovely wife and mother."

But Marianne honestly regretted reminding him of a former love. Especially in their last week together, when they would so soon be parted again. When she was behind the stone walls of the Farnham Academy she did not believe she wanted him to be alone here at Kingsbrook, thinking of a beautiful woman with whom he had once been in love.

Chapter Nine

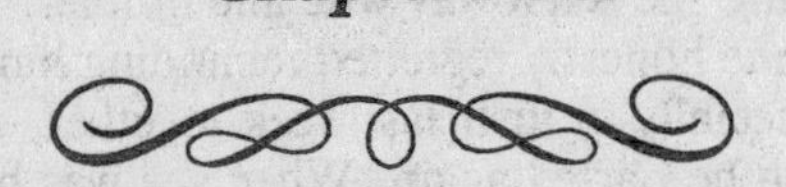

Mr. Desmond was away quite early the next morning. He stayed at Kingsbrook long enough to have breakfast with his ward, but when he rose from the table and said he thought he would be off, there was a farewell in his voice they both recognized. They would most probably not be seeing one another until Christmas, and six months seemed like a very long time.

After he had left, Marianne wandered listlessly through the rooms on the ground floor of the manor, usually in Mrs. River's wake, quite often in the housekeeper's way.

Mrs. River would have exiled her to the out-of-doors, but exasperatingly, at the end of a month of uniformly fair weather, this day was damp and rainy. Mr. Desmond had not been gone a half hour when rain began to drip from the clouds. Not with the furious intensity of a sudden storm, quickly over, however. These clouds were somehow more petulant, settled in to pout over the whole day.

Marianne gazed through one of the tall windows in the receiving hall. She shuddered from a sudden damp chill.

"Come away from the windows, Miss Marianne," Mrs. River coaxed. "James has a nice, warm fire burning in the library."

"The library will be so gloomy today," Marianne said, not turning yet from the window.

"I will have Alice light all the lamps and bring you a cup of hot chocolate."

To Mrs. River's relief the young woman turned from the window. If Miss Marianne would only stay in the library, she would be warmer, and more importantly, she would be out of Mrs. River's and Alice's way.

"Oh, very well," the girl sighed with resignation, as if she were agreeing on liver for dinner.

By the time Marianne reached the library, Alice was already busy putting a flame to the several lamps set about the room, on every flat surface, it seemed, to allow a person to read his selected tome from any chair he chose.

"It brightens right up in here, miss," Alice said hopefully. "Sure, there is not a thing so pleasant as a toasty fire on such a day as today."

"Not a thing," the young lady agreed, though her tone hardly matched Alice's cheerful voice.

"If that will be everything, Miss Marianne?"

"What? Oh, yes. Thank you," the girl murmured impatiently.

But once she had the room to herself, she was discontented with the quiet. She wished someone was here with her. Oh, not Alice, and not Mrs. River, either. She wished...

She ran her hand back and forth over the smooth brown leather of the arm of the chair and admitted to herself who it was she wished was there. She could see his tangled hair, incongruent with his careful apparel, hear the deep timbre of his voice in her mind.

She pushed herself out of the comfortable chair. It was too easy to imagine its supple confines as his embrace. But if her goal was to avoid thinking of him, she had chosen the wrong room. Everything in the library was reminiscent of him. The hassock in front of his favorite chair, the worn volumes of Homer and Virgil taken down from the bookshelf, little piles of papers all over the room, on every table, on the seat of one straight-backed chair, on the mantel shelf.

She glanced at his desk, another mass of confusion, but she did not step in that direction. She remembered only too well the letter she had discovered there from Uncle Horace. As she had spent the past weeks with Mr. Desmond, that letter and Carstairs's insinuating remarks when she had seen him at the academy preyed on her mind. How could she allow herself to find such pleasure in her guardian's company, knowing what she did about him? And yet she *had* enjoyed his association, his wit, his intelligence, the flattering interest he had shown in her. Just as she appreciated his intense gray eyes; his mane of hair, which seemed to belie his perfectly civilized manner; the broad expanse of his shoulders; the strength of those muscles, which she still remembered well. Sometimes, as she watched him, her fingers had tingled with the phantom sensation of the feel of his skin.

Absently she picked up the *Iliad,* which was lying on the low table between the two leather chairs. It, too, was bound in fine leather, and when she opened the cover she could detect its faint, pleasing odor.

There was a folded paper inside the book, and Marianne was surprised to recognize her own handwriting. She could not remember leaving a paper inside one of Mr. Desmond's books, certainly not in a favorite one. She picked up the sheet and unfolded it. It was a letter to Nedra she had forgotten to mail. It spoke of classes they'd shared and, typically, mentioned one or two of the girls at the academy and the various traits they displayed that annoyed Marianne and Nedra. She spoke in particular of Sylvia Prince and how she did go on about her father, the ship's captain, and where he traveled and what he would bring when next he sailed into home port. Marianne had also written that Kingsbrook was as lovely as ever.

She scanned the lines hurriedly and sighed with relief when she confirmed she had had the good luck not to have mentioned Mr. Desmond at all. She smiled to herself, refolded the paper and tucked it into her bodice. She would not bother to mail this now. She would be seeing Nedra in two days and could tell her everything in person.

As much as she loved Kingsbrook and the pleasure she had taken in Mr. Desmond's company, she was actually quite anxious to return to the academy. Besides Nedra, she was anxious to see Grace, Elinor and Beverly, and the rest of the students at the academy, though the girls who associated with Judith Eastman and Sylvia were always a bit standoffish. Still, she had nothing against them and was mildly surprised and disappointed when Mrs. Avery announced, on their second day back, that Miss Prince would not be returning to the Farnham Academy.

"What?" Judith cried in alarm.

Poor Judith looked positively stricken by the news. Quite obviously her friend had not informed her of her plan not to return to the academy. Marianne thought it a curious coincidence that she herself had referred to Sylvia Prince in the letter she had failed to mail to Nedra. And the thought crossed her mind that she had found that letter tucked into a book of Mr. Desmond's that she could not remember ever opening.

"I assume you have something for me."

It was Peter Desmond making the assumption, sitting across the desk in the office of two interesting gentlemen. The placard on the door identified this as the office of Cranston and Dweeve, Confidential Inquiries.

Without noting the two names on the door, one would very likely have overlooked Mr. Dweeve entirely. It was Mr. Cranston, sitting directly opposite Mr. Desmond and leaning forward, his hair cropped aggressively close, his face red, his voice loud, who so dynamically occupied the office. One would have expected a man of more refined nature, certainly more restraint, to be making "confidential inquiries." Someone like Mr. Dweeve.

Dweeve sat back from the desk, to one side of the larger man. He was small and pale, with bland eyes and a fussy manner that made one discount him automatically as also being trivial and unimportant. Mr. Dweeve could go anywhere without being seen, listen to any conversation without being noticed, ask any question without really being heard.

Desmond had come to see Mr. Cranston and Mr. Dweeve because of a letter his solicitor had received from "a Mr. H. Carstairs, sir," Mr. Bradley had told him. In it, in terms that Mr. Bradley described as "distinctly belligerent," Carstairs protested the transfer of Miss Marianne Trenton's guardianship from his "legally recognized" trusteeship.

Mr. Bradley had carefully reviewed the papers he had drawn up, putting Miss Trenton in Desmond's care. He confirmed that they were perfectly legal, but admitted they might not be permanently binding, as Carstairs had suggested in his letter. If, for instance, Mr. Carstairs was a blood relation of the girl, he could still claim guardianship, until the girl either turned twenty-one or married.

Since Mr. Bradley himself knew his client saw the girl only on rare occasions and had no personal correspondence with her, that so far his guardianship had occasioned nothing but expense and effort on his part, the solicitor might have wondered why Mr. Desmond was so determined to keep her in his charge and out of Mr. Carstairs's. But the solicitor was not privy to the other letter, the one Desmond had received.

That letter from Carstairs had arrived months ago, before last Christmas, if Desmond remembered correctly. With a grunt of distaste, he had tossed it aside. He'd believed he had thrown it away, and was surprised to find it still in his pile of pending correspondence when he came upon it a month or so ago, when he did throw it away. But at the time he first read it, even when he finally disposed of it, he had believed he was reading merely the dirty little fantasies of a warped old man. Even still, if that was all it was, Desmond wanted to keep the girl out of Carstairs's unhealthy clutches.

"He does not say in his letter why he has waited so long to make his protest," Mr. Bradley told him. "If I remember correctly, this business was addressed almost a year ago. If Mr. Carstairs had misgivings, he should have voiced them at that time."

"He has waited too long, then? He can do nothing now?" Desmond asked hopefully.

"I did not say that, Mr. Desmond. If you will recall, I drew up these papers rather hastily, at your insistence," the solicitor said. "On another occasion I might have made more careful inquiries about the young woman and her familial ties."

"And if I wanted to make such inquiries now?" Desmond asked.

"This firm has done business with—" Mr. Bradley flipped through the pages of a small address book atop his desk "—Cranston and Dweeve, confidential investigators."

Which explained Desmond's first visit to these offices. This was his second.

"What is it you have found out?" he continued.

"About the girl, you mean. Miss..." Cranston paused, trying to remember the name. Mr. Dweeve leaned forward and murmured softly, and Cranston nodded. "Ah, yes, Trenton." Not for the first time the idea occurred to Desmond that Cranston and Dweeve were like a well-oiled machine with perfectly intermeshing parts. "Marianne Trenton. Yes. Well, now. She is, or was, ward of Mr. Horace Carstairs, put in his care some—" again he leaned back to catch his partner's words "—two years ago, upon the death of her parents."

"Yes, yes, but what about Carstairs? Is he a blood relation to the girl? Does he have some legal hold on her?"

"About Carstairs now." Cranston looked over his shoulder at Dweeve, whose bland eyes conveyed nothing to Desmond. "While we have not been able to determine Mr. Carstairs's *exact* connection to Miss Trenton, we have discovered some very interesting things about Mr. Carstairs himself."

"Oh? Is that right?" Desmond asked, his curiosity piqued.

Mr. Dweeve leaned forward and passed a small notebook over his partner's shoulder.

"You commissioned us to investigate a Horace Carstairs, moneylender. The Mr. Carstairs we have investigated has other, less savory business dealings," Cranston said.

"Such as?" Desmond prompted.

"The trafficking of opium and liquor. The receiving and selling of stolen goods. He has connections with the Asian ivory market, the African slave trade. He can even, for the right price, put one in contact with an assassin—some thug who would stick a knife into someone for the price of a cigarette. Mr. Carstairs is, in short, a busy man."

Desmond's brow had furrowed during this recitation of Carstairs's illegal dealings, but suddenly his eyes filled with genuine alarm. "Prostitution?" he asked.

"Does Horace Carstairs deal in prostitution, do you mean?" Cranston turned a page or two in the notebook. "That does appear to be one of his more recent enterprises."

Desmond fell back heavily in his chair. "I paid no attention to what he suggested. But you are telling me he has the unsavory connections to pursue such a scheme."

Cranston glanced back at his partner, who merely shrugged his shoulders. "Mr. Carstairs has the connections to pursue any scheme he chooses," Cranston confirmed.

Suddenly this meeting and the investigators' success gained a grim urgency. Desmond had come to Cranston and

Dweeve to make certain his claim on the girl was legitimate. Carstairs had hinted that he and Miss Trenton were closely related, and Desmond himself had heard Marianne refer to Carstairs as "Uncle Horace," but he had not believed the connection, if any, could be very close or binding. At Mr. Bradley's suggestion, he was willing to confirm that fact, though he, like this solicitor, did not know why Carstairs had waited until now to lodge his protest.

Suddenly it all made perfect sense. Carstairs had been busy in the intervening months, making connections, locating the young innocents he planned to prostitute, getting the workings of his hellish machine in order. Evidently he was prepared now to undertake the operation he had suggested to Desmond.

Desmond had never imagined that Carstairs could actually implement such an undertaking. The man was talking about kidnapping and prostitution. Now Mr. Cranston was telling him kidnapping and prostitution were crimes easily within Carstairs's purview.

"Crime," Desmond said suddenly. "That is the answer."

Cranston raised a questioning eyebrow, and even Dweeve looked more alert.

"Well, surely with what you have there—" Desmond nodded toward the notepad Dweeve had produced "—Mr. Carstairs could be imprisoned. In fact, it appears you have the evidence to put him in prison and leave him there to rot until Miss Trenton is out from under his power."

Cranston cleared his throat and Dweeve brushed a bit of lint from his trousers. "I am afraid we could run into a problem there, Mr. Desmond, sir," the former said. "Knowing is one thing and proving is another. Mr. Carstairs's various business concerns would be...elusive. He is, as they say in the back alleys, 'mobile.'"

"What do you mean?" Desmond asked, looking from Cranston to Dweeve and then back again.

"I mean Mr. Carstairs's business is, according to the only record available, moneylending. His interest rates are usurious, but lending private money at individually determined interest is not illegal."

"But what about those other things you mentioned? The drugs, the killers?" Desmond demanded.

"Ah, but those are not businesses of record."

"*You* know about them," Desmond said.

"Everyone knows about them. Anyone who wishes to may do business with Mr. Carstairs, but legal authorities cannot imprison him or even stop him. He simply moves his operation, leaving no evidence behind."

Mr. Desmond sat studying the men before him as seriously as Mr. Dweeve was studying the cuff of his jacket.

"What about Miss Trenton, then?" he asked at last. "Is she in any danger from him?"

"Perhaps," Mr. Cranston said. "If he were to find a judge in need of ready cash, for instance, or one willing to *accept* ready cash, the court could demand her return to him."

"And once in his clutches . . ." Desmond began.

"Once in his clutches, I suspect he would liquidate his properties as quickly as possible."

Desmond looked up sharply into Mr. Cranston's face. "Liquidate his properties?" he repeated. "What do you mean?"

"Turn them for an immediate profit," Mr. Dweeve said behind Mr. Cranston's shoulder, his voice very cool and soft.

"An immediate profit? Do you mean sell the girl?"

"Rather sell her services," Cranston replied. "I do not believe Mr. Carstairs would be so shortsighted as to bargain the girl away completely again."

"No, I do not suppose he would be," Desmond agreed heavily.

"Though, of course, he could not demand full price for used merchandise," Cranston said.

"Why you..." Desmond cried, half rising from his chair.

"Mr. Cranston is correct, Mr. Desmond," Dweeve said with a curious dampening note in his voice that caused Desmond to drop back into his chair. "Mr. Carstairs is having it conveyed around town that for top price he can provide virginal schoolgirls. Evidently a Monsieur Phillipe de Rauchenout has contracted for just such a young lady."

"Impossible," Desmond said, though he did not believe it anymore.

"Not at all. Though Carstairs's sources are not yet known, Monsieur Rauchenout has been assured that Miss Prince is completely unsullied or his money will be returned. And Mr. Carstairs would never make such an offer if there was any chance of that." Cranston's look dared Desmond to refute his claim, which, of course, he could not.

Desmond narrowed his eyes. "Did you say Miss Prince? Do you know the girl's given name?" he asked, his memory nudged by the name Cranston had mentioned.

Cranston looked through his notebook, then turned to consult with Mr. Dweeve. His partner took the notebook, flipped the pages, stopped a time or two to read the scrawled lines, before finally finding the reference for which he was searching. He pointed it out to Mr. Cranston, who took the notebook again and squinted to decipher the writing.

"It looks like Sylvia," he said, "though I cannot be sure."

"I am sure," Desmond said, his voice as hard as stone.

Both Cranston and Dweeve looked up at him curiously. "You know Miss Prince?" Cranston asked.

"I know *of* Miss Prince. She is an acquaintance of Miss Trenton's from the Farnham Academy. And you say Mr. Carstairs has delivered her to your Monsieur Rauchenout?"

"Has or soon will," Cranston confirmed.

"Stop him," Desmond said.

"Stop him?"

"Find the girl and get her away from him," Desmond said impatiently. It was blatantly obvious to him what they must do.

"Our sources were vague, our information more in the way of whispers and rumors than statements of fact. To find a lone girl in the city will require time and money," Cranston warned.

"We do not have much time," Desmond reminded them.

He did not have to remind himself that he did not have much money. It was true he had brought up production of his estate, but the rents provided only enough money for the upkeep of the manor house and park. Desmond was tempted to believe he could earn any phenomenal amounts necessary at his games of chance, but he was not so young or so obsessed as to really believe that anymore. Nevertheless, he did not hesitate when Mr. Cranston voiced his caution.

He simply repeated, "Find the girl. Take her from Rauchenout's bedroom if you must."

He would get the money from somewhere. That was not important now. What was important was saving the girl from Carstairs's clutches.

Sylvia did not return to the Farnham Academy. No one gave Miss Prince another thought when it was announced she would not be returning, no one but Judith and Marianne.

Marianne could tell the other girl missed her friend. Judith could not understand why Sylvia did not write, or at least send one of those picture postcards one scrawled a few words across, presumably because one was too busy to write more. But no word came, and in a few weeks Sylvia's memory became nothing more than a pale shadow.

Judith Eastman and Myrtle Thane struck up a close friendship. Marianne thought Judith must recognize the fog of hyperbole through which Myrtle viewed the world, but perhaps found it amusing after months of association with the humorless Miss Prince to be with someone who always saw more than was there.

For her part, Marianne was not finding her studies nearly as interesting as the student intrigues on her little campus. She was one of the older girls in the school now and had begun to suspect the Farnham staff could not teach her much more. The lessons were easy and often repetitious, and Marianne found herself bored by her classes. Her thoughts were filled with images of Kingsbrook and its intriguing owner. She could not trust the man, certainly. But she was ruefully amused by her anxious anticipation of the letter from Mrs. River telling her when Rickers would arrive at the academy to bring her back to Kingsbrook for Christmas. Last year Marianne had been so nervous about returning. This year she could not wait, and when Mrs. River's letter finally arrived early in December and said Rickers would not be there for another week, she thought the wait would drive her mad.

It was a crisp, frosty day when the carriage from Kingsbrook finally carried her onto the estate. The ground was covered with a few inches of snow, grimy in the traffic lanes but pristine in the Kingsbrook park. The sun sparkled across it, making it appear that the lawn and meadows around the manor were strewn with shattered crystal.

Mrs. River hailed her from the sitting room when she entered, the housekeeper alerted to her presence, no doubt, by the heavy opening and closing of the door, the gust of cool air and the pounding of Marianne's feet as she tried to dislodge the snow clinging to her heavy winter shoes.

"We are in here, Miss Marianne," Mrs. River called.

Marianne was aware that the tiny shiver she experienced at Mrs. River's words was not from the cold, but from eager anticipation. She pushed a strand of wet hair back from her face and glanced down the front of her dress to make sure her sash was straight and the mud was brushed from her hem. She wished there was a mirror at hand and wondered with irritation why there was not. There were times when a woman wanted to be sure she looked her very best.

"Miss Marianne, this is Candy Miller. Candy's family is from over near King's Crossing," Mrs. River said. She was sitting on the divan with a girl who was faintly familiar to Marianne. Marianne had seen her and her family, she was sure, here at Kingsbrook or in Reading. Candy had a pleasant expression on her plain, rather heavyset face.

Caught unawares, Marianne offered her hand to the girl, who had jumped to her feet when Mrs. River introduced her and now pumped her hand vigorously.

"Pleased to meet ya, miss. Course, I've seen you and the gentleman around plenty places, though you don't know me from Adam, I know," she bubbled.

"Candy Miller?" Marianne repeated blankly.

"Candy has come to take Alice's place," Mrs. River said.

"Alice is gone?"

"She was married this last month. I would have written, but I knew you would be here for Christmas. To a nice boy, David Trout. They have known each other since they were children, but David grew half a foot all of a sudden and little Alice claimed she was swept off her feet," Mrs. River said with an indulgent chuckle.

"I see. Well, I must send her something. I shall miss Alice, but you are very welcome, Miss Miller," Marianne responded dutifully.

"Just Candy. And thank you, miss."

Marianne turned to Mrs. River. "Where is Mr. Desmond? I was expecting...I thought he would be here." She attempted to keep the disappointment out of her voice, but did not succeed.

"The master went into London on business, and then he was going up to Reading for a few days. To stay with the Dudleys."

"The Dudleys?" Marianne asked. The name was unfamiliar to her.

"Casual acquaintances, though I understand Mrs. Dudley's cousin is staying with them through Christmas, which may explain this sudden rekindling of old friendships," Mrs. River said. "You may go, Candy. Mrs. Rawlins will need you in the kitchen, now that Miss Marianne has returned."

"I don't..." Candy began, and Mrs. River pushed herself off the divan with a sigh of resignation.

"I had better go with you," the housekeeper conceded. David and Alice were a happy couple, too young to realize there were challenges before them and too much in love to give any challenges much heed. Mrs. River wished them all the happiness in the world, of course, but really, could they not have waited until Alice had shown the new girl her duties? Love could be frightfully inconvenient at times.

Marianne was left alone in the sitting room. Mrs. River was off to help the new maid. Alice, who had been here since Marianne arrived at Kingsbrook, who had been her only friend that first terrifying evening Mr. Desmond had brought her here, was married and gone away. And Mr. Desmond was staying with friends in Reading.

Casual acquaintances, but evidently more important to him than she was.

"You found her?"

Once again Desmond was in the office marked Cranston and Dweeve, Confidential Inquiries. Once again he sat on one side of the desk, with Mr. Cranston on the other, while Mr. Dweeve seemed to materialize and dematerialize like a phantom of mist, depending on whether or not Desmond was giving him his full attention.

"I believe we have, Mr. Desmond. As I warned you, the search was not quick or easy. And Monsieur Rauchenout is a formidable opponent. But with Mr. Dweeve's mind and my muscle, we managed to extricate Miss Prince from his clutches. Our question now..." Cranston paused uncomfortably.

"Our question, Mr. Desmond, is what do we do with her now that we have her? Her father is somewhere on the Indian Ocean until sometime in the spring. *We* cannot care for her, nor could we return her to Farnham Academy without running the risk of losing her again. Particularly now that Monsieur Rauchenout has become a player," Mr. Dweeve explained.

"Bring her to Kingsbrook," Desmond said.

"You intend on keeping her at your estate?" Dweeve asked doubtfully. Then he cleared his throat. "Not to put too fine a point on it, Mr. Desmond, but the girl's reputation..."

"Yes, I see. Well, her presence will be kept strictly confidential while she is at Kingsbrook, and as soon as possible I will—I will..."

Cranston and Dweeve looked at him expectantly. Suddenly his brow cleared. "Why, I will send her to stay with Mother until her own father returns," he said. "Mother would never refuse to help a young woman in difficult straits. She did not even refuse help to her worthless son when he took her money and broke her heart," he murmured to himself.

"Very good, Mr. Desmond. If that will be everything then..." Cranston began.

"Oh, but that will not be everything," Desmond said grimly.

"You require our services further?" Cranston asked.

"I do. I want you to put Mr. Carstairs out of business," Desmond said. "If the law cannot stop him, then we must."

"We must?" Cranston asked.

"Absolutely. You must remember that I spoke with Mr. Carstairs, that he proposed this very enterprise to me. You have taken Miss Prince from him, but that does not change his plan to enslave other innocent young girls."

"How are we to put Mr. Carstairs out of business, Mr. Desmond?" Cranston asked.

"You say he deals in illegal drugs and liquor, receives stolen property...."

"And ivory," Mr. Dweeve reminded him.

"Oh, yes, and poached ivory. You must interrupt his supply. Intimidate his clients. Steal or destroy his stock. If Mr. Carstairs does not have to stay within the boundaries of the law, I see no reason why we should, either."

"What you are suggesting will take time," Cranston warned.

"Then the sooner you start the better," Desmond replied.

"Mr. Carstairs could simply pull up stakes and disappear if we came upon him on several fronts at once," Cranston reminded him.

"Then be discreet. I leave the particulars to you gentlemen."

"And this will take money, Mr. Desmond. Are you prepared for that?" Cranston asked. Cranston and Dweeve were good investigators, but they were also good businessmen. It was important to know who would pay the bill when the piper required his due.

Desmond took a slow breath to steady his nerves. "I am prepared to seek gainful employment if necessary, sirs," he told them. He did not know if Cranston and Dweeve understood from that declaration the sacrifice he was willing to make. But once given, his word could have been no more binding if it were written in blood.

Chapter Ten

Christmas was less than a week away when Mr. Desmond finally returned. In his absence, Mrs. River and the new girl had hung the hall and the library with ropes of cranberries and wreaths of evergreen.

Marianne helped Mrs. River and Candy wind ropes of popcorn around the tree James and Rickers brought in, and carefully position the few porcelain ornaments Mrs. River produced.

The neighbors learned that Marianne had returned from Farnham and paid visits, which Marianne was obligated to return alone. They always asked after her guardian, expressing more disappointment at his absence than any joy they might have felt at her presence.

Finally Mr. Desmond returned, to be followed that same afternoon by Mr. and Mrs. Dudley and Mrs. Dudley's cousin. The Dudleys obviously did not subscribe to the old adage, "Absence makes the heart grow fonder," but rather feared the possibility of "Out of sight, out of mind."

"My cousin has been on the continent," Mrs. Dudley told the little party assembled around the tea table. Marianne had been quick to order the serving of tea in the faint hope their guests would leave soon after. "She has only just returned, in fact. What was your comment about Brussels, Erica?"

"I found Brussels a very busy place," Miss Erica Leeming said.

"Ah, yes, a *busy* place," Mrs. Dudley repeated with emphasis and a slight laugh, attempting to turn her cousin's colorless comment into a bon mot.

Miss Leeming was perhaps not a great raconteur, but she had blazing red hair and liked wearing things that sparkled around her neck and on her wrists. Marianne fancied she could actually feel herself fading away when the lady entered the room.

Though Mr. Desmond and his ward called upon the Romer family and Sir Montmare Grissam, the Steepletons and Parson Dooley, the Dudleys were their most relentless guests during the holiday season. The Dudleys and Miss Erica Leeming. Evidently Mrs. Dudley had determined that her cousin and Mr. Desmond would make the perfect couple.

And Mrs. Dudley used some ingenious ploys to further her campaign. On two occasions she remembered pressing engagements for herself and Mr. Dudley and entreated Mr. Desmond to see her cousin home. If it would not be too much of an inconvenience?

To a gentleman, no request to be a lady's escort was inconvenient, but Marianne knew Desmond better than Mrs. Dudley and might have warned her that Mr. Desmond was not always a *perfect* gentleman. However, he never balked at taking Miss Leeming home, which irked his ward. She suspected the brilliance of Miss Leeming's hair color was due, in some degree, anyway, to the generous application of henna.

The Dudley party even dropped in on Christmas Eve, when Marianne had been hoping to enjoy a quiet evening at Kingsbrook. She might have excused herself and retreated to her room, but Miss Leeming was in a shimmering green silk dress. Marianne simply could not leave her to her own devices.

The Dudleys stayed until midnight, when Mrs. Dudley laughed and clapped her hands and instructed her husband to bring in the presents. The Dudleys' gifts were large and extravagant, and in Marianne's opinion rather tasteless.

Finally, around two o'clock in the morning, when Marianne had frankly given up and gone to sleep with her head on the arm of her chair, the Dudleys left.

"We are having a small get-together the evening after next, and of course we are expecting you. You cannot disappoint us, dear Mr. Desmond," Mrs. Dudley told her host in an undertone as the party was standing to leave.

"We shall be happy to attend," Desmond said.

"Oh!" Mrs. Dudley gasped softly. "Oh, no. I meant... that is, I thought you might come yourself. Alone," she added hopefully.

"I would never consider depriving Miss Trenton of the pleasure of your hospitality, a pleasure I have so enjoyed myself these past weeks," Desmond said, his voice smooth and curiously intractable.

"Then certainly you must bring your ward with you. And we will endeavor to find something to amuse her," Mrs. Dudley said weakly.

"I think you will find Miss Trenton equal to any of your entertainments. And if she is not, I doubt I would be, either," Desmond said, again with that satiny quality to his voice and smile.

"I dare say," Mrs. Dudley said. It occurred to her in that instant that Mr. Desmond could be a dangerous man. Perhaps a man too colorful even for Erica. But then she glanced around at the dark wood and tapestry-covered walls of Kingsbrook and decided her cousin would be equal to a great deal of color if married to the owner of this.

After they left, Desmond shook Marianne's arm, which had been dangling across the chair, cutting off the circulation. His vigorous shaking was exquisitely painful, and Marianne cried out and sat up, blinking her eyes.

"It is Christmas Day. Time to go to bed," Desmond said, smiling.

"Very amusing," she said, taking a moment to coax a kink out of neck. Then she looked around the room carefully to make certain they were alone. "Have our guests gone?" she whispered.

"They left to prepare their own entertainment. We are attending a get-together in their home tomorrow evening. Something for their most intimate acquaintances," Desmond told her.

Marianne groaned and sank back into her chair. "Could you not go without me? Tell them I am sick. Tell them I am away. Tell them I am too callow to enjoy their sophisticated company." She smiled up at him.

"I am sorry," Desmond said, pulling her to her feet. "Mrs. Dudley specifically asked that you be there."

The private little gathering to which they were invited the evening after Christmas had grown to include all of the near and even reasonably close neighbors of Mr. and Mrs. Dudley. Mrs. Dudley had decided it was easier to occupy Miss Trenton if there were a dozen or so additional guests in the party. By the careful maneuvering of chairs, tables and events, Miss Leeming and Mr. Desmond were practically isolated all night.

Mr. Wynder, who lived a mile west of the Dudleys and who Marianne knew only slightly, brought his younger brother with him. Although Mrs. Dudley was not at all concerned with Miss Trenton's enjoyment of the evening, she recognized that one way to keep the girl away from her guardian was to occupy her attention, so she directed the younger Mr. Wynder in Marianne's direction.

Joseph Wynder was a lanky young fellow who looked as if he would be more comfortable behind a plow than at Mrs. Dudley's buffet table. Marianne, feeling like another castaway in the festive confusion, undertook to ease the young man's introduction to local society.

Not without effort, though, was she able to engage him in conversation. Eliciting personal history, interests and opinions from him was like pulling teeth, a strain for her and absolutely excruciating for young Mr. Wynder. But she persevered. Eventually she learned that he was from a family of five brothers and sisters, he being the youngest. He was staying with his brother for a month or two, he liked to fish and he did not think much at all of "damned pasty-faced bookworms."

"There is a damned sight more to do with your life than spend it shut up in some fool classroom," he told her, in one of his lengthiest speeches of the evening.

Marianne smiled and nodded, and guided the young man away from some of the more intellectual conversations going on around the room.

"This Mr. Wynder. A pleasant enough fellow, I gather, though he seemed a bit rustic," Mr. Desmond commented.

They were finally returning to Kingsbrook. The sky was overcast, so the air did not snap with the bone-creaking chill of a clear night. Still, Marianne wished her guardian would talk less and drive faster.

"I suppose," she mumbled into the woolen scarf wound around her throat.

"Perhaps you prefer someone plain, someone with ordinary 'horse sense,' I believe they call it."

"Do they?" Marianne asked.

It was hard to gauge her response through the layers of fleece and heavy material surrounding her head. "Do you?" Desmond repeated.

"Do I what?"

"Do you prefer the country lad to the more sophisticated sort of gentleman?" he said.

"I really do not know," Marianne replied impatiently. Could he drive this trap any slower? She felt like jumping down and pulling the horse along by the bit to get it moving.

"That was the impression you gave tonight," Desmond continued relentlessly. "Indeed, you seemed quite taken with the younger Mr. Wynder. I was surprised. He seemed somewhat less than articulate when I spoke to him. But evidently you find men who do not speak so much appealing."

"Right now I do," Marianne said with exasperation in her voice. "And how do you know *what* I did tonight, or with whom? Every modicum of your attention was devoted to the ravishing Miss Leeming. Though I do not think purple is a particularly becoming color on her."

Marianne wrapped her cloak tightly around her, as if to shield herself from more questions, and Mr. Desmond finally jiggled the reins and encouraged the horse to a faster gait.

"It was violet," he said at last.

"Purple is purple," Marianne returned grumpily. "And speaking of articulate, I have not noticed Miss Leeming to be particularly brilliant in her conversation before tonight."

"Miss Leeming has traveled farther than the cowshed. She has been on the Continent, if you will remember."

"And found it busy," Marianne said.

Somehow Mr. Desmond's measured comments about Mr. Wynder had turned into a snapping contest between him and the girl. "Which is more than can be said of Sleepy Vale, or wherever it is Mr. Wynder hails from," he told her.

"Though he did not have thrilling tales of his world travels to tell me, I am relieved Mr. Wynder was at Mrs. Dudley's charming gathering. I might have been placed in a corner and had cloaks thrown over me like a hall tree for all the notice you took of me tonight, or been a fly on the wall, for that matter. Then at least I could have buzzed around your head and found out what was so engrossing about Miss

Leeming's narrative," Marianne said. "With her dress cut so low it was positively indecent, there is little question what it was about Miss Leeming herself that was so engrossing." Now a pouting quality had crept into her voice.

"If you had been a fly, I would have swatted you," Desmond growled, then he glanced at her sideways. "I may do that anyway."

Marianne turned her head away petulantly, and Desmond paid stricter attention to the roadway. "She was telling me about her aunt in Liverpool," he mumbled at last.

Marianne turned to him with a confused expression. "What did you say?"

"I said she was telling me about her aunt in Liverpool, Mrs. Stagway."

"Miss Leeming?"

Desmond nodded.

"Do you know her aunt? Do you know a Mrs. Stagway in Liverpool?" Marianne asked doubtfully. She herself had never heard of the woman.

"No," he said.

"Not at all?"

Mr. Desmond and Miss Leeming had been sequestered in their corner for most of the evening, and anyone present could not have helped but notice Miss Leeming had been talking rapidly and most sincerely to the gentleman throughout that time. Now a smile began to tug at Marianne's lips.

"Not when I arrived at the Dudley home tonight, no," Desmond said. "Now I know where she was born and the names of her brothers and sisters. I can tell you her husband's name and occupation and share a scandalous rumor or two about him, you may be sure. I also know her children and who they married—at least, the three who are married. Cathie, I am afraid, is frightfully plain, and as they have no money to speak of, she may very likely remain single, the poor dear. I can also tell you Aunt Winnie's hat size, her dressmaker and the name of her cat."

Marianne burst out in a merry laugh at the last and in a natural motion turned to Mr. Desmond and hugged his arm in both of hers to help warm her. With her cheek pressed against the heavy twill of his winter cloak, she looked up into his face, still smiling.

"And here I thought I had a trying evening. At his most articulate, Mr. Wynder spoke only in monosyllables and quite often in unintelligible mumbles. It was an effort to get an answer to any of my questions, but at least he allowed me a moment's peace when I wanted it."

Desmond groaned softly. "You lucky little devil. You must promise me, if we are ever in the same company, that you will exchange partners with me."

"I doubt Mrs. Dudley would allow that. And in any case, Miss Leeming would not have as much to say to me," Marianne said. "And I must warn you, Mr. Wynder considers men of letters 'damned pasty-faced bookworms.'"

"Then in all probability he would not want to talk to me at all." Desmond looked down into her eyes and sighed dramatically. "What utter bliss!"

Marianne clung to Desmond's arm for the rest of the ride back to Kingsbrook. He could almost feel the shape of her smile through the heavy material, and occasionally she would giggle a bit when she thought of Miss Leeming and her two-hour lecture on her Aunt Winnie Stagway, from Liverpool.

Mrs. Dudley and Miss Leeming managed to occupy Mr. Desmond for most of the week between Christmas and New Year's Day. But for New Year's Eve, Mr. Desmond refused all the invitations delivered to Kingsbrook, stating that it was his intention to welcome in the New Year in his own home, in the company of his ward.

Marianne was touched. New Year's Eve in Kingsbrook had a special significance to her, but she had not been sure Desmond was aware of that. Last year she had been so afraid to come here from Farnham, afraid to see *him* again, to be in the same place, under the same roof.

Then when she got here he had been perfectly pleasant, had even invited his neighbors for Christmas when she suggested it. The day after Christmas Mr. Desmond had left Kingsbrook for a few days, and now, a year later, Marianne was able to admit to herself she had missed him when he left. He had returned on New Year's Eve with a few friends from Reading. They had been a rowdy lot who sang dancehall songs, laughed loudly and kept Mrs. River and Alice running to and from the kitchen for foodstuffs all night long. She had felt like a perfect infant at the time, in such boisterously grown-up company, but Mr. Desmond had not sent her to her room. He had allowed her to stay, to listen to the songs and stories, though he stopped a few of them as they got started, for her sake.

That was the first time she had ever heard him laugh out loud, too. It was a full, deep laugh, rarely employed, but unmistakable when heard.

At midnight Mrs. River had given Marianne a glass the size of a thimble full of pale sherry.

"Mr. Desmond says you are to have that," Mrs. River had said, shaking her head with disapproval.

The men were toasting each other with great whoops and bellows, but Mr. Desmond had turned to her, raised his own glass and said, "May the coming year be the best of your life."

She had come to think of it as a sort of blessing during the past twelve months.

"We will toast in the New Year together again," Mr. Desmond told her now.

Marianne smiled to think he remembered the occasion, her cheeks turning a pretty shade of pink.

"Though if I can have the day to myself it will give me a chance to catch my breath," he added. "Miss Leeming is returning to Manchester on Tuesday. I believe I know how the innocent woodland creatures feel when hunting season is nearing an end. If I can just survive a few more days, Miss Leeming will have to go home without a trophy to hang on her wall."

Marianne laughed and closed the door to Mr. Desmond's library.

Mrs. River was busy with Candy, going through her duties with her, and Marianne did not feel as if she should interfere there, either. That left her on her own, and with the day too chill for the out-of-doors, she began to feel in something of an exploratory mood.

She did not often have the opportunity to wander through Kingsbrook's unused rooms, and the house was very large, with whole sections of the upper floors shut up for decades. Marianne was carrying a candle, but wished she had brought two or three, and a heavier cloak besides. She pushed open several doors along the third-floor hallway in the north wing, disturbing dust and cobwebs, forcing the doors ajar on protesting hinges.

But one door, near the back staircase that led to the kitchen, opened with surprising ease. The flickering light of her candle did not highlight the expected cloud of dust. Curious, Marianne pushed the door all the way open and stepped into the room to inspect it. The first thing she noticed was that the bed was made up, not draped with the heavy burlap coverings that shrouded most of the furnishings on this floor. The quilt on top of the bed was not new, but it was serviceable. She stepped forward to inspect the blanket, and her candle further revealed that the floor was swept, the chest of drawers was relatively dust free, the pitcher and bowl sitting on top of the chest had been cleaned of the thick gray film that covered unprotected surfaces in other rooms.

Marianne's brows furrowed in puzzlement. Why on earth had this room been tidied and scrubbed? It had obviously been in use quite recently—perhaps as recently as a few weeks ago.

Mrs. River's room was on the ground floor, behind the sitting room. James's room was on the second floor, near Mr. Desmond's, and though Candy had not taken Alice's old quarters, she had chosen one even closer to the kitchen stairs, in the back hallway on the second floor. Mrs. Rawlins, naturally, slept near the kitchen and could not get the smell of cooking out of her clothes, and Rickers and Tilly did not stay in the main house at all, but had been afforded a little cottage farther down the lane. That accounted for all of the household staff at Kingsbrook, and Mr. Desmond would never put a guest up in these small, third-floor rooms.

Marianne was completely mystified. Who had been staying here? She held her candle high and turned slowly, studying everything in the room with interest.

The glimmer of her candle highlighted some object on the floor just under the chest of drawers. Marianne stopped and picked it up and found herself holding a thimble. An ordinary metal thimble, except for the engraving on the tip. She held it closer to the candle flame, and with a start realized she recognized the little sewing device she held.

In quiet evenings at the academy, the girls would often gather by the big fireplace in the common room downstairs, to work on their sewing projects. Marianne recalled an evening when she had been sitting near Sylvia Prince. She had commented on Miss Prince's skill, and quite seriously, Sylvia had looked up and told Marianne what she lacked was the proper equipment.

"The proper equipment?" Marianne had asked with a smile. "I have needle and thread. What more do I need?"

"A thimble," Sylvia said. "A proper thimble. Fitted and custom-made. They produce such things in the Orient. My father, of course, brought this one back for me." And she held out her thimble for Marianne to see the *S.P.* engraved on the end.

"I see," Marianne had said. "Well, then, I may never be as accomplished a seamstress as you are. My father is passed away, and even when alive the farthest east he ever traveled was to Shoeburyness."

"That is unfortunate," the other girl had replied, still perfectly serious. Marianne was not surprised the irony of her own response had been wasted on Sylvia.

Now in the clean, aired room in the ostensibly abandoned north wing of the third floor of Kingsbrook Manor, the words came back to Marianne.

The candle in her hand flickered, highlighting the markings on the end of the thimble she had found there. The initials *S.P.*

Chapter Eleven

The fire could not warm her, though she kept it burning brightly and sat directly before it.

Marianne was in the sitting room—she always thought of it as Mrs. River's sitting room—and had set a match to the kindling as soon as she came in, had even asked James to bring in a large log, which was halfway burned by now. And still she could not get warm. She had not been aware that the third floor was cold, yet when she came downstairs she was chilled to the bone.

Mrs. River and Candy were upstairs on the second floor, the housekeeper showing the new maid where to put this and that. Marianne was alone. She sat on the hearth rug directly in front of the fire, staring into the flames with unseeing eyes.

Mr. Desmond was still in the library, where he had spent the day. He might be reading, though Marianne suspected he could be dozing now in the afternoon, sleeping the peaceful sleep of the just. Or the amoral.

She had not opened the door to discover what he was doing. She had, in fact, veered away from the library when she came downstairs again, as if plague and pestilence threatened within.

Instead she sat in this other room, staring into the flickering fire, her thoughts as frantic and erratic as the flames.

It was not only the thimble—*Sylvia's* thimble—that troubled her. It was everything else, all the pictures and scraps of conversation floating through her head, like a puzzle attempting to put itself together.

As she gazed at the leaping red-and-yellow tongues of flame, she fancied she could see before her, written in a familiar and hateful hand, "It is therefore my proposition to procure young women, fresh and unsullied . . . you providing the customers and myself providing the girls."

After Marianne had read that infamous letter she had buried it in the stack of mail on Mr. Desmond's desk. But she could not bury the words deep enough in her memory to forget what they said, or to misunderstand what Uncle Horace had been proposing.

She lowered her eyes to look at the black coals in front of the flames and found herself in the damp and dark of the forest. It was the woodland just beyond the academy.

"I can see you and the other pretty little girls from up here," she heard a voice snarling in her ear. Marianne shivered again, as if she felt Uncle Horace's clammy hand around her arm, felt his fetid breath stirring the fine hairs of her neck.

She thought of the book in Mr. Desmond's library, the copy of the *Iliad,* and could almost smell the scent of fine leather as she recalled discovering in it the letter she had not sent to Nedra, the one that talked about Sylvia Prince, and Sylvia's father, the ship's captain, who was away at sea.

And from long ago, more than a year, a picture came to mind of a street in Reading, and a restaurant table set on the sidewalk to tempt passersby in the warm summer weather. Mr. Desmond was nodding toward the stack of banknotes he had placed before Uncle Horace. . . . Marianne shuddered helplessly. Almost simultaneously there was a noise in the doorway. "Heavens, child, it is as dark as the inside of a cave in here. Why do you not light a lamp?"

She jumped violently, startled from her reverie, and scrambled to her feet, blinking uncertainly. The afternoon had faded as she sat there. "I did not know it had grown so late," she said.

"You and the master, two peas in the same pod you are. There he is in his library, squinting through the shadows to read his book, and you sitting in the dark here."

Fussily, the housekeeper went around to several of the lamps and put a flame to their wicks. With the room lighted to her satisfaction, she lowered herself with a slight groan into her favorite chair.

Marianne listened with half an ear. Mrs. River's presence had drawn her out of herself, and now she was alert to any sound that might come from the library. Doubtless it was cold as well as dark in there, and Rickers, she knew, would be complaining under his breath about having to bring more wood into the room, and would Mr. Desmond not be more comfortable in with the ladies?

But Mr. Desmond had kept strictly to himself all day today. They had spoken after lunch, and Marianne had smilingly promised not to disturb him, but that had been hours ago. Since then he had not come out for a drink or to stretch his legs, to her knowledge. He must have heard her when she came downstairs, but he had made no effort to see her. She could not be sorry.

But if she did not want to see Mr. Desmond, why did her eyes wander so often to the heavy doors of the library across the hall there?

Eventually Candy summoned them to the dining room. Mrs. River nodded her approval at the new girl's announcement and stood up. Marianne had no choice but to lead the way.

Mr. Desmond was there before her, standing near his chair, watching the doorway, obviously waiting for her so dinner could be served. He nodded in her direction and sat down. "Have Mrs. Rawlins send in *something,* before I fade completely away," he told Candy with a playful smile.

The maid giggled slightly as she hurried out of the room. Mrs. River frowned after her, but could not blame the girl. Mr. Desmond was incorrigible at times, especially when Mrs. River was trying to break in new help. He had been an unconscionable flirt when little Alice started working here, and the poor girl had spent the first year in his service hopelessly infatuated with the man.

"Well, this has turned out to be a rather quiet day. Probably now you wish I had not turned down all those invitations," he said to Marianne.

"I do not think I was up to socializing today, anyway," she replied glumly. In fact, she would have felt quite sociable now if something had kept her occupied and out of the north wing today.

After dinner, just when Marianne was relieved that Desmond would be retiring to his room and she to hers, Mrs. River put on her jolliest cajoling manner and insisted the master and sweet Miss Trenton join her in the sitting room. "Let us not be scattered to the four winds tonight. There is nothing drearier than spending a festive occasion alone," she said.

Into the sitting room they dutifully trooped, and still the dear woman would not leave Mr. Desmond and Marianne to their own devices. Nothing would do but that Marianne must sing them a song, and then Mr. Desmond had to recite one of those clever verses he knew so well.

"What would you have, Mrs. River?" he asked.

"Oh, anything at all. I do declare, Miss Marianne, Mr. Desmond has every book in the library memorized!"

"Perhaps not *every* book," Desmond said.

"Something for the New Year," Mrs. River said.

Desmond pondered a moment.

"Milton," he said at last. "John Milton, scholar and poet. What could be more fitting for the New Year than a passage from *Paradise Lost*?" He stood and cleared his throat, pausing for a moment to recall the words to memory.

"'... What hinders, then,
To reach, and feed at once both body and mind?'
So saying, her rash hand in evil hour
Forth-reaching to the Fruit, she plucked, she ate.
Earth felt the wound, and...
Sighing through all her works, gave signs of woe
That all was lost."

The two women sat silently for just a moment after Desmond ended his rather solemn recitation. Then Mrs. River clapped her hands eagerly and nodded for Marianne to join her, though the young woman's applause was far from enthusiastic.

It had been a curious passage for the gentleman to select. Eve's tasting of the forbidden fruit and the fall of man.

With Mrs. River's questions and suggestions, and Mr. Desmond's quiet contributions, eventually the evening passed.

"Look at the hour," the housekeeper finally said, yawning. "The New Year came in forty minutes ago and has surely made himself comfortable by now. You and Miss Marianne may stay up as long as you like, but some of us have things to do tomorrow. Miss Marianne, Mr. Desmond." She was up from her chair and out of the room before Marianne could think of a way to delay her.

"I am afraid Mrs. River was correct," Desmond said. He was standing next to his chair, having risen when the housekeeper left the room. "The New Year came in without our notice. I am afraid we did not make our toast. Perhaps you would rather we did not this year?"

He was watching Marianne curiously. He had noted her changing mood. As far as he could tell they had started this morning as friends, smiling, talking, exchanging pleasantries and the commonplace things close associates share with each other. But when they met this evening they were strangers again, as cool and distant as the first time they had seen each other. More so, in fact, since he had been trying to seduce her then and she, in her ignorance, had seemed perfectly willing to be seduced.

"Oh, no! Do let us toast in the year," Marianne cried. There was a touching, plaintive note in her voice.

"Very well," Mr. Desmond said hesitantly. He waited for an instant, just in case Marianne changed her mind and mood again. When it appeared she really did want to exchange the toast, he turned to the sideboard where the liquor was kept. With an experienced hand he poured the drinks, his a generous two fingers of good Irish whiskey, and hers a pale pink liquid in a slender-stemmed, crystal glass.

He handed her the glass and raised his in salute. "To the New Year. And may it be the best time of our lives."

They were standing face-to-face on the stone hearth before the fireplace. Desmond looked down into the girl's eyes. The light from the fire danced across the green irises, and he could see the moisture glistening near her lower lids. It was not just a trick of the light; there were tears in her eyes. She reminded him of a frightened, forlorn puppy, abandoned and afraid. His heart pounded painfully with sympathy for the girl and anger at whatever had brought the tears to her eyes.

Why did she do this to him? he thought with impatience, tossing back his drink, heedless of the burning that made his own eyes water.

He wiped his lips and put his tumbler on the mantel. Marianne was sipping at her glass tentatively and might have been drinking it drop by drop for another ten minutes. She did not look at him, but kept her head bent, exposing the lily-white nape of her neck. Something clutched at Desmond's heart. He knew desire, had felt it often enough before in his philandering days. But this was different. The sight of her bent head and the defenselessness of her posture summoned a kind of primal need to protect and care for this creature. What had Adam said? "How can I live without thee? how forgo/Thy sweet converse, and love so dearly joined,/To live again in these wild woods forlorn?"

Wordlessly Desmond extended his hand and took the half-filled glass from her. He put it beside his own on the mantelpiece and then, for a moment, stood looking down into her eyes.

"And was your last year?" he asked softly.

"Was it what?" she whispered. The picture of poor Eve and the subtle serpent flashed into Marianne's head. Surely Satan had been a handsome creature, breathing strange promises into the girl's ears.

"Was it the best of your life?"

"I... do not know," she answered. It was not simply a vague reply, made without thought, just to get her through one moment and on to the next. She believed the truth was an emphatic no. But standing here with him, close enough to hear his breathing and to study the charcoal color of his eyes, she was not sure. Had the academy been her reprieve and safeguard, or had she tolerated her schooling because she knew she would see him again?

"Do you believe the next one will be?" he asked.

"I do not know that, either," she said.

"It could be," he murmured.

Marianne's eyes grew very wide and slightly unfocused as she gazed up at him, totally mesmerized. When Desmond spoke again his voice was deep and low, heavy with a dark invitation.

"It could be the best year either of us have ever known," he purred. Now his words were an irresistible magnet that drew her to him. "*Tonight* could be the best night of our lives."

He did nothing more than lean toward her, and their bodies came together, the mounds and curves meshing like elaborate machinery, fitting like a hand and glove.

With his fingertips under her chin he guided her lips to his. She felt the warmth of his breath against her mouth before he closed the space between them.

His kiss was as silken as his voice, as seductive as his eyes. The pressure of his mouth was neither demanding nor frantic, but there was a dense inevitability about the kiss that both excited and frightened her.

She had no choice but to yield her mouth to him. He claimed her lips, and then his hands grasped her shoulders, and the long, strong muscles of his thighs rubbed against her own shaking legs. he pressed himself against her in a strange, yet powerful ritual of possession, as if he were marking her as his. His hands caressed her shoulders, back and neck, and the slow movement of his torso and legs was a caress as well, a more intimate, urgent caress.

In a moment his lips left hers, and as she gasped for air, they trailed across her chin and down to the hollow of her neck. He pushed the material of her dress off her shoulders, out of his way, and was gratified to hear one of the buttons of her dress pop off and feel the garment loosening.

His nostrils were filled with the scent of her; his hands tingled at the soft touch of her skin. He ached for her. He wanted her, he *needed* her. He would take her tonight and keep her forever.

For those brief minutes she returned his kisses, moved against him in a sweet submission he recognized.

She wanted to experience the pleasure she knew would wash over her and immerse her as completely as a warm bath. "What fear I, then?... Here grows the cure of all, this Fruit divine."

And unlike Mother Eve, Marianne was not completely without knowledge of good and evil. She had felt these sensations before, but she was no longer a child of sixteen. Now she was older and not frightened by his desire, nor confused by her own. He would take her in his arms and place her on his wide bed and remove, piece by piece, the clothes she wore. With hesitant efforts she would pull his clothes from him, as well. Their limbs would intertwine, their hands explore; they would drink deeply.

Her body throbbed with longing. She wanted to lie with him, to *be* with him.

To be one of his doxies?

The question popped rudely into her mind, in such a rough inner voice she barely recognized it as her own.

How long would he keep her in her room, or rather his, before he moved her up to the bare room on the third floor in preparation for sending her on? Would she go on to another client, or back to Uncle Horace, or merely disappear, like Sylvia?

"No, Peter! Please no!" she moaned. "You must not. You must never. I cannot…oh, do not do this to me again!"

"Do what to you again?" he asked. "What have I ever done to you that was so repellent?"

"This!" she cried. He thought she meant his display of passion, but she meant the passion he ignited in her.

Her protest had drawn him up short, and now his hands, which moments before had held her so closely to his chest that she could not breathe, now held her away from him so she could no longer feel the heat that threatened to overpower her. But it had been a comforting heat, a protective heat, a heat that easily held thought at bay.

"I would like to take you to a place you cannot imagine," he said.

"You would take me against my will," she said, a thickness of tears in her voice.

"I hoped it would not be against your will this time," he said. He spoke reasonably, calmly, no small measure of the man who had, moments before, been inflamed with passion. "I thought you had grown to care for me."

"Not that way. Never that way," Marianne said.

When he had first taken her in his arms and put his lips to hers, she had lost herself in that kiss. She wanted him to be the knight in shining armor she had imagined. But she knew he was not.

"Never *that* way," she repeated.

She might have delivered the words from a gun. He dropped his hands from her shoulders and staggered backward, and she fled from the room.

They barely spoke to each other for the remainder of the time they were together at Kingsbrook. Desmond would leave early in the morning and not return until late at night, usually drunk. Miss Leeming had left her cousin's house by then, and Marianne wondered what the young lady and the scheming Mrs. Dudley would think of the splendid matrimonial candidate they had so desperately pursued if they saw him now. When Marianne and Desmond were forced to be together, he would offer her no more than grunts and monosyllables, and when speech was absolutely necessary, he would convey his message through Mrs. River, even if they were both in the same room.

Marianne was too immersed in her own self-pity to pay him any heed the first day, and when she did notice him she grew very angry that he should be behaving this way towards her. *He* was the one in the wrong. He had no business making her feel that *she* had injured *him*.

As a matter of fact, Desmond *did* feel injured. Nor was it merely his pride that was bruised and his desire frustrated. When the girl told him, in plain and painful English, that she did not want him, could never want him, desire him, *love* him, it had been like a blow forcing the air from his lungs, like a knife plunged into his belly. He was honestly surprised by the pain. He would not have thought he could feel that, considering the depths to which his morals and character had sunk.

Two days later Mr. Desmond announced that business would be taking him to London and then to Reading, and that he trusted Miss Trenton could get herself reenrolled in her school. He made the comment to Mrs. River, who turned to Marianne, sitting at the other end of the table, for her reply.

"I suppose I can," Marianne said.

She slept fitfully that night and heard the disturbance of Mr. Desmond taking his bags down the stairs very early the next morning. He was leaving Kingsbrook for an extended period of time, evidently, though he had given no explanation of the business that called him away.

She could not go back to sleep, but stayed in her bed for several hours, until Candy tapped at her door and called softly that breakfast was ready.

Marianne put her belongings in her two valises, and Rickers carried them to the coach.

And thus ended Marianne's second Christmas at Kingsbrook. The first one she had feared so, and it had been a wonderfully happy time. This one she had been eagerly anticipating, and it had resulted in two dreadful discoveries: that Mr. Desmond was in some way involved with the disappearance of Sylvia Prince, and that that terrible fact could not completely obliterate her fond emotions for the beast.

Chapter Twelve

Marianne returned to the academy determined to do something about Miss Prince and what she knew about her disappearance, little as it was. She was helpless at Kingsbrook, under Desmond's frightful influence—which she could only term "frightful" when she was away from him—and unsure about what action she should take.

But at the Farnham Academy there were people who could help her, persons of authority who would find Sylvia and bring Desmond to justice.

Squaring her shoulders, Marianne wasted no time. She left her bags in her room and went to find Mrs. Avery. Marianne was quite certain a wronged young woman could find no better champion.

"Mrs. Avery, there is something... I need to talk to you about. You see, I discovered something while I was away at Christmas. Something you need to know...." For all her determination, Marianne paused, painfully reluctant even now to bring harm to her guardian.

"What is it, Miss Trenton?" the headmistress prompted.

"Well, I found something that has led me to believe my guardian, Mr. Desmond, has something to do with—"

Marianne was interrupted in her wavering accusation by a knock at Mrs. Avery's door. Without waiting for an invitation to enter, Mrs. Grey stuck her head into the office.

"There is a gentleman to see you, Mrs. Avery," the little woman said timidly.

The headmistress looked up in surprise. Those gentlemen with whom she dealt regarding the business of the school came at appointed times for appointed reasons. There were no appointments scheduled today. "Who is it?" she asked.

"It is Captain Prince. Come for his daughter's things," Mrs. Grey said.

Marianne turned to stare at Mrs. Grey in disbelief. "Sylvia's father?" she asked bluntly.

Mrs. Grey nodded. "He said Miss Prince will not be returning to the Farnham Academy and needs her clothes and books."

"Well, certainly," Mrs. Avery said. "Though I was not aware Miss Prince was dissatisfied with the academy. Has she been unhappy here, Mrs. Grey?" Distracted by this surprising development, the woman rose, forgetting Miss Trenton for the moment.

"Not that I am aware. Though she did leave us rather suddenly," Mrs. Grey affirmed.

The two instructors left together, exchanging surprised comments. But they could not have been as surprised as Marianne, who stood gazing after them with jaw agape.

Sylvia's father here? To collect her things? Because she would not be returning? Was it all as simple as that?

The headmistress was gone for a long time. Marianne should have returned to class, but she sat in Mrs. Avery's empty office instead, engaged in imagining completely unlikely explanations.

Finally Mrs. Lynk looked into the room and told her everyone was being allowed a free hour, but to be in class directly after lunch.

As far as Marianne knew, no one had seen the headmistress since she left her office. Yet as soon as Marianne stepped from the building with her shawl about her shoulders, Myrtle Thane detached herself from the group of girls around Judith Eastman and hurried to her side.

"Did you hear?" Miss Thane asked under her breath.

"Hear what?" Marianne asked.

"Captain Prince, Sylvia's father, came himself, personally, to the school and collected all of Sylvia's things," Myrtle said.

"I was in Mrs. Avery's office when he arrived," Marianne replied.

"I heard that words were exchanged, words that left Mrs. Avery pale and shaken," Myrtle told her, with the certain eagerness with which women share particularly juicy morsels of gossip.

"From whom did you hear that?" Marianne pressed.

Myrtle waved her hand in the general direction of the girls behind her and the township of Farnham beyond.

Marianne was totally confused, but the fact was undeniable that Captain Prince had been at the academy to get all of Sylvia's things, and evidently there had been some kind of heated discussion. No one knew what the captain had said to the headmistress, but the girls were assembled that evening and sternly instructed never to leave the academy grounds, nor even wander too far from the main buildings, alone.

"Now, Miss Trenton, I am afraid we were interrupted this morning. What was it you wanted to tell me?" Mrs. Avery asked, stopping her as the assembly dispersed.

"I wanted to tell you... I wanted to say... I just wanted to let you know I and most of my fellow students are very happy here at the Farnham Academy," Marianne told her weakly.

It was not convincing, but Marianne truly did not know what it was she had to tell Mrs. Avery now. If Miss Prince was with her father, how had her thimble—and it *was* Sylvia's thimble—gotten into a third-floor bedroom of Kingsbrook Manor? And if Miss Prince were with her father, of what could she accuse Mr. Desmond?

Marianne Trenton was an exceptionally intelligent young woman. Even as classes got underway that winter, all her teachers, even Mrs. Lynk, with her exacting concept of proper mannerisms, allowed that Miss Trenton had thoroughly learned all they had to teach her. One did not have to be exceptionally intelligent, however, to know that what they knew was not all there was to learn.

"You ought to attend the university in Reading," Mrs. Avery told her.

Marianne was taken aback. University attendance was not something young women of her time usually considered. Certainly she had never considered it.

"I—I do not think..." she sputtered.

"Oh, but you do, Miss Trenton. And very well. You would be an exemplary university student. I have no doubt you could easily pin back the ears of most of those young popinjays who call themselves 'college men,'" Mrs. Avery affirmed.

"My guardian..." Marianne began, making another useless attempt to get a word in edgewise in a conversation with the headmistress.

"Who do you think made the proposition in the first place, if you please?"

"Mr. Desmond?" Marianne asked doubtfully.

"None other," Mrs. Avery said. "Now I am depending on you, Miss Trenton, to prove that women are as smart, as quick, as studious and as serious as any man who ever lived. Will you do that for me?"

Marianne hesitated to make the promise. She did not feel as if she had anything to prove, and only wondered what it was her guardian was attempting.

Not a week later, she received her answer.

A letter came for her from Kingsbrook—a thick envelope, full of documents and applications and a very off-putting missive from Mr. Desmond.

"Miss Trenton," it began. The colorless salutation seemed to put a vast distance between them, yet Marianne was forced to admit it was she who had put the distance between them, with her own declaration, "Never *that* way."

> By the spring of this year you will have completed two full years of instruction at the Farnham Academy. When I first spoke with Mrs. Avery, she said girls usually leave the academy when they are eighteen. As of November you have reached the age of advancement. The question remains, of course, advancement to what? I suggest you consider taking a few classes of university study.

In the margin of the paper he had jotted a personal note that almost sounded like the old Mr. Desmond: "I know you always thought Mrs. Grey was preparing you for your passage to heaven with Dante's *Inferno, Purgatorio* and *Paradiso,* rather than your entrance to college." But the body of the letter was very businesslike.

> As you know, I am not in a position to introduce you to society. Here at Kingsbrook you cannot—I believe "come out" is the proper term. I have no close female relative or friend who can perform the service for you and oversee its intricacies. I have given the matter much thought, as you can see, and now that you have reached the age of some maturity I can think of no better way to get you into the marriage arena than to have you enroll in the university at Reading to meet some of the young men there.

Marianne stared blankly at the paper for a moment. Marriage arena? Well, of course. It was perfectly logical. If she had categorically refused him, Mr. Desmond's main objective now would be to rid himself of the encumbrance she represented.

> I have enclosed an entrance application to the university in this letter. Please look it over and consider seriously my suggestion.
>
> Your humble servant,
> P. Desmond

The papers Mr. Desmond had sent were comprehensive. They explained the courses of study offered, praised the university's faculty and expressed in no uncertain terms what was expected of students attending. Nowhere was it suggested that the university would welcome young women, but then again, nowhere did it say women were *not* allowed in the hallowed halls.

Feeling numb and disoriented, perversely hurt by Mr. Desmond's sensible and, considering his other options, very humane course of action, Marianne studied the documents, though she did not punish herself so much as to reread the letter.

At last she took the papers to Mrs. Avery, who pounced upon them with the eagerness of a large spider finding a fly caught in its web, and immediately accepted the challenge of getting Marianne enrolled in the university.

Letters were written. Mr. Desmond sent word that he would use his influence to guarantee the young woman's acceptance. Mrs. Avery raised her eyebrows over that, perhaps wondering, as did Marianne, what Mr. Desmond's influence was with Reading University.

At the end of May, just when summer began to bring out the most charming aspects of the Farnham Academy, such as they were, Mrs. Avery called the girl into her office and solemnly presented her with a letter confirming her acceptance as a student at the university in Reading, classes to commence in the autumn. Marianne was evidently not to be welcomed to the "temple of education" with open arms, but her presence would be tolerated.

"It has not been our regular practice, Miss Trenton," the letter read, "to include women in the Reading University student body, but by the urgings and assurances of Mr. Desmond, we have been persuaded to allow your attendance."

So Marianne gravely shook hands with her teachers and hugged Nedra fondly, accepting their warm congratulations. But Marianne was not the only student who would be leaving the academy at the end of term. Judith, like Alice back in Kingsbrook, would be married later that year and already had the pleased and placid look of a seasoned matron about her. The other girls in her class were all to be "presented." There would be balls and fetes and carefully chaperoned outings, and by Christmastime most of her friends from the academy would have had a nibble or two from that great fish tank Mr. Desmond called the marriage arena.

Even Marianne's fishing from a less frequented pier should have met with some success. Mrs. Avery called the university students "a lot of ignorant, callow, rosy-cheeked boys," but Marianne supposed that if they were sufficiently ignorant and rosy cheeked, she should be able to finagle a proposal from one of them by the end of the year. And if she were to be as easily satisfied as her anxious guardian, any proposal at all would do. But Marianne valued herself too much to accept with gratitude whatever offer of marriage came her way. She wanted more for her life than an ignorant, rosy-cheeked boy. She wanted a man of experience, maturity, with strength of purpose. And gray eyes . . .

Marianne drew herself up short. Such thoughts would never do. The decision was made, the die was cast—by her, as a matter of fact. And if he wanted to see her married and out of his life, she would not fight him, though she would at least be selective.

Toward the end of August, the carriage arrived to take her away from Farnham for good. She would stay at Kingsbrook for the rest of the month, but on September 1 was expected at Reading University.

The short time she spent at Kingsbrook was filled with Mrs. River's frantic attempts to ready Marianne's wardrobe and possessions for her new enterprise, one that the housekeeper considered a great deal too adventurous for a lady of quality, in any case.

As usual, Mrs. River had not been consulted in the matter, and what with getting Miss Marianne off, and the other things going on in the house these days, the poor woman felt quite besieged.

On the eve of Marianne's departure, with all in readiness at last, the housekeeper was finally allowed a few moments of peace in her sitting room. The young lady had joined her, and the two of them sat together companionably.

The house was still, the air heavy with the warmth of late summer. Mrs. River's head began to nod. But before she could close her eyes for a well-earned nap, Marianne disturbed the quiet.

"Mrs. River," she began, trying to make her voice sound light, her question inconsequential. "Has anyone been staying here at Kingsbrook? A friend of Mr. Desmond's, perhaps?"

The woman looked up sharply. "Why do you ask?" she demanded.

"I noticed one of the rooms upstairs has evidently been in use recently."

There was no question that Sylvia Prince was reunited with her father, but there was also no question that the thimble Marianne had found here last Christmas had been her schoolmate's. In an attempt to find some answers,

Marianne had returned to the room on Kingsbrook's third floor as soon as she could do so without being detected. Instead of answers, she found only more questions. She had expected to look through a bureau and wardrobe covered with six months' worth of dust. But the room had once again been recently cleaned, leading her to believe it had also been once again recently occupied.

After sitting on the comfortably made up bed in that room for many minutes, the young woman was forced to admit she was completely befuddled by the conundrum. She had no idea what was happening in this house, but she knew someone who did. Someone who knew *everything* that went on at Kingsbrook. She finally determined to ask for the answers to some of her questions.

"I would not suppose a cleaned room necessarily meant anyone has been staying in it," Mrs. River returned.

Her quelling tone did nothing to discourage the girl's probing. "Well, no, not necessarily. But I found a personal article in there," Marianne said, in dogged pursuit.

"You could not have. I myself—" Mrs. River stopped suddenly, catching too late the slip of her tongue.

Marianne had not put a stitch in the little sampler she was working on since before she asked her first question of the older woman, and now she set it to one side, abandoning completely the pretense of sewing. "What is it, Mrs. River? Who is the young woman who has been staying at Kingsbrook?" she asked in a wheedling tone.

"Now why would you think it was a young woman, even if a room *had* been used upstairs?" Mrs. River asked.

"I found a thimble there last Christmas, so I naturally assumed some female had been in residence. And as for the room having been used at one time, I believe it still is. Regularly. You cannot deny this, dear Mrs. River," Marianne said.

Mrs. River was a simple, honest soul, unequal to Marianne's grueling inquiry. She gave a slight whimper and her self-discipline crumbled. "Oh, miss," she cried, "I don't know what to make of it! Mr. Desmond has never done anything like this before. He did bring a girl in here before Christmas. For a week it was, maybe ten days, and since then there have been two others. Mr. Desmond hustles them in when no one is about, usually at night. They are poor little things, scared to death, it seems to me. The master tells me to feed them and keep them comfortable and otherwise leave them alone. Oh, miss, I do not like it."

"Who are they?" Marianne asked.

"I do not know. Mr. Desmond is especially strict on that point. 'You must not ask them any questions,' he says to me, but that is all."

"What happened to them?" she asked in a bewildered tone.

Mrs. River shrugged and shook her head. "Mr. Desmond brings them in, and Mr. Desmond takes them away."

"In the coach? Does Rickers drive?"

"No one here knows any more about the young women than I do. If they leave in a carriage, and I assume they do, it is a carriage from somewhere else, though I have not seen it myself."

The two sat looking at each other for a few moments.

"They must be old friends of his," Marianne said at last, uncertainly.

"They must be," Mrs. River agreed, with the same lack of conviction.

Mr. Desmond was still away when the time came for Marianne to leave Kingsbrook. She had not seen him at all since arriving from the academy, which Mrs. River said was also out of the ordinary. In years past Mr. Desmond's one regular time of residence at the manor had been late summer, when the summer gamesters had returned home and the winter crowd was not yet out and about.

He had left word for Mrs. River to assist Marianne and see that she got to Reading by September 1. A place had been secured for her in town in the home of a widowed lady who had a room to let to a "proper young lady." Marianne, with plans to attend a men's university, hoped she would still be welcome as a boarder.

But she was required to make the move from Kingsbrook to Reading by herself. By herself, if one did not count Candy or James or Mrs. Rawlins and her basket of "necessaries," which were to sustain Marianne on the perilous trek to town. Or Rickers. Or the omnipresent, fretful Mrs. River.

"You have your pocketbook? Your gloves? Where did James put Mrs. Rawlins's basket? Ah, yes, there on the floor. Rickers will take you directly to the home of this Mrs. Simmons. Mr. Desmond left careful instructions. Really, I do not know why he could not come himself."

"I shall tell him you were very put out," Marianne assured Mrs. River, who was fluttering about the waiting carriage.

"Rickers, is this trunk tied on securely? I do not want you to leave a trail of Miss Marianne's clothes behind you when you go."

Marianne gave a sad little smile. Such a trail would be like the one left by Hansel and Gretel and might, if she became lost, help her find her way back here. If there was a way back.

"Tied it on myself, Mrs. River," Rickers was saying. "And checked all the straps. It will get to Reading safe enough, if we are ever allowed to leave."

"I suppose . . . yes, well, everything appears to be ready. Now you write to me, Miss Trenton. I am certain if Mr. Desmond can pull himself away long enough, he will see to your well-being, but you know how folks here worry," Mrs. River said, nodding hesitantly.

"I do know," Marianne said, smiling. "But Rickers will see me safely to Widow Simmons, and we learned from her letter that she is at least as careful as you are, so you must not fear. This is only half as far as it was to the Farnham Academy."

"Yes, but the academy was a quiet institution for young ladies. Now you are going to a large town, to a *men's* university. Do not tell me there is nothing to worry about."

"I would not dream of it. Even if I were going to a convent you would find something to worry about," Marianne teased.

"Doubtless I would." Mrs. Rivers smiled and patted her cheek. "Take care of yourself," she said.

Marianne and Rickers arrived in Reading as the lowering sun began to cast long shadows behind trees and buildings. After two misguided passes up and down residential lanes, Rickers found the address and the little house belonging to the widow Simmons. Waiting at the roadside in front of the house was a strange man, just the sort of menacing figure of which Mrs. River had warned her. When Rickers drew the carriage to a stop, Marianne could see that, besides being dark and suspicious looking, the young man was also undeniably rosy cheeked.

"Miss Trenton?" Before Rickers would climb down from his box, the young man had pulled the door open and was peering inside, trying to see through the gloom of the interior.

"Yes?" Marianne replied.

"The lecturer sent me over to see you get settled."

"The lecturer?"

"Yes, miss. Oh, I am sorry. The name is Bernie Brewster. Let me take that basket. Here we go. Watch your step there. How was your trip? Let me help you there."

Marianne smiled and took the hand he offered as she stepped down from the carriage. Besides the healthy glow on his cheeks, the young man had a healthy form, one that would likely lead to a paunchy middle age. He had reddish brown hair and a generous spattering of freckles across his face.

"I thank you for myself, sir," Marianne said, once she had both feet on solid ground. "And I know Rickers will appreciate a hand to get my things in, if you do not mind."

"That is why I am here," he said cheerfully.

Marianne left Rickers and this most timely helper to get her bags and unstrap the trunk from the back of the carriage. She went to the door and knocked, though she had seen a curious face watching from the window and could not believe her summons would be a surprise.

The door opened a crack.

"Mrs. Simmons? I am Miss Marianne Trenton."

"And who is that with you?"

The door was open enough now for Marianne to see a head nod toward the road and the carriage.

"Mr. Rickers drove me up from Kingsbrook. He is retained by Mr. Desmond and is an old friend. The younger man was evidently sent over by the university."

"You do not know him?"

"He seems perfectly pleasant," Marianne replied calmly.

"Hmm. We shall see," Mrs. Simmons said, sounding as if she saw much already. It was a tone that would have gratified Mrs. River.

The men were approaching the door now, carrying the trunk between them, so Mrs. Simmons was obliged to open the door to let them pass.

She wore a gray cap on her head and a gray frown on her face. Though doubtless she had not begun life unhappy, the years had taught her that lesson. She let the men in, but followed them closely, barking directions after them. "Up these stairs. Past the landing, that way. Now down this hall. Second door on the left. Right in there. Put it down at the foot of the bed. Come away now. This is a lady's room."

Just as closely, she followed them out again, passing Marianne, who was still standing at the bottom of the stairs.

"So, you are Miss Trenton?" Mrs. Simmons asked when the door closed behind the two men. She was running her eyes down the length of Marianne's form as if trying to discover some hint of duplicity, some evidence to prove she was not who she said she was.

"I am," Marianne said.

"From Farnham, I believe."

"I went to school in Farnham. My home is an estate south of here called Kingsbrook, the property of Mr. Peter Desmond, with whom, I believe, you have spoken."

"Yes, Mr. Desmond. We have corresponded, though I have not met the gentleman personally," Mrs. Simmons said.

Marianne could not be surprised. If Mrs. Simmons had ever seen her guardian, with his dark eyes and unruly mane of hair, Marianne surely would not be staying in this house.

"I suppose you had better dismiss your gentlemen. And you may tell them, and any other callers, that I do not allow men in my house. Beaux may call for you, but you are to meet them at the door."

"I have no beaux, Mrs. Simmons, and only my guardian will come to call, I am sure, though I will tell him your regulations," Marianne promised.

"Mr. Desmond, of course, may come in," the widow lady said, but Marianne thought she would wait until Mr. Desmond had actually presented himself before she took Mrs. Simmons at her word.

Following her landlady's advice, Marianne stepped outside to send Rickers on his way and to thank the young man again.

"We will wait to hear from you, Miss Marianne," the driver said, touching his cap, which was as much deference as Rickers ever paid her.

"And tell Mrs. River all is safe and sound here," the girl called after him as he climbed onto the carriage. "You tell the gentlemen at the college, too, that I appreciate the help they sent, and your thoughtfulness,'' she told the young man still waiting on her.

Brewster furrowed his brow for a moment, then smiled at her. ''It was just the lecturer, miss. But I will give him your message. Is there anything else I can do for you?'' he asked, looking around hopefully. But there was nothing to be seen except Mrs. Simmons's neat little yard.

''I do not think so,'' Marianne told him.

Mr. Brewster assumed a whimsical expression of disappointment. ''I suppose I had better go then.''

Marianne smiled, not verbally agreeing, but certainly not disagreeing.

''But I had forgotten,'' he said, brightening, ''I may very well see you in class tomorrow.''

''In class?'' Marianne asked.

''Perhaps,'' Brewster told her. ''You are enrolled in the literature class, as am I.''

Marianne was distressed to think her presence in Reading, her enrollment in the university, even her scheduled classes, were of general knowledge, but if her life was public domain, there was nothing for it now but to second Brewster's hope that they would meet at the school.

After another comment or two about the school and the teachers that she did not understand, the young man retreated down the walk and out onto the road. But he went slowly, as if hoping to think of some brilliant topic of conversation that would lengthen his stay.

He did not, and when he finally turned onto the roadway, Marianne went back inside Mrs. Simmons's house.

''You will want to get settled,'' the widow said as Marianne turned from the door.

Actually, she was hungry for human contact, but she was given no choice, so she went up the stairs to her room.

Marianne spent a fitful night. She could not seem to get comfortable in the small bed, the unfamiliar room, and by morning her eyelids were so heavy she hardly had strength enough to lift them.

But the liberal application of cold water from Mrs. Simmons's pump helped, and by eight o'clock she was bathed, brushed and dressed for her first day of college classes.

With the brave squaring of her shoulders so characteristic of her, Marianne was preparing to walk down to the university alone, feeling both excited and frightened. As she was wrapping her shawl about her, there was a loud knocking at the front door. She jumped and Mrs. Simmons came scolding from the kitchen to answer the rude summons.

Standing in the doorway was the bright, beaming figure of Mr. Brewster. "Morning, ma'am. I have come to show Miss Trenton to her classes," he announced.

Mrs. Simmons frowned slightly, but Marianne hurried to the door, weak with relief. "Oh, thank you, Mr. Brewster," she said, and any inconvenience Bernie might have experienced was amply recompensed by her grateful smile.

Once in the little trap, Brewster offered bright bits of conversation for consideration. "I've not had a girl in any of my classes before," he said. "I think it will be a great lark, don't you? Not that you would usually be in my same classes. I am a second-year man, you know. But you qualified for studies in my literature class. The fellows were impressed. And they haven't even seen you yet." Brewster grinned as roguishly as he was able, and Marianne gave in and returned his smile.

Evidently, she was a news item and her entire scholastic history had been broadcast over the school. But if all of the scholars were as guileless as young Mr. Brewster, there was no serious harm done, she supposed.

"We are on our way to classic literature right now," the young man said. He was interrupted by the clock in the tower chiming the third quarter hour. "In fact," he continued when the bell had stopped, "we might very possibly be late for your first class."

He gathered the reins and flicked them urgently. The horse broke into a rapid trot, but could not be hurried into a gallop.

Marianne clung to the side of the carriage as it bounced along the road. Her heart had plummeted at Brewster's words. She really did not want to make a noisy, late entrance at this first class, filled with a score or more of curious young men and one disapproving teacher.

Brewster seemed determined to prevent that eventuality, which due to the lateness of the hour had become almost a certainty by now. Still, the young man recklessly guided the horse along the narrow lanes of the campus, missing by inches more than one tardy pupil hurrying to class. The lanes were deserted, though, by the time he stopped the horse in front of one of the old brick buildings and jumped down and tied the horse to the hitching post.

The boy pulled her from the trap and then, taking her hand in his, ran up the stairs and pushed open the heavy door.

The hall was dark and cool, with the weighty odor of ages past emanating from its walls. The ceiling was high and every sound was amplified. These halls were meant to be trod with silent feet, heads bowed in contemplation. Instead, Brewster continued to tug her hurriedly behind him, so their steps clattered noisily through the cavernous building.

At last he stopped in front of a door, yanking his vest into place and smoothing his hair back with both hands. It gave Marianne a chance to straighten her bonnet and tuck a strand or two of her own hair into place.

When he opened the door, she discovered they were at the back of a room where ten or fifteen young men were seated. Those who had not turned around when they entered were intently watching the lecturer, who was listing on the blackboard the various works they would be studying that year, Aeschylus's *Orestia,* Euripides's *Iphigeneia in Tauris,* and Cicero's *Five Canons of Rhetoric.*

"You are late, Mr. Brewster," the teacher said, without turning around.

Now the rest of the class turned to gaze at the latecomers. They aimed mocking expressions at old Brewster, but their eyes widened in surprise when they saw Marianne with him.

"And this is our newest pupil, Miss Trenton. I will expect her to be treated with your full consideration and respect. Do I make myself clear, gentlemen?" the teacher asked, turning from the blackboard to face his class.

"Yes, sir, Mr. Desmond," a number of the students responded, those who were no longer staring in amazement.

Chapter Thirteen

"I trust you found your first day of studies interesting, a good deal more interesting than your deportment and elocution lessons at Farnham. At least, I assume so after your stories of the academy. The roast beef is a little stringy, I am afraid, but this inn caters to university students and teachers on limited budgets. The Yorkshire pudding is excellent."

Mr. Desmond had found Marianne when his classes were finished, which was not too difficult, she being one of only three women on campus. He had invited her to join him for supper. Now they sat together at a small table in the Treemore Inn, a modest little restaurant filled with raucous young scholars. The young men were talking loudly, calling to each other from table to table. There was even a small group at the other end singing sentimental love songs.

The noise and Mr. Desmond's comments helped disguise the fact that Marianne was not saying anything. Two people, though, were aware of her reticence: Marianne herself and her guardian.

At the end of his latest monologue, Desmond pointed to the chewy popover on Marianne's plate. Dutifully, she broke off a morsel and swirled it through the gravy before putting it into her mouth.

Desmond drew in a breath and was about to launch into

another series of observations Marianne would neither refute nor second, when he was enthusiastically interrupted.

"Desmond, old man! Good to see you here at last. And do I find our newest academician dining with one of our celebrated new students? Which one are you, my dear?"

"May I present my ward, Miss Marianne Trenton. Miss Trenton, this is Dean Brimley," Desmond said quietly.

"Your ward, you say? Come to the university to keep an eye on our new professor, are you? I have been telling Desmond for years now he ought to put that sterling education of his to some use. Brimley, my dear. Warren Brimley. Dean of the College of Ancient Studies."

The man seemed too large for the crowded room—not his physical person, but rather his personality, which seemed to push Marianne back into her chair with the same force a gale wind would have. Now he loomed over her and shoved his pale, meaty hand into her face. Having no choice, she gave him her hand in greeting and watched in dismay as it was swallowed up in his.

"Immersing yourself in campus life, I see. Best way to get acclimated, I suppose, though young Rogers and Williamson there get to be something of a tidal wave at times," Brimley said, indicating the singers on the other side of the room and the whooping audience surrounding them.

"Actually, we only came in for a bite of supper," Desmond said coolly. His tone was not unfriendly, just not inviting. He could see by the look in Marianne's eye, even if Brimley could not, that she was already nearly overwhelmed.

"Oh. Yes. Of course," the other man said, his verve dampened by Desmond's aloofness. "Good to meet you, Miss Trenton, and a delight to finally have you here, Peter, my boy. I suppose I had better look for a place to sit down. It appears we are crowded tonight." Brimley glanced down at Marianne's and Desmond's table. It was set against the wall, with the two of them facing each other, but Desmond did not offer the fourth side to Brimley, and the gentleman finally turned to force his way through the crowd in quest of another table.

When he was out of range, Marianne leaned forward. "Can we please leave?" she asked in urgent undertones.

"Have you finished?" Desmond asked doubtfully, looking down at the roast beef and Yorkshire pudding almost untouched on her plate.

Marianne pushed the plate away impatiently, and Desmond shrugged and rose. The bill had been settled when he ordered the food—"Money first, then food" was the establishment's wise rule in the university town—so now he had only to claim the girl's elbow and usher her out of the bright, noisy inn.

Once in the cool air, Marianne breathed a deep sigh of relief. She had been feeling as if she were about to explode in there, and now she took several more calming breaths before attempting to speak.

Desmond, who until now had been maintaining a steady stream of light, inconsequential talk, was silent, too. Evidently he sensed the girl's need for quiet, for the chance to organize her thoughts.

"Why did you not tell me you were a teacher?" she asked at last.

"I have not been a teacher for long," Desmond told her.

"How long?"

He smiled. "What time is it now?"

Marianne was confused rather than amused by his sally. "You have not always been a teacher?" she asked carefully.

"Good heavens, no!" Desmond exclaimed. "Until a month ago I was always exactly what I appeared to be, a good-for-nothing rake."

"But Dean Brimley suggested he has known you for years," Marianne reminded him.

"Well, yes, the dean was my teacher of literature when I was a student at this very institution. I have always been interested in classical literature, and what he called brilliance on my part was merely a natural inclination," Desmond explained modestly.

"Then you have not been a professor?" Marianne asked. "This is a new position for you? You have come to university to keep an eye on me."

"Doubtless that is the way it appears—" Desmond began.

"To monitor my studies and to oversee my social encounters," Marianne accused.

"Not precisely," Desmond said.

"Why else would you suddenly take a teaching position, a position for which you are so poorly suited?" Marianne demanded.

"To put it succinctly, because I needed the money," Desmond said with a note of embarrassment in his voice.

Marianne made a derisive, mocking noise in her throat, indicating how much stock she put in *that* answer.

"I swear, it is the truth. My finances have met with a . . . drain in recent months. I was forced to seek some sort of gainful employment," he said.

"What about your gambling winnings?" Marianne asked.

"I needed a more reliable income, I am afraid. London and the European capitals are very glamorous and exciting at times, but they are *always* expensive, and most of the monies I made at the tables I returned to the hotels in which I stayed. No," he continued, shaking his head as he spoke, "I needed to make money. And I will admit that when you were accepted at the university, it occurred to me to dip my bucket in the same well."

"And just like that you became a university professor?" Marianne asked doubtfully.

"Not 'just like that.' Dean Brimley oversaw my qualifications as a teacher when I attended school here and, since my graduation, has reminded me of those qualifications regularly. As for my being poorly suited to the profession, I am no less surprised than you are to be forced to take umbrage at your charge. I find I *am* suited to be a teacher. I am very well acquainted with the subject matter, and I find the young men—and women—personable, their willingness to learn invigorating. Good heavens, I am beginning to sound like old Brimley himself," Desmond said, finishing his speech with a rueful chuckle.

Marianne refused to return his smile, and they walked in silence for a few moments more. Desmond did not keep a carriage here in town, and hiring one seemed an unnecessary luxury. He had considered the extravagance tonight, but now was actually glad his recently acquired parsimony had discouraged and ultimately decided against the horse and buggy. The lengthy walk back to Mrs. Simmons's house would give the girl a chance to vent her anger.

"I cannot imagine why you should be out of temper," Desmond said innocently. "Teaching is hardly a heinous profession. You would think I had revealed myself to be a slave trader."

His tone was light, but looking up under her lashes at his dark eyes and tangled hair, Marianne could not dismiss him as a harmless university teacher, and she was disturbed he had called himself a "slave trader," even in evident jest.

"I found it very interesting," she said suddenly, apropos of nothing they had been discussing.

Desmond furrowed his brow, trying to recall the question to which she was responding. Despite herself, Marianne smiled at his expression of comic concentration.

"My first day of studies at Reading University, that is. And more than my discovery that you are a professor of classic studies. I also sat in on Mr. Howard's poetry and Mr. Ingle's natural science, though I gathered from Mr. Ingle and his students they would rather I had not disrupted their class with my disquieting presence. Even if the hallowed halls of the university are to be desecrated by the attendance of females, surely the sanctum sanctorum of science should remain undefiled."

"Poppycock," Desmond muttered.

"I thought so," Marianne agreed.

Once again they lapsed into silence as they walked briskly along the narrow lanes. The cobblestone walk was rough and treacherous in the dewy night air, so to steady her step, Marianne finally accepted the arm Desmond offered. To accommodate her shorter steps and the layers and lengths of material confining her legs, he slowed his pace until they appeared to be simply a gentleman and his lady out for a leisurely evening stroll. The suggestion was not accurate, and Marianne was impatient with herself for even thinking about the impression they presented.

"My decision was very sudden. There was not time," Desmond said.

Their conversation was oddly out of synchronization, and they took several more steps while Marianne worked her way back through their exchange to find the question *he* was answering. "Why you did not tell me you were a teacher?" she supplied, then shook her head. "No, I cannot wholly accept that. You might have written. You might have returned to Kingsbrook and brought me here to Reading yourself. I think you were looking forward to my surprise when you presented yourself as the teacher in my classroom."

Desmond could not suppress his telling smile. "Your expression was all I had been hoping for," he admitted.

By now, they had nearly completed the walk from the student inn to the quiet street on which Mrs. Simmons's house was located. After they linked arms, they had walked slower and slower as they talked, but now Desmond drew back even more until it was Marianne pulling them along. He had another question to ask her.

"And the other students?" he inquired. "The young men not in Mr. Ingle's class of natural science? What did you think of them? Mr. Howard's students, or young Brewster? Quite a creditable crowd, all in all, excusing the occasional dolt and nitwit, which you must expect in any group of young men. Still, not a bad lot, would you not agree?"

"I suppose so. I really was too nervous today to give particular attention to any of them."

"Quite understandable. In the future, though, I believe you will find the selection quite presentable here at the university. It should not take long at all for you to make some sort of conquest," Desmond said, a note of self-congratulations in his voice. "Mr. Brewster—now there's a fine fellow," he continued encouragingly.

"Mr. Brewster was most helpful, and if he had not dragged me into your classroom ten minutes late this morning, I might have been more generous with my gratitude. As it was, I was too humiliated to thank him properly," she said with a touch of irony.

"Yes, I will admit your entrance was rather dramatic, but Bernie tends to the thoughtless uproar now and then. A good sort, though. You must allow him that," Desmond said indulgently. Young Brewster was obviously a favorite of his. "You could do worse."

"Oh, doubtless I could do much worse."

"I think you should see Mr. Brewster again," Desmond said.

"In all probability I will. We share two or three classes, I believe," Marianne said.

"I meant socially," he amended. He wanted her to understand his exact meaning.

Marianne was not stupid, nor were Desmond's hints so subtle as to be misconstrued. She fully understood his meaning and, she believed, his motivation. She sighed heavily.

"Yes, yes, Mr. Brewster is a darling of a lad and I would be flattered if he were to call upon me. Please tell him so for me," she said, capitulating.

They had come to a standstill in front of the gate to Mrs. Simmons's walk. Desmond released her hand slowly from his arm.

"You may tell him yourself," he said. "I think you and Mr. Brewster will be spending a great deal of time together."

Despite Marianne's desire to learn and her guardian's able assistance, the pathway to higher education was not an easy one for young women in the latter half of the nineteenth century. Marianne and the two other female students enrolled at Reading University had a hard row to hoe.

One was a bespectacled, timid young woman who trod the cobblestone walks with head bent, who sat quietly and anonymously in her classes and whose performance and test scores surpassed those of every young gentleman at the school. Miss Tamberlay would not have said boo to a goose, though she could have discussed the egg-laying process in great detail and dissected the goose as well. She, too, invaded the natural-science classroom, but the trail had been blazed by Marianne, and Mr. Ingle and his male students were reconciled, more or less, to the collapse of their fortress.

The other female at the university was a buxom woman of middle years and brassy presence. She was of Mrs. Avery's school of thought and had enrolled primarily because women did not generally go to college.

"Women belong in colleges," she declared. "Women belong in politics, on the governing boards of businesses, on the forefront of science, even on the legal bench. Why, Mr. Nebling and I were talking the other day, and I said, 'Mr.

Nebling, does the woman belong in the home? Would you want me to stay home with you all day?' and he said, 'I would not, Mrs. Nebling.' Here I am, then, nor will I be turned away, so teach me something, Mr. Desmond."

Mrs. Nebling made her impassioned speech when Mr. Desmond acknowledged her as new to his classroom. Marianne, who was more favorably impressed by Miss Tamberlay's example, sat quietly to one side. She was compelled, though, to turn her head and smile at Mrs. Nebling's bravado and challenge to their teacher.

And Mr. Desmond would be hardpressed to meet that challenge, it turned out. Of all of Mrs. Nebling's stony features, her head seemed the most solidly impenetrable.

It also turned out that the young men who were students had an easier time accepting women, even Mrs. Nebling, in their midst than did the instructors, excepting Mr. Desmond. Most of the teachers ignored Marianne and the other women, or biased their questions toward a male viewpoint. They corrected the women's papers more stringently, demanded more, allowed less leeway—in short, used every method possible to discourage their continued attendance. Unfortunately for the teachers, they were up against three of the least tractable opponents they would ever encounter.

Miss Tamberlay had undisputed brilliance, Mrs. Nebling had unmitigated gall, and in her nearly nineteen years, Marianne had become a chameleon in her ability to adapt to difficult situations. Without a single absence or even another tardiness, she attended her classes daily.

Mr. Desmond often took her to supper in the evening, but he almost always invited another one or two of his students to join them. The table conversation consisted of Marianne's polite comments and questions, which Desmond handily fielded, tossing the ball into his young guests' court.

"'*O tempora! O mores!* Oh the time! The customs!' You recognize that quotation of Cicero, do you not, Miss Trenton? What do you think of the times and customs, Mr. Collins?"

Or "Miss Trenton finds the accessibility of the English translation of the *Iliad* compensates for any inaccuracies. Do you agree, Whitney?"

Or "Brown was saying to me just the other day he finds it difficult to apply himself to his books in the gloom of our English autumn. You expressed nearly the same sentiment, is that not true, Miss Trenton?"

Desmond encouraged and promoted Marianne's acquaintance with any and all young men attending the university, it seemed, and, Marianne, for her part, endured her guardian's heavy-handed matchmaking attempts with a pleasant smile and a quiet voice. However, though Mr. Desmond had been perfectly frank about his goal in enrolling her, she did not feel obliged to be romantically drawn to any of her fellow students.

Her warmest emotion tapped was for young Bernie Brewster, and that emotion was friendship, not amour.

Though Mr. Desmond had assumed his teaching position in late August, he had spent a great deal of time there during the summer, transferring personal affects, taking occupancy of his rooms, preparing himself for this latest, and it appeared most challenging, venture. Dean Brimley, his own former teacher here at the university, had directed him to the young Mr. Brewster to help him in his move, and the two of them, Brewster and Desmond, had struck up a friendship that suggested they had known each other for years instead of months.

Not surprisingly, it was Brewster Mr. Desmond invited most often to join Marianne and him for dinner. And he deferred every question to Bernie, even those Marianne asked specifically about teaching or even Kingsbrook, subjects about which Brewster knew nothing. Finally Marianne gave up trying to include her guardian in the conversation. She and Bernie discussed classes, fellow students, other teachers. Desmond would lean back in his chair and listen quietly, wearing a mask of indulgent amusement.

Later he would insist that young Brewster accompany Marianne to Mrs. Simmons's, and Mrs. Simmons, for her part, having met the agreeable young man, allowed him inside the front door to bid the girl good-night.

As the weeks advanced, more and more often Desmond would find an excuse that kept him from joining Marianne and Brewster for supper. "You two go ahead. I have papers to look over. Here Brewster, my boy, slip this into your pocket there. Take Miss Marianne uptown," he would say, passing a pound note to the young man, who came from a well-to-do merchant family and usually had more ready cash than his teacher.

Marianne and Brewster were "shooed" away to theatrical performances, to dramatic readings, to formal dinners and casual student socials. Mr. Desmond was too busy, or too tired, or suddenly too old to accompany them.

So Marianne bowed to the unavoidability of the situation and allowed her guardian to make herself and Mr. Brewster a couple. She trusted Desmond found it gratifying, and she, for her part, knew she was in no real danger of being coerced into matrimony. Not with Bernie, anyway.

Mr. Bernard Brewster, it seems, had found love without the assistance of his professor. He found it in the form of the bewitching, bespectacled Miss Rachel Tamberlay.

Chapter Fourteen

Desmond believed he was being subtle and noble, but Marianne had to smile to herself over the plaintive note in his voice, the wistful expression on his face whenever he bade her and Brewster farewell. It really was quite endearing and Marianne might have put forth more effort to convince her guardian to join them, had Mr. Brewster not been sharing certain confidential matters with her.

Poor Bernie really believed he was the soul of discretion and subterfuge, but Marianne did not need to be thrown into his company more than twice before she began to notice his frequent comments, compliments and questions about their fellow student, Miss Rachel Tamberlay.

"Miss Tamberlay is a charming young woman, do you not think, Miss Trenton?" he asked the very first time Desmond left them alone together.

"Rachel?" Marianne asked. "Miss Tamberlay? Why, yes, perfectly charming. A little shy, perhaps."

"That only adds to her charms," Brewster said, suppressing at the last moment a soulful sigh.

In subsequent meetings, Marianne learned that Brewster could imagine nothing more lovely than Miss Tamberlay's pale blue eyes magnified unnaturally behind the lenses of her glasses. Her voice to him was like the song of a lark, which was interesting to Marianne, since she herself could not recall ever having heard Miss Tamberlay speak above a whisper. But to Bernie Brewster, Miss Tamberlay was all that was beautiful, refined and adorable.

Far from being insulted by Brewster's obvious preference for the other girl, Marianne was greatly relieved and, in fact, found his infatuation with Miss Tamberlay quite delightful.

Eventually, when he suspected his secret was known to Miss Trenton, Brewster confessed he had made certain overtures toward Miss Tamberlay, such as nodding his head and even turning up his lips into a small half smile when their eyes met.

"Those have been your advances to date?" Marianne asked dubiously.

"It is all I have dared, but I must admit they have not proven particularly successful. What I need is a friend at court, if you see what I mean," he told Marianne in the middle of October, when Mr. Desmond was not making a show of accompanying them anymore. "Someone to foster my cause. An aid, an ally."

"Would you like me to talk to Miss Tamberlay?" Marianne supplied at last, and Brewster's relieved smile was answer enough.

By the end of October, she had conveyed his first note. Marianne, scrupulously principled, had not peeked at what he wrote, but Rachel Tamberlay blushed prettily when she read the slight epistle, and Marianne was sure it was some pleasing bit of flattery that only Bernie Brewster could have believed.

She was able to report only that Miss Tamberlay had seemed pleased, since the girl did not send a reply. But over the next few weeks, Marianne transported letters back and forth between them, and finally a silver locket from Mr. Brewster and a bar of soap—which Marianne found a curiously unflattering gift—from Miss Tamberlay to the young gentleman. And all this was done under the auspices of Mr.

Desmond, in his campaign to bring Marianne and Brewster together.

Marianne viewed her guardian's heavy-handed role of Cupid with what she believed was resignation. In Bernie's case, even with tolerance. But Marianne Trenton was a very young woman, still under twenty, who had been buffeted about a good deal in her youth and was still trying to get her bearings straight as she entered adulthood. She was surprisingly cool and levelheaded about most things, but Mr. Desmond had always been a source of confusion for her.

At Kingsbrook she had believed he was a wild, thoughtless, devil-may-care sort of man. Handsome, yes; romantic to some—Marianne included—but not what her father would have called "a pillar of society." Yet at the university, in his class, she found he was a serious scholar, skilled as a teacher, mindful of his pupils.

But every time she tried to accept the decent image he was protecting, the memory of her last discussion with Mrs. River reared its ugly head and she could not forget that her guardian, her teacher, the man to whom her heart insisted on being drawn, was spiriting girls to and from Kingsbrook Manor, very likely in conspiracy with Uncle Horace.

And all the while, Desmond believed that his scheme to get his ward safely married was exactly on course.

In November, Marianne turned nineteen. Though younger than both Bernie and Rachel, she felt like Mr. Shakespeare's conspiratorial Friar Lawrence, abetting the two of them in their clandestine romance. Brewster could, and often did, go on for hours about Miss Tamberlay and her numerous admirable qualities. Rachel was much more withdrawn, and yet she conveyed an even deeper level of emotion with her sighs and smiles and blushes.

"Really, Miss Marianne, I do not know what I shall do if Miss Tamberlay fails to return to the university after

Christmas. You do not believe there is any danger of that, do you?"

The two of them, Bernie and Marianne, were seated at a little table in one of the taverns popular with the university students. In fact, it was the same inn, even the same table, to which Mr. Desmond had brought her after that first harrowing day of classes. It was at least as crowded and noisy this evening, so young Brewster had to lean across his plate of corned beef and cabbage, practically dipping his tie into his mug of dark ale, to make himself heard.

"I think Miss Tamberlay is not comfortable here at the school, but she would greatly regret halting her education. She is a very bright girl, you know," Marianne said seriously.

"Bright? By heavens, the young lady is a star! She is the sun!" Brewster cried rapturously.

"I mean she is intelligent," Marianne told him.

Brewster sobered immediately and took a sip from his mug. "I know," he said, having fallen from the heights of ecstasy to the depths of despair. "She is a good deal smarter than I am. I am not so great a fool as not to realize that. Has she told you, then, that she wants nothing to do with such a perfect idiot as me?"

"Oh, Mr. Brewster, you are ridiculous," Marianne said with a laugh.

"I am in love," the young man explained simply.

"Exactly. Now pay close attention and do not go into your histrionics before I am finished. You asked if Rachel Tamberlay would be leaving the university after Christmas. My reply was that, on the one hand, she is very shy, but on the other she enjoys the opportunity to learn. Now I will tell you something else. If these were the only two considerations, I believe Miss Tamberlay would, with relief, quit our happy little school. But as you know, there is another attraction here that keeps her in Reading, that keeps her attending classes."

"Me?" Brewster asked, a note of cheerful conspiracy in his voice.

"You," Marianne confirmed.

It was the first week of December, with only three weeks left until the Christmas break, and Brewster had worked himself into a lather over whether or not Miss Tamberlay would be coming back.

"Why do you not simply ask her?" Marianne demanded of him now.

"If she will be returning?" Brewster asked.

"If she will be returning because of you," Marianne corrected. "Square your shoulders, raise your chin and tell her how you feel. And you really are a stupid fellow if you cannot see she feels the same about you."

Bernie furrowed his brow in doubt, while at the same time beaming a pleased and flattered smile. Marianne laughed out loud at the resulting expression on his face.

She reached across the table and squeezed his hand. "I think you should ask her to marry you," she said, her voice low and sincere.

"Marriage?" he gasped.

She nodded solemnly.

"I could never...do you think...? Oh, no," he sputtered.

"Ask her," Marianne urged.

Bernie looked into her eyes, and she saw a desperate resolve fill him. Suddenly he banged his fist on the table, rattling the plates and silverware and drawing attention to himself, even in the noise of the Treemore.

"By George," he cried, "I will do it! You have been a brick and all that, Miss Trenton, but there comes a times when a man must be a man. Next week, then."

"Today. After Mr. Rogers's chemistry class," Marianne said firmly.

"I do not take chemistry," Brewster protested breathlessly. Miss Trenton was being terribly impulsive about this, was she not?

"Miss Tamberlay does," Marianne told him.

"There. You see what I mean? A girl bright enough to study chemistry would not want to marry a dolt who struggles to understand Mr. Lear's limericks," the young man said with a fine defeatist tone.

"She is, but she does, and you must ask her today."

Peter Desmond sat behind his desk. His office was empty, cold and dark, except for the lamp he had lighted right above his head.

The papers he was shuffling through were various student interpretations of the conflict between Paris and Menelaus from the *Iliad,* but he was not devoting his full concentration on the scholastic opinions, which varied little from paper to paper. He was congratulating himself, or at least trying to, on how well his plan was working. Marianne and young Brewster had become practically inseparable. Their preference for one another's company was even being commented upon by the teachers, so it certainly must be an accepted and highly publicized fact among the student body.

The Christmas break was approaching, when Desmond assumed they would make their intentions public. Every time young Brewster came into his classroom, Desmond steeled himself to be called aside, his blessings entreated. But the days came and went. Brewster did not approach him. Marianne greeted him every morning with the freshness and innocence of a daisy, and it was driving him mad.

Cranston and Dweeve had been very circumspect in their movements, and they reported that Horace Carstairs's business had taken a downward plunge, though the moneylender was still ignorant as to who was responsible. That was all to the good, of course, but Desmond was determined to be finally and permanently free of Carstairs, and have Marianne married off. He might once have hoped to provide that protection himself, but the young woman had made it abundantly clear to him she could never think of him romantically.

He put his hand to his forehead and was distressed to see that his fingers trembled. He had been able to master himself well enough that when he was away from the girl, she was—for the most part—out of his mind. Even when they were together at Kingsbrook he had convinced himself that their relationship was maturing into a platonic stability that would not threaten either of them. But having her here, in Reading, in his classroom every day, bringing the sunshine with her when she came through the door, filling his every sense with her smile, her voice, the pressure of her hand on his arm, the delicate scent of her person, had fired again those longings he thought he had quieted.

"Mr. Desmond?"

He jerked his hand away from his face in startled surprise and found the girl directly in front of him, her image blurred in the uncertain light, like a desert mirage. "Marianne?"

"Oh, I hope you were not sleeping," she said with a laugh, aware of but not understanding his confusion.

"Certainly not. Merely correcting a few papers. What time is it?"

"It is quite late. Almost seven o'clock. I have been waiting for you near the library," she said.

"Waiting at the library?" Desmond demanded. "On a night like this? And where is that young popinjay, Brewster? He should have had you home an hour ago."

"Bernie had an important matter to see to. I told him not to worry about me, that the good Mr. Desmond would see me to Mrs. Simmons's."

"Well, he *should* have worried about you," Desmond said, arranging the papers into a neat pile and then standing. "Perhaps I ought to have a talk with our friend and remind him of his responsibilities." He turned down the wick on the lamp and the room grew dark.

"What responsibilities?" Marianne asked as she reached through the darkness for his arm. Desmond was surprised that blue sparks of electricity did not ignite when their hands met. He felt the sparks, even if he did not see them. "He is not my nursemaid, and if you have not abdicated your duties completely, he is not my guardian, either. Come away now. I am tired and cold, and you are hungry. I know, because you always become as grouchy as a bear when your meals are late."

Desmond growled ominously and Marianne laughed. Together they left the old brick building. The night was clear and cold. If Marianne had been waiting long at the library, he could understand her chill.

"Where do you want to eat?" he asked. "The Treemore Inn?"

Marianne shook her head. "Somewhere quieter. I do not feel . . . exuberant tonight."

"I understand completely," he said, nodding. He had been dreading the thought of the lights and laughter of the noisy tavern. He and Marianne would not share many more quiet hours together. "Would you mind awfully eating day-old bread and cold meat and cheese? What the place lacks in the menu it more then compensates for in peace and warmth."

"Sounds perfect. What is this mysterious nook you have been keeping to yourself?"

"My rooms. I keep a modest supply of foodstuffs on hand for evenings just like this, when my age catches up with me and I do not feel equal to being 'one of the boys,'" he said.

"These rooms of yours. Am I allowed in them by your landlady, or is she another Mrs. Simmons and I shall have to be spirited in through an upstairs window?" Marianne asked. She spoke quickly, hoping to cover any misgiving she might have about Desmond's invitation. After all, she had lived the past three years of her life under his roof.

"My rooms consist of the lower story in an older home, relegated to my exclusive use. I am at liberty to entertain any sort of riffraff I choose. And this evening, at least for as long as it takes to warm your hands and eat a cold sandwich, I choose you, Miss Trenton."

The house to which Mr. Desmond was referring was a two-story stone cottage near the campus, with decades of ivy covering one wall. It took only a few minutes to reach it, and Desmond opened the door and showed her in. It was a place as unlike Kingsbrook as ocean is from land. Everything was neat, orderly and expected. There was the mirror above the knickknack table, complete with ceramic figurines. The sitting room, which Marianne gathered, from the dust on the shelves and the cleanliness of the hearth, was not often sat in, had a low divan upholstered in pink-flowered material with two delicate-looking chairs facing it. The room might have been furnished by Desmond's grandmother, and had no doubt come intact from the previous owner and never been given a second thought by the present owner. The students and teachers who visited Mr. Desmond in this room did not know the man.

He turned carelessly away, taking the light with him. "Let us picnic in the kitchen. You and I have known each other too long for me to attempt to entertain you in the front room," he said, leading her down a short hall.

"You would not want riffraff in your more formal rooms, anyway," Marianne reminded him.

"Too true," Desmond agreed.

The kitchen was more Mr. Desmond than the sitting room, but it was primarily utilitarian. Quickly, hardly moving his feet to do so, he produced the bread and the promised meats and cheese. Marianne assembled the sandwiches, and together, by the glow of the only two candles he had bothered to light, they ate their plain fare.

There was a little stove that Desmond had lighted before Marianne was all the way into the room. It quickly heated the small space, and as Desmond had promised, within thirty minutes she was warmed and fed, reveling in the peaceful, homey quiet.

"I assume Brewster's intentions are serious," Desmond said unexpectedly, disturbing her revery, taking her by surprise.

"Quite serious," Marianne answered with a casual disinterest that irritated her guardian.

"And honorable," he added grimly.

Marianne was forced to smile. "Oh, entirely honorable," she said, remembering how Bernie had "screwed his courage to the sticking place" earlier that afternoon in his determination to ask for Miss Tamberlay's hand.

"He has not spoken to me, but I assume a formal declaration will be forthcoming in the near future?"

"I believe so," Marianne said.

"Brewster is a fine fellow. Solid. Perhaps not brilliant, but he has a good heart, which is better than any sort of shallow wit," Desmond said, sounding as if he were trying to convince someone.

Marianne did not need convincing. "I agree completely."

"Of course you do," Desmond said, bending his head over his plate, which had been empty for a long time. "He will make a very decent husband," he continued.

"More than decent. I believe it is his desire and ability to make his wife entirely happy," Marianne said.

"And *are* you happy?" Desmond asked. Her answer would be like nails in his coffin, but he had to ask the question, to be sure.

"The way I feel is immaterial," she said.

"What do you mean, the way you feel about him is immaterial?" Desmond demanded. "Damn it, girl, you are about to join with the fellow in wedlock."

"Not I," she said quietly. "If my words of encouragement achieved their aim, Mr. Brewster is this very evening proposing marriage to Miss Tamberlay."

Desmond sat staring at her, completely dumbfounded. Marianne drank a swallow of milk from the cracked mug he had provided.

Desmond saw his dream collapse around him like a child's sand castle caught in an incoming tide. He liked Brewster. Brewster was safe, the sort of fellow who could protect Marianne behind an impenetrable shield of respectability. He would make an inoffensive, terribly sincere husband. And his family's business was located in Reading. He would not be moving halfway across the country when he married, but would set up housekeeping right here in town. Desmond had never consciously admitted it to himself, but that was perhaps Bernie's most telling recommendation.

But young Brewster was not going to marry his Marianne.

The dream castle was smashed asunder and carried away by the waves, and Desmond could not have been happier. He felt like jumping up, clicking his heels and shouting "Huzzah!" Instead, he raised one eyebrow.

"Indeed?" he asked.

"Oh, yes. They are mad about each other, but shy as two titmouses—titmice? Anyway, I have been instrumental in their romance," Marianne told him with a congratulatory note in her voice. Then she smiled wickedly at the man sitting practically brow-to-brow with her in the small kitchen. "It appears one of us, anyway, has been successful in his role as Cupid," she said.

She stood before he could voice any sort of denial and stacked the two plates one on top of the other. "Here, allow me to help you do up these dishes."

Desmond had arranged his kitchen to accommodate one man and his bachelor attempts at cooking. There was barely room for two people to be working at the same time. While Marianne washed the plates and few utensils and passed them to Desmond to dry, they could not help but brush shoulders. Both became uncomfortably aware that they had not been this close in such a limited area since New Year's Eve.

"Are you disappointed—about Brewster?" he asked, carefully and quietly. He was replacing the pitcher of milk in the ice box, not noticing that the block of ice was nearly melted and the milk would turn sour if he didn't do something about it.

"Not at all," Marianne said. "But thank you for asking. That shows more consideration for my feelings than you showed when you arbitrarily selected Mr. Brewster for me in the first place."

"I thought you and he would have something in common, would enjoy one another's company. Was I wrong?"

"No, of course not." Marianne sighed wearily.

"My only concern is your happiness," he said with quiet sincerity.

Of necessity they were standing very close to each other, and Marianne was able to gaze deeply into his eyes. There was no deceit there, no dishonesty.

The room was silent and the moment grew very long. Slowly Desmond leaned toward her, and Marianne tilted back her head, offering her lips to him.

But he did not accept the invitation. Instead, he reached behind her for the basin of dishwater and took it out the back door to empty.

When he was out of earshot, Marianne whispered after, "*You* could be my happiness, Peter Desmond, if only I knew what sort of man you are."

Chapter Fifteen

Within a week the news was all over campus that Bernie Brewster and Miss Tamberlay were to be married.

"Miss Rachel thinks she will not return to the university, but I told her we would be living here in Reading, and if there ever comes a time when she, like Mrs. Nebling, wishes to pursue her studies, she shall have my full and enthusiastic support," Brewster told Marianne a week later.

The happy couple had bumped into her after classes and insisted she join them for an early supper.

Marianne smiled at them, and to herself, trying to picture mild little Rachel Tamberlay with Mrs. Nebling's strident personality. "And when will the wedding be?" she asked.

Rachel blushed, and Brewster patted her hand affectionately.

"After the first of the year. There is Christmas to be got through, during which my family and Miss Tamberlay's will meet. Visits, teas, house parties, evenings out, evenings in. Well, really, you can see there is simply no place in there to fit a wedding. Then after Christmas I have to go up to London for a few days on a business matter for my father. But directly after I am returned, we shall be wed. You will come, of course. Miss Rachel and I do not see how we could be married without you there," Brewster said earnestly.

Miss Tamberlay murmured something, no doubt along those same lines.

"You could be married very easily without me there," Marianne said, smiling indulgently. "But yes, if I am here in Reading, I will be there."

"What do you mean, if you are here in Reading?" Brewster asked.

"I do not know that I will be returning to the university, either," Marianne said.

"No? What does Mr. Desmond think of that?" Bernie asked.

"I have not..." Marianne began, but then broke off her explanation. "Whether I am attending the university or not, I will make it a point to be at your wedding," she concluded instead, handily diverting Bernie's attention.

"It will be a grand affair, you may be sure," he crowed, putting his arm around his fiancée's waist and giving her a squeeze.

Marianne smiled warmly, and Miss Tamberlay blushed furiously.

Classes ended the second week in December.

In the last week of school, examinations were taken and passed. By Marianne, not with flying colors: she was a woman being judged by a prejudiced male faculty. But she did complete the classes, and she felt successful in having learned what she'd come to university to learn.

Mr. Desmond was required to stay on for a few days to complete the grading of his students' final papers, and he encouraged her to hire a coach and return to Kingsbrook without him. But as anxious as she was to get back to Kingsbrook, Marianne did not like to leave Desmond, to desert him at this season of the year. She was feeling very sentimental these days, due either to Christmas holidays, her decision not to return to the university or the curious lump that had risen in her throat when Desmond assured her Bernie would take good care of her.

At last Mr. Desmond had finished his midyear work and was free to enjoy his own month of Christmas vacation. He and Marianne left Reading early in the morning a week before Christmas. It had snowed and melted just enough to make the roads a muddy wasteland. By the time they arrived at Kingsbrook, not until evening due to the traveling conditions, both of them were tired, hungry, aching and spattered with mud from head to foot.

"Good gracious, sir, what has happened? And Miss Marianne, what a sight you are."

"I am perfectly well aware of the picture we present, Mrs. River," Desmond snapped as he climbed down from the carriage and pulled Marianne into his arms in an unnecessarily rough attempt to assist her.

"And tired, too, I would wager," Mrs. River clucked, while Marianne was still trying to regain the breath Mr. Desmond had crushed from her.

"You would win your bet, Mrs. River. Remind me never to gamble against you. *Rickers!*"

The outdoors man appeared immediately from the other side of the wagon and Desmond threw him the horse's reins and gave some curt instructions for the disposition of the carriage. Then the master of the house disappeared within its portals, leaving Mrs. River to see Marianne into the manor.

"It must have been a terrible ride," Mrs. River said, looking after the gentleman, who was not acting like one, and shaking her head.

"It is not that," Marianne said, gathering her muddied skirts into her hands to follow the housekeeper up the front steps.

"No?" Mrs. River asked, turning to look at the girl behind her as she opened the door.

"Mr. Desmond and I... had words, I am afraid," Marianne explained, though it was hardly an explanation that satisfied Mrs. River.

"Did you, miss?"

Marianne recognized the inquiry in the woman's voice, but she did not feel up to satisfying her curiosity. Not just then, anyway.

Halfway between Reading and Kingsbrook, axle deep in mud on a winter day had perhaps not been the ideal occasion to tell Desmond of her decision, but he had asked about her schooling plans for the coming year and had made some sugary comments about Howard Collins.

"I will not be returning to the university," Marianne had said.

Mr. Desmond did not take the announcement well. "Not returning? What do you mean, you will not be returning? You must return."

"Why must I?" Marianne had demanded.

"To pursue your studies, to enjoy the social life—"

"To select a suitor? It seems a duplication of effort for me to be there, when you have already selected the next sacrificial lamb," she said sarcastically. "But perhaps you do not want me to be at Kingsbrook?" she asked, and then was appalled at herself for the cloaked accusation.

Now, having arrived at the estate and Mrs. River's protective wing, she wished she could take back most of what she had said as they traveled.

"I will be in my room, Mrs. River. If Mrs. Rawlins has any hot soup, have Candy bring me a bowl," she said, as she put her foot on the step to go up to her room.

Mrs. River said she would see to it, and though she would rather have followed Marianne up the stairs to find out exactly what words she and Mr. Desmond had exchanged, she turned toward the kitchen. If Marianne would not explain the altercation, then Mrs. River and Mrs. Rawlins would just have to speculate on the matter.

Once in her room, Marianne pulled off her muddied clothes and poured some water from the pitcher into the basin on her bureau.

Impatiently she picked up the soap and scrubbed some of it onto a washcloth. She was glad the water was cold, that slapping the wet cloth against her bare bosom and back made her gasp. She cleaned her face and hands and dabbed the mud as well as she could out of her hair, trusting that she could brush the rest out when it dried.

After drying herself, she slipped into a long, loose, flannel nightgown, prepared to spend the rest of the evening alone in her room before she retired early. The gown was warm and comfortable, and the cheery room, with the familiarity of home, calmed her pique a bit. She was not a choleric person and did not enjoy being angry. Especially not with Mr. Desmond. Even though, considering how she had come to live in his house, the tyrannical control he had exercised over her life since and the suspicions she entertained concerning him, she should certainly have gotten into the habit of being angry with him. With a sigh she dropped to her bed and acknowledged, as unaccountable as it was, that she had not.

There was a soft tap at her door. Finally Candy was here with her soup. Marianne was starving, and hurrying to the door, she flung it wide.

It was not Candy standing in the hallway holding a tray. It was Peter Desmond.

"Mr. Desmond!" Marianne gasped, and then looked down at her nightgown in horror. "I..." She turned to hunt for her bathrobe. Locating it on the floor by her bed, she fought with it for several seconds, trying to get her arm through the sleeves. "I was not expecting you."

"Mrs. River said you wanted some soup in your room. I volunteered to bring it up," he said, still standing outside the door, waiting to be invited in.

"That was very good of you. Come in. Put it there." She gestured toward the bureau, where her basin of dirty water rested.

"Why don't I put it here, at the foot of your bed, instead?" he suggested.

"Yes. All right. That would be better. Thank you."

Desmond gingerly set the tray down, then straightened, but did not move to the door.

"Marianne," he began, in a calm, reasonable tone he had spent the last half hour, since their arrival at Kingsbrook, trying to master. "We need to resolve our differences regarding the university."

"I am perfectly resolved," Marianne said, with infuriating implacability. "Now it is up to you to reconcile yourself to the fact."

"I think—"

"I am very well aware of what you think. You have made that abundantly clear to me. But I have no intention of returning to the university. As I said, I appreciate the unique opportunity you provided for my attendance these past few months, and now I believe I can pursue my interests and studies here, in the Kingsbrook library."

"I do not doubt your personal capability and initiative, and if it were only a question of letters, I could certainly allow your independent studies. But there are other, more pressing, more *personal* considerations. We have already discussed this," Desmond said.

"No! No!" Marianne snapped, suddenly lashing out. "*You* have decided. *I* was expected to comply. There was no discussion. There has never been any discussion between us on the matter. I have finally acknowledged that fact. I would think you would be very pleased with my proposal. It would satisfy your requirement and allow you the absolute control you have always enjoyed."

"You are being unreasonable, Marianne," he said, trying to calm her and keep his own semblance of self-mastery.

"On the contrary, I am being eminently reasonable. I do not want to return to your university, where I am to be exhibited and paraded about like prize livestock."

"I do not know why you say that. The young men at the school are, for the most part, well-bred gentlemen. And I explained to you I have no other way to introduce you to society. I thought you understood that," Desmond protested.

"Your aim is not my introduction to society. Your aim has been my marriage and your final disposal of me. *That* is what I understand perfectly. It is an accepted fact. I went to Reading. I enrolled in your university. I met your school full of matrimonial candidates. And I am not interested in any of them."

"If you would just come back, get to know Collins, or even Mr. Dowling better, perhaps—" Desmond began, but once again Marianne cut him short. He remembered the good old days, when the girl, instead of blazing with impatience, had allowed him to finish a thought now and then.

"*You* get to know them better. *You* make the choice. You will choose for me, anyway. I really am an unnecessary encumbrance. The boys have met me. I have met them. You pick out who it is you want me to marry, whose money you want me to have, whose family name I am to acquire."

"You make it sound so cold-blooded," he protested.

"It is cold-blooded. I am sorry if you do not like the sound of it, but I, at least, am reconciled to the fact," she responded.

"I cannot leave you alone here at Kingsbrook," he said, trying a different tack, recognizing, for the time being anyway, that she was immovable on the other question. He had chosen, though, a topic even more sensitive than the last.

"Oh? That would not be wise? There are things here you would rather I did not see or know about?" she asked suspiciously.

Desmond's expression was a study in surprised confusion. "Not at all," he said. "Not usually, that is."

"Aha!" Marianne cried. "So there is something going on here at Kingsbrook."

"What are you talking about? I think the ride home from Reading has exhausted you," Desmond said, searching for an explanation for the girl's raving.

Marianne turned away from him. "I suppose you are right," she murmured. "I am tired and hungry."

"Of course," Desmond said. "We will talk about your returning to the university later."

Marianne looked at him again, the wild light no longer in her eyes. Now they were filled with a forlorn entreaty. "Do you not understand?" she asked. They were standing in the center of her room, the bowl of soup forgotten, grown cold now at the foot of her bed. "I *want* to be here. How can I make you understand?" she asked desperately.

"I do understand, Marianne," he said. "You love Kingsbrook. It is as if only here are you completely alive. Other things, other demands may take you away, but there is always an invisible string linking you with this place, giving you stability and substance."

A soft gleam was in his eyes, and Marianne was surprised to hear her vague feelings expressed in such exact terms. "Yes. Yes," she whispered.

"And is it only Kingsbrook?" he asked softly.

"It is the place that has become home to me," she said, evading his question, afraid of her answer. "I do not want to leave."

He reached forward and took her hand. His fingers were large and strong, but they held the delicate bones of hers as gently as a mother holds her baby. "Even though your time here has not always been happy?" he asked.

"I have been happy here," she said, but she dropped her eyes when she spoke so he could not probe the truthfulness of her expression.

Desmond sighed. "Oh, my dear little Marianne, I have led you on a merry chase since first we met, have I not? Look what I have done to your life, and through it all you have remained pleasant and cheerful—and as young and beautiful as the first time I set eyes on you."

"Not quite so young," Marianne corrected him. "And what have you done to my life? You rescued me from Uncle Horace, you have seen to my care and my education. You have been a dear."

"But never quite dear enough, it seems," he said.

He continued to hold her hand, but did not draw her to him or make any further demands. He spoke quietly, without urgency or hope, and though there was no more than twelve inches between them, they might have been separated by a deep, wide chasm. His whole attitude was one of regret, and Marianne felt the sting of tears in her eyes over the sorrow she shared with him.

"I will admit I have made some monstrous mistakes since knowing you. And before I knew you, too. Believe me, Marianne, I would do anything to wipe the slate clean between us. Is there any possibility of that?" he asked with genuine humility in his voice.

He looked down at her, but she did not raise her eyes, would not meet his gaze. His heart sank when she shook her head.

"How can that be? How can you ask me to ignore what I know about you?" she whispered. She meant the secret he was keeping at Kingsbrook, but he heard an accusation of his behavior the first night she had come here.

He released her hand and stepped back.

"You cannot, of course," he said coolly. "It was foolish to ask. But you must see, then, that it is my duty to provide for your future security as well as I am able. You must be safely married—" At that Marianne jerked her head up, her eyes rebellious again, but he stopped her before she could launch another tirade. "For your sake, not for mine, I assure you. The young men at the university seemed a logical place to start, but I would not dictate your decision." He forced a smile that did little to lighten the heavy mood in the room. "We will talk more about this later," he said.

He had moved back a step, but they still stood close to one another, and now she reached up and pushed back a heavy lock of his hair.

"I wish . . ." she whispered.

"The time for wishes is past," he said, capturing her fingers as they left his brow. He held them to his lips and kissed them softly, but with a finality that broke her heart. "Your soup is getting cold."

Marianne had long ago forgotten her late supper, and now glanced toward the foot of her bed, where the tray sat, with distaste.

"My soup is already stone cold," Marianne said. "I do not feel hungry, anyway."

"Nonsense. You have had a difficult day and you need to eat something. Come down to the kitchen with me and we will see if Mrs. Rawlins can warm this up for you. Perhaps she will have another bowl for me," Desmond said, lifting the tray once again. "And a slice of bread," he added.

"And maybe some cheese," Marianne offered.

"And a bit of ham or cold beef."

"And a slice of pie," Marianne concluded.

As they always did, they wrapped their personal feelings up very tightly and hid them away. If Marianne Trenton and Peter Desmond were not very careful, they were going to protect themselves so completely they would never be happy.

Chapter Sixteen

Marianne's feelings of loss, abandonment and distrust were amplified by Mr. Desmond's strange behavior this holiday season, probably her last at Kingsbrook.

The Dudleys and the Romers sent them Christmas invitations, but Desmond refused them both, insisting they spend the days alone at Kingsbrook, though he spent his in the library and Marianne spent hers apart, too, or unwillingly with Mrs. River in the sitting room.

In years past, Mr. Desmond had said he had invited neighbors in on New Year's Eve. It had been one of the festive observances he had participated in.

But this year, in the days after Christmas, Marianne noticed no particular preparations being made in the house.

"What are the plans for New Year's Eve this year?" she finally asked Mrs. River.

"There are no plans, Miss Marianne," the housekeeper said.

Marianne drew her brows together. "Nothing? But Mr. Desmond always—"

"Not this year," Mrs. River told her, shaking her head. The master's departures had not gone unnoticed by the housekeeper, either. "*This* year our Mr. Desmond will be joining a party in Reading, I understand."

And Desmond did leave, with no particular word of

farewell. Instead of the happy neighborhood gatherings of years past, Marianne found herself alone, plagued by her troublesome thoughts, required to see in the New Year, and whatever it was going to bring, by herself.

December 31 was cold and bright. The King's Brook was frozen over. Rickers told them in the kitchen over breakfast that that was something of a rarity.

"Three, maybe four times that I can remember it ever happening. Has to be cold *and* dry. 'Tis a wonder," he said, shaking his head.

It was too cold to go out and "too hard to heat the whole place!" Mrs. River scolded. But Marianne liked the library and enjoyed its exclusive use when Mr. Desmond was away, while the housekeeper stubbornly remained in her sitting room, so James and Candy were obliged to keep the fires going in both rooms, with Rickers hauling in the wood, complaining loudly over every log. Mrs. River, peeved that the girl had been so intractable all day—usually Marianne could be convinced to join her in the brighter sitting room—retired early. It was the signal, whether justified or not, that the house was going to bed and James and the serving girl could retire as well. Marianne was required to keep her own fire ablaze, even crossing the darkened receiving hall to get the wood unused by Mrs. River when all of the wood Rickers had brought into the library was burned.

But Marianne did not want to go to bed yet. It was New Year's Eve. She might be alone, but she knew where the sherry was kept and was determined to drink her own forlorn little toast at midnight.

She read some and did a bit of handwork, and as the hour grew late and the house settled for the night, she dozed now and then in the big leather chair in front of the fire.

Mrs. River had bade her come into the sitting room, but tonight—tonight especially—she wanted to be here in the library. This was the room she loved most, just as the gazebo was the place on the grounds she preferred. They were part of her life, part of *her.* These places had contributed to forming the woman she had become.

And now Mr. Desmond, who had brought her here for his casual enjoyment so long ago, was doing all in his power to separate her from Kingsbrook. To sever forever the ties that bound her here. So he could turn this beautiful old manor into—what? A bawdy house? An exchange market? It was too horrible.

She was especially plagued by her conscience when she realized what she dreaded most was losing Kingsbrook herself.

She nestled snugly into the chair, putting her cheek against the thickly padded arm. As sleep stroked her forehead, it occurred to her in a half dream that she could smell Mr. Desmond here. She dreamed it was his arms around her, his shoulder she was resting her head against.

Was it the house she feared to lose? *Was* it Kingsbrook?

With what sounded like thunderbolts, the clock struck three-quarters of the hour. It was almost midnight. Marianne was pushing herself up in the chair, so she would not sleep through the arrival of the New Year, when there was a commotion at the front door.

"'Resist beginnings,' Ovid said. 'Prescription comes too late when the disease has gained strength by long delays.' He was either talking about the bottle or the blasted New Year."

It was Mr. Desmond. Marianne scrambled to her feet and was facing the door to the library, wide-eyed, when he pushed it open. There were only two lamps glowing in the dark room, and the one behind Marianne gave her a gentle nimbus.

"You look like an angel," he whispered.

"And you look like you have been drinking," she replied.

His clothes and hair were thoroughly disheveled, and his expression was a combination of bemusement and painful gravity.

"Well, yes," he admitted. Then his eyes slid to the tabletop and the tiny glass of sherry she had poured for herself at ten o'clock, waiting for the stroke of midnight. "I see, though, that I am not the only one imbibing tonight." He squinted his eyes to bring the fluted glass into focus and then smiled broadly when he recognized it. "But no," he said. "That is our New Year's toast. We want to make sure the coming year is a good one, don't we? The best one of our lives. We will both need an extra portion of our magic potion to see us through the year. I am glad you waited for me to drink it."

"*You* obviously did not wait to drink until our toast," Marianne said.

"Shh!" Desmond hissed, putting his forefinger against his cheek, though he was no doubt aiming for his lips. He turned and with exaggerated care closed the door behind him. "It is true I and a number of my closest companions—well, you know them, Miss Trenton. Mr. Greg, who, I might mention, does an uproarious imitation of Dean Brimley, and Whitney and Dowling and Mr. Collins, of course. Mustn't forget old Collins, what? He's practically one of the family now. Or will be soon, when you quit this foolishness and come to a decision. Oh, and that other fellow, you know the one—who has the affected speech and sports that perfectly ridiculous and superfluous pince-nez . . . ?"

"You mean Mr. Brown?" Marianne supplied the name easily from Desmond's description.

"Yes, of course. Mr. Brown. One of my closest companions. Well, the lot of us, you see, wanted to make sure the infant New Year had a soft landing, so we decided to drink enough liquor to fill a bathing pond. At least, that is what I *think* we were doing."

Mr. Desmond had remained standing by the door during his long and slightly slurred speech, but now he began to sway dangerously, and Marianne hurried to his side to help him to a chair. There was a stiff, narrow seat by the door she meant to settle him on, but the larger, heavier man guided them irresistibly to the soft chair Marianne had just quitted.

"You are pie-eyed drunk!" she said accusingly, with pious disapproval.

"My eyes can't be so very pied. I pronounced both *ridiculous* and *superfluous,* did I not?" he claimed proudly. "*And* used them in the proper context." Then doubt filled his bloodshot eyes. "At least I think I did. I know I meant to say something like that. Oh, it is awfully warm in here," he cried weakly, dropping his head onto the arm of the chair.

Marianne was at a loss. She should probably go wake Mrs. River. Or should she summon James first? Mr. Desmond would have to be helped to bed, and she supposed James would have to do that, but should *she* get James, or should she have Mrs. River summon the man? And could she leave Mr. Desmond alone in here? So close to the fire? The fumes of his breath might very possibly ignite a blaze.

As Marianne stood irresolutely near the gentleman, he began to speak, not in a loud, drunken voice, but softly, with a touching note of wonder. "You know," he said, his head still resting on the upholstered arm, "sometimes when I sit in this chair I imagine I can detect your scent. Not just your bath soap or your cologne. It seems I can smell you, your unique, delicate air." Now he raised his head and gazed into the fire, which was reduced to a single fitful flame and glowing coals. "And sometimes, when I sense you, I close my eyes and imagine these arms are yours." He rubbed his hands along the sides of the chair, his fingers caressing the soft leather. "That the softness, the surrender I feel is yours."

Marianne caught her breath. He had just described her own dream to her. Those were her thoughts, her fantasies about him.

"I had better go get Mrs. River," she murmured.

Before she could move, he reached out and grasped her hand. "Do not leave me, Marianne," he whispered fiercely.

She struggled, fruitlessly, to free her hand from his painful hold. "You need Mrs. River," she said.

With his other hand he reached up and grabbed her shoulder, forcing her to stoop toward him. "I do not need Mrs. River!" he growled. "I need *you!*"

Suddenly he released her hand and threw his arm around her waist. From her already awkward position she was swept off balance and fell into his lap.

Desmond kissed her forcefully, capturing her lips as she tried to turn her head. She could not breathe for a moment with his mouth covering hers and had no choice but to yield her lips under the pressure of his. Her mouth opened, but before Desmond's kiss could become more intimate, she pulled her head away and, with a sob, took a breath of air.

He buried his face in the soft indention between her neck and her shoulder. His mouth was like a devouring flame as it seared the flesh of her throat, her collarbone, the rise of her breasts above the bodice of her dress.

"I need you," he repeated, raising his head and moving his hand to unfasten the front of her dress. "I want you. I have wanted you since the moment I laid eyes on you three years ago. Has it only been three years? It seems like an eternity. You were always near, but infinitely far from me. And now you are going to leave me forever. I cannot let you go, Marianne, without ever tasting the fruit."

Marianne, though she heard what he said, had not been lying motionless in his grasp. She had been twisting and turning and kicking her legs. Despite the steadiness of his voice, Mr. Desmond was still drunk, and now, when he loosened his grasp to undo her dress, she managed to roll off his lap and onto the hearth at his feet. Quickly she scrambled up and away from him, but Mr. Desmond had not loosened his hold on the bodice of her dress and now held most of it in his hand. Marianne was not entirely bare breasted, but he had also torn the top of her camisole, and the fabric fluttered as she moved, giving Desmond tantalizing glimpses of her ivory skin, glimpses he hardly needed to fan his desire.

He stood, too, and grabbed for her, but she kept out of his reach. She would have run from the room, but Desmond had managed to position himself between her and the door. She stood, a hapless fawn at bay, watching him nervously, panting for breath.

He held his hand out to her again, but not to seize her. Rather, it was a pleading gesture.

"Oh, Marianne," he crooned gently. "Why don't you want me? Have our years together not managed to put the slightest scratch on that porcelain heart of yours? Oh, yes, I am sure you think of me now as a kindly mentor, even a favored uncle. But I do not want to be your uncle, nor your mentor, nor even a *trusted friend.*" He practically spat out those last words, as if a bite of fruit gone bad. "I want *you.* And I thought if I was kind, if I was careful, if I gave you time, I could melt your icy barrier." His knees buckled and he sat down with a thud on the chair by the door, where Marianne had originally tried to seat him. "Or failing that," he said, sighing wearily, "I hoped to build up an icy barrier of my own. To forget you, to ignore what you had done to my life, the part of my life you have become."

The girl's breathing had slowed now, and she held the torn material in place as well as she could. "Let me go, Mr. Desmond," she said, trying to sound reasonable, trying to disguise the panic in her voice.

"'Let me go, Mr. Desmond,'" he said mockingly. "That has always been your one plea. Marianne, I have given you my *heart.* If you leave me for another, without my ever having you, it will kill me. The best in me will die anyway when you go. So give me this much. One night is all I ask—for you to come to my bed willingly, without any of those damnable tears that have haunted me for years. Is it too much?"

His own chest now heaved painfully. He rested his head against the hard wall behind him and closed his eyes. "I have given you my soul. Will you not give me anything in return?" he murmured.

"I will play you a game of cards for it," she said.

Desmond opened his eyes and raised his head to look into her eyes. "What did you say?"

"I said I will play you a game of cards," she repeated. "If you win, you may have me. I will come to your bed willingly, wearing nothing but a smile of invitation. There will be no damnable tears."

"And if you win?" he asked.

"I get Kingsbrook."

There was a stunned silence. One could almost see the workings in Desmond's head as he tried to collect his faculties.

"You would get Kingsbrook?" he finally asked, very slowly and carefully.

"Or you would get me," Marianne said.

Desmond narrowed his eyelids and appeared to be considering very seriously. "You value yourself highly, Miss Trenton, to judge your worth equivalent to this grand estate," he said.

"Rather it is a question of how highly *you* value me, Mr. Desmond," the girl said coolly.

"That is true. And I *do* value you." He was silent for another moment and then nodded his head. "I consider it an equitable wager," he said at last. His voice, though still slightly slurred, now had the smooth, neutral tone of the seasoned gambler.

"Shall we play, then?" Marianne asked.

"Now?" Desmond sounded surprised again by the immediacy of the proposal. But his eyes, focusing on the girl's torn dress, on the silky material she tried to hold in place with one hand, burned with a steady fire.

She, too, looked down at her dress. "I could borrow your jacket, if you do not mind. Unless you would prefer another time and the chance to sober yourself. I believe we will both want all of our wits about us to play this game."

"My wits are perfectly collected, and I fear if I were completely sober I would not take this chance. There is no time like the present, as impetuous fools are wont to say. And I believe I have waited for my prize long enough."

Desmond removed his jacket and handed it to Marianne.

"As have I," Marianne said, her grim tone matching Desmond's.

They sat on opposite sides of the little card table Desmond pulled out from against the wall. He produced a box of cards.

"The seal is still intact," he said, offering the box for Marianne's inspection to satisfy her that the cards were new. His hand wandered a little, but he was able to hold the box relatively steady.

The girl nodded, and Mr. Desmond pulled the cards from the package. Swiftly he shuffled the deck twice, even in his inebriated state with practiced skill. Before he could shuffle a third time, Marianne touched the back of his hand with her fingertips.

"You obviously have more experience than I have," she said. "You might even be able to employ such sleight of hand as to insure your winning. You must not cheat, Mr. Desmond. The stakes are too high for the game to be determined by fraud."

"I would not cheat, Miss Trenton. You have my word this will be a fair and honest game."

Mr. Desmond's present sterling sincerity could not be taken as proof positive that the idea of a little bottom-of-the-deck dealing, or a well-hidden ace or two, had not occurred to him. He loved Kingsbrook almost as much as he wanted this girl, and the idea of losing both of them was almost more than he could bear. But he had been forced from his home once before and had managed to survive. He could do it again if he had to. He was going to lose the girl, anyway. If not to a young man of his choosing, then sometime, somewhere to another young man who would come into her life. This was his only chance to satisfy the longing she had ignited when she was a tender schoolgirl, those endless years ago.

She was right. The stakes were too high for the outcome to be determined by fraud.

He pushed the cards across the table. "You finish the shuffle and deal," he told her.

At a much slower pace, with much less skill, Marianne cut the cards and reshuffled them. She shuffled them enough times, in fact, that even with her inexperienced mixing of the deck, any positioning Desmond might have managed was surely foiled.

She glanced at his arms, resting on the tabletop, and dutifully he unfastened his shirtsleeves and pushed them back, leaving his forearms bare. She might not have been skilled enough to cheat herself, but she had learned by listening to Mr. Desmond how such things were done.

"We will play a single hand of five cards. That is a sufficient foundation upon which to base one's life, do you not agree, Mr. Desmond? Was that not the way you won me?" Marianne asked. If there was a professionalism in his voice she found disconcerting, he did not like the harshness he heard in hers.

In silence now she dealt the cards—five to him and five to her. Then she laid the remainder on the table. Desmond squinted his eyes to bring the cards into focus and, with no alteration whatsoever in his expression, silently studied the disheartening hand he held. Hearts, spades, diamond, face cards, numeric cards—he had rarely seen a less promising display. Fate should have been kinder to him. This was his life and his happiness at stake here.

"Mr. Desmond? Cards?" the girl asked. She held the deck invitingly in her hands again, forty-two chances to win or lose—everything.

"Three," Desmond said.

He gave up a jack and two number cards, keeping an ace and a two. But with the first replacement card Marianne gave him, he saw there was no possibility of a straight. The card, a ten, dashed his hopes. But the other cards were twos, and his hopes rose again. Three twos. There were five combinations that would beat three of a kind, plus any higher-valued three of a kind. But it was better than one or two pairs.

"I will take one card," Marianne said.

Desmond's hopes plummeted again. One card. He glanced at her face. Where had she learned to guard her expression like that? She was only a schoolgirl.

A young woman, he quickly amended. Not only to ease his conscience over what he was playing for, but because she was no longer a child or a schoolgirl, she was very much a woman. Especially as she sat holding his fate in her hands.

"We know what the stakes are, Miss Trenton. There is no use holding back any longer or trying to bluff one another. I have three twos," he said, laying out the cards in front of him.

Marianne studied his hand carefully for a moment, still holding her own close to her body.

"What do you have?" Desmond demanded impatiently.

Still without saying anything, she looked at him with a small, enigmatic, infuriating smile. One at a time she began to put her cards faceup on the table. The first was a queen of clubs. Desmond was fearful. The second was a five. He was relieved. The third was the fourth two. It, like the queen and, he noticed with a start, the five, was a club. A flush would beat his three of a kind. Five clubs would take the girl and the only solace he had ever been able to find, Kingsbrook, from him.

The fourth card she put down was the eight of clubs.

Desmond felt as if the world had come to a standstill. He did not know if he ever wanted time and motion to start again, but the suspense of not knowing was enough to drive him mad.

Marianne took the last card between her thumb and forefinger and tapped it enigmatically against her cheek.

Chapter Seventeen

On the day after Christmas, Bernie Brewster kissed the cheek of his fiancée and boarded the public coach that would take him to London to attend to that little matter of business for his father. He told Rachel he would return within a week.

"Ten days, at the very outside limit, my pet. This is a financial matter, and men of business always take their time about parting with money. It may therefore take a few days, which is to say, an eternity away from you."

"Hurry back as quickly as you can. Mother is growing anxious for the wedding," Rachel told him.

Bernie put his lips against her ear. "And I am becoming anxious for the wedding *night,*" he whispered.

Rachel was getting so she did not blush over every word Brewster said, but some things, like this, still summoned the blood to her cheeks. "Oh, Bernie!" she cried softly.

That was when he kissed her cheek soundly and climbed into the carriage.

The coach was advertised for six passengers, but it seemed crowded now with only five. Bernie was a gregarious lad, and long before he reached London he knew all his fellow passengers' names, occupations and current errands in Londontown. The Forsythes, seeing their son off as a midshipman in the Royal Navy. Mr. Hardy, a horse dealer, on his way to a sale of two-year-old Arabians outside of the city. "Finest horseflesh in the world, my boy," Mr. Hardy told him.

The fourth passenger was a Miss Chase. "Miss Mellifluous Chase," she said, in a thick country accent. "I'm off to make me fortune on the London stage, I am. I sing, and I dance some, and I can play any of those characters in the bur-le-que shows, too."

Brewster might have mentioned his business in London, but his primary theme was Miss Rachel Tamberlay and his upcoming nuptials.

It took two days to get to London on the coach, which stopped at every town and watering trough between Reading and London. It was still early in the afternoon, though, when they reached the city, and Brewster jumped from the passenger carriage, eager as a schoolboy—which, strictly speaking, he was—to be about his business and hurry back to his lady love as quickly as possible.

The senior Mr. Brewster's business was hats. He sold hats not only in Reading, but in London and Rochester, as far south as Winchester and as far north as Oxford. He had just received word that a late shipment of beaver pelts were to land in Liverpool right after the first of the year. Mr. Brewster was a canny businessman, and he saw a comfortable profit there for the taking if he could only raise the capital to buy the furs to make the hats to sell during the winter months, when men's heads were cold and the cost of a beaver hat was not a consideration.

The problem, of course, was the capital. And he was required to leave immediately for Liverpool with what earnest money he did have, which would hold the pelts for him until the funding could be arranged.

It was Bernie's job, therefore, to secure the cash. Mr. Brewster had assured his son the Brewster Hat Company was solid enough that he would be able to secure a bank loan on his father's letter alone. However, another problem was the required speed of the transaction. Bernie had not been exaggerating when he described the difficulty of getting money from rich and powerful old men. There would be checks and confirmations and a ream of letters back and forth among London, Reading and Liverpool.

"They will not guarantee the sale to me past the middle of January, Son. If you cannot complete the transaction with a bank then, you will have to go to one of the private moneylenders."

Bernie listened carefully and nodded his understanding. He had been a part of his father's business almost from the day he was born, and he was cognizant of the alleys and back streets one occasionally had to tread when dealing with financial matters.

With those instructions, then, he arrived in London and went directly to the London National Bank. He explained his business, produced his father's letter, stated the amount required and gave the reason for the necessary speed of the transaction.

He was directed to Mr. Biggins, manager of business loans.

Bernie shook hands with Mr. Biggins, once again explained his business, unfolded the letter, wrote down the amount needed this time and urged the bank officer to all possible speed.

Mr. Biggins murmured thoughtfully and studied Mr. Brewster's letter and the amount written on the paper.

"Mrs. Riley, will you have Mr. Yarnell come in here?"

Mrs. Riley left. Mr. Biggins offered Bernie a cigar. The two men lit up and discussed the situation in India. In a few minutes Mr. Yarnell entered the stuffy little office, now dim with smoke.

"Ah, Mr. Yarnell. This is Mr. Brewster."

"Yes. Of course," the newcomer said, proceeded to listen in silence to the continuing discussion of the Colonies, until Bernie was not at all convinced of the necessity of his presence.

"It seems to me, Mr. Brewster, that, in all likelihood, the London National Bank will be able to loan the Brewster Hat Company of Reading the amount you have requested," Mr. Biggins finally said. It was now growing very late in the afternoon.

"Jolly good!" Brewster cried, jumping to his feet and thrusting his hand across Mr. Biggins's desk.

"We will discuss it at the board meeting in the morning," the bank officer said, ignoring the proffered appendage.

"Yes. Of course," Mr. Yarnell added.

In his naive optimism, Bernie had hoped that his business could be completed this afternoon, in which case he could have hired some sort of transportation and begun his return journey that night. Instead, he left the London National Bank to spend a long, lonely evening in his hotel room.

Bright and early the next morning, he hurried down to the impressive brick building that housed the London National Bank.

"Well, I've some very good news for you, Mr. Brewster. The National is prepared to lend you the money—as soon as we receive a reply from Liverpool. We need to have a confirmation of the value of the pelts in question before making a loan of this size," Biggins said.

"Yes. Of course," Bernie replied woodenly. He put his hat on his head and left the bank.

A letter to and from Liverpool would take at least a week, and who knew what delay Mr. Biggins would manufacture next? Bernie would have to get the funds from one of the private moneylenders in the city and repay it when he was finally awarded his already approved loan from the bank.

"If you do need to go private," his father had told him, "I took out a loan a number of years ago from a man named Horace Carstairs. He may remember the transaction."

Mr. Brewster had given him Carstairs's address in East Coventry Lane, but it was only now, when he needed to find the place, that Bernie realized he was not acquainted with the area.

"Lost, guv?"

A young man was standing on the steps leading to the doors of London National Bank. He was one of several young men waiting outside the money house for some loose change going in and out the doors.

"I need to find East Coventry Lane," Bernie replied frankly.

The boy, not more than in his early teens, nodded his head sagely. "You didn't get your loan, then," he said.

Bernie looked surprised, then smiled. Obviously there was no point in trying to hide anything from this fellow's acumen. "I will be getting a National loan all right, but I need the money today."

The boy nodded again. "Then you want to go down to the money pits, and you'll need a guide to take you."

"And that would be you?" Bernie asked.

The young businessman pulled his cap from his head and grinned. "Tom Moffitt's the name, and I know the money pits like the back of me 'and. Course, nothin's free, mister," he warned. Bernie nodded and and pulled a handful of change from his pocket. He began to pick over the coins.

"What is your going rate?" he asked.

"What you got there looks about right," Tom said, nodding at the whole handful.

Bernie shook his head, but passed across all of the coins, totalling nearly a pound.

Forty minutes later, standing in the dirty little lane they had reached by a serpentine route Bernie doubted he could duplicate even now, he decided his money had been well spent. He would never have found his way down here and as he looked around him, he wondered how his father ever had. The neighborhood was mean and rundown, hardly suggesting the availability of money behind the sooty walls. Perhaps this Mr. Carstairs had taken his business elsewhere in the years since Bernie's father had taken out his loan.

"This is East Coventry Lane?" he asked young Tom doubtfully.

"East Coventry, number sixteen, just like you said."

"Yes, well, I suppose this is the place, then," he said. He had been looking up at the dark, dilapidated building and when he turned to say something else to his young guide, the boy was already halfway down to the corner.

Bernie reminded himself of the importance of the transaction, and there was nothing for it now but to make his inquiry.

"Halloo?" he called from the street, and then climbed the stairs and poked his head in the gap created by the leaning door. "I say, is anyone here?"

"Wha'd'ya want?" someone answered from overhead.

Quickly Bernie went back into the street and tilted his head to look up at the second floor, where a shutter was now open.

"I am looking for—"

"Wha'd'ya say?" the voice called, interrupting him.

"I am coming upstairs," Bernie said loudly.

He pushed aside the door and stumbled through the rubble just inside. There was a rickety-looking set of stairs against the wall, which the boy gingerly mounted. At the top was another door, this one closed securely. Bernie knocked.

"Who is it?" the same voice called sharply from inside the room. At this close range it sounded scratched and harsh.

"A Mr. Bernard Brewster, sir. I believe you know my fa—"

He was cut off abruptly. "I don't know any Bernard Brewster."

"No, sir, but as I was saying, I believe my father and you transacted some business a few years—"

The narrow door was pulled open. "Business?"

The man peering at him from the other side of the door was very lean, his face pinched, his nose almost beaklike. He was balding and had unhealthy-looking scabs on his head. His face and clothes appeared dirty, and when he opened the door, a gush of foul-smelling air was released.

"Mr. Carstairs?" Bernie asked doubtfully, sincerely hoping this was not the man for whom he was looking.

"Horace Carstairs. Yes. You said something about business." When the man spoke of business there was a keen edge to his voice, like a well-honed knife that cut to the heart of the matter.

Bernie cleared his throat. "I said you and my father had transacted some business a number of years ago," he said, "and now he finds himself in a situation at present, a *temporary* situation, that requires a similar transaction. . . ."

"You have come for money," Carstairs said, reducing Bernie's fumbling explanation to a single pithy sentence.

"Well, yes."

"Come in. Sit down." Mr. Carstairs picked up a jumbled mass of papers and dirty clothes, which he threw into a corner of the room.

"Brewster . . . Brewster. Hats, if I'm not mistaken. A hat company. Now I remember." Carstairs squinted, studying the young man before him. He noted the sharp cut of his clothes, the superior quality of the material. It did not take an appraisal as careful as Carstairs's to see from Bernie's comfortable girth, smooth face and soft hands that he came from a prosperous home. "I guess Brewster has done rather well for himself since my little advance covered one of his foolish overextensions. Brewster is your father?"

"Yes," Bernie said.

"That's right," Carstairs said, continuing his close inspection. "I see he gave you his big nose and fat face."

Bernie again cleared his throat nervously under the other man's unflattering study. "See here, Mr. Carstairs," he protested, "I do not believe we need to get personal. I have come to do business. Perhaps I have come to the wrong address. Do you have an office uptown where I can apply?"

Bernie had no intention of going to the man's office once he was out of here. There were other private moneylenders, he was sure. And even if he were unable to find one of those, or secure a loan if he did, he could always wait for the bank to come through.

"*This* is my office, boy," Carstairs told him. "And you apply to me. Maybe my business has not enjoyed the same healthy increase as Brewster Hats, increase and profit which, I might remind you, are directly due to my timely financial aid. I have met with certain . . . reversals." Carstairs's voice was bitter, so bitter it made Bernie wince. "But one good deal could get me back on my feet. Just one good deal."

The light in Carstairs's eyes gleamed so harshly now it made Bernie squint in turn. "Perhaps I had better leave and come back another—more convenient—time," he said, putting his hat back on his head.

"Sit down!" Carstairs snarled, and Bernie sat.

"Really, I do not like to bother you, sir," the boy offered.

"You came to do business, now let us do some business," Carstairs ordered.

"Really, Mr. Carstairs. I am afraid I have caught you at a rather awkward time. Please, you must not trouble yourself. The matter is not pressing. A small *minuscule* cash advance is all I need. Barely a profitable transaction for you. It occurs to me I might just as easily apply to a personal friend for aid and save you the annoyance. I have a friend, Mr. Desmond . . ." Suddenly he stopped. He *did* have a friend, Mr. Desmond.

Though Mr. Desmond taught literature at a small university, he owned that fine estate, and it was said his family was very wealthy. Bernie knew for a fact there were some Monday mornings when money was positively falling out of Mr. Desmond's pockets. The youth was not, of course, aware of Desmond's success at private gambling tables over the occasional weekend. It did occur to him, though, that surely he could secure a short-term loan from his comfortably situated tutor. Why had he not thought of good old Desmond before?

"Desmond?" Carstairs asked, suddenly refocusing his attention. "Would that be a *Peter* Desmond, of the Kingsbrook estate?"

"Why, yes. He's my tutor at Reading University." Bernie was surprised that a man like this would know a person of Mr. Desmond's quality.

"Fancy that. He has decided to become respectable. Or maybe he just puts on a show for the college board, though I would be willing to bet he makes a little money off you boys, does he not?" Carstairs winked slyly at Brewster, who squirmed like a worm being prodded with a sharp stick.

"Really, Mr. Carstairs, I cannot think what you are implying. Perhaps we are not talking about the same person."

"Mr. Peter Desmond, of Kingsbrook Manor, a rascally villain who tempts the limits of the law, but who so far has possessed confounded good luck," Carstairs said.

Bernie nodded with some hesitation. "Yes..." he said slowly. "Mr. Desmond is master of Kingsbrook, but he has said himself there is no such thing as good luck, only applied intelligence and insight."

Carstairs cackled unpleasantly. "'Applied intelligence and insight,' does he call it? Well, well, I had heard Desmond had all but given up the table. I think, though, that he must be making money somewhere. Perhaps supplying some of you young fellows with willing female companionship, eh?" Carstairs gave a thin smile, as unpleasant as his laughter, revealing several gaps along his gums where some of the old, dark teeth had fallen out.

Bernie would have liked to look away, but was strangely mesmerized by the unpleasant old man. "If you are suggesting what I think you are suggesting," he said, "I am more convinced than ever that we are discussing two different men. Far from dealing in such unsavory business, Mr. Desmond is actively involved, with the authorities, I might add, in fighting against just such activities. He does not discuss it with undergraduates, of course, but it is known about campus he has rescued several young women from a fate worse than death, as they say." Bernie grinned himself now, a much more endearing expression than Mr. Carstairs's unhealthy smile. "I have heard the story that one girl was taken, half-clothed, from the very bedroom of a peer of the realm, his lordship being brought up on humiliating charges later. It quite reaffirms one's faith in the judicial system, does it not?"

Carstairs seemed distracted and did not answer the young man directly. "Desmond? Peter Desmond, you say?" he asked instead.

Bernie nodded resolutely.

"Then it is Desmond who has done all this?" Carstairs inquired, looking about him at the cold, bare, filthy room.

Bernie gazed at the man blankly, unable to answer his question, since he had no idea what Carstairs was talking about.

"I might have guessed. He has his girl, so he does not want to allow the same privilege to others. He was always spiteful and vindictive. But I think he does not know me, if he believes I cannot be as vindictive in turn. I will require *full* restitution." Carstairs had been mumbling under his breath, his words largely unintelligible to Bernie, but his threatening tone unmistakable.

The young man hitched himself forward in his chair, preparatory to rising. The idea strongly presented itself that it would be well for him if he left.

Carstairs had been gazing across the room, but Bernie's movement alerted him, and suddenly his dark eyes were on the young man again, the lids narrowed intently. "You say you are a good friend of Mr. Desmond's?"

Bernie gulped. Perhaps he had spoken too freely. Just because this Mr. Carstairs knew Mr. Desmond did not mean they were fond of each other. Perhaps his teacher would not want his private business affairs discussed with this moneylender, who reminded Bernie of a gaunt bird of prey. In fact, just the way Carstairs said Desmond's name suggested he would not.

"I—I would not call him a *close* friend," Bernie stammered. "An acquaintance. Less than an acquaintance, really. He was my teacher. Taught me Plato. How close can a friendship be if a man who has been dead for two thousand years is your only mutual acquaintance?" Bernie asked, ending with a weak smile. "Well, I must be on my way. Sorry to have troubled you, Mr. Carstairs, sir."

The boy stood and turned toward the door, but Carstairs stopped him. "Sit down," he commanded again.

Bernie turned back toward the man, to protest this time, and found himself looking into the muzzle of a wicked-looking pistol.

"I said sit down," Carstairs told him again.

Bernie sat. The thought uppermost in his mind was that it was a shame to die so near to his wedding day.

As Marianne took the last card between her thumb and forefinger and tapped it against her cheek, there was a loud banging at the front door.

Both she and Desmond started violently in surprise. It was past midnight on a dark, frozen night. The year had barely begun, and other than the life-determining drama taking place in the library, they were not expecting anything to disturb them.

The noise at the front of the house continued. Mrs. River called from her room, "Mr. Desmond? Is that you, Mr. Desmond?"

Mr. Desmond pushed back his chair and rose. "One moment," he said. He looked pointedly at the card Marianne still held turned away from him, but she did not offer to reveal it, and Mrs. River called again as the banging continued.

"Mr. Desmond?"

"I will get it, Mrs. River," he called loudly. "You may go back to sleep."

He hurried out into the receiving hall, and Marianne heard him unlatch the front door. The loud knocking ceased. She laid the card facedown on the table and went to the library door.

"What do you mean, pounding like that in the middle of the night?" Desmond was demanding.

He had taken one of the lamps with him, but even by its glow Marianne did not recognize the fellow to whom he was speaking.

"Sorry to disturb you, guv," the stranger said, touching the brim of his hat apologetically. "But I had firm instructions to see that you got this tonight. I was told you would want to read it and wouldn't mind bein' woke."

The man took a folded scrap of paper from inside his coat and handed it to Mr. Desmond.

Desmond, holding the lamp in one hand, clumsily unfolded the paper with the other and held it close to the light. Immediately he looked up at the messenger again. "Was this delivered today?" he asked.

"Just this afternoon, sir. Had a devil of a time gettin' here, what with one thing and another." The man wiped his mouth, and Marianne deduced that at least one of the things that had delayed him had been a stop at a tavern along the way. She was sure the excuse of it being a cold night and New Year's Eve, besides, would, to the man, justify completely any delay in delivering whatever dire news the note held.

That it did contain dire news was evident from the change in Desmond's expression and manner. "Can you take me?" he asked urgently.

"That's what I was sent for," the man replied.

"Well, come in for a minute. Close the door. Let me just..."

Desmond pulled the man through the doorway and shut the door, but now stood gazing about him in confusion, struggling to throw off the fog of alcohol and collect himself.

"Did you want to pack anything?" the man prompted helpfully.

"No. No, I will not take time for that," Desmond replied. "My coat... Wait here. I will be right back." He turned first to the stairs, then started toward the half-open library door instead.

Marianne stepped back when Desmond entered. "What is it?" she asked fearfully.

"Something I have to take care of. Nothing. Do not worry," he told her distractedly.

"Do not worry?" she cried incredulously. "Peter, what is that?" She looked down at the note he still held in his hand.

"A matter of business," he said. "Just business." He opened the top drawer of his desk and took out his leather purse. Quickly refolding the note, he put it in the purse and then, opening another drawer in the desk, drew out a surprising handful of banknotes, stuffing them in as well.

"I shall need my jacket again, I am afraid," he said, turning to her and glancing down at the coat she held around her.

As she struggled out of it, barely aware now of her half-exposed bosom, she watched him with dismay. "Where are you going?" she asked, handing him his jacket.

"Up to London," he said.

"Tonight?" she gasped.

"I should be back in a day or two."

"But—"

"No questions," he cautioned her, pausing in his haste for just a moment to look her directly in the eyes. "I haven't the time nor the answers. Not tonight."

She followed him as he started from the room and nearly stepped on his heels when he stopped in front of the playing table and looked down at the nine exposed cards, the one still facedown. He reached for it, to flip it over, but Marianne stopped him by putting her fingertips on the card, holding it flat to the table.

"I will show you when you come back," she said.

"Things might not be the same when I get back," he told her.

"Just return."

In her torn dress, she stopped behind the library door, concealed from the stranger's eyes. She heard Mr. Desmond take his heavy winter cloak from the hall tree and then the door open and close as the two men left together. She went to the library window and pushed aside the drapery to see the glow of light from the coach lantern. In only moments it started to grow smaller, and moments after that she could not see it at all.

Chapter Eighteen

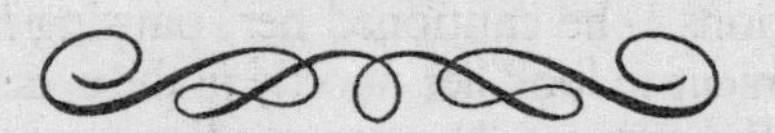

"Well, Mr. Desmond is not here," Mrs. River said in greeting the next morning, while Marianne was still descending the stairs. "Gone in the night. With not a word of explanation about the commotion. You heard the ruckus, too, I imagine. Sometime in the wee hours of the morning. It sounded like someone had taken a battering ram to the front door."

"Actually, it was just a little after midnight," Marianne said.

"You heard it from your room, then?" Mrs. River said, nodding with grim satisfaction.

"From the library," she corrected.

"The library?" the housekeeper asked in surprise.

"Mr. Desmond and I were..." Marianne's voice faded. She had not stopped to consider that this might be a difficult explanation.

"Oh, of course. You and the master were seeing in the New Year," Mrs. River supplied. "Well, what was all the noise about? Who was it, waking the whole neighborhood? And where is Mr. Desmond this morning?"

"I do not know," Marianne said softly.

"You do not know what was the cause of such an uproar, or you do not know who caused it?" the woman said.

"I do not know the answer to any of your questions. I did

not see the caller, and Mr. Desmond offered no explanation when he left."

The housekeeper gave a short, unamused laugh. "Is that not just like the man?"

But Mrs. River had not seen Desmond when he left last night, and Marianne did not think he had been himself at all.

She did not make that observation aloud, though. Instead, she silently took a muffin from the woven basket on the sideboard, to accompany her stewed fruit and the last chop, cold and dry by now, and turned, not to the dining table, but toward the receiving hall.

"Now where are *you* going?" Mrs. River asked, fearful, perhaps, that Marianne would suddenly disappear the way Mr. Desmond had.

"To the library."

"To eat your breakfast? Don't be foolish. Come and sit down here, and you may lock yourself away with your books after Candy has had a chance to clean the room," Mrs. River chided.

"She mustn't do that!" Marianne cried.

"Mustn't do what?" Mrs. River asked in surprise. "Clean the library? Whatever do you mean, child?"

"There is a card game laid out on the playing table that must not be disturbed," Marianne said, softening her voice and endeavoring to sound perfectly reasonable. "The table may be moved back against the wall, but no one is to touch the cards. They are to be left *exactly* as they are now."

"For how long?" Mrs. River asked.

"Until Mr. Desmond returns. It is a . . . card trick I want to show him, and the cards must be just as they are for the trick to work." From somewhere, Marianne produced a smile.

"We don't know when Mr. Desmond will be back," Mrs. River reminded her.

"He will be back shortly, no doubt. But whenever he returns, the cards must be exactly as they are now. Do I make myself clear?"

"Perfectly clear. I have very good hearing." The housekeeper was a bit put out by the girl's insistence on the silly card trick. But if she said the cards were not to be disturbed, they would not be. Probably. "Candace!" Mrs. River suddenly called loudly, making Marianne jump and inadvertently slosh a bit of the fruit juice from her bowl onto the floor at her feet.

"Perhaps I will eat in here," she said, glancing apologetically down at the mess before turning back to the dining table. She could check the cards after breakfast, she supposed.

Actually, she checked them several times during the day.

The early darkness of the winter night filled Kingsbrook, and Marianne instructed Candy to light candles and lamps in all the downstairs rooms, so their welcoming glow could be seen through the windows.

But early evening became late evening and Mr. Desmond did not return. Mrs. River stepped into the library where Marianne sat brooding over Sophocles's *Antigone*.

"James, Candy and I all thought we would go to bed," the housekeeper said.

"Yes, yes," Marianne replied impatiently.

"Do you want me to leave on all the lights?" the housekeeper asked, finally getting to the point.

"No." Marianne sighed. "You may put them out. I suppose if you are all going to bed, I may as well join you."

Mr. Desmond did not return the next day, or the day after that. Three days passed, then four; then they were a week into the New Year. Classes would be starting at the university in another week, and the cards still lay, undisturbed, on the table in the library.

Marianne started at the sound of every passing carriage and raced Mrs. River to collect the post every day.

A week from the day Mr. Desmond left Kingsbrook, Marianne finally received a letter, though not from Peter. It was from Miss Rachel Tamberlay.

My dear Miss Trenton,
I do not know if you can help me, but Mr. Brewster has been gone for almost two weeks now, and I am very worried. You and Bernie have been such good friends, I thought you might know of something that would keep him in London for so long without sending a word of explanation to me. Probably I am suffering from the anxiety of my approaching marriage. I certainly hope so. But I would appreciate any word of comfort, explanation or advice you could give me. Write to me as soon as possible, as I am in an agony of suspense over dear Bernie's whereabouts.

Sincerely and humbly yours,
Rachel Tamberlay.

Marianne reread the letter several times, forcibly struck by some of the phrases Rachel had used in her epistle. "Gone for almost two weeks now, and I am very worried." "Something that would keep him in London so long without sending a word of explanation to me." "I am in an agony of suspense."

Marianne might have written this very letter to Rachel Tamberlay. What could it mean? The circumstances of Mr. Brewster's and Mr. Desmond's disappearances were too parallel to be a coincidence.

As she sat frowning over the paper, there was a knock at the front door, which Mrs. River hurried to answer. From the surprised tone of recognition in the housekeeper's voice, it sounded as if she knew their caller.

After a minute or more, Mrs. River appeared at the door of the library and then stood to one side, allowing the door to open wider. A fine-looking woman with a quiet assurance entered the room. She appeared to be about fifty years of age.

"You are Miss Trenton," the woman said, stepping forward and offering her hand to the girl. "I am Mrs. Desmond, Peter's mother."

"Mrs. Desmond?" Marianne asked uncertainly. "I am honored...and surprised." She shook the lady's hand briefly and then said, "Your son is not here." She spoke apologetically, as if Mr. Desmond's absence and his mother's fruitless journey were somehow all her fault. "I am quite certain Mr. Desmond was not expecting you, or surely he would not have gone away."

"No, I do not imagine I was expected. I have not come down here to Kingsbrook since Peter took it over. There were...feelings between Peter and his father, though I have begun to hope..." Mrs. Desmond stopped, disconcerted for a moment. Marianne could see it was an uncertainty from which she did not often suffer.

"Do you know where Mr. Desmond—Peter—is now?" Marianne asked hopefully. Perhaps the lady could answer her questions, though she was willing to admit Mrs. Desmond would probably have some of her own concerning her son and herself.

Mrs. Desmond, a mother with grave moral misgivings about the living arrangements of her son and this young woman whom he called his ward, put her questions and any accusations to the side, for the time being, anyway. "You do not?" she said instead, in response to Marianne's question. "I was expecting, hoping you would... he would have..." Again Mrs. Desmond floundered and halted uncertainly. "It is just that Miss Morely has been with us a month now, and Peter has sent no word from her people or told us what we are to do with her. I have written to the address in Reading, our usual correspondence route, and have received no reply for more than two weeks now."

"Miss Morely?" Marianne asked in surprise.

Mrs. Desmond was too worried at the moment to be amused by the girl's obviously unconscious note of jealousy. There had been times in the last several years when Peter had left Kingsbrook, suddenly and unannounced, to be gone for months at a time. And Mrs. Desmond might have worried then, but she had not been particularly surprised. Now, though, Peter was so changed, his actions in recent months so selfless, that his mother had begun to hope for a reconciliation at last between her husband and her only son. Yet Peter had disappeared again, with no word, and worse, leaving one of his "damsels in distress" still in his mother's care.

"Miss Helen Morely, one of the young women my son has been assisting," Mrs. Desmond said.

"You know about the young women your son has been involved with?" Marianne asked incredulously. True, Desmond had never talked about his parents enough for Marianne to form more than a vague impression of them, but having met Mrs. Desmond in person, she could not believe this gracious lady would countenance such villainous actions. From anyone, her son included.

"Certainly. Well, the ones since he wrote to me for help," Mrs. Desmond said.

Marianne stared at the women agog. Her jaw actually dropped and her eyes opened wide. "You have been *helping* Mr. Desmond?" she asked at last.

"I do what I am able," Mrs. Desmond said. "It is Peter, of course, who masterminds the whole operation. I merely provide quarters for the girls until someone picks them up."

Marianne dropped to the divan. Mrs. Desmond sat next to her.

"Miss Morely's disposition has not been provided for yet, so you can see why I am so surprised my son would have left now. Leaving no word, finalizing no arrangements."

Marianne stared at the other woman for a moment. "Mrs. Desmond, what is it you believe your son *does* with the young women you house?" she asked at last. The question was blunt, perhaps indelicate, but she had decided it was time for the truth to come out.

"I know perfectly well what he does with them," Mrs. Desmond replied. "My darling boy has taken it upon himself to return the poor creatures to friends and families, rescuing them from lives of sin and degradation." She sounded a bit triumphant, suggesting that his actions were more than the salvation of a number of innocent girls; they were also the salvation of her son.

For just a moment Marianne paused. "Really?" she asked at last, in a meek, wonder-filled voice.

"Well, certainly. But I thought . . . were you not . . . ? Excuse me, Miss Trenton, but I assumed Peter brought you here to Kingsbrook to provide you the same protection," Mrs. Desmond said.

Marianne drew in her breath suddenly, but released it very slowly. "Yes," she replied at last. "He did."

Mrs. Desmond dismissed the topic, to return to a discussion of her son's present whereabouts, unaware that Marianne's life had been completely redefined in the last few moments, her mind cleared of suspicions, her heart and intellect at last brought into synchronous harmony.

"You cannot give me any idea as to where Peter is then?" she asked.

Marianne shook her head helplessly.

Mrs. Desmond, in her distraction, had removed one of her gloves, and now she began to put it back on. "I really am at something of a loss, I am afraid. I came expecting to find Peter, but if he is not here . . ."

"Mrs. Desmond, this is your son's home. I know he would want you to stay. I must run up to Reading myself, but Mrs. River will be delighted by your company, and doubtless Mr. Desmond will be returning in another day or two and will want to see you."

"Oh, my dear, I would never *think...*" The older woman began, demurring a bit longer, but finally accepting Marianne's invitation.

Mrs. River was summoned at once and was, as Marianne promised, delighted with Mrs. Desmond's determination to stay at Kingsbrook for a few days. The housekeeper was not a little surprised, however, to hear Marianne announce, "And tell Rickers I am going up to Reading."

"Now, miss?" she asked.

"Immediately."

Both Mrs. Desmond and Mrs. River watched dumbfounded as Marianne hurried from the room, calling for Candy and sending James out to alert Rickers.

Rickers, though in the midst of some repairs he was making on the fence, still had the horse caught and hitched to the carriage by the time Candy followed Marianne downstairs again with her packed valise. And Marianne had been very quick in her packing, scarcely noticing what she was taking, style or color, merely trying to get tops with bottoms, rights with lefts and underwear to go with outerwear.

In less than thirty minutes everyone—Marianne, Mrs. Desmond, Mrs. River and all the servants—had gathered outside the front doors.

"Miss Marianne, what can you be thinking? Where are you going?" Mrs. River asked, glancing behind her at the master's mother. Deserting her at the moment of her arrival seemed terribly gauche to the housekeeper.

"I must go up to Reading to see a friend of mine. I am hopeful, Mrs. Desmond, that she or her fiancé will know where Mr. Desmond is. I will send word to you as soon as I have learned anything," Marianne announced hurriedly.

Neither of the women appeared to be reassured by the girl's sketchy explanation and vague promises, but then, neither was Marianne. But she simply could not sit here at Kingsbrook any longer, waiting for a message from the man she loved. She knew in her heart that what was preventing Bernie's return to Miss Tamberlay was the same thing detaining Peter. She could not explain it, but she hoped Rachel could.

So she smiled down at Mrs. Desmond and Mrs. River and told them not to worry, realizing that that was what Mr. Desmond had told her when he left that night. Then Rickers jounced the reins and they were away.

It was well past nightfall when she reached Reading. Miss Tamberlay lived with an aunt near the university campus, but Marianne had only been there a time or two with Bernie, so she hoped she could find it again. In the dark. In the middle of winter. Rickers hoped she could, too.

"Try this house," she called up to him twice before they found the home of Mrs. Curtain.

Once Rickers had inquired and Mrs. Curtain had confirmed that this was the place, Marianne got out of the carriage to see Rachel coming down from upstairs. "Miss Marianne! What on earth are you doing here?" her friend asked.

"I received your letter," Marianne told her. "Mr. Brewster has not returned?"

"No, but I did not mean for you to come all the way into Reading. As I told you, I am probably being silly," Rachel said.

"I do not think so. Mr. Desmond has disappeared, too."

"What?"

Marianne told her about the late-night delivery of the note and Desmond's immediate departure, saying that it could only have been a matter of the direst importance to call him away at that particular moment.

"That was more than a week ago. We have not heard anything from Mr. Desmond since. Then this morning, Mrs. Desmond, his mother, came to Kingsbrook. She has not heard from her son either, and she had definite expectations that he would be contacting her. I cannot help but think there is some connection between Mr. Desmond's mysterious disappearance and Bernie's," Marianne explained, unable to keep the note of urgency out of her voice.

Rachel had led them into her aunt's front parlor as Marianne talked. When she finished, she grabbed Rachel's hand, and now the two of them sank down to sit knee-to-knee on the divan.

"I do not see how our two situations can be connected," Rachel said. "Bernie's departure was hardly mysterious. His errand was simple, and he warned me it might take a few days. Of course, I was not expecting him to be gone a fortnight. I do not think he was expecting it, either. But he has gone to secure a loan for his father. The elder Mr. Brewster is in Liverpool, hoping to take possession of some beaver pelts, I believe."

"And he said nothing about Mr. Desmond when he left?"

"His business did not have anything to do with school, or even his friendship with Mr. Desmond or yourself."

Marianne released Rachel's hand and turned to look across the room. "Mr. Brewster has been gone two weeks, not one?" she asked.

"Two weeks," Rachel affirmed.

"But he has not written to you. Do you not find that strange? I would not have thought he would go two weeks without writing to you. Indeed, I had not thought he *could.*"

"I had not thought so myself," Rachel said. There was a quaver in her voice, and behind the lenses of her glasses Marianne saw tears shimmering in her eyes.

"Mr. Desmond has not written, either," Marianne said, patting Rachel's hand comfortingly. Then she smiled. "Of course, that he has not written to me is not so very unusual, but he has not written to Mrs. River about the estate, which is as unlikely as Mr. Brewster ignoring his fiancée."

Rachel could not return her smile. "Bernie would not ignore me," she said.

"No, he would not, would he?" Marianne said thoughtfully. "Just as Mr. Desmond would not absent himself right now without leaving word with his mother."

"I was right, was I not? Something has happened to him, to them," Rachel said fearfully.

"We do not actually *know* anything," Marianne told her. "We do not even know whether Bernie has been awarded the loan or not."

"But we can find out," Rachel said, sounding like someone grasping for straws. "Bernie gave me the name of the bank. . . ." The girl stood and began looking through the drawers of the small secretary near the door of the little sitting room. In only a few moments she withdrew a slip of paper from one of the compartments. "The London National Bank," she announced.

Marianne held out her hand and read the three words over carefully to herself when Rachel delivered the note to her.

"Very good," she said at last. "Then I will just go to the London National Bank and find out what they can tell me."

"Go into London? Yourself? I thought we could write to them," Rachel suggested timidly.

"I do not want to rely on a letter. I am tired of waiting for people to write to me to determine my fate," Marianne said bitterly.

Chapter Nineteen

It was decided that Marianne would spend the night with Rachel in Mrs. Curtain's house. There was nothing Marianne could do tonight, and she would be more effective tomorrow with a night's sleep and a good breakfast.

She was determined, though, to be away bright and early the next morning. She was also determined to go alone. But Miss Rachel had surprising determination of her own.

"I cannot possibly wait here in Reading while you go off to discover what has become of my betrothed," she said.

"What are you thinking?" Marianne cried.

"I am thinking I am at least as anxious as you are to find the gentlemen, and you may need some help," her friend told her, pushing her glasses up the bridge of her nose.

Marianne made a show of protesting, but relented easily and acknowledged she would feel safer plunging into London's murky depths with someone at her side.

"London's murky depths?" Rachel said. "I thought you said we were going to the London National Bank?"

"Exactly," Marianne said, in a voice suggesting danger and intrigue.

Miss Tamberlay laughed nervously. She hoped Marianne was joking, and Marianne was quite sure she was. But they were to discover London had some *very* murky depths.

Rachel told her aunt that Miss Trenton was an old and dear friend who had invited her to spend a few days in

London with her. "You do not think this will keep us away longer than that, do you?" she asked in an undertone.

"Oh, no," Marianne assured her.

Mrs. Curtain gave her consent with some hesitation. She would have liked to confirm the arrangement with Rachel's parents, but they lived in Bedford, and Rachel's delightful friend was leaving in the morning. The aunt said she supposed it would be all right, if Miss Trenton was a *very* old and dear friend of the Tamberlays and the girls were to be met in London.

"We shall certainly be met in London," Marianne said sincerely. Nor was there any duplicity in her response. The City of London was teeming with people. They were sure to meet someone there.

So the two young women boarded the public coach. They were more reticent than Mr. Brewster, so they did not say more than five words to their fellow passengers, parted without learning their names or anything about them and missed the opportunity to become acquainted with one of the most celebrated authors of their day.

When they disembarked from the coach, Rachel produced the slip of paper Bernie had left with her, and the two young ladies had only to hail a hansom cab to be driven to the bank.

Marianne fervently blessed Mr. Desmond's generosity and her own parsimony. She had brought with her the fat envelope with the unspent allowance Mr. Bradley had sent faithfully every week to the Farnham Academy. With that tucked in her reticule, the girls had practically unlimited funds at their disposal.

Twenty minutes later, with two of the bills from her envelope in his pocket, the driver let them off in front of an imposing brick structure with London National Bank written in large metallic letters above the double doors.

Clinging to one another's arm, they pushed open the heavy doors and entered the building. The ceiling of the main hall was two, perhaps even three stories above their heads. There were many men in black suits behind glass windows and sitting at the desks about the room, but they might have been wax figures, judging from the noise they made, and every tap of the two girls' shoes was distinctly heard in the echoing chamber.

Marianne pulled Rachel with her as she made her way to a young man sitting at a desk marked Loans.

"Yes?" the pale young man inquired. "May I help you?"

"We would like to know if a Mr. Bernard Brewster has received a loan from your bank," Marianne said, in the naive belief that she could receive a straight answer to a direct question in this place.

The young man looked up a them with an expression of haughtiness on his pinched face. "I am sorry. And this has to do with . . . what?"

"With a loan for which Mr. Bernard Brewster applied," Marianne repeated, surprised she had not made herself understood the first time.

"And with whom was your appointment?" the gentleman asked.

Marianne and Rachel looked in bewilderment at each other. "I was not aware . . . we—we did not think—" Marianne stammered.

Having established his position of petty authority, the young man cut her off. "You will have to see Mr. Henner," he said, indicating the other side of the long room and another desk, behind which sat another pale young man.

The young women approached Mr. Henner, who, after hearing their complete story thrice, sent them through a heavy door into an inner office. Evidently they were making progress. At least their steps did not echo resoundingly here.

"Mr. Brewster, Mr. Brewster, let me see . . ." They were speaking to an older gentleman this time, his eyes sunken, his skin as colorless as an onion skin—the fate that awaited the young men in the public room if they worked very hard at their profession and were regularly advanced, Marianne thought. "Mr. Brenner, was it?" he asked over his shoulder as he looked through some papers in the long wooden cabinet behind his desk.

"Brewster," Marianne reminded him. "Mr. Bernard Brewster."

"I see an Alfred Bingham and a Gerald Bunyon, but no... ah, here it is."

What he found the young women were not shown. The clerk closed the drawer without withdrawing anything.

"You may see Mr. Biggins," was all he said, indicating with a nod of his head which door they were to enter.

"Mr. Biggins, certainly." The woman on the other side of the door replied immediately to their request, then stood and opened one final door for them, revealing a large gentleman in a small office. Or perhaps the office was not exceptionally small, but Mr. Biggins's substance merely made it appear so.

"These young ladies have a few questions concerning Mr. Brewster," the woman said.

"Mr. Brewster... Mr. Brewster..." Mr. Biggins said doubtfully.

"Brewster Hats, the shipment of pelts in Liverpool," the woman reminded him.

"Brewster Hats. Ah, yes. That will be all, Mrs. Riley," Biggins said, dismissing the secretary.

Marianne was sorry to see the lady go. Mrs. Riley had been the only bank employee who seemed to remember Bernie and would answer their questions in plain, concise English.

With a sigh, Marianne repeated her story to Mr. Biggins. The gentleman listened to their request, gave it a good deal of thought and then called to Mrs. Riley to ask Mr. Yarnell to step into his office.

Mr. Yarnell entered the room a moment later, to make his own valuable contribution. "Yes, of course," he said twice—once upon being asked to hear the young ladies' request and again when Mr. Biggins asked if they might reveal the status of Mr. Brewster's loan to the girls.

"The loan has been approved," Mr. Biggins announced.

"Oh, I see," Marianne said with a note of surprise in her voice. She was expecting something more dramatic, after their afternoon of interrogation.

Now, though, there seemed little else to be done here at the London National Bank. They had learned what they had wanted to and found they knew as little as ever.

"Well, thank you, Mr. Biggins," she said, rising, with Rachel standing next to her. The two girls looked at each other for a moment. Suddenly a light was ignited in Miss Tamberlay's eyes.

She turned eagerly back toward the loan officer. "Can you tell us if Mr. Brewster's loan was approved immediately?" she asked.

"Oh, yes indeed. With the greatest celerity. Mr. Brewster told us of the pressing nature of the transaction in Liverpool, so I personally sped things along. One letter to Reading, a brief check in Liverpool, and at the following appropriations meeting, the loan was approved. In less than a fortnight, I assure you," Mr. Biggins said.

Rachel gave Biggins a scornful look, then turned back to Marianne. The two girls exchanged a few words before Marianne addressed the loan officer.

"Miss Tamberlay tells me her fiancé said something about going to a moneylender if he was not able to get the money from the bank quickly. We believe that is what he may have done. Do you have any idea to whom he may have applied for a *private* transfer of funds?" she asked.

Mr. Biggins drew himself up with the same look a clergyman might have worn had Marianne asked him if he had directed Mr. Brewster to a house of prostitution. "Indeed I do not, young lady. If your Mr. Brewster got a loan on the street, I am afraid that is where you will have to go looking. Now if you will excuse me?" In a huff, he closed the door behind them.

The two girls stood there at a loss. Marianne found she was completely out of ideas. Until now, there had always been one more place they could investigate.

"What are we to do?" Rachel asked, and Marianne had no idea what to tell her.

"I could not help overhearing."

With a start, the young ladies looked across the room. Mrs. Riley sat behind her desk, and Marianne was more than ever convinced the woman must be personally responsible for the smooth operation of the London National Bank.

"Can you help?" she asked her eagerly.

"I do not mean to pry," Mrs. Riley said, "but your Mr. Brewster came out of that office two weeks ago with an expression very like the ones you are wearing yourselves just now."

"Do you know where Bernie is?" Rachel asked tremulously.

"I am afraid not, my dear. I can only tell you what I told your gentleman. He said he had the street number of a private moneylender, but he was not well enough acquainted with the city to locate it. I suggested there are certain lads outside this very institution who, for a slight recompense, will guide unsuccessful applicants to other, more accommodating lenders. You might inquire outside if anyone remembers the young man."

Marianne thanked the woman profusely and then, pulling Rachel behind her, worked her way back through the obstacle course of the bank and out onto the street again.

Just as Mrs. Riley had said, there were a number of young fellows outside, lounging about the steps and walkway in front of the London National Bank. The girls had barely noticed them when they arrived.

Marianne paused for a moment, not at all sure how one went about approaching such people. To her utter astonishment, Miss Tamberlay did not hesitate at all, but went directly to the nearest boy and asked, "Do you remember taking a Mr. Bernard Brewster to see a private money-lender approximately two weeks ago?"

It was a shocking departure for Rachel, as was the apparent relish with which she posed the question. Except for the fact that they were searching for her dear Bernie, this was turning into a marvelous adventure.

Miss Tamberlay, being exceptionally intelligent, had always taken very seriously what she had considered to be her responsibilities. She must be sober, studious, shy, quiet, intent, plain and as humorless as possible.

Then Mr. Brewster had unexpectedly fallen in love with her. He told her—often—it was because she was so beautiful. If Mr. Brewster was to be believed, she was the most beautiful creature ever to walk the earth. Since Bernie had entered her life, she'd discovered that she had a wonderful sense of humor and, not surprisingly, a very quick wit. And now, in her search for her sweet love, she was discovering all sorts of thrilling things about herself—her bravery, her derring-do, her sense of adventure, all of which would delight Bernie. If they found him.

When they found him, her new, stronger inner voice insisted.

"We takes 'em where they wants to go, miss," the boy told her, in answer to her question. "But I can't tell you who or where. Lots of folks go down to the other end of town from here."

"Mr. Brewster had...has," Rachel corrected herself firmly, "red hair. He is about your height, though a little heavier, I would say."

"Quite a bit heavier, actually," Marianne amended. "And freckled. Bernie is very freckled."

"Freckled? And heavy, you say? 'Ay! Any of you blokes take a fellow down to the money pit two weeks ago?" the boy called to the ragtag lot lounging around the bank entrance. Several of them rose and came closer to hear the questioner better. "The ladies say he was big, with red hair."

Now most of the gathered audience turned their backs with murmurs of disinterest, but one boy came forward.

"The bloke you're looking for, beefy sort, with a face like he'd been sprinkled with red pepper?" the boy asked. He was wiry and thin, but his eyes were sharp and his expression keen. The two young women had the distinct impression that very little went on in this boy's world of which he was unaware.

"Yes," Rachel said, nodding eagerly. "That is the gentleman we are seeking."

"Well, now," the lad began slowly, tilting his head to one side and withdrawing his hand from his pants pocket. "I might be able to help, and then again, I might not."

"But you said—" Rachel began in protest, but Marianne grasped her arm to silence her.

"I have a pound note in this bag," she said, touching the little cloth purse attached to her waistband. "You may have the entire amount if you tell us where you took Mr. Brewster."

"A quid!" The boy Rachel had first approached whistled in wonder at the reward Marianne promised. "Gar, miss, ol' Tom there would have taken you across the Channel for a bob." He laughed derisively, with a special note of rancor in his voice because these two fledglings were not going to be his to pluck.

The lucky fellow who was to receive the princely reward stepped forward and touched his cap. "Tom Moffitt at your service, ladies," he said.

"Can you tell us where you took the gentleman?" Rachel asked breathlessly.

"Well, now, miss, I could tell you right enough, but you'd be lost before you made your first corner, and in danger before then, what with that bag you're carrying. The best plan would be for me to show you."

The lad turned, and the ladies looked at each other. Rachel's eyebrows lifted and Marianne replied with a shrug of her shoulders.

"Well, you comin' or not?" young Tom Moffitt called back to them, and with no further hesitation they followed him.

The London National Bank was located in a monied section of the city where the stores were smart, the carriages grand, the houses sedate, reserved and suggesting taste, style and wealth.

But Mr. Moffitt soon took them away from the wide, clean streets near the London National Bank. The early nightfall of winter had begun to settle, and the lamps that created a semblance of daylight outside the bank, then of twilight a few blocks farther along, soon became like the faint glow of starlight, glittering in the darkness at great distances from each other.

Finally the boy turned off the more or less main thoroughfare he had been following into one of the dilapidated side streets, where no lights shone at all, except for dim candlelight glimmering inside one or two of the buildings.

The young ladies had slackened their pace as their surroundings deteriorated. Marianne had spoken of London's murky depths, and they had most certainly found them. The lad they were following continued boldly and soon outdistanced the two young women. In fact, he was so far ahead of them that Marianne began to fear that they would lose sight of him. As the thought was going through her head, Tom disappeared around a corner ahead.

They were suddenly alone in the darkness, and when they began to hurry to catch up with the lad again, their footsteps clattered in the empty street like marbles across a kitchen floor. When they reached the corner, it was Rachel who emerged first from the black shadows.

Once out onto the walkway, with a clear view of the street, Marianne held back. "I know this place," she said. "I—I lived here once."

"You lived *here?* On this street?" Rachel asked incredulously.

"When my parents died I became the ward of a man who lived here. There was a bookseller who kept his cart on this corner, and old Mrs. Daniel lived there," Marianne said, pointing up to a window in the house opposite, a window now dark and blank and obviously long deserted. "She scolded me every time I passed her doorway, on my way to the bookseller. I always called her the lion in the Daniels' den."

There was wonder in Marianne's voice as she spoke. These were memories she had not called to mind for years. They hardly seemed real to her, especially looking down this black, empty street. "But it was not like this then," she protested.

Rachel pulled on her friend's arm. "Come along. I think I see young Mr. Moffitt waiting for us, but I cannot be sure in this uncertain light. I do not want to lose him again, not in this place," she urged.

"I know where he went," Marianne told her, with a trancelike conviction in her voice. "East Coventry Lane, Number 16. The apartment on the second floor."

Rachel glanced at the girl beside her with a puzzled expression, but there was no time now to discuss how she knew the things she said she did. The boy they were following was barely distinct now, and Rachel broke into a run without releasing Marianne's hand.

Marianne was necessarily required to follow, and in a few moments they were standing beside their guide, breathing heavily. The boy indicated the shabby building before them. Number 16.

"In there," he said. He was not precisely whispering, but his voice was low, and the young women automatically followed his example when they spoke.

"What happened when Mr. Brewster got here?" Marianne asked.

"Nothin' happened," Tom said. "I brought the gen'l'man to East Coventry Lane, he give me a bob and I left."

"And Mr. Brewster stayed?" Rachel demanded. Her voice was more suited to purring than to snarling, but like a lioness when its young are threatened, she was fully capable of clawing and scratching to protect the ones she loved.

"Yes, ma'am."

"For how long?" she asked.

"I can't say for certain, miss. I just know we came here and he went in."

"Who is that? Eh? Who is that down in the street there?" They were startled by a voice overhead, coming from one of the open windows upstairs. The voice was old and cracked, but with a chill, Marianne recognized it. Fearfully she ducked back into the shadow of the overhanging eaves, pulling Rachel with her.

"Who is that, I say?" the voice demanded again.

"It's..." Tom Moffitt began, but Marianne motioned frantically to get his attention and then shook her head vigorously when he looked in her direction. "It's Tom Moffitt, guv'ner," the boy finished.

"Tom Moffitt? Master Moffitt? Is that you? Do you have someone with you tonight?"

"Not tonight. Just out for a stroll," the boy said.

"A stroll? Humph! Out to rob some poor dolt, I'd wager. Well, if you've nothing better to do, come up here. I have an errand I want you to run. And do not think you are going to be awarded a king's ransom, either. If I give you a farthing it will be many times what you are worth," the voice demanded.

"I've got better..." the boy began, but Marianne motioned for him to lean toward her so she could whisper without being overheard.

"If you will go up and distract the gentleman, it will give us a chance to look around without being detected," she told him.

"'E'll 'ave me run 'alfway to Birmingham and back, and tell me the fresh air and exercise is my reward," Tom complained, in a halfhearted way. The pitiful expression on the faces of both young ladies would have melted the heart of the Sphinx. "Oh, all right. But I'm thinkin' you're gettin' your money's worth and then some out of a quid note."

The boy stepped out into the street again. "Comin' up, guv'ner. But remember I promised to meet Bob Killmer next Saturday when you send me on this errand of yours." With a scowl, Tom pushed open the loose door and entered the building, but his scowl was not as deep as it might have been if Marianne had not smiled so sweetly at him as he went in.

They heard the lad's solid footsteps cross the floor and then become less and less distinct as he mounted the stairs. Yet they were still quite audible, as Tom was making no effort to lessen the noise of his progress.

In stark contrast to the young man's bold entrance, the two girls gathered their skirts and tiptoed through the littered doorway. After each creak of wood under their feet they became as figures sculpted in marble, waiting for some cry of suspicion overhead.

No cry came, and eventually they reached the stairs. The faint murmur of voices rose and fell and Marianne pointed upward. Rachel nodded. Crouching low and grasping the railing, they slowly mounted the stairs, until their eyes grew level with the second story. Before them was the door to a dingy apartment, which the boy had thoughtfully left ajar.

"Post this letter for me, boy," the man was saying. Marianne did not need visual proof to recognize the speaker as Horace Carstairs. Uncle Horace. Grown old and skinny and as decrepit as his living quarters since she'd seen him last, but unmistakable for all of that.

"You can mail it yourself on the corner," Tom reminded him petulantly.

"I do not trust the local delivery man. You take this to the main branch, downtown. And see that it is sent, too."

"But that'll take—" the boy began.

"And what else do you do with your time? Loiter about street corners, frightening away honest gentlefolk? Do it now, with no further protest," Carstairs scolded.

"Not for nothin'. You know the deal, guv. I do your runnin', but not for nothin'."

"Oh, very well then, here is a penny. Now see that you do as I say, and do not try to cheat me. I shall know if the letter is sent, and if it is not." There was a familiar note of threat in the old man's voice that raised gooseflesh on Marianne's arm.

After a slight shuffling sound as the letter in question was transferred, the girls heard footsteps approaching the partially opened doorway. They were strong and steady: those of a young man.

The door opened, and Marianne and Rachel sank back to keep out of Carstairs's sight. Tom stood in the doorway, looking around him. Finally he located their crouched figures and smiled and nodded in their direction.

"What are you doing?" Carstairs demanded. "Who is out there?"

Now other footsteps crossed the floor to the door, shuffling steps, yet surprisingly swift, so the girls barely had time to scramble softly down the stairs and hide on the landing before the old man reached Tom Moffitt and the doorway.

"Who is out there?" the man asked again, peering into the gloom of the stairwell.

"Nobody's out here," Tom said with derision, though his tone was just a shade short of convincing.

The old man took another long look down the stairs. "I heard something," he said.

"Probably just rats," the boy said.

Carstairs continued to peer out through the doorway. "I will go down with you all the same," he said.

Marianne and Rachel had time enough to stand, gather their skirts and tiptoe down the rest of the stairs, producing only a whisper of sound as they hurried before the man and boy. They ducked under the stairs as the two came down from the second floor apartment.

At the loosely hanging door, Carstairs stopped the lad. "That letter must be posted tonight, boy. Do not forget," he snarled.

"Tonight," Tom repeated stoutly. Carstairs was waiting for him to leave, so he really had no choice, but he looked over the man's shoulder into the gloom of the building one last time before he left. The young ladies were nowhere to be seen, and he was forced to conclude they had gotten away. He was certainly concerned about the pound he had been promised and never received, but he was also surprisingly sincere in his hope that they had gotten away safely.

The man stayed at the doorway several moments to make sure the boy was gone before he turned back into the building. Both girls expected him to go on up the stairs, but he came around the side of the staircase instead and headed directly for their hiding place. The shadows where they stood were so dark he could not possibly see them huddled against the wall, but Marianne glanced down nervously to make sure the tip of a shoe or the light-colored hem of a petticoat were not visible.

Though all was in blackness, the man took another step or two toward them before drawing up short. He murmured a curse and then turned again, but still did not go up the stairway, but entered a room on the other side of the staircase.

The girls did not dare go out the front door while Carstairs was down here. Neither could they go up the stairs again. But Marianne suspected if they stayed where they were they would be discovered. She was frantically trying to think of a way out, when Rachel tapped her on the shoulder. Glancing back, her eyes now accustomed to the near total blackness, Marianne saw an opening appear behind Rachel.

"Is that door open?" she whispered in surprise. She knew about the door under the stairwell, of course, but in the two years she had lived in this house it had always been locked tightly.

Rachel replied softly, "I think it goes to the cellar."

Wherever it led, they slipped through it eagerly, to find another set of stairs leading downward. Rachel felt along the wall for a banister. In relief she grasped the rounded piece of wood and stepped down onto the first step, with Marianne pulling the door shut behind them. When she did, Rachel gasped and stiffened, though it could not have gotten much darker than it already was on the cellar steps.

"So Uncle Horace will not notice," Marianne whispered into her ear.

Rachel nodded, and when her legs would once more function, she proceeded. They had taken eight or ten steps when Rachel stumbled, on a suddenly flat surface she hadn't been expecting. It took her a moment to comprehend the meaning of the large, level area in the dark, but at last the solution presented itself. "The landing," she whispered over her shoulder. "The stairs continue—"

Before she could say more, the door above them opened noisily. Looking up, Marianne recognized Uncle Horace's silhouette. She put her arm around Rachel's waist and pulled her back against the damp cellar wall.

They could feel the movement of air as Carstairs reached the landing, and when he passed them to continue down the next flight, Marianne saw he was carrying something. It must have been what he had forgotten and gone into the other room to get.

Fortunately, she thought, it had not been a candle.

But Carstairs was like one of the narrow-faced, long-snouted, red-eyed bats that hang from the ceiling in black places like this—perfectly at home in the darkness, familiar with his surroundings, most comfortable when he could not be seen.

They heard him reach the bottom of the stairs, then the rattle of a door being unlocked, unlatched and opened.

The door closed and Marianne tugged on Rachel's arm. Her friend almost cheerfully stepped behind her, willing now to venture into the fires of hell if only she did not have to blaze the trail.

At a much faster rate than before, Marianne hurried them down the remaining stairs. At the bottom, with Rachel leaning against her shoulder, Marianne put her ear against the door. She was not sure what she expected to hear, but did not want to yank open the door to find Mr. Carstairs alone in a very small room, facing them. His eyes, Marianne knew, would glitter with a scarlet glow, even in the blackness.

What she had not expected to hear was voices. Voices of more than one person. She dared to open the door a crack and squint through the slit.

There appeared to be a fairly open area, without rooms and doors, but broken up by support beams and partitions. She could not see Carstairs or who he was speaking to, but there was a faint glow from about fifty feet away, probably from a single candle.

She opened the door just wide enough to slip through, and felt Rachel follow her closely. With the fluidity of eels they moved into the shadows, working their way closer and closer to the light and the voices. Finally they were close enough to understand the words, and they froze, hidden behind one of the parted walls.

"That's enough. Take it easy. Here's a piece of bread, too. Until I get word from your father, I suppose I will have to keep you alive," Carstairs said, ending with his repulsive laugh.

"What about my friend?" someone asked, and Marianne stifled a horrified gasp. She recognized the voice, though it was ragged and hoarse, pain filled and unutterably weary. It was Mr. Desmond who spoke.

"He doesn't matter," Carstairs said. "It's probably too late for him, anyway."

"No," Desmond croaked. "No more for me until you check on Brewster."

Now Rachel gasped and even opened her mouth to cry out in alarm, but Marianne pressed her hand tightly against her friend's lips, keeping her silent.

"Very well, but that is all the water. What he drinks you will not," Carstairs threatened. His words did not alter Desmond's decision.

They heard a moan. It was Bernie, and Marianne felt hot tears fall on the hand still covering Rachel's mouth.

"It's water. Take a drink," Carstairs said.

There were the sounds of a struggling body, probably Brewster turning, and then heavy gulps, choking and sputtering.

"There now," Carstairs said, "the water is almost gone, and your friend spat half of it out onto the floor. I warned you."

"The bread," Desmond muttered.

"I didn't bring a banquet for two. If you want the bread, you eat it. If not, I will take it back upstairs."

"Give him my portion. And the rest of the water," Desmond said, his voice suddenly strong, the words an irresistible command.

"Fool!" Carstairs spat, but they heard his footsteps and Bernie's soft moan again as the command was carried out.

"Why do you not just kill us?" Desmond asked, real pleading in his voice. "That is your ultimate intention."

"Oh, you mustn't imagine I find pleasure in this," Carstairs said. "I do not like it any more than you do." He stopped, and the very air in the cellar was chilled by his malicious laugh. "Then again, perhaps I like it a little more than you do. But do not despair, as soon as your father sends something to recompense me for my losses, I shall be perfectly willing to kill you. Though I think even then I shall take my time about the matter. I find that the suffering of others holds an undeniable fascination."

"I told you my father will not send any money for me," Desmond muttered.

"Not willing to redeem his favored, his *only* son? Oh, I think you undervalue a father's devotion," Carstairs muttered.

"I am hardly a 'favored son,'" Desmond said. "I am afraid I have been something of a disappointment."

"How thoughtful of you to attempt to ease my conscience. You really must not concern yourself, though," Carstairs said, dismissing the gentleman's warning. "It will be perfectly easy taking your father's money and your life. But in case he demands some proof of my possession, you must be kept alive a few more days. Do not despair. Your end is in sight." Carstairs chuckled, and in the amused laughter there was a note of madness.

"At least put poor Brewster out of his misery," Desmond said, a real note of pleading in his cracked voice.

"Him? Why bother? He will die on his own soon enough," Carstairs said carelessly.

"You could let him go once you have killed me," Desmond suggested.

Carstairs laughed chillingly again. "I do not think so."

There were sounds of movement at the end of the cellar where the men were, beyond the wall where the two young women stood huddled together.

"The candle is nearly gone," Desmond said. "Did you bring another?"

"I will tomorrow, if I think of it," Carstairs said carelessly. He sounded closer, and Marianne guessed he was about to depart.

"Do not leave us down here in the dark again," Desmond said, with a humble entreaty in his voice that to Marianne sounded totally foreign. "We shall go mad." It was the first personal request Desmond had made.

He was answered with a laugh that suggested Carstairs understood madness and the dark all too well.

The young women saw the black figure pass the little alcove where they huddled. They heard him cross the long cellar to the heavy door, which opened, then shut. Even from where they stood, they heard the grate of the key in the lock. Though Rachel strained against her, Marianne held her friend motionless and silent against the wall until they heard Carstairs climb the cellar stairs and shut the door at the top.

Finally Marianne released Rachel, and the two girls rushed around the remaining partition toward the end of the cellar.

"Who is it?" Mr. Desmond asked in alarm, trying to make out the figures bearing down upon him from the darkness.

"It is I, Marianne. And Rachel Tamberlay. Oh! What has he done to you?"

Marianne found herself looking down on a gaunt specter, a man who, a week ago, had been her beloved Peter Desmond, though she had not dared admit that last to herself until now.

"Marianne? Is it really you? Or are you a phantom come to plague me before I die?" Desmond asked weakly. He was so tired and hungry he might have been hallucinating, but Marianne dropped to her knees at his side and touched his poor sunken cheek with her hand.

"It is I," she told him.

He raised his hands together and fearfully ran his finger down the side of her face. "Oh, my darling," he whispered.

"Shh," Marianne murmured. "I am here now."

"But what are you doing here, Marianne? How did you get in?"

"We came through that door back there," Marianne said, glancing toward the other end of the cellar. "And we came to free you and bring you home."

"I do not know how you can free us. More importantly—" and this truly was a more important consideration to him, he realized "—you are now locked in here as well."

Chapter Twenty

Rachel rushed passed Marianne and her guardian to Bernie's side, where she struggled to turn him onto his back. When at last she succeeded, she cried out in dismay. Bernie had been in this cellar for two weeks, and as Carstairs had indicated, very little attention had been paid the boy once he had been used as the lure to bring Desmond here. The comfortable reserve of flesh Brewster had had when he came to London had melted away. Loose skin hung from his cheeks and arms and belly. His eyes were dark and sunken and his lips were pulled back from his teeth because of his severe dehydration.

"Go see to Bernie," Desmond urged Marianne, before he allowed any more words to pass between them. "I know there is water somewhere down here. I hear it dripping sometimes and it has nearly driven me wild. That is what he needs most. Find the water."

Marianne might have protested, but like Carstairs, she was driven by Desmond's will. So she rose and began to wander through the cellar, trying to listen for the dripping sounds Mr. Desmond had claimed he heard. She heard nothing. He must have been...no, there it was...yes, from that direction.

She found a pool of water near one of the outer walls. Carefully she tasted it. It seemed relatively fresh, and she decided it must be rainwater or melting ice seeping through from the outside, which explained why Mr. Desmond heard dripping only sometimes.

She hurried back to the light.

"You found it," Desmond said, as soon as he saw her face.

"Back there," she said. "I must have something to carry it in. I did not want to waste any of it by trying to carry it in my hands."

Desmond indicated the broken dish holding the bit of candle.

"Be careful," he cautioned nervously, when she took up the dish. "Do not let the light go out."

She managed to break the dish along an existing crack. She returned to the little pool of water, and after using her skirt and petticoat to clean the bit of pottery, she scooped up as much water as it would hold.

Back and forth she traveled across the damp, slippery cellar floor, taking water to Bernie, until he nodded his head weakly and told her he'd had enough. Only then would Desmond allow her to bring him any.

Meanwhile Rachel sat on the floor, holding Brewster's head in her lap, rocking gently and crying softly. After Marianne had brought him two drinks, his eyelids fluttered open and he looked up into Miss Tamberlay's face. "Rachel?"

She nodded.

"Oh, Rachel." He sighed happily. "I have missed you."

He called himself Tom Moffitt. His mother's surname was Moffitt, so he supposed it was his, too, since there had never been a father around to contest the matter.

He was not a bad sort, really. The company he mixed with were a rough lot, true enough, and as for himself, he liked to pick up what money was available, nor did it matter to him on which side of the law he earned his bread. But he was not a bad sort at heart.

And he liked a pretty face. He was apt to allow a great deal of leeway for a pair of bright eyes and a lithesome figure. So it was not only the pound note that interested the boy.

He had expected to catch up with the two young women farther up the street, but he was halfway back to the London National and had seen neither hide nor hair of them.

He stopped and peered up the dark street as far as he was able, trying to catch a glimpse of a fluttering petticoat. Then he looked behind him. The streets he had just traversed were deserted, except by drunken old men and the type of ladies whose petticoats did not flutter, if they wore petticoats at all. He scratched his head. He took another step toward town, then stopped and looked behind him again. Finally, with a sigh, he turned back the way he had come.

The men's wrists were held in iron cuffs attached to chains fastened into the wall. The place had probably been used to hold African slaves bound for the American market. Desmond pulled on the chains to demonstrate how securely they were bound.

"Believe me, you cannot free us. Our concern now must be to get you out of here. When Carstairs comes back, you can hide yourself again and sneak out the unlocked door, the way you came in," he said.

Marianne shook her head. "We will not leave until you are freed," she said stubbornly.

"And how do you propose to accomplish that?" he asked, with a smile twisted into a grimace by the dryness of his lips.

"We will get you free with one of these." It was Rachel who spoke. Her hands went to her hair and withdrew a hairpin. She held it out to Marianne, who took it, but sat staring at it blankly.

"A hairpin. To unlock the handcuffs," the other girl prompted. "Do you not know anything about the mechanism of a lock?" she asked incredulously, when comprehension did not immediately light up Marianne's face.

"Allow me," Rachel said. She moved over to Mr. Desmond and began to fiddle with the iron cuffs binding him. "An uncle of mine, Uncle Thadeus, used to work for the London police, and despite my mother's disapproval, he was pleased to answer all my questions. 'The child cannot learn a thing if she does not ask questions,' he used to tell Mama. The handcuff, you see, is held in place by a series of metal teeth," Rachel explained as she worked. "The teeth are pushed into this sleeve and are held in place by the catch. What the key does is flip that catch so the metal teeth are released. Of course, in an instance like this, where the cuffs have been on so long as to interfere with the circulation of the blood, the hand and wrist swell, and for the hairpin to spring the catch..."

"Ow!" Desmond suddenly cried out in pain.

"I am sorry, Mr. Desmond, but to spring the catch I have to squeeze the cuff to tighten it before it...releases!" Rachel ended triumphantly.

The iron circlet fell open, and gingerly Desmond pulled his hand free. In another moment the girl had the other cuff loosened as well.

Rachel turned to Bernie, while Marianne gently rubbed Desmond's swollen, tender wrists, and in a moment had Brewster free and was performing the same service for him.

"How often does Uncle...does Carstairs come down here?" Marianne asked Desmond.

He shook his head. "It cannot be more than once a day," he said. "I really cannot judge time by any means other than watching the candle. He usually brings a new one with him when he comes. This is the second time he forgot." He shuddered involuntarily. "We watched it sputter out together, Brewster and I. What I took with me into the darkness was the look in the poor boy's eyes."

Brewster moaned softly. "The walls come alive in the blackness," he murmured.

Marianne swallowed heavily, and Rachel held her love more tightly in her arms.

"We talked," Desmond said simply.

"No, you talked," Brewster amended. "You talked of the sun and sea, you described foreign sights and sounds so I believed I was in those places. It was mesmerizing."

"It was talk off the top of my head. There was no importance in it," Desmond said.

"You saved my sanity. And my life," Bernie said with a simple conviction that could not be doubted.

"You talked, too, Mr. Brewster. Or have you forgotten? He talked about you, Miss Tamberlay. If anything mesmerized the boy, and saved his sanity and life, it was the picture of you he was able to conjure up before his blinded eyes," Desmond said with an indulgent tone. "But to answer your question, Marianne, I think Carstairs comes down once a day, though I do not believe it is always at the same time. Sometimes when he comes the candle is almost burned down completely, as it is now. Other times it is only three-quarters burned. Does that information help you at all in your plans for rescue?" Even in his weakened, pitiable condition, he could be infuriatingly condescending.

"It means," she said with a slight chill in her voice, but only slight, "we have several hours to find a way out of here. At least twelve, if you are correct about his appearances, and possibly as many as twenty-four."

"We do not have twenty-four hours of light left, or even twelve," Bernie reminded them nervously.

"Then we must search carefully while we have light, and work diligently when the light is gone," Marianne told them.

"The walls are solid rock and dirt. There are no windows. There are no other openings into this dungeon but the door through which you entered and which Carstairs locked behind him," Desmond said.

Marianne looked thoughtfully in the direction of the door. "I cannot believe that ancient wood is impregnable," she said.

"Perhaps not impregnable, but sturdy. We could not break it down without creating a great deal of noise," Desmond explained. "Noise that would attract Carstairs."

"And Carstairs has a gun," Brewster added.

Though the idea discouraged everyone else, Marianne was spurred on by the seeming hopelessness of their situation. To her it was only a challenge.

"We shall certainly not find a way out sitting about telling each other it is impossible," she said, at last releasing Desmond's hands to push herself to her feet. "And you gentlemen look like you could use a little fresh air and healthful exercise," she said, mimicking Mrs. Avery's tone and voice precisely.

Reluctantly, Rachel released Bernie and stood, after which slowly and painfully, with many gasps and groans, the two men gained their feet. The chains that had held them were only a few feet long, and they were bolted into the wall at floor level. Mr. Desmond and Brewster had not been able to stand fully erect to stretch their limbs since their incarceration, and now the limbering and readjustment of their arms, legs and spinal columns took several more pain-filled minutes.

When the men appeared to be as flexible as they could get in their condition, Marianne carefully picked up the candle from the floor. "Come along," she said.

"Where are you going with that?" Bernie asked, nervously watching the flame in her hands.

"To try to open the door."

"If we do that, Carstairs will come down here with his gun," Bernie said.

Desmond did not repeat his own warnings. He had explained the obstacles once, but now watched in admiration as Marianne rose to the challenges and attempted to overcome them. He did not allow himself to hope, and dared not imagine what it would mean for both Marianne and Miss Tamberlay when Carstairs discovered them both down here. But for the time being he was content to admire and revel in his ward's indomitable spirit. As Bernie with his Rachel, oh, how he had missed Marianne.

"We shall work quietly, with whatever implement we can find. There are four of us. Surely we can accomplish something," she told Brewster. "Look about you on the floor for anything that might be used as a tool."

In a few moments Brewster exclaimed, "Here!" But when he bent down to pick up what looked like a good-sized rock, a mass of wet clay crumbled away in his fingers.

Rachel did find a smaller stone, and Mr. Desmond detected a glint of metal that turned out to be a nail.

Marianne had been hoping to find a whole trove of useful treasures on the cellar floor, but when they reached the locked door they had only the stone, the nail and a rusty old piece of metal. The latter had been wedged under the edge of one of the support beams, where Bernie quite literally stumbled over it. He was very weak from lack of food, leaning heavily on Rachel, barely able to lift his feet enough to shuffle along. When Marianne turned with the candle, to see how he was, they all noticed the metal.

With great expectations, Marianne and Desmond dug and pulled at it, hoping for a valuable tool, but when they finally got it loose they found it was no more than half an inch wide, eight inches long and an eighth of an inch thick.

"It was probably used as a retaining slide in the slave chains down here. They could run the lead chain through those bolts in the wall and secure it at one end with a slide like this," Desmond explained.

"This does not appear as if it would secure anything," Rachel said, examining the rusty scrap. One end was broken off unevenly and the rest so twisted and oxidized it looked like it would disintegrate under no more pressure than what Bernie had exerted to crumble his ball of clay.

"Not now, I don't suppose," Desmond said, carelessly dropping it on the cellar floor again.

Marianne snatched it up, even at peril to their light, and after both metal and candle were secured, Desmond shook his head. "Why hang on to that? It is too brittle to work with. The nail is a much more useful tool. My *teeth* are a more useful tool than that thing."

"We are not in a position to choose only those tools most to our liking. We kept Rachel's stone and we shall keep Bernie's piece of metal," Marianne said.

When they reached the door, she and Mr. Desmond used the candle, sputtering by now, as it was about to burn itself out, to minutely examine the barrier, to determine its strength and any weaknesses, and the job that would be theirs when the cellar was plunged into darkness.

The door was not only constructed of thick oak panels, but the panels themselves were bound together with strips of iron. The lock on the door was massive, and, they knew, had a metal bolt on the other side.

"The only possibility I see is to try and work the hinges off from this side, and open the door that way. But it does not appear these hinges have ever been disturbed, and this door is several decades, if not centuries, old," Desmond said.

He held the candle close to the hinge side of the door and studied the massive pieces of metal. "This nail can be used to dig some of that rust and accumulation away, and we can use the stone as a hammer to loosen the worst spots. But that bit of slide will not do us a bit of good. You should have left it where we found it so we would not have to fumble with it now," he told Marianne, half seriously and half teasingly, in an effort to keep her fighting spirit alive.

"Rachel, will you hold this for me?" Marianne asked, passing the scrap of metal to the other girl. "My extravagance is offensive to Mr. Desmond."

Desmond smiled to himself. "While we have the light, Marianne, lift it up here for me to see, and I will work with the nail."

With the four-inch nail in one hand and the stone in the other, and working above his head to reach the top hinge, Desmond began pounding and prying and vainly struggling to get some play in the solid barrier. But he had been without sufficient food or water for several days, and he was only slightly stronger than Mr. Brewster. In a few minutes he dropped his arms in exhaustion.

"Here, let me try," Marianne said, reaching for their primitive tools.

"You cannot... too hard," Desmond said, shaking his head again.

But Marianne took the tools from him and handed him the light to hold.

For a while she worked on the top hinge, then switched to the lower one, more to give Mr. Desmond a chance to put the candle down than because she had made any actual progress.

"I—I think...I am getting...something...here," she said, her sentence broken by her exertions.

She felt the tiniest bit of movement between the layers of metal that comprised the hinge. "Ah!" She sighed in satisfaction.

And the candle went out.

They had all been concentrating so hard on her efforts and her promise of some success that they had forgotten their candle was burning low. It flickered fitfully for a few seconds and then simply winked out.

In the sudden darkness Rachel screamed softly and Bernie groaned. Marianne felt a hand on her arm and realized it was Mr. Desmond locating her, trying to reassure both her and himself.

"We are all here together," Desmond said, with a calmness in his voice that had not been evident in the hand searching for her arm and then fingers, which he held very tightly now. "Take a few deep breaths, Bernie, old chum, then hang on to Miss Tamberlay. She is right there beside you."

"Yes, Bernie," Rachel said, "I am right here. I will never leave you."

After a few minutes, when they had become more accustomed to the dark, which was absolutely complete darkness, Desmond spoke again. "Can you work on the hinge without any light, Marianne?" he asked.

"I am not sure," she said.

She could understand how terrifying this blackness must have been to someone chained to the wall back there, alone. They had free use of their hands and legs and were all together, yet she still felt chill tickles of panic in the pit of her stomach. And more than that, it was impossible for her to get her bearings in such total darkness. She really did not know if she could find the hinge or be able to judge the placement of the nail, much less hit the nail with the rock in this blackness.

"Let me try," Desmond said, stumbling around her.

She managed to pass the tools to him and thought she was standing away from the door. Actually, she had moved to Desmond's side, near the hinges. She was still standing with her ear almost against the wood of the door.

Desmond was trying to get the nail situated in his hand and find the hinge when she thought she heard something. "What was that?" she hissed.

Brewster was startled out of a half doze and moaned slightly when he opened his eyes and could not see anything. Rachel shushed him softly and pressed the length of her body against his.

"What was what?" Desmond whispered over his shoulder.

"Shh! I thought I heard something."

It became as still as a tomb in the cellar, which was a very apt comparison. Faintly, but loud enough that both Desmond and Rachel heard it this time, came a faint tapping from the other side of the oaken door.

"Who is it?" Marianne asked softly. To her surprise, a response came instantly.

"This is Tom. Is that you, miss?"

The voice was low and muffled, but they all heard the words clearly.

Marianne, who had by now discovered how close she was to the door, began to knock on it softly. "Let us out!" she urged. "Let us out!"

Desmond found her hand to stop the knocking. "Can you open the door, young man?" he asked.

"'Oo's that? That you, guv? 'Ere now, why would you lock yourself and the ladies in there?"

"No, this is not Horace Carstairs. He has imprisoned us in here," Desmond said.

"This 'oo you were lookin' for, miss?" the boy asked.

"Yes," Marianne replied. "These are the two gentlemen we were hoping to find, though we had no idea they were being held prisoner."

"*Two* gentlemen? I thought we were just after a hefty fellow with red hair," Tom said.

"This is where you last saw Mr. Brewster, and I suspected Mr. Desmond's absence was connected with his—" Marianne began, but Desmond impatiently cut her short.

"Listen," he said sternly. "Carstairs is keeping us prisoners down here. He means to kill Brewster and myself. He does not know about the young ladies yet, but when he finds them here perhaps killing them is the kindest thing he could do to them. Can you help us get out?"

"I don't know, sir. I really don't know," Tom said. He spoke very soberly at last, understanding for the first time the gravity of the situation. "I can unfasten the bolt, but there's still the lock. I don't see a key anywheres around."

"Carstairs." The groan came out of the darkness. It was the first contribution to the conversation Bernie had made, and Marianne was relieved to hear his voice. It was weak and ragged, but lucid.

"The old man?" the boy called, not having heard clearly.

"Yes," Desmond replied. "Carstairs has it. He carries it in his pocket. We have seen him drop it in there when he came down."

"'Is pocket, you say?" the boy repeated thoughtfully. "Well, now, Tom Moffitt's nothin' if he ain't a pickpocket, now is 'e? First class, I am. If gettin' a key from the old man's pocket is all that's keepin' you down 'ere, you're almost up and out now."

The voice was suddenly moving away, and Bernie called out, much louder than they had been speaking. "Light!" he cried. "We need a light down here."

Rachel hushed him again, but from halfway up the stairs they heard Tom's "Right-ho!" in response.

It was suddenly quiet, and so seemed blacker to them. The voice from the other side of the door, out of the darkness, might have been from a dream.

"How long has he been gone?" Rachel whispered. Like bearings and depth perception, it was hard to judge time with their sense of sight so totally deprived.

"Only a few minutes. It has not been long enough," Desmond replied calmly.

"*Can* he do it, do you think?" Marianne asked fearfully.

"He believes he can," Desmond said, with a smile in his voice, and in the dark air of the cellar, stinking with mildew and rotten timbers and ages of accumulated fear, the sound was as fresh as a mountain stream.

They were quiet again, straining to hear some sound from above, on the stairs, at the other side of the door.

Marianne felt Desmond lean toward her. "I have dropped the nail and the rock," he said softly, too softly, he hoped, for Rachel and Bernie to hear. "I think I dropped them when the boy first spoke. Help me find them. They must be right around here."

Before Marianne could reply, she saw a glitter of gold out of the corner of her eye. "Look!" she whispered.

"It looks like the boy brought your candle, Bernie," Desmond called softly over Marianne's head.

In just a moment they heard a soft scratching on the other side of the door again.

"Is that you, Tom?" Desmond asked.

"Ay," the boy said.

"Did you get the key?" Marianne asked.

"It's right 'ere."

They heard the grating sound of metal against metal, and then the distinctive click of the mechanism releasing.

The door swung toward them, so they were forced to step back, but before they could crowd around the opening, the boy shouted, "Look out!"

He suddenly stumbled through the doorway, followed by a flash of light and the deafening roar of a gun at close quarters.

The boy lay sprawled on the floor, facedown. In horror Marianne looked from his figure to the one still standing in the doorway. The one holding the candle in one hand and the pistol in the other. The one whose eyes glittered with a cold fire, even in the darkness.

Horace Carstairs.

Chapter Twenty-One

Rachel screamed and Brewster stumbled backward. Desmond leaned forward as if to lunge, but Carstairs swung the muzzle of the gun so it pointed directly at Desmond's chest.

"Back," he snarled. Desmond stopped, and Carstairs waved the gun in a semicircle in front of him. "All of you, step back! The first one who tries anything will join my young friend there on the floor."

Carstairs advanced and his four prisoners retreated. Marianne had backed up far enough so that she was standing next to Tom Moffitt's body. Out of the corner of her eye she saw a slight motion and could hear, if she diverted her attention away from the gun facing them all, his labored breathing.

"Well, well, well," Carstairs was saying. "What a happy party, and all together. You. I do not know you." He swung the gun in Rachel's direction, and she followed with her myopic eyes, hypnotized by the borehole. Carstairs smiled thinly. "But the more the merrier, that is what I have always said."

"Let the ladies go, Carstairs," Desmond said.

Carstairs returned his attention to Desmond, though he had been careful never to dismiss him entirely, regardless of to whom else he was talking.

"Let them go?" he asked incredulously. "And break up such a happy little foursome? You must think me mad."

About that there could be no doubt.

"You can have Kingsbrook," Desmond said. "You cannot expect my father to send you any money for my release, but I own Kingsbrook outright, and you may have it—the house, the lands. I am not even asking for my release, only for that of the young women."

"Oh." Carstairs shook his head slowly, thoughtfully. "I think this has gone past a consideration of money or property now. There comes a time, Peter, my boy, when revenge becomes the most valuable prize. You shut down one operation of mine after another—the loans, the girls, guns, drugs, ivory. But you didn't take my hate. Oh, I still have my hate," the man crooned.

The two couples had shifted their attention from the gun in Carstairs's hand to the expression on his face, acknowledging as they did so which was the most dangerous.

"Turn around. Back the other way, down to the other end," he ordered, motioning broadly with the pistol.

Obediently they turned and retraced their steps, Carstairs following with the feeble light. Desmond had his hand at Marianne's back, and Rachel was helping Bernie. When they reached the far end once more, near the chains and handcuffs, Carstairs stopped them.

"I don't know how you got those cuffs off, but we will make sure they do not come loose again." He nudged the chain and iron bands with the toe of his shoe. "Marianne, put those back on Mr. Desmond. And you there, put those on the boy."

The young women had no choice but to fasten the handcuffs around the gentlemen's wrists again. Rachel kept murmuring, "Oh, Bernie, I am sorry. I am so sorry."

"What are you doing?" Carstairs growled, suddenly looming over the girl and the weakened young man, pushing the gun directly under her nose.

"Fastening the—the cuffs," Rachel stammered.

"I think you are trying another one of your little tricks. Out of the way!"

Rachel backed away fearfully, and Carstairs, setting the candle on the floor, grabbed the chain that held the two cuffs together and jerked Brewster roughly, so the boy sprawled forward. Two weeks ago Carstairs would not have been able to do that, as Bernie had weighed twenty pounds more and would have had the strength to resist.

Rachel cried out in alarm and leapt forward. She gave no consideration to the retaliation she was inviting or the minimal threat she posed even at her most outraged. With no more thought than he would have given to swatting a fly, except that he was aware of a flash of pleasure when his fist encountered the girl's soft flesh, Carstairs turned and struck Rachel, knocking her, too, off her feet. The back of her head hit the hard clay floor with a heavy thud and she lay motionless.

Marianne watched Carstairs's treatment of her friends in horror. At the same time, though, she could not help but be thankful for the distraction, which kept Carstairs's attention away from her while she fastened the cuffs on Mr. Desmond.

She slid the locking mechanism into the metal sleeves, but did not apply enough pressure to engage the locks. She looked into Desmond's eyes and then down at the cuffs, communicating silently with him.

Unexpectedly, Carstairs's clawlike hand was gripping her shoulder. He pulled her roughly out of the way and grabbed the cuffs to test them. A sneer twisted his thin lip when both bands came loose in his hand.

"What is this?" he said softly. "Another wolf in the fold?"

Holding the muzzle of the gun to Desmond's chest, Carstairs snapped the cuffs shut. But he worked quickly, because he did not like to stand close to the man, even bound and threatened with a gun. He closed the cuffs securely and tightly. They would be excruciating after only a few hours, but Desmond did not think he would have to worry about that.

Marianne, when pushed away from Mr. Desmond, had gone to Rachel. She knelt beside her friend and took her hand, attempting to rouse her. Rachel did not open her eyes. And then Marianne's attentions were engaged elsewhere.

"What a sly one you are, Miss Marianne." Carstairs was standing over her, sneering down at her. "What a wily vixen. And so brave. So valiant. You thought to set your lover free, did you? What do you think now, eh? What do you think now?"

She watched him fearfully, every reason and instinct shrieking for her to run, to get away. He had left the cellar door open, and she ached to escape.

It was not only that Carstairs held the gun on her that prevented the attempt, though. She would not leave Desmond. She would not leave the other girl. She would not leave any of them down here while she tried to save herself.

Carstairs suddenly reached down and grabbed a handful of her hair, pulling her head back painfully. He bent toward her and screamed into her face, "Who will free you? Him? In a moment he will be dead. But I think I will leave him alive, chained up like a butchered side of beef, to watch while I take you. While I strip those clothes from your body, until you huddle there naked, your flanks quivering like a freshly killed deer's, your breasts hanging heavy, your nipples taut in the cold air. But will it be from the cold, or from desire, do you think? Did you used to lie in your bed and imagine, as I did sometimes, my hand on you? You probably never thought of the sweet agony of hot coals or a sharp blade, like I did, but you will experience it all tonight. While he hangs there and watches, and the others lay around you dead and dying."

A glaze had come over the man's black eyes. He ran his gray tongue hungrily over his lips, then reached forward and ran one skeletal finger down Marianne's cheek, chin, neck, cupping his hand around her breast as it rose and fell quickly with her fear.

"So soft. So firm. So perfect," he murmured. Without warning, the glaze on his eyes changed to mindless rage and he raised his arm and struck the girl. She fell heavily to the floor, the side of her mouth split open and bleeding. She turned onto her stomach and attempted to crawl away. Carstairs swung his foot back and kicked her in the side.

Marianne crumpled, but as her assailant reached forward, a roar like that of a wild beast shattered the air behind him, raising the hair on the back of his balding head.

Carstairs swung around, and Desmond charged like a mad bull. The old man fired wildly, in panic, and the chains that stopped Desmond short also saved his life. The bullet meant for his heart lodged in his thigh instead.

"Keep away from me!" Carstairs screamed, using both hands to steady his aim on Desmond, who had fallen to the floor when the bullet struck him. "One more sound from you and I will shoot you in the other leg. Or perhaps the arm..." The pistol shifted to Desmond's elbow. "But would that stop you?" he asked thoughtfully. "I could shoot you in the knee. In both knees." The muzzle was lowered to Desmond's legs. "That would stop you, but would it be enough pain? I find I like inflicting pain very much. I am not sure which I would prefer, shooting off both your knees or receiving a trunk full of gold. What an interesting question. Or," he continued, raising the tip of the gun just a little, "I could shoot you *there.* What a perfect revenge. I would have your blinding agony and you would watch Miss Marianne and me, and die knowing you had lost everything. You would die knowing you were less than a man."

There was great satisfaction in Carstairs's voice and he pulled back the hammer.

Marianne was dazed when Carstairs struck and kicked her, but she was not knocked unconscious. As he began threatening to shoot Peter in various parts of his body, she struggled to regain her full faculties.

She pushed herself up from the floor. The room spun before her dizzily, but her vision cleared as Carstairs said, "You would die knowing you were less than a man."

She sprang forward and threw herself on the villain's back.

Jarred, Carstairs jerked back his index finger and fired, but his aim was off and the bullet spat into the wall behind Desmond's shoulder. Marianne clung desperately to his back while he thrashed his arms and screamed curses. Finally dislodging her, he turned on her in baffled rage, his eyes wild, his thin lips pulled back in a snarl. Forgetting his calculated scheme of torture and revenge, he pulled the trigger once more. As he did so, Marianne rolled.

The bullet once again struck the floor without inflicting any damage. Marianne, though, had rolled instinctively, without conscious thought, in Carstairs's direction. Her legs and skirts suddenly struck his ankles and he was knocked to the floor. The gun fell from his grip. On hands and knees, in a panic, the old man scrambled to recover his weapon.

Marianne, meanwhile, was trying to put as much distance as possible between herself and their captor, and in the process came across Rachel's inert form. As she bumped into her friend, Rachel made a little sound of protest, struggling out of her own oblivion. She was alive, Marianne was relieved to know, even though she realized that if Carstairs succeeded in killing her now, he would take out his frustrated rage on her friend.

Carstairs found the gun. Grasping it in his hand, he held it aloft like the token of victory it surely was. "Aha!" he cried. "It appears the day is mine, after all."

He staggered to his feet, then turned toward Marianne. In wild despair, Marianne lunged once more toward him, and in the wild flailing of legs and skirts and falling bodies, she upset the candle, and the cellar was plunged into total blackness.

A second later her form slammed into Carstairs's legs again, once more sending him to the floor. But this time he held onto his gun, and with his other hand he grabbed for her. She had risen to her knees, but Carstairs found one of her ankles, and before she could crawl away from him, he jerked her legs out from under her and started to pull her toward him. She threw her arms above her head, her fingers grabbing for any handhold on the smooth, hard floor. But there was nothing but packed clay....

Her fingers closed around a flat, narrow object. With her mind clouded with panic, it took her a few moments to recognize the metal piece Bernie had stumbled over and she herself had given Rachel to hold. When her friend was knocked to the floor, it must have fallen from the waistband of her skirt, where she had slipped it and then doubtless forgotten about it herself.

With the same tenacity that Carstairs had shown in keeping hold of his gun, Marianne wrapped her fingers around the rusted metal, refusing to let go even when she felt the skin of her knuckles and the palm of her hand break, sensed the warm trail of blood she was leaving on the clay floor as Carstairs dragged her to him.

He released her leg to grab her arm. He did not want to waste another bullet, and he wanted to be the author of death. It had by now become a black, unreasoning need. He would not kill just this girl, he would start with her, then kill each of the others in turn. It would be the supreme act of avarice.

But when he let go of her leg, she kicked wildly. Carstairs struck out in defense, then went sprawling. They grappled together. There were confused grunts and gasps as the combatants twisted and turned.

Desmond thought he would go mad, straining to see something in the blackness.

There was a groan.

There was a blast from the gun.

There was utter and complete silence.

"Marianne?" Desmond whispered.

Now he heard labored breathing. It was not his own, but whose was it?

"Carstairs? Is it you?" he whispered again, softer this time, dreading the answer he might hear.

"I think... I think he is dead."

It was Marianne's muffled voice, and Desmond fell back against the wall in relief and joy and humble thanksgiving. "Are you all right?" he asked.

"He did not shoot me, if that is what you mean. But I cannot get... cannot get his body off... mine!"

With one last heave she pushed herself free of the dead weight. Then, still on her hands and knees, she crawled to Desmond, hugging his ankles, then his hips, his torso, until she finally held his dear face in her hands.

"Is it you?" he asked again.

"It is. I am here. We are alive. As far as I can tell, Rachel and Bernie are alive. I think even young Tom Moffitt is alive." She laughed with just a hint of hysteria.

Desmond was restrained by the chains, but he had enough play to lean toward the young woman and find her smiling lips in the dark. He kissed her, but it was not the kiss of a guardian to his ward, nor was it the kiss of inflammatory passion Marianne had from the man twice before. This kiss was light and soft, not demanding, but lingering. It was a simple act, yet despite Desmond's years of experience, he had never kissed anyone in quite that way before.

Since Marianne had come into his life he had quitted the gaming tables of London to remain at Kingsbrook, and had been surprised to find pleasure and gratification in the change. He had been forced to take up teaching, and had found a purpose to his life. And now, with his gentle kiss he was devoting himself to the woman, exclusively and for the rest of his life. She was his one greatest joy.

Marianne sensed some of that in his kiss, and when their lips parted and he spoke there was a gruffness in his voice..

"I love you," he murmured. "I was afraid I had lost you and would never have the chance to tell you that."

"To ease your mind, I give you permission to tell me that as often as you like for the next fifty years," she told him, smiling once again.

"But how...?" Desmond asked. The scene which had been imprinted on his eyes when the candle was extinguished was Carstairs, pointing the muzzle of his gun directly at her.

"I stabbed him. With the piece of metal Mr. Brewster found."

Of most immediate concern was the care and recovery of the injured.

Desmond told Marianne the hole in his leg was a superficial flesh wound, and he insisted she help him to his feet. Together they went to find some help for Brewster and the boy who had been shot. They commissioned the first person they met to take food and water to Bernie, and to direct them to a physician.

When they reached the office of Dr. Manley, it was closed, but the doctor lived in the flat upstairs and answered the loud summons. He listened to their tale and agreed to go back to East Coventry Lane with Marianne, but first ordered Mr. Desmond to lie down in his infirmary. Confirming Desmond's opinion of the wound, he cleaned and bandaged it, though the patient protested vigorously that the doctor should go at once to those more in need. Dr. Manley ignored him, and even roused his housekeeper before he left with instructions to warm up some soup for the gentleman and see he had all the water he wanted to drink.

In the cellar, young Tom Moffitt was given a cursory examination and declared to be in no immediate danger. The bullet Carstairs had fired at him had grazed his skull, broken the skin and caused quite a bit of bleeding, but by now the boy was sitting up, trying to get his bearings.

For poor Bernie, Dr. Manley enlisted the aid of a few men from the street above to carry him to his office, where the young man was washed, put to bed and given food and drink. Just one day later he was able to get up and walk around his room, and in two days he was leaning more heavily on Rachel than he really needed to.

Word was sent to his family in Reading, and another letter was mailed to his father in Liverpool. The elder Mr. Brewster had suspected something must be amiss with his son, and would have begun looking for him sooner, but he'd been contacted by the London National Bank and forwarded the loan, in time for him to purchase the beaver pelts. All of which had kept him in Liverpool.

As soon as Mr. Brewster received word, he rushed to London to be with his son. What is more, and to Peter Desmond's complete surprise, his own father also came to London.

Dr. Manley had arranged quarters for the recuperation of his two patients, and though they were not bedfast, they both were content to sit quietly and rest. Peter had been reading and dozing and wondering when Marianne would be back when a dark form filled the doorway. It was not the slight figure of the girl, and for a moment all he could make out was the silhouette. In the next moment he recognized the shape and believed he was looking at the same stern expression he had last seen.

"Father?"

"How are you, Peter?" Mr. Desmond asked, hesitating on the threshold. He, too, thought he recognized the tone and expression of his son.

"Getting better."

There was a pause, and then the elder Mr. Desmond took a hesitant step in his son's direction. "I have been out of the country. On the Continent. Business. Your mother forwarded Carstairs's letters, believing the man was a business acquaintance of mine. I—she—we neither one of us had any idea."

"When Carstairs did not receive a reply to his demands, I thought—" Peter began.

"I came as soon as I read the first one," Mr. Desmond cut in. "But it had come through three countries, and then the trains and ships I took home were damnably slow. I was afraid I would be too late."

"I warned Carstairs not to expect money from you. I did not think you would pay for me," Peter murmured.

"I would have paid anything," Mr. Desmond said gruffly. He stopped and cleared his throat. "May I?" he asked, glancing down at the boy's bed.

"By all means," the younger man said.

Mr. Desmond sat on the edge of the bed, since Peter was sitting on the only chair in the room. "You mother told me, finally, what it is you have been doing. I was not blind to the steady drain on our finances, but I thought I would not interfere. A mother's worrying, I assumed..."

"I did not ask for money," Peter said defensively. "But I could hardly keep the young women with me until their people were contacted."

"Yes, yes, I understand all that. And I understand, too, what your mother meant when she said you have changed. Your irresponsible behavior has changed, but not, I think, the fine young man you always were."

Peter caught his breath. It was time to say what needed to be said. What was, he realized, finally the truth.

"I am sorry, Father. Can you forgive me?"

"Oh, my boy!" Mr. Desmond cried, standing and drawing his son up to stand in front of him. "The only thing you ever had to do was ask."

The two men, father and son, embraced, and the years of animosity and estrangement melted away.

Mrs. Desmond had gone to speak with Dr. Manley while her husband went to see Peter, and while she was conferring with the physician, Marianne returned. The two ladies exchanged bits of conversation as they both waited tensely for the outcome of the meeting taking place in the sick-room.

Mr. Desmond finally opened the door and motioned his wife to join them. Mrs. Desmond took Marianne's hand and pulled her forward.

"Dear, I would like you to meet Miss Marianne Trenton. She is..." Mrs. Desmond hesitated. Her husband was smiling, and she did not want to say or do anything to darken his pleasant expression, an expression suggesting a reconciliation had taken place. But how was she to explain this young woman?

"Miss Trenton is my fiancée." It was Peter speaking. He had come to stand next to his father and now held his hand out to the young woman. "We are to be married as soon as possible."

Mr. Desmond took the girl's slim fingers into his large hand and smiled. She did not find his expression forbidding, and he in turn could not imagine how his wife had ever thought ill of this charming girl.

Suddenly the door of the room burst open.

"Oh, sure Pete'll see me. You just go stick your needles into somebody else," the speaker called loudly into the hall behind him before turning his grinning countenance on the people in the room. "What 'ave we 'ere, Mr. Pete? Miss Marianne?"

"Father, Mother, allow me to introduce Master Tom Moffitt," Desmond said.

The boy quickly pulled the cap from his head and stepped forward, bobbing his head ingratiatingly toward the older couple.

"Tom Moffitt? You are the young man who saved my son?" Mrs. Desmond asked. Her voice was low and genteel and young Moffitt's cheekiness was momentarily checked by the fine lady's gratitude.

"I didn't do much, ma'am," he said. "Mostly laid on the floor and bled, if I remember me rightly."

"Tom is as reluctant to take credit as he is to accept reward," Marianne spoke up, coming to the lad's rescue.

"Indeed?" Mrs. Desmond said, nor was there any irony in her voice.

Tom felt unexpectedly flattered and pulled himself up with a touch of pride. "Professor Pete there wants to educate me, but I says to him, what the 'ell am I supposed to do with book-learnin'? I'd be laughed off the streets, I would. And bein' able to write my name won't earn me any brass when I'm out with the lads."

"If you could read and write you might be able to get an honest job," Desmond said.

"And oo'd want to 'ire the likes of Tom Moffitt?" the boy asked with a note of derision in his voice.

"As a matter of fact, I will be looking for a clerk myself in a few months," Mr. Desmond said.

"You'd give me the job?" Tom asked.

"If you could read and write and do some simple figuring," Mr. Desmond said.

Tom grinned a grin so wide it seemed as if it would split his face in two. "It looks like I'll be takin' those lessons from you after all, Mr. Pete," he said, laughing and shaking his head. "What did I get myself into hitchin' up with you folks?"

"I guarantee you will like the change better than you imagined," Peter said, as he took Marianne's hand in his and smiled down into her eyes.

It was not three weeks later when Peter Desmond and Marianne Trenton were married.

They were married in Reading. Desmond's parents would have preferred their son's marriage to take place in Birmingham, but Peter insisted on Reading, where his students and fellow faculty members could attend.

Peter and his pretty new bride then returned immediately to Kingsbrook. Very wisely, Mrs. Desmond told her son she and his father would not join them, but would go directly to Birmingham from Reading. Mrs. Desmond wanted her two men to part while still on speaking terms, which would not be the case unless they parted immediately.

The very day the couple arrived back at Kingsbrook, Mrs. River had arranged for a small social, where their neighbors could offer their congratulations.

The party was a great success. Everyone laughed and cooed and winked. One might have thought this union of Mr. Desmond and his erstwhile ward had been a community effort of the Kingsbrook neighborhood. Marianne and Peter did not have the heart to tell them they had been brought together by the late and completely detestable Horace Carstairs.

At last their friends and neighbors left, and Mr. and Mrs. Desmond were relieved to be alone in this house that was a haven for them both. From the front door, where they waved goodbye to the ever emotional Mrs. Jacobs and her indulgent husband, Peter took Marianne's hand and led her away from the sounds of Mrs. River and the staff straightening up after the party, to the quiet seclusion of the dark library.

Mrs. River had given instructions for a small fire to be kept up in this room, as if she was aware there was one final piece of business to be carried out before the master and new mistress could claim the full partnership of marriage.

"What a lovely gathering for Mrs. River to have arranged," Marianne said.

"Grand," Desmond agreed.

Marianne playfully retreated to stand in front of the fire, and Desmond cornered her there. He put his arms around her and began to nuzzle her ear. She turned her head and glanced down.

"Oh!" she exclaimed softly.

"What is it?" he asked, only half interested, his lips against the pulse in her neck at the moment.

"Our card game," she told him.

He stepped back and looked down in turn. The card table had been moved to one side of the fireplace, almost hidden by the large stuffed chair placed to catch the heat from the fire. The cards were exactly where they had been when the note from Carstairs, threatening young Brewster, had called Desmond away from this game so suddenly those many nights ago.

He reached down to flip over Marianne's last card, but once again she put her fingertips on top of it to stop him.

"Let me see," he protested.

She shook her head.

"You said you would show me when I came back," he reminded her.

She shook her head again.

"Well then, tell me whether you won or lost."

With one hand behind his neck, she pulled him toward her. "It appears I did," she said, and then placed her mouth against his.

He folded his arms around her, excited by her body, her spirit, the neverending thrill she was to him.

Marianne returned his ardor, but with her free hand she gathered the cards from the tabletop and threw them into the fire.

* * * * *